LOVERS, PLAYERS, SEDUCER BOOK III

LOVERS, PLAYERS, SEDUCER BOOK III

The Betrayal of Nicholas La Cour

J. A. JACKSON

Contents

I

Dedication
Thanks to Alpha & Omega.
The First & The Last.

2

For this son of mine was dead and is ALIVE AGAIN: He was Lost but Now is Found.

Luke 15:24

The Prodigal Son Returns

Luke 15:24

3

4

Preface

Acknowledgement

Thank You...
All the beautiful angels God gave to me as family, and best friends...
Dorothy & Jerry Henson, Rossi V. Jackson Jr., Phillip Duran Green-Henson, Grandmother Viola and Grandmother Ruby, Aunt Bessie, Jocelyn Lewis, Mary Shields, Lenise Gibson, Petra Ramirez, Donna Jackson, Johnny Ray James,, Stephan Earl Carter, and a host of many others, you know who you are. Much Love to you all, always.

6

Thank You

Thank you for all that you do. I truly appreciate you!

7

Prologue

"Power must not be allowed to triumph all the time!" Nicholas had heard these words often enough growing up from his father Louis. It wasn't until he was watching an old gangster movie on TV that he realized his father had borrowed the phrase he often said to him. Still, for some reason he had memorized his words and now sitting in the courtroom, his father's words tormented him.

The courtroom was located in the Federal building in downtown San Jose. Nicholas sat at the defense table and his mind wondered. His eyes fell on the courtroom stenographer as she walked in. She was just what he needed to take his mind off of his situation. He marveled with his thoughts thinking her naturally caramel tanned skin was beautiful, he was sure she had acquired it at birth, no tanning booth could make such a perfect even skin tone. Her skin accented excellently against her chocolate tailored suit.

He had used the courtroom stenographer to take his mind off things on several occasions. She'd become the highlight of

Nicholas' days since his trial had started. He'd heard her speak often enough and knew that she had a soft -spoken pleasant voice that was soothing to his senses. Besides, it didn't hurt that she was professionally dressed in a form fitting outfit that accented her curves every day.

Today she wore a classic chocolate brown elegant ladies' blazer paired with matching tapered ankle length straight leg pants that showed off her delicate ankles. He smiled softly enjoying the fit of her tailored blazer as it highlighted her ample breasts. She made him wish he was somewhere off alone with her, with a chilled cup of thick whipped smooth chocolate with a crown of whipped cream on top with a drizzle of caramel, he could see himself pouring the drink over her naked breast and licking it off . The thought was so sensual, he licked his lips.

Lucky for him when his mind wondered too long like he was doing right then or if he fell asleep, his trusted attorney, Ross Goldman, would give him a nudge.

Ross Goldman was a tall gray-haired man in his mid-sixties, he had been a good friend of his father Louis La Cour.

All at once, Ross leaned over and patted Nicholas's hand and gave him a reassuring glance in a fatherly manner.

Nicholas took his focus off the courtroom stenographer as he glanced around the court room, just at that moment the bailiff opened the main doors of the court room and the public entered. The courtroom hummed with noise as the press began setting up their cameras and positioning their lighting to get the best shots.

As the courtroom bustled with excitement Nicholas took it all in. He quickly grew bored and let his gaze settle out the window next to the table where he sat. The window afforded him a glimpse of the courtyard in front of the Federal court building.

Several rows of the Kwanzan trees were planted there. The Kwanzan tree, is the Japanese Flowering Cherry. It blooms with deep pink colors during its peak season the last week of April. *The blooms had come early that year*, Nicholas thought, as he stared out the window. The early bloom made him think about his life. He could envision in his mind the last few years of his life. His rise to grace and riches had afforded him to live a life filled with power, and flamboyant debauchery but now it was at the cost of a jail cell. He thought often about it and realized his real problems had all began when he lost his father Louis, he hadn't realized Louis had been more to him than just his father, he'd been his mentor and very possibly his best friend, only it took his father's death for Nicholas to realized that.

His case had instantly thrust him into fame in the local newspapers. He still hadn't gotten used to the celebrity status his case had brought him. His case had garnered headlines in the local paper every day for almost a year now. The local newspaper had described him as the handsome local boy next door, right down to his good looks, broad shoulders, and lean muscled frame. They had even done their research on him discovering that in high school he was the type of kid everyone loved and said that he had a nice personality and got along well with others. The kind of kid you knew would succeed.

Nicholas' attorney, Ross Goldman, leaned over to him in a fatherly manner, and patted his hand.

Nicholas glanced up at Ross Goldman just as he was giving him a reassuring glance.

His act of kindness made Nicholas feel a little better as he sat beside his attorney in the court room. Because today was the day, he would discover his fate. Still the conflict inside of him was raging in full force as his thoughts wondered, while he sat silently in the courtroom. He wondered how he could have been so naive to think he could have trusted Dante Channing in the first place. He could see Dante clearly now for what he was, a cold-hearted manipulative user. In an instant the scene flashed right before his eyes as his mind wondered back in time to the moment, he knew he had been betrayed by Dante Channing as the vivid memory took hold.

"Dante, you can't be serious?" Nicholas shouted but didn't wait for an answer. "Is this really what you want to do expose us all to a lawsuit or worst yet criminal charges?"

"Not me, you, Nicholas," Dante venomous voice laughed out. "What was that old corny Cajun dumb line you used to say that you thought was so funny" Dante asked but didn't wait for him to respond. "Oh yeah! It was Winner! Winner Chicken Dinner!"

Dante' threw back his head and laughed again. "Looks like I won the chicken dinner! You dumb ass gator back fool!"

Hearing his sinister laughter Nicholas felt a gut-wrenching knot forming in his stomach as he realized he should have never trusted Dante Channing. He felt paralyzed and could only stare back at Dante in disbelief.

Dante stared back at Nicholas victoriously. "You seem to forget I never put my signature on anything. What fool would? I mean come on Nicholas you knew what shady business deals we made, what with the price fixing false financial statements and with our inter-

national businesses failing. Hell, I made sure my name wasn't on everything."

"Are you serious?" Nicholas asked in disbelief.

"You, dumb ass!" Dante laughed hysterically as he focused his sinister gaze on Nicholas. "You should have been more thorough with checking the facts."

Nicholas looked at the piece of paper in his hand. A tragic look of despair flashed across his face. His eyes twitched as he stared back at it. It was all there in plain sight, every last business transaction unloading the millions of dollars in stock. What had been done was totally unethical and illegal. He'd known it when he'd agreed to Dante's scheme, but he'd never knew Dante was setting him up. He knew the trail would lead straight back to him and he would be ruined for it. He couldn't believe he had been so trusting, so stupid. He felt used and betrayed. This couldn't be real. "Dante, this was your idea! I thought we were in this together?"

"You thought that we were in this together!" Dante vehemently song back at him. "Nicholas! Stop whining like a little bitch!"

Nicholas shrugged helplessly. "Can't you put a stop to this?"

Dante gazed back at Nicholas uncaring. "Bad things happen to good people all the time," he shrugged. "Right now, you are just angry, because I outsmarted you!"

While you're sitting in jail facing all that time, maybe you'll get over it. But, hell, I doubt it," he taunted him. I sure in hell wouldn't!"

Rage filled Nicholas as he lunged forward. "You motherfu-..!"

Instantly Dante sprung forward pulling a led pipe from his sleeve aiming high and landed it to the side of Nicholas' head.

Nicholas felt like he had been hit by a train and as the blow sent him crashing to the floor. He felt something running down the side of his face and his fingers automatically reached out and touched it.

It was blood, Nicholas couldn't believe it. He was in shock. It was his blood running down the side of his face.

"See you in court! Or should I say I hope you get yourself a great lawyer!" Dante laughed out as he made his exit.

It was the last thing Nicholas remembered before hearing the bailiff's strong stem voice echoing as he woke out of his thoughts.

"The jurors are returning," the bailiff yelled.

The door just to the right of the judge's desk opened and the jurors walked in and took their seats. The bailiff went into action and started restricting access and soon had the room quieted down.

Suddenly, the door to the judge's chambers opened wide and the judge walked in, his black robe bellowing behind him, instantly the room went quiet.

"All rise, hear ye hear ye, the court is now in session in the Federal courtroom of Honorable US Magistrate Judge Edward Joseph George." The bailiff bellowed. "Silence in the courtroom any outburst will be dealt with post haste."

The bailiff waited until the judge was seated and then yelled. "Everyone be seated."

The judge than took center stage in the courtroom and turned his full attention to the jury. "Has the jury reached a verdict," Judge George asked.

"Yes, the jury has," the jury foreman said, as he handed the verdict to the bailiff.

The moment was tense as the bailiff quickly walked over and handed the verdict to the judge.

Judge George's voice was sturdy when he asked. "What does the jury say?"

"We the jury, in the case of The State of California versus Nicholas La Cour, find the defendant guilty of the charge of federal larceny and securities fraud."

At the sound of the jury's verdict Nicholas felt all was lost as he heard his mother, grandmother and sister piercing sobs filled the air he felt the tears swell up in his eyes.

The out of control crying sob that escaped his lips was not his voice, Nicholas prayed as the tears ran down his face and the agony words rolled off the tip of his tongue. "Mamma! Grand *mere*!" He openly sobbed. "Oh, my God! No!"

"So be it," Judge George declared. The defendant will be sentence to five years in Federal Prison at Lompoc, with a chance of parole after three years for time already served."

Grand *mere* Catherine's voice rung out across the room. "Your honor, please have pity on this old grandmother and this child's mother. We beg of you!"

Judge Edward Joseph George was not unfeeling to the voice that pleaded with him. Catherine Marie Rousseau-La Cour was a woman he could never forget. He knew the woman well and could deny her nothing.

"Bailiff, clear the courtroom of everyone except the defendant's grandmother and mother and be sure you lock the doors."

Grand *mere* Catherine's eyes swelled up with grateful tears as she looked into the eyes of Judge Edward Joseph George and mouth the words thank you.

She took her daughter-in-law by the hand and said, "Come Pearl, let's give our son encouragement for this journey he must endure."

Pearl La Cour looked into the eyes of the old woman beside her and knew her strength would be her saving grace as they walked over to where her son stood. Instantly she pulled a handkerchief from her purse as she headed toward her son.

"Nicholas... Nicholas...My baby!" Pearl's voice was laden with tears as she hugged her son tight and reached up and wiped the tears from his eyes.

"Mom, please don't take this the wrong way," Nicholas said, pulling the handkerchief from his mother's hand. But could I please just have a private moment with Grand *mere*," Nicholas pleaded.

Pearl knew her son Nicholas and his grandmother had a special bond, as she kissed her son's cheek and nodded her head gently. "Nicholas, I understand, just know I love you."

"I love you too," Nicholas said giving his mother a quick hug and watching as she pulled out of their embrace, turned and swiftly headed for the exit door.

Grand *mere* Catherine stood silently in front of her grandson. She knew him well. His tear stained face stared back at her with a look she knew by hard. "What is it Nicholas?"

"Grand *mere*, what was the proverb number of that old saying you used to say to me, when I was a kid? You know the one about taking your plan to God?"

Curiously Grand *mere* Catherine's eyes flashed. "You mean proverbs 16:3 *Commit to the Lord whatever you do, and he will establish your plans?*"

"Yes! That's the one." Nicholas replied. "Can I have a tight hug, before the Bailiff returns?"

"Of course, you can my son," she said wrapping her arms around him.

Grand *mere* Catherine squeezed Nicholas tight. She knew her grandson well.

"Nicholas, you should also reacquaint yourself with Proverbs 19:21 for it says, *many are the plans in a person's heart, but it is the Lord's purpose that prevails.*"

Grand *mere* Catherine pulled out of their embrace and stared hard back at her grandson's face. She reached up her hands and cupped the side of his face. "Nicholas always remember vengeance is mine, so says the Lord."

"Mam, I'm sorry but it's time, I must ask you to leave," the Bailiff declared as he walked over and cuffed Nicholas, before leading him over to the side door.

Instantly Nicholas tilted his head and gave one glance back at his grandmother just before he disappeared through the side door. The door that led to the jail cell they housed prisoners in before taking them back to the main jail.

8

Chapter 1

Receiving Line...

Nicholas stood behind a man in the receiving line and tilted his head to see if they had left. They were still standing there. His mother Pearl was standing next to his real father, Sherlock Bailey Garrison.

It was over a couple of years ago, that he'd found out Louis La Cour wasn't his biological father. No words can describe the engulfing, all-consuming shock he had experienced once his mother Pearl told him the truth.

Nicholas' remembered the first time he and his biological Dad, Sherlock, were alone without his mother Pearl present, they went for a long walk and they talked about everything.

At the end of their long walk, Sherlock help him deal with the fact that he had been systematically lied to by his mother, who really had no choice but to lie. His victimization was the ultimate betrayal by the people around him who were sup-posed to love and support him.

Sherlock had even helped him see that those other family

members who had enabled his mother Pearl's lie by maintaining that lie. All were thinking they were doing the best thing for the situation at hand, him.

But it was Sherlock, his real father, who had helped him to see that all of them had been wrong and that they had wronged him. At the end of their conversation Sherlock had put his arm around his shoulder and apologize to him for everyone's behavior and told him the best thing that he and his mother could do for him was to go to counseling together with a vetted therapist.

It was those therapist sessions together that had help Nicholas see clearly and get closure. His, Dad, Sherlock didn't know how much that had meant to him.

Nicholas looked back at Sherlock a second longer and thought, now that I have a lot of time on my hands, may be the first letter I write will be to Sherlock to let him know how much he means to me.

He shifted his vision and captured his sister Lacey's face. His sister Lacey was standing beside her husband Kienan. His grandmother, Grand *mere* Catherine, was standing beside his attorney Ross Goldman.

Nicholas was glad his mother, sister and grandmother had someone to watch out for them, while he was stuck in prison. It meant he had less to worry about. The men standing beside his mother, grandmother, and sister were capable of taking care of them and more.

His thoughts turned to his attorney, Ross Goldman was a good man, Nicholas thought. *"How many attorneys accompany their clients to their first day of prison?"*

There they were. All still standing where he'd left them

at the big glass window, next to the door, he'd just walked through.

They were staring out of the wide window the women in his family were teary eyed. Just like all the other crying sad relatives and friends coming to say their goodbye to their loved ones as they entered the California Department of Correction.

All at once a loud bell sounded and a gigantic precision metal door, resembling a garage door slowly rolled out of the ceiling and closed over the huge window where the families all stood.

An eerie quietness fell over the room. Nicholas felt like it was the most defeating and heart wrenching moment of his life. For one moment that he couldn't understand, he'd wished Maëlle had been there to say goodbye to him. But no sooner had the thought entered his mind. He erased it knowing it was the best thing, her not being there. Not after he'd broken her heart leaving her at the altar.

"Nicholas La Cour! Did you hear me calling your name?"

The next thing Nicholas knew a guard was standing in front of him.

Nicholas shook out his thoughts. "I'm sorry, what did you say?"

"I said, I need you to take off all of your personal effects and put them in this box," the Trustee said. "If any of your personal possessions are permitted, I'll let you know. Otherwise, they will be here in this box for you when you get released."

After the Trustee accounted for Nicholas' personal effects,

he handed him a bundle of prison clothes and on top of them sat a Bible.

"Excuse me," Nicholas stated. "But you handed me a Bible."

"Yeah all the new inmates get one," the Trustee said. "Consider it a gift, courtesy of Prison Fellowship."

"What am I supposed to do with it?" Nicholas asked.

"I suggest you sleep with it under your pillow. It'll give your pillow that extra height of comfort and who knows, maybe one night, you just might want to pray to God and ask him to get you out of here," the Trustee laughed. "Now go and get dressed, picture time is coming up next!"

A half our later, Nicholas stood fully dressed in his new prison clothes waiting to have his hand fingerprinted and his picture taken.

Nicholas heard the fingerprint guy yell. "Next!"

He stepped up still holding the new Bible he'd been given. He was told to put his hand flat on the table in front of him. He put the Bible down and for the first time really looked at his hands. It was as if he was noticing his hands for the first time. He noticed the scar on his left hand. The scar was from when he'd cut himself with his first pocketknife. The knife his father Louis had given him.

The fingerprint Trustee was careful and quick taking his prints. The next thing Nicholas knew he was passed down to take his picture, and just as quickly as the finger printing went the photo session was over too.

"They take your keys. Your phone. Your clothes. Your humanity and then they take your fingerprint and your picture," the guy ahead of him turned back and said. "I see you're hanging on to that Bible."

"Yeah, I thought I was supposed too?" Nicholas answered as he looked up to see who was talking to him.

"It's up to you, but it's not a bad idea to hang on to it. The Christians, they love to see you hanging on to your Bible."

"Is that a fact," Nicholas stated. "Thanks for the advice, by the way my name is Nicholas. Nicholas La Cour."

"Good to meet you Nicholas, my name is Jesus Martinez.

Jesus Martinez was a tall lean handsome looking Hispanic man with deeply slanted dark eyes that gave him an Asian look. His face was formed of converging planes that gave him a rugged, feral look. On the right side of his neck was a very distinguish looking silver and red dragon's head tattoo with a realistic looking jade pendant trapped in the jaws of his mouth and some words tattooed in Chinese that read ?? ??.

Nicholas stared at the dragon's head tattoo and wondered at it, but it was the words in Chinese that really caught his attention. He'd seen the symbols before and knew their meaning. He didn't have long to wonder if it was alright to talk to Jesus about it when he heard Jesus say.

"I had the red dragon tattoo done in Chinatown in San Francisco. Pretty cool, huh?"

"Yes, that tattoo is one of the finest I've ever seen. Whoever did it is a real artist. Can I ask if your mother is Chinese?" Nicholas asked.

Jesus smiled. "Yes, she is. What gave me away? My eyes? Or my dragon tattoo?"

Nicholas nodded in disagreement. "No, not the dragon tattoo but the words written in Chinese. Those are Chinese symbols that stands for what I believe is the words my *geek Robin Hood*."

'Yeah, that's actually my real middle name in Chinese," Jesus laughed out. So where did you learn Chinese?"

"I had lessons as a kid. We had a Chinese tutor who was more like a second mother Nanny most of the time. My father insisted his children learn more than one language growing up," Nicholas said.

"Looks like you had a smart father," Jesus replied. "What Chinese I know, my mother taught it to me. Anyway, my mother gave me geek Robin Hook as my nickname growing up too. You know how Chinese mothers are."

Nicholas smiled with understanding. "So, Jesus who are the Christians? You were talking about, if you don't mind my asking."

"No problem, they are the Holy ones. The ones who believe their purpose on this earth is to save your soul. Don't worry they'll find you. Them and the rest of the welcome wagon."

"Welcome wagon," Nicholas repeated with a curious tone in his voice.

"Yeah, the Christians, and everybody else who will drop in on you to tell you that they want to help you," Jesus paused and then continued. "Let's see you've got the psychologist, and then there's a cuckoo guard or two, there are crusader guards some who are real, people who want to help, then there are the crusader guards with something to prove, now those just want to hurt you."

Nicholas nodded. "So, you're saying I can trust the Christians?"

Jesus nodded. "Hell, yeah! The Christians they are truthful, they just want to save your soul and on a positive note they will hook you up with some good stuff. Like better soap, tooth paste and stuff like that."

"So that means it's good to talk to them? The Christians, I mean?" Nicholas asked.

"Hell yes! And you don't have to believe in religion. Just don't tell them," Jesus exclaimed. "And don't forget some of the guards are cuckoo, some guards are crusaders and some crusaders are just snitches. Then you have the goon squad, guards who will write you up for anything."

"Wow!" Nicholas exclaimed. "You are a wealth of information."

Jesus chuckled. "I'm sure you've guessed, this ain't my first time here, at *the big house of chess.*"

"The *big house of chess,*" Nicholas repeated, with a puzzled stare. "I don't see it."

Jesus nodded. "You play chess Nicholas?"

"Yeah, sure I do."

"Well, think about it this way. When you're playing chess, the game unfolds while you're playing, right before you, wouldn't you say?"

"Sure," Nicholas agreed. "I follow you so far."

"Since you're following me so far. Think about it this way," Jesus replied. "When you're playing chess, you have to think really hard if you want to win and it's the same way while you're in prison. You have to think and think hard, plot out some things, study everything and everyone around you. You have to do this, that is if you want to survive."

Only half listening Nicholas thought that having to think really hard every day wouldn't be such a bad thing. It would give him time to think about the thing he wanted most right at the moment and that was the best way and place he could have his revenge against Dante Channing.

After a few moments, Nicholas shook out his thoughts and said. "So, what I hear you saying is while in prison, we are like playing some type of prison war games, plotting, scheming... Planning things like revenge..." he abruptly stopped talking right in the middle of his sentence when he realized he was about to give away his plans.

"Believe me, Nicholas, *Prison Chess*, is a war game and it's the biggest, badassed, saddest war game you will ever have to play, in your life. Rest assured you must be prepared for it every second, minute, and hour while your ass is in prison and whatever you do, Nicholas, never forget that! Because you never know what others are thinking. Hell, for all you know you might be just minding your own business one minute and the next minute you're getting swept up in somebody's desire for revenge, or other stupid drama."

Nicholas found what Jesus was saying was intriguing, as he heard the stern tone in Jesus' voice and knew he was serious. He let his words sink in. He watched Jesus waiting to see if he had read his mind or heard him say the word revenge and wondering if Jesus was making a point with him.

At that moment the only thing Nicholas could think of to say was. "Well, on that note, I guess I need to be hanging out with the Bible toting Christians. Looks like they are my only chance for survival in this prison game of chess," Nicholas replied.

"I'm serious, Nicholas," Jesus said. "Even the Christians can't save you from this hell hole, that prison is. Just remember they issue you clothes and stuff and tell you it's your stuff.

But in reality, they own it. They tell you when you can shower, when you can shit, when you can eat. But they can't tell you when you can pray. So, I suggest you start memorizing a few prayers from that Bible of yours. It will help you get through this once you wake up every day and realized you don't have a choice. You have to get through this, until you can get released."

Nicholas thought about what he was saying and then his stomach started making some loud gurgling noises.

"Sounds like your belly is ready to eat," Jesus replied. "They usually take us and show us around once we're done here and the chow hall is one of the last stops."

Jesus rubbed his jaw as if he was thinking. "Oh, before I forget. One thing you don't want to forget to do once they take you down to the chow hall."

"What's that?" Nicholas inquired.

"Scram, and I do mean scram. Eat fast and get the hell out of there. Believe me, the chow hall, is a dangerous place to linger, *hell-of* drama can start in there in seconds."

Nicholas nodded. "Thanks, for the tip."

"Inmate Jesus Martinez to line P!"

"Looks like it's my turn to talk to the head doctor, that "P" is code for the psychologist," Jesus stated and then joked and laughed. "Some just call him Dr. P. Well, I should get going. I'll see you around Nicholas, don't be a stranger."

Chapter 2

Lacey La Cour-Egan...

Lacey had been devastated when the verdict had been read in court that sad day, weeks ago. It seemed like yesterday when she heard the jury declaring her brother Nicholas, guilty.

People everywhere she went had had something to say about her brother, and his so-called crimes. Their tight knit family, who had once been admired and honored by practically everyone in Silicon Valley had been reduced to being treated like lepers by their neighbors and even some friends.

If it hadn't been for Grand *mere* Catherine, Lacey would have been content to stay shut-up in the house hidden away from prying eyes of all those who sat on thrones to pass judgment. But her Grand *mere* Catherine was the strong one in the family, and had insisted, everyone in the family go on about their life as if nothing had happened.

Lacey smiled thinking about Grand *mere* Catherine and her barrage of Bible quotes. *"This too shall pass,"* which Grand *mere* Catherine was fond of saying regularly, but when asked where it was found in the Bible she had quickly stated it was only partially stated in the Bible in Act 2:21 and really could be credited to common belief that stems from a fable written by Persian Sufi poets and also said to have originate with King Solomon.

Still, Grand *mere* Catherine's words were the reason Lacey had ventured out of her safe haven and signed up for an evening class. She'd been attending now for several weeks. She was glad her grandmother had suggested she attend. She'd been right it been just what she needed to keep her mind busy.

That evening, Lacey excitedly made her way across the parking lot to the Silicon Valley Culinary Cooking School. She'd been glad she was able to sign up for the class at the last minute. The day and time fit her schedule perfectly. She knew it was the best thing to do to keep her mind busy

Lacey adjusted the apron she was required to wear as she entered the classroom and found her station to place her bag holding the materials, she was told to bring for today's class, all that was missing was her large mixing bowl.

Quickly Lacey made her way over to the cabinets in the back. Each cabinet was labeled by station number. She shared her cabinet with the station next to hers. She knew cabinet five-six labeled cabinet, housed her mixing bowls and whisk, as she walked over to her cabinet and opened it.

Grabbing her bowls and whisked she was just about to close her cabinet door when it shut abruptly just barely missing her fingers.

"Ouch!"

"Stop it! I didn't hit you!"

It was Shawna Zamora, she sat at workstation six, right next to hers. "It was a reflex, my saying ouch, that is. You could have hit me."

"Yeah, well I didn't," Shawna raucously declared. "What you going to do? Start crying like your brother, Nicholas did when he got sentence at court?"

"Excuse me!" Lacey said finding her voice.

Shawna grinned turned into a sneer. "Sounds like you're a chicken just like your brother."

Lacey didn't feel like being harassed by Shawna Zamora. She knew Shawna was a bully straight up. She knew her type. She also knew, iIf she didn't address her, right there on the spot she'd have to deal with Shawna's stupidity for the duration of the class. She swallowed hard and tried to look away, self-conscious as she tried to think of something to say.

Lacey hated being reminded of her brother's last day in court. "I... I... Shawna, you don't have a right to judge my brother, or me!"

"Lacey is everything alright here," Mrs. French vociferously called out as she closed the distance between them.

Mrs. French walked over and stood right next to Shawna Zamora. "Ms. Zamora! Do you need my assistance in minding your own business?"

"No, Mrs. French," Shawna answered.

"Good, because my cooking class is not some reality show. I do not allow bullying of any kind in my classroom. If you want to be on that reality show, *Restaurant Impossible*, then I suggest you go and get started auditioning. I would hate to have to give you an "F" and fail you in my class because you don't know how to conduct yourself. Do I make myself clear?"

"Yes, Mrs. French," Shawna answered.

"Good," Mrs. French replied. "Now get your bowls and get back to your station."

Mrs. French watched as Shawna did as she was told and then turned her attention to Lacey and gave her a knowingly wink. "Take your seat Lacey, I don't think Shawna will bother you again."

Judy French, the instructor, walked to the head of the class and immediately took over the room.

Judy French looked like she loved to cook. She had salt and pepper hair tied neatly in a bun at her neck, pouty red lips that would pucker when she wanted to express the taste of something good. She was short and round with the look of someone who enjoyed cooking and eating what she cooked.

"Hello Class, no time to waste. Today we will master the Souffle'. As you may have heard the Souffle' is the one legendarily light and fluffy dessert that is notoriously confounding for cooks to prepare. But today all of you will master it."

The next thing Lacey knew she was busy preparing her Souffle. It took her over a half hour in assembling her ingredients and mixing them as Mrs. French had instructed. Now it was nearing the end of the half hour cooking time. She stood in front of the window of her oven and watched the golden-brown color her Souffle had become. It had puff high just as it was supposed to do.

Lacey was sure her Souffle was ready to face the world, when her instructor Mrs. French walked over.

"Your Souffle᾽ looks superb, Lacey," Mrs. French stated pouty her lips. "I believe it is time to take it out."

Quickly Lacey followed her teacher's instruction and retrieved her Souffle᾽ from the oven. She placed it at her station.

Mrs. French looked over her Souffle᾽ with her eyes taking in every inch of it before finally blurting out. "Ahhhh! *Parfait!* Lacey,*très bon!*"

Lacey stood there smiling. "Thank you, Mrs. French."

Mrs. French quickly walked over to the next station and said. *"Shawna, please take your* Souffle᾽ *out of the oven."*

Shawna did as she was told. The Souffle was lop sided as she placed it on her station. In the blink of an eye Shawna's Souffle flopped as the little air it had popped out.

"Hmm, Shawna," Mrs. French condescendingly said. "It does look like you need to pay attention to the air in your Souffle᾽, perhaps you could apply some of that hot air you're filled with to your eggs when you beat them," she said as she walked to the next station.

Laughter erupted all around.

Lacey's eyes met Shawna's; she could see the rage boiling in Shawna's eyes. She mouthed the words. *"Take that you Bit—-!"* Then she gave Shawna her meanest sneer and rolled her eyes.

Chapter 3

Lunch and Punch ...

Lompoc Prison the next day...

Nicholas and a bunch of other inmates were heading toward the chow hall. The first thing he notice was that there were two lines that snake between long serving lines. The second thing he notices was there was no pleasant aromas of a cooked meal filling the air. It didn't matter how long Nicholas had been in prison, the one thing he was sure of was he was never going to get used to the taste of the food served in the chow hall.

Quickly his line arrived at the food counter. Splatters of dried food greeted him. He watched as the food service helper heaped a large portion of gray gump on a tray laden with over-cooked green beans, a lettuce salad and a rock-hard looking dinner roll. He soon learned the gray glob was called *Chicken Ala King.*

A laden tray was thrust at Nicholas' hands and he quickly placed his Bible on his tray and walked over to along dining room table and sat down. He watched as everyone around him quickly choked down their food. He tried to do the same and felt his throat gag.

"Eat the salad and the green beans," someone called out to him. "You'll get used to the rest another time."

"Thanks," Nicholas replied and then quickly did as he was told.

Once he finished eating, he made his way toward the exit door leading out of the chow hall securely holding his Bible in his hand.

He had just made it to the entry of the threshold when he heard a loud commotion behind him.

"You motherfucker!" An inmate yelled.

Nicholas paused at the exit and turned around just in time to see who was yelling.

"Look, man! I don't want to fight you!" Another inmate yelled, and then took a step back and dropped his shoulder.

The aggressor grinned a toothless grin and laughed out. "Yawl hear that. Pretty Ricky doesn't want to fight me! How about I give you some punch to go with your lunch!"

Immediately Pretty Ricky dodged the aggressor and then let out a solid left punch squarely on his jaw and then continued with a right punch. He continued to hit the toothless aggressor with everything he had.

As if on instinct Nicholas felt like his legs wanted to take him back inside. Instantly a hand grabbed his shoulder.

"Uh, oh! Ahhhh! You're going the wrong way. Besides, Pretty Ricky can take care of himself."

Nicholas looked up into a familiar face. It was Jesus Martinez.

"Remember what I told you Nicholas? Come on let's get out of here before the guards lock this place down."

Nicholas quickly followed Jesus.

Once Jesus thought they were safe he turned and said. "The toothless guy you saw hitting Pretty Ricky is called Fresno Bob. Basically, once you are in here, you have two types of inmates. Wolves and sheep. Now, Fresno Bob, he's what you would call a wolf agitator."

"A wolf agitator," Nicholas repeated with a puzzled expression on his face.

"Yes, he is. And he's a dump-ass coward wolf agitator at that," Jesus replied. "You see Nicholas a coward wolf won't attack another wolf, they only want to attack sheep and they will attack a sheep every chance they can get, especially if they think he's weak."

"So, why did you say Fresno Bob was dumb?" Nicholas inquired.

Jesus rubbed his jaw. "I heard from a Spider Monkey, who said he was and if he said he was believe me he is."

"Spider Monkey?" Nicholas inquired staring off into thin air as if he was trying to figure it out.

"Yeah, a Spider Monkey is just another name for someone doing hard time and this Spider Monkey happens to be a well-respected O. G. and if you don't know what O. G. stands for it means old gangster. This O. G. normally walks the yard with Fresno Bob and a few of his friends. Now, O. G. told me Fresno Bob was one dumb asshole because Fresno Bob thought Pretty Ricky was a lame duck."

"Lame duck?" Nicholas repeated with a puzzled expression.

"Yeah, a lame duck is someone who keeps to himself, so some folks think they are weak," Jesus said and then paused and looked at Nicholas. "Don't you know who Pretty Ricky is?"

"No, sorry, I don't, "Nicholas replied.

"Well, you, I can understand you're not knowing, Nicholas, you came from the Silicon Valley, but Fresno Bob came from Central Valley, he ought to have known, who Pretty Ricky was."

He stated but didn't wait for Nicholas to respond. "Well, I guess if you don't know then it's safe to say O. G. was right Fresno Bob is one dumb ass hole, because he didn't know either."

"That's why Fresno Bob just got his ass kicked, he didn't know either," Jesus chuckled and shook his head. "In fact, you can say Fresno Bob just had some punch to go with his lunch," he laughed to himself taken by the joke running through his mind.

Jesus chuckled to himself a little more and then said. "Pretty Ricky's real name is Enrique Calderon Jimenez. He comes out of the Eastside Boxing Club in Stockton. He was on his way to becoming the middle -weight boxing champion when he got busted for being an accomplice to his certifiable lunatic cousin bank robbery idea. Did you know that the man who started the Eastside Boxing Club, is Chuck Jackson and he's been an inmate here for over a year?"

"Really? Is he a trainer too, or just the owner?" Nicholas inquired.

"Who, Chuck Jackson? He's an outstanding trainer, everybody knows that and his fighters have performed at their highest for years. It's been said he can train a man to kill another man with his bare hands."

"So, what is he here for?" Nicholas inquired.

"Something to do with illegal firearms possession," Jesus replied. "Hey, speaking of the man, here he comes now. Do you want to meet him?"

"I sure do!" Nicholas exclaimed.

Nicholas turned where Jesus was looking and saw a tall, over six-feet four-inch tall man approached them. He had a lean, athletic build with precision muscle tone with a boyish handsome face with a crown of salt and pepper hair cut to a even fade with a part on the side.

"Hey Jesus, I heard you were back. Who's your friend?" Chuck asked.

"Hey Chuck, this is Nicholas La Cour," Jesus replied.

"Nicholas, I've been hoping to meet you," Chuck said. "Your father Louis was a very well-known and respected man."

"You knew my father?" Nicholas asked in awe.

"Yes, and I wish I had time to stay and chat with you and share some stories, about your father, but I'm supposed to be on the other side of the yard in five minutes," Chuck said.

"Okay, no worries. I understand," Nicholas replied.

Chuck focused his attention on Nicholas. "Tell you what, tomorrow at this time, I'm free. How about you look for me at this spot and we can talk about some of the crazy stories I have about your dad?"

"Sure, thanks, I'll see you tomorrow," Nicholas replied, watching Chuck walk out of sight. He was thinking to himself he wanted to talk to Chuck Jackson alright, but it was about asking him to teach him how to be a fighter.

"Wow, Nicholas, looks like you've made friends with a legend," Jesus said. "I've never seen Chuck Jackson make an appointment to meet with a guy. He must have really liked your father."

"I'm in awe myself, I can't believe Chuck Jackson, knew my Dad, " Nicholas blurted, shaking his head. "Not to mention I'm in awe of you too, Jesus, and your wealth of information. Looks like you know practically everybody who is somebody in this prison," he said out loud.

Nicholas stood there spellbound to the spot and then he thought about what could have happened if he had gone back into the Chow hall. He shook out his thoughts and said. "Thanks again, Jesus, for looking out for me in the chow hall and introducing me to Chuck Jackson. I owe you one."

Jesus just smiled. "Don't thank me I'm just doing an old crusader a favor or two. Now Nicholas, you just try and stay out of trouble. And open that bible, of yours, and maybe learn a few prayers," he paused. "Look I've got to get going, I'll catch you later."

Nicholas watched as Jesus made his exit. He decided it wouldn't be a bad idea to learn some prayers, while he contemplated revenge against Dante Channing for putting him there. But then a thought ran through his mind. He thought he'd heard Jesus say he was just doing an old crusader a favor. He wondered if he had just imagined hearing him say that. His eyes glanced down at the bible in his hands. It was time to get down to reading it. Maybe he'd look up some of *Grand mere Catherine's old Proverb sayings.* He thought to himself as he hurried down the corridor.

II

Chapter 4

Lacey & Mamma Pearl...

Later... That same day back in San Jose, California.

That Thursday afternoon, Lacey arrived at her mother's house excited about helping her clean out her closets in several bedrooms. She left her children at home with their nanny. Since her brother's incarceration Lacey had worked hard at making sure her mother didn't spend too much time alone analyzing where she'd gone wrong raising her brother.

She thought back to that dark moment months ago, when Lacey had first learned of her mother's deep depression. That sad dark moment had ended with Lacey taking her mother to see a well-known local therapist. Who had suggested her mother take medication for her depression but when her mother had refused and asked for an alternative treatment, her therapist had recommend that her mother keep herself busy with lifestyle changes, like exercising, changing her nutrition, adding a social support system, and adding *to do* projects that made her keep her mind busy. That was when her mother Pearl decided she wanted to clean out every closet in the house and reorganize them. This had resulted in her daughter Lacey reading every book she could find on the subject of reorganizing and closet cleaning.

Now armed with all the tips she could find on the subject, Lacey parked her car in the driveway and quickly strolled around to the back of her mother's house, toward the kitchen. She just walked the length of the back deck when she saw her mother standing on the deck with her back to her.

Her mother Pearl was a doll of a woman, beautiful, exquisitely. Toned and delicate curvaceous build, on the outside. With a soft, Southern-polite, well-bred, genteel feminine, on the inside. She was always a lady however, if the moment called for it, Pearl Fanay Andries-La Cour, could be a real bitch.

As Lacey approached the deck. She heard her mother's intake of breath and heard the soft sob. She watched her mother in earnest and realized she'd been crying.

"Mother? Mother? Are you crying? Is something wrong?"

Pearl looked back at her daughter. She didn't know which of her questions to answer first. Then she thought better of it and just said. "Oh, goodness Lacey... Where did you come from? I didn't hear you arrive. I thought I was alone out here,"

"Are you alright?" Lacey asked.

Pearl replied, pulling a handkerchief out of nowhere and dabbing her eyes before blowing her nose. "I'm okay. I'm so sorry your finding me this way. You've caught me completely off guard. Forgive me, I must look a mess."

Quickly Lacey closed the distance between them and gave

her mother a reassuring hug. "You always look beautiful to me, mother."

"Thanks, baby. Mother's alright," Pearl replied pulling out of their embrace and taking a deep breath.

Lacey steered her mother over to the patio seating on the deck. "Come, Mother, sit down and tell me why you are crying, on such a fine beautiful day."

Pearl let her daughter lead her over to the sitting area. She settled herself in her seat before she said. "I feel like I failed him," she took a deep breath suppressing a sob. "Daughter, my grief is that of a mother feeling like she failed her only son. Nicholas... My beautiful creative son is sitting in prison and it's all my fault."

"No, Mother," Lacey scolded. "I won't let you blame yourself."

"But I am to blame," Pearl declared with a sob. "And who should feel the bulk of this whole devastating experience but me?"

"Mother stop saying that. Think of the stress and anguish you're putting yourself through. Not to mention what your being upset is doing to your blood pressure. Your health."

"I know Lacey and you're right," Pearl declared slouching over. "The stress is unbearable. But as a mother I know I must stand by my son. And here I am doing nothing to help him."

Lacey lean over and took her Mother's hand's in hers and softly said. "Help him," she shook her head. "Mother I understand you think you must help him. But you've done all you can. You forget that this is a choice that Nicholas made. Yes, I understand, and I know you have a firm belief that you must stand by your son," she stated "But Mother, not to the detriment of your health.

"Oh... What's the use of my health," Pearl exclaimed in anguish?

Instantly Lacey interrupted her she knew she had to talk some sense into her mother. "Mother, calm yourself. Don't you remember what the Honorable Judge Edward Joseph George said to you, when he called you into his office after he'd sentence Nicholas?"

Pearl looked up into her daughter's face. "What?"

"Judge George, remember." Lacey said and then started to quote him. He said. "*The biggest mistake most parents make is thinking they, too, have to "do time" with their child. Your son made a bad choice. Not you. You must get this through your head, or you'll never be any good to yourself or your son. The first thing you have to do is make sure you don't let your son's incarceration be the detriment to your health. If you don't do this one thing. You'll never survive, Nicholas' incarceration. And what good will you do for him, if you are dead?*"

Instantly, Lacey's words had an impact on her mother Pearl.

Pearl sat up straight, and she took a deep breath as she composed herself. She took out her handkerchief and dabbed at her eyes. "Will you look at the time Lacey? It looks like I 'm toddling away the day and with your coming over to help me clear out those closets. Come now, let's get a move on it. I'm done feeling sorry for myself."

Lacey was startled by her mother's change in attitude, but she was glad she'd changed. Her mother face looked a lot calmer. "Sure, thing Mother, lead the way. I'm all yours for to-day."

12

Chapter 5

Four months later...

The massive, razor-wire-topped gates opened signaling it was time for the afternoon-controlled mass-movement to the yard.

Nicholas waited his turn as the guard frisked the man standing in front of him. He was starting to get used to this way of life. He knew each time he'd went to the yard or other places on the prison grounds where prisoners hung out the guards would have to search him. He glanced behind him and notice he was the last person left in line to enter the yard.

"Inmate step forward!"

Nicholas knew the guard his name was Raul Di Silva. He'd seen him before. In fact, for some reason Di Silva was always where Nicholas had plans to be. Sometimes it seemed uncanny.

Quickly the guard patted him down. "Alright inmate you get four hours on the yard today. Any plans?"

Nicholas was caught off guard. He'd never been asked

that question before. "No, sir. I just thought I'd do a little weightlifting."

"Huh, I've noticed that, you seem to make it a point to stick to yourself. And I also noticed, from time to time Chuck Jackson drops over to the weights and gives you some pointers."

Nicholas just stood there not saying a word. He wondered where this was going. He thought back to his friend Jesus Martinez and what he had told him the first day he'd entered. He'd seen Jesus from time to time and he had been right. He wondered what category to place the guard standing in front of him.

The guard relaxed. "Look Nicholas, my name is Di Silva, Raul Di Silva and I know that may not mean anything to you. But I believe in making sure I look out for inmates. Help them stay out of trouble. I noticed you've spent a lot of time with Chuck Jackson, I also know he's been helping you learn some fighting routines, stuff like contact fighting."

"I just wanted to be able to take care of myself while I was here," Nicholas replied.

"Well, I'm sure Chuck has given you plenty of pointers on how to do that," Di Silva replied. "But that's not why I'm worried about you. You see Chuck has also told me you are a very quick and sharp learner. And that worries me."

Nicholas thought back to Jesus, one day he'd asked him about Di Silva, and he'd remember that Jesus had said Di Silva was one of the good guys. He had to wait and see. He kept his mouth shut. He shook out his thoughts and paid attention to what Di Silva was saying.

"Look Nicholas," Di Silva stated. "I believe that if a man

spends too much time alone in a place like this, he starts to get bitter and worst, he starts to think of crazy stuff, getting revenge And that ain't good."

Nicholas wondered if Di Silva could read minds. Every day since he'd been there all he thought about was ways to get back at Dante once he was out.

Di Silva steadied his gaze on Nicholas. I can see that mind of yours moving. Don't worry, I can't read minds. Not yet anyway."

Nicholas studied Di Silva for a long moment. He couldn't make out what he was thinking. He was certain Di Silva had no clue about his plans for revenge against Dante Channing.

"Well inmate did you hear anything I just said?"

All at once Nicholas realized Di Silva was talking to him and he realized something else he'd called him inmate again.

"Yes, sir. I heard you loud and clear. I need to mix in more with the locals," Nicholas replied, with a hint of sarcasm. "Any suggestions on who my new BFF should be?"

Di Silva smiled. "As a matter a fact I do," he grinned. "In fact, I'm going to pretend I'm your mommy and that I'm going to book you a play date, so you can find you next best friend forever."

Then Di Silva turned and yelled. "Archibald Boarman come over here!"

Archibald hurried over and paused just as he reached Di Silva. "Boss you called me?"

"Archibald this is your new friend, Nicholas. Nicholas say hi to Archibald," Di Silva stated.

Nicholas did as he was told. "Hello, Archibald, glad to meet you."

"Glad to meet you too Nicholas," Archibald replied nodding.

"Excellent," Di Silva stated. "I can see you too are getting along already. By the way Archibald, Nicholas is interested in joining your card game. Hook him up for me and introduce him to a few of the guys. Tell them I'll pay Nicholas' buy in. His box of Top Ramen, is on me."

"Sure thing. No problem, Boss," Archibald stated.

"Good!" Di Silva replied. "Well I'll leave you to your card game," he stated turning and walking away.

Nicholas and Archibald stood there and watched the guard walk away.

All at once Archibald turned to Nicholas and said. "Whatever you do, Nicholas. Don't ever call me Archibald. I hate that name. Arch or Archie will do just fine."

"Sure... Sure! Does that mean I don't have to play cards with you?"

"Oh, hell no!" Arch laughed. "You are playing cards with us. In fact, me and the fellas are going to be your best friends. Because Raul Di Silva told us so and you don't say no to Di Silva."

Nicholas gazed at Archibald for a second longer and then said. "What's it with Di Silva? He's got some kind of power around here or something?"

Archibald laughed. "Yeah, he sure does. The fact is his mother is a practicing Hoodoo priestess of the Oshun of Santería Cuba and his older brother is a catholic priest and then he's got one brother that's a Federal judge and another brother who's a Federal Marshall."

Archibald chuckled to himself letting his words sink in. "And Nicholas do you know what that means?

Nicholas shrugged. "No, I haven't got a clue."

"It means that they've got God, the devil, and Lady Justice in their back pocket. Now that's a powerful trinity."

"So, is a practicing Hoodoo priestess pretty powerful? I mean she must know a lot of things?"

"Yes, alright but you know she's not the most powerful woman. She's only good for the area she lives in."

"Really?" Nicholas asked. "There's others?"

"Yeah, take for example where you come from probably has a different one, more powerful than a practicing Hoodoo priestess. Say where do you come from?" Archibald asked.

"Silicon Valley, you know San Jose," Nicholas replied.

"Oh yeah, you got a pretty powerful one only she ain't no practicing Hoodoo priestess."

"Really?" Nicholas replied. "I'm curious to know just what Silicon Valley has that's more powerful?"

"You all got, Madame Annie Mae!"

"Really?"

"Nicholas, you sure use the word, really a lot. Anyway, I take it that you didn't know about Madame Annie Mae?'

"Nope!"

"It figures, cause if you did, I'm sure you would have gone to her to ask her help on your case."

"So, tell me. If Madame Annie Mae isn't a practicing Hoodoo priestess, what is she?"

"Well rumor has it she used to be a real madame of a brothel, some say she was a stripper. I don't know, what I do know is she is some kind of hidden Angel, more powerful than any practicing Hoodoo priestess. She helps people that's all I know."

Archibald looked thoughtful for a moment and then said. "You know I hear if folks want to reach her all they have to do is go to some magic shop on Murphy street in Sunnyvale."

"A magic shop," Nicholas repeated. "There's only one magic shop I know of on Murphy street in Sunnyvale, and that is *Magickal Enchanted Gift* run by a lady named, Joan."

"That's the one," Archibald said. "There's a little guy with Bart in his name who hangs out there, some say he can get word to her and some say he can't. I don't know which is true. All I know is that if you go to the magic shop and you're looking for her. You can find Madame Annie Mae."

All at once Archibald laughed out. "You know they say that guy named Bart something is one ugly looking dude. They say he uses his ugly to scare away evil," he laughed. "Boy I'd love to see that."

Archibald kept laughing at his own joke for what seemed like a long time before he stopped and said. "Well, come on Nicholas, it's dangerous to linger out in the open like this too long. Let me introduce you to the fellas in our poker game."

***

A few months later...

Nicholas found himself looking forward to playing cards with Arch and the rest of the gang. Briskly he walked to the end of the line at the massive, gate and watched it opened and signaling it was time for the afternoon-controlled mass-movement to the yard.

Nicholas waited his turn as the guard frisked the man standing in front of him and then it was his turn. He finished and he quickly entered through the gates and headed for the gang's favorite area.

"Hey Nicholas!"

Nicholas paused it was Vincent Lopez he had met him at the Bible study group.

"Hey Vincent, how's it going."

"I'm good, thanks for asking. Did you get started on reading the Chapter, Ruth in the Bible?"

Nicholas grinned. "I sure did. It's an interesting chapter I can't wait to talk about it at our next Bible Study group."

"Me, too," Vincent replied. "What did you think about that "kinsman" redeemer stuff? You know the taking off a shoe to redeem?"

"Yeah, that stuff was pretty cool for its day," Nicholas agreed. "I can't wait to talk about it more!!"

"Me too!" Vincent replied. "I see you are going to hang out with your friends. I'm on my way to play some dominoes. Check you later."

Nicholas nodded and made his way toward the group of men sitting and standing around the far tables.

"Looks like the gangs all here," Nicholas joked as he greeted his friends.

The gang consisted of several regular guys including Archibald Boarman, who everyone called Arch for short.

Arch was a fast talker and a whiz at calming down high tense situations. He had strange eyes — a clear, pale brown, like rare amber found in a tall forest in a land distant across the sea.

Next, came Daniel Wolski, a real big dude that everyone

called Heavy D because he was over six foot six-inches tall and weighed over three hundred and twenty-five pounds.

Then you had Sir George Blackstone. He was a thin tall, pasty man with a quiet manner and a noticeable slouch. Who held dual citizenship in Great Britain and America? He was called Sir George because he really had received a title of "Sir" from The British Honors System. Next, came Theodore Brunansky who everyone called Bruno. And no one could forget Heinie short for Heinz, which was his last name. His first name was Orel, Orel Heinz.

Then there was Maddog. Whose real name was Leroy Maidu-Johnson. His skin was dark as if it had been kissed by the sun and his long straight jet-black hair was plaited neatly in one braid hanging down his back with the most perfectly cut chiseled bangs lying flat against his forehead. Maddog was a man that no one messed with.

Leroy Maidu-Johnson was a multi-racial part African American part Picayune Chukchansi Native American, who was a full member of a federally recognized tribe of indigenous people of the Blue Gold Rancheria Casino. Leroy was in federal prison, for charges stemming from a violent casino takeover, where he had assaulted, battered and falsely imprisoned casino security guards.

The story has it Leroy had become upset because he had not been sent his full monthly allotment check, after a group of Tribal Council had unanimously decided to send Leroy and his full-blooded mother Ruby Dondero Maidu-Johnson, disenrollment letters and terminate their monthly allotment checks that totaled $40,000, for the two of them.

Leroy then took matters into his own hands and stormed

the Casino with a few of his most loyal friends, an AK-47, a FAMAS a bullpup-styled assault rifle designed and manufactured in France, grenades, a bomb vest and enough explosives to blow the casino to the ground. But it was his mother Ruby Dondero Maidu-Johnson that kept her son alive when she learned what he had done. She immediately contacted her lawyer to make the Blue Gold Casino and rest of the tribal members aware of who really owned the land that the casino was sitting on.

Mother Ruby's quick thinking kept her son alive, got their monthly allotment checks increased and resumed and negotiated her son a short eighteen month sentence in Lompoc Federal Prison. Momma Ruby Dondero Maidu-Johnson was no one you wanted to mess with.

Maddog showed up to play poker when he wanted to, and no one questioned him. There was always a seat left open for Maddog, just in case he wanted to play.

That day Maddog was dealing. "Seven... King gets a three."

Nicholas wasn't playing he was watching the pros handle the cards.

Hennie was taking the card game serious as usual y. Though you couldn't tell by the calmness of his disposition.

But Nicholas could tell, because Hennie had told him that the only way to play poker was to play it with a blank face that no one could read. It was also the key Hennie had shared with him on how to bet any adversary, never show them any emotions.

Nicholas smiled with his thoughts. Hennie had taught him many things. He focused on the game and noticed Sir George.

Sir George leaned over and whispered. "What you got?"

Bruno showed him his hand. "Got a pair he mumbled."

Sir George nodded at him. "Go for it."

"I call!" Bruno yelled.

Maddog slapped down a new card all around.

Sir George leaned over and nudged Bruno and whispered, "What you got in your hole?"

Bruno showed him his pair of Kings

They both smiled.

Next thing you knew Hennie called.

Orel Heinz, or Hennie as everybody called him, had a mafia pedigree that read like the who's who of criminal network stretching from the East Coast to the West Coast. He'd been born one of six sons to an immigrant father who started out working as a street sweeper in New York City, for the Department of Sanitation. But it was his brothers who like Hennie were rumored to be worth hundreds of millions, who held the power. Hennie and his brothers had amassed a wealth of real estate properties and had their hand in several criminal connections consisting of nightclubs and restaurants they owned in San Francisco, Los Angeles, Miami and even Vegas. From what Nicholas had learned Hennie had taken the jail time for his family's operation, he'd been caught money laundering through his nightclubs in San Francisco and L.A. Because he had two brothers who worked for the IRS, headquarters, and one who worked for the FBI. It was rumored that they had fixed it Hennie got less of jail time. Whatever the case Hennie was said to have only gotten sentence to two years in Federal Prison, for his money laundering charge.

But it was Hennie skills playing poker that was amazing. Hennie knew how to play poker like a boss.

Nicholas stood their studying their faces. Losing to these guys many times over had taught him a lot. He remembered back several months ago, when their group had sat around talking. The topic had been revenge. It had been Sir George Blackstone who brought up the topic, talking about the most famous revenge plan he'd ever heard of was done by a set of twins he'd met while living in Quebec Canada.

"That story is the truth," Sir George stated. "Those two twins were famous in Quebec, and they perfected the art of torture revenge on their victims. You could always find them hanging at the notorious Montreal Social Club it was a famous mafia hangout."

"Yeah, but the Montreal Social Club was even more famous for their beef Wellington. It was so good it melted in your mouth," Archibald Boarman replied. "I have been there a time or two. But you know Sir George, I think you have the Quebec twins confused with the Britain twins, the Kray brothers. Now those dudes perfected the art of revenge torture."

"I agree," Heavy D. replied. "The Kray brothers were the worst. I heard those two nailed some unlucky guys kneecaps together. Those guys were brutally evil. They used brass knuckles, with blades on them, swords, hammers with nails welded to them. Yeah, those guys were diabolical with their torture."

"Yeah, I heard about that. Those two were heartless and coldblooded, when they went after someone for revenge," Archie declared.

Eagerly Nicholas listened to every word. The talk about revenge torture piqued his interest. He hadn't known there were so many ways to extract vengeance on a person.

Unbeknownst to him, Hennie was studying Nicholas face and watching his card game at the same time. He knew he needed to have that talk he'd been putting off having with Nicholas. It was just about the right time. He turned his attention back to the card game and waited.

Nicholas thought he'd felt eyes watching him and glanced up at Hennie at just that moment. Immediately he noticed nothing was out of the ordinary.

Earnestly he studied Hennie and knew he was the one to watch during a card game. There was nothing that Hennie couldn't do well.

Hennie had even become Nicholas' sort of mentor. He was the one who had told Nicholas in confidence that he knew he had plans to seek revenge against his business partner, Dante Channing.

Nicholas focused his gaze. He knew the look on Hennie's face. He was going in for the kill the card game would be over soon.

"I call!" Hennie declared loudly.

"Dam! Hennie, we know you ain't got a hand that's worth a damn!" Heavy D yelled, as he rubbed his jaw and looked around the table, before he threw out more money.

Bruno looked back at Sir George and they both nodded. He then threw out more money. "I call."

As Nicholas stood there his daydream took over. He remembered the day Hennie had walked up to him with wisdom in his voice and said.

"I heard from Chuck Jackson, that your fighter skills are first class. Chuck doesn't think there is much more he can teach you."

"Really, Chuck said that about me?"

"Chuck is proud of your skills. But he's worried just like me. You know Nicholas, I see it in your eyes. You're tormented. Day in and day out. All you think about day and night is revenge. You need to understand why you seek revenge against your business partner."

His remarks had caught Nicholas off guard that day. "Okay, Hennie, Mr. Wisdom, what it is that I need to understand?"

"Well, what you don't understand is why you feel that way, but it is not really you that feels the pain, but the little boy inside yourself, who is named Nicholas, who is feeling that hurt. You see, he is the reason you feel the pain and hurt your old business partner Dante, has done to you, because in reality Dante represents the school bully who bullied the little Nicholas inside of you, when he was a child."

Nicholas shrugged. "Sorry, Hennie, I don't see it."

"Of course, you don't because you don't want to get quiet for a moment and ask the little Nicholas inside of you why he is hurting. Because right now all you see rolling through your mind is different ways you can blow Dante your bully, up with a bomb, or shoot him until he's dead, or poison him or whatever your mind is plotting to do. But what you don't see is that before you know it, you've spent your whole time here imagining ways to pay your bully back for all the pain they have caused you and all you really succeed in doing is giving away your power, your time, see?"

"My power?"

Yes, Nicholas, your power," Hennie replied. "By giving your bully your time, by thinking about them all the time. You give away your power and doing this makes them the winner."

Hennie paused and took a moment to gather his thoughts.

"Tell me Nicholas. Do you really think your life will be better after you get revenge? Because if you actually looked at the big picture you will see that if you get your revenge, your life would be worse than it is now. Think about what I'm saying Nicholas. Use your mind. The best way to get revenge is to turn your tormentors from winners into losers."

Loud yelling broke Nicholas out of his trance.

"Dammit Hennie! I knew you were bluffing!"

"I may have been bluffing Heavy D, but I still beat all of your asses," Hennie grinned and looked back at Nicholas and winked.

Nicholas wondered if Hennie had the ability to read a person's mind.

He watched as Hennie got up and gathered his winnings of several boxes of top ramen and some cash and then walked over and closed the distance between them.

Hennie thrust a couple boxes of top ramen into Nicholas' hand. "Here!"

"Thanks, Hennie, but you didn't have too," Nicholas replied.

"That's for that girl of yours, what's her name..." He popped his finger. "Maëlle...Maëlle Moulard. You can use one to keep your place in line tonight, when you call her to night to remind her visiting day is next week."

Nicholas had told Hennie about his relationship with Maëlle Moulard and ever since he had, Hennie had been helping the two of them get to talk every week a couple of times and Maëlle had even started to come out to see him during visiting hours. "Thanks Hennie, I know Maëlle would want me to thank you too, for her."

13

❧

Chapter 6

One year later...

That morning Nicholas was jolted awake by the whooping and hollering outside of his cell. He took a few minutes to center himself and climbed off the top bunk.

The bunk below him was empty. Early that month he'd lost his cellmate, Dave Waldman. Dave had been released after completing his two-year sentence for embezzlement. Dave had been an accountant at a high-tech company, he'd embezzled $350,000 from his employer.

Nicholas gather his clothes, and his hygiene kit that consisted of his toothbrush and soap and walked to the entrance of his cell. The door opened it was time to head down to the communal bathroom he shared with other inmates and shower, brush his teeth and get ready for the day.

"Hey Nicholas! Do you know what day it is?"

Nicholas looked up at the familiar voice. It was Jesus Martinez.

"Hey Jesus, no, I don't know what day it is. What day is it?"

"Man, it's a *Taste of Soul Food Day* in the dining hall. They are serving Southern Fried Catfish, grits and eggs. I think they have collard greens too. You know in honor of *Black History month*."

"Oh, yeah!" Nicholas replied. "Sounds good."

"Man, it sounds delicious," Jesus blurted. "I'm headed that way now. You want me to save you a place in line? It'll only cost you one box of top ramen."

"Thanks Jesus, but no thanks," Nicholas shook his head. "I'm saving my top ramen for the phone line this evening."

"Suit yourself. See you later, I'm heading to the dining hall."

Nicholas gave Jesus a nod and watched him turn and make his exit.

***

That same morning, back in San Jose, California.

Late, the night before, Ross Goldman got a call from the Santa Clara County District Attorney's Office and was told to come to their office the next day.

The office was on the corner of West Hedding and First Street. He took the elevator to the 8th floor of the west wing. Ross had had no idea what their meeting was about when he arrived and he was dumbfounded when he walked into the office and saw the Attorney General for the State of California, standing there.

"Julien! Julien Broussard!" Ross stated in disbelief. "My goodness what are you doing here?"

Julien extended his hand. "Ross Goldman, I'm here to see you. The Santa Clara County, District Attorney has been kind enough to let us use their conference room, this way, please."

Julien Broussard was a tall slender man, with lightly graying hair in his mid-fifties.

Ross knew Julien Broussard, well, he was a man with a brilliant mind and family connection going back to the Broussard's of the great state of Louisiana.

Ross walked in the direction Julien waved him to follow as they walked down the hall.

An open conference room door stood waiting for them to enter. The huge windows in the room afforded spectacular views of Mountain Hamilton.

"Wow! Now that is one excellent view," Ross stated as he walked in.

"Yes, I noticed it also. Julien said sitting in front of a file folder. "Would you care for a cup of coffee," he offered. "As you can see Santa Clara County is really treating us well."

Ross took in the refreshment table. Fresh coffee, bagels, donuts were teamed with apples, bananas and oranges. There was enough food to feed a small army. He'd recall hearing attorney friends who had dealings with the Santa Clara County District Attorney's office refer to Santa Clara County as Santa Claus County for the generous way they had been treated when visiting. Now Ross, knew what they'd meant.

"Thanks, maybe later," Ross replied, taking in his surroundings. He leaned back in his chair and looked around the room. "This is something big. I mean, look at all of this and it's just you and me."

Julien smiled. "I suppose it looks big. But really, it's just the hands of justice working, to correct a wrong."

Ross laid his hand on the table. "I'm curious to know why I'm here sitting with the Attorney General for the State of

California. In the Santa Clara County District Attorney's Office."

"Well, like I said the hands of justice move slow, but they move," Julien paused letting his words sink in. "I guess I should get to the point. It is the duty of the D. O. J. to locate those whom an injustice has been done too, and letting them know, they may be eligible and, in some cases, have charges dropped against them."

Ross interlaced his fingers as if he was going to pray. "Get, to the point Julien."

"Well, Ross, it appears I have been task to be the mechanism to reach out to you and let you know that the charges against your client, have been dropped due to the fact that the evidence used against him was indeed planted. Because this information has been brought to the attention of the D.O.J. it was determined your client was framed and is indeed innocent, all charges have been therefore dropped against him."

Ross Goldman closed his eyes. "Now, Julien would you please tell me the name of my client that all charges have been dropped against!"

"Why, I thought you knew I was referring to Nicholas... Nicholas La Cour!" Julien declared. "Since you were the one who sent the letters to Federal courtroom of Honorable US Magistrate Judge Edward Joseph George, about the movie clips showing Dante Channing confessing."

Ross Goldman leaned back in his chair and smiled. "Well, Julien, I guess and will have some coffee and a bagel, would you care to join me. I think we should talk some more."

"If I was to inquire. Exactly what would the topic be about" Julien asked but didn't wait for a response. "I assume

you want to discuss compensation for wrongful imprisonment of our client."

"You and I both know if a Jury would be called to hear
such a case, especially since it involves a much beloved local
family, the jury would be ask to award compensatory damages, false imprisonment, physical suffering, mental suffering
and of course humiliation by my client and his family, loss of
time, interruption of business and of course my attorney fees
and all of those other necessary incurred expense, etc., etc."

"There's no need to call a jury," Julien stated.

Ross stared Julien straight in the eye. "Now Julien you
and I both know an individual subjected to a false arrest
and added with false imprisonment is entitled to two types
of compensatory damages. One for loss of liberty and two
for loss of physical and emotion distress. And since we both
know that there are aggravating factors..."

"Okay, Ross. I hear what you are saying. But let's be reasonable."

Ross took out his pen and a small note pad. He began vig-
orously writing and then abruptly stopped and pushed the
pad over to Julien.

"Ouch!" Julien replied shaking his head. "Ross! My Friend.
Can we be reasonable?"

Ross looked Julien dead in the eyes. "I am being a reasonable man, Julien. Besides, the coffee and bagel didn't taste that
great."

***

At dinner that night, Nicholas quickly choked down the
overcooked collard greens, green beans and macaroni and

cheese with the limp fried catfish they'd served in honor of Black history month.

With his new skills Nicholas had acquired he was starting to not dread dinner time. The trick Nicholas had learned was never stare at your food. Just start eating.

His new skill afforded him extra time for other things, he thought as he quickly and efficiently headed out of the chow hall toward the telephones.

Quickly he headed to the front of the line. He'd paid his friend Vincent Lopez two boxes of top ramen to hold his place in line. Now Nicholas, stood front and center and quickly dialed the number.

The phone picked up on the first ring.

"Nicholas, I know it's you, the prison name came up on the caller ID, "Goldman blurted.

"Hey Ross, how's things?"

"I'm fantastic! Look, Nicholas I've got some great news! You're getting out."

"Yeah, right when my times up," Nicholas joked.

"No, Nicholas, this is not a joke. I mean you are really getting out. Apparently, the State of California received information that you had been framed, by Dante Channing," Ross declared and began filling him in on all the details.

Nicholas stood there holding the phone with a look of shock and disbelief. He couldn't utter a word. He felt like he was walking in a cloud. A thought hit him. He wondered if God had heard his prayers, if he had, then he also knew about his plan. His plan for revenge.

14

Chapter 7

Freedom...

A distant rumble of thunder sounded on the horizon as Nicholas La Cour, walked out of Lompoc Federal prison a free man. He could smell the poignant smell of sweet peas growing in the fields nearby as he looked down at the bible he held in his hand. Since he'd entered prison, he'd slept with the bible under his pillow every night.

He looked up at the sky as billowing white clouds against the blue sky all at once an ethereal bright white clouds stream across the skies seemed like a movie screen as a sudden rush of memories flooded his mind as the day dream hit him hard right in the middle of the day.

It was vivid and real.

Loud buzzer sounds and the master locks were thrown — KA-THUMP!

A prison sentence is called "hard time" for a reason — there's nothing cushy about it," Nicholas thought as he looked around. "The first night I arrived I remember being waken up at two o'clock a.m.

by a guard with a flashlight in my face. I, as well, as my cellmate, a man who spelled his name, Waldman, but pronounced it Wildman. We were both stripped and searched. Apparently, they were looking for some home-made thongs someone had made that they called testicle crushers.

When it was all over, I felt like I needed a shower, I felt dirty as I put my clothes back on and climbed back under my itchy wool blanket on my bunk and hit the sack again. It was just the first of many things he came to dislike about being locked up, in Lompoc Federal prison.

From that moment on Nicholas plotted and planned his revenge. It was all he'd cared about as he went about living out his sentence at Lompoc, Federal prison.

Nicholas shook himself out of his daydream and looked around, he was still at Lompoc.

"Hey Nicholas," A guard yelled. "I see you're getting out."

Nicholas looked up at the familiar voice, it was Raul Di Silva. He was the guard that stuck the flashlight in his face when he'd first arrived.

"The men are out in the yard, preparing for their couple of hours of free time." Di Silva said. "They are going to be sad when they learn you can't make it to their regular poker game."

Nicholas shrugged. "Yeah, well, it looks like I made other plans."

Raul Di Silva closed the distance between them fast. He glanced around to make sure they were alone. "Look, Nicholas, I know you think I was kind of rough on you in here. But the truth is I was looking out for you. I owed your old man, Louis. So, I did what I did to keep you safe."

"You knew my father?"

Di Silva shook his head as he pushed his hands into his pockets. "Yes, your father Louis La Cour, was a good man. He did a lot of good for people and he had a lot of friends. I consider myself one of them."

Nicholas stared back at him in stunned disbelief. Was this the same man who had threaten him every morning. Yelling at the top of his lungs. *Be standing beside your bunks and be visible! I repeat, be standing beside your bunks and be visible by 7:00 a.m. sharp or it'll be no breakfast for you!*

All at once Raul Di Silva thrust out his hand in friendship to Nicholas.

Nicholas looked down at Di Silva's hand and hesitated before finally grasping it.

"Look, Nicholas," Di Silva, stated shaking his hand hard. "I want you to know, I'm glad you're getting out, and I'm sorry you got framed for something you didn't do," he let out a deep breath. "Just remember the past is behind you now. Don't make the mistake of plotting revenge. You'll only end of back in this place."

Di Silva let his words sink in and then added. "I'm sure your father Louis, wouldn't want you coming back to this place. Think of it this way. You had a little adventure in life. Take that experience and make something good happen with it."

"Something good," Nicholas repeated. "Yeah, sure. Sure thing."

"Well, I've got to get back to work. You take care Nicholas and remember God has a bigger plan for your life," Di Silva said as he turned and walked away.

"God has a plan," Nicholas repeated under his breath as he watched Di Silva disappear behind a loud locking gate.

"*Well, God,*" Nicholas said to himself. "*I know one thing for sure you heard my prayers when you got Dante Channing to confess to framing me with* federal larceny and securities fraud..".

Nicholas couldn't believe the elaborate scheme Dante had set into action. He was thankful that Yanni Smirnov had filed a civil action against Dante, once in court she had admitted being his consensual sex slave, confidant and friend.

Unbeknownst to Dante, while he was high on drugs and alcohol. Yanni had systematically video tape all his drunken drug induced confession. She made sure her cameras had been on while they were making love. She brought her collections of videos to court and played them for the judge in his private chambers with her attorney present.

When Yanni had thought the court would not welcome her videos and testimonies she had summoned the help of local news agencies who had been more than happy to show partial clips of her video on live air.

Those scenes clip she filtered to the local news stations had been better than reality TV and had opened the way for their admission into the court.

In Yanni's desire to prove she had been telling the truth about Dante breaking her arm. She had systematically sneaked the actual tape showing Dante committing the act into the courtroom.

An unknowing judge had allowed the video, to be shown in a darken court room, the audience sat spelled bound and once the video started it showed Yanni, clad naked except for a leather thong, a pair of black leather thigh high boots with spike heels and a black leather chain collar around her neck. Her hands and wrist were bond together and suspended from some kind of strong hook hanging from the ceiling. It was evident she was sharing a mutually consensual bondage game with Dante Channing. Because Dante was shown clearly standing there playing the starring role as he hammered out discipline, spanking her with a small leather whip in a perverted sexual dominance game where he could be heard telling Yanni to say his name or he would spank her. Yanni was heard saying Dante's name softly until he would order her to say it louder. Throughout the video Dante was heard telling Yanni to state he was her Daddy and he provided for all of her needs. Even stressing to her to say he took care of her financially. Dante arrogance was astounding as he confessed to be a brilliant man. A man so smart there was nothing he couldn't do. Nothing he couldn't get away with.

In Dante's drugged up stupor he bragged about snarling his business partner and sending him to jail. Watching the video, there was no denying Dante thought he was the greatest man that ever lived.

But the final scene was the one that showed Yanni had told the truth when she stated Dante had broken her arm. The video showed Dante gagging Yanni before lowering her arms from the ceiling all the while keeping her arms secure behind her as he entered climaxing moments of his sex act.

The jammed packed courtroom witnessed the scene of Dante coming all over Yanni's broken arm.

The audience in the courtroom looked on aghast as Yanni's gagged muffled screams did little to mask the pain of her broken arm shown clearly in the video.

The judge had immediately seized the evidence and contacted the district attorney. Once Nicholas's attorney, Ross Goldman, had seen the story unfold on the evening news, he used every favored ever owed to him and sat to work on securing Nicholas' release. He immediately filed a motion asking that all the charges against Nicholas be dropped and dismissed.

Their judge had allowed those same video tapes to be played in court once Dante had proven himself to be a hostile witness. Those videos had supported Yanni's accusations. In court everyone heard Dante assert in his own voice how he had had plenty of money to take care of Yanni, since he had betrayed his best friend and sent him to prison.

Additionally, Yanni's videos were thorough. Many showing Dante bragging about his involvement with the selling of bogus stock options and how he'd framed Nicholas for all of it. Over and over the video tapes of Dante showed him to be a loud, unfeeling narcissist, hell been on destroying Nicholas La Cour because he had been jealous of the level of privilege, Nicholas had been born into. Then after his trial, Dante Channing had vanished into thin air. Law enforcement couldn't locate him.

Now Nicholas was stepping out the doors of prison into freedom. He didn't even mind waiting for his favorite girl to pick him up as he pulled out one of the few possessions he had hung onto. The local newspaper was badly worn from his many handling. It had permanently been folded to the article with the colored picture of the blue-eyed Russian woman named, Yanni Smirnov. He had immediately remembered her. She was one of the girls he had introduced Dante to at a party at an old historic mansion off Golf Links road, high up in the Oakland Hills.

It was all like a blur to him now, Nicholas thought as he stood there outside the prison waiting. He couldn't believe he had ever taken Dante Channing under his wing and tried to help him only to be betrayed. He remembered how he thought he and Dante had become friends. Each of them enjoyed the parties at the mansion and they both enjoyed making lots of money. It was their love for making money that got the two of them to create the investing holding company. It was the reason the two of them had had the dispute. A dispute Nicholas never could have imagined would send him to Federal prison for a white-collar crime that he never committed. All because Dante had got it into his head that Nicholas should just hand over their company to him. Well now that he was a free man, Dante Channing was going to have to pay plenty for what he'd done.

Nicholas wanted something else, but he didn't have a name for it yet.

Nicholas was so deeply engrossed in his thoughts he didn't hear the car until it slowly pulled in front of him.

"Hey Nicholas, didn't you hear me call your name?"

Conflicted with a heavy heart but full of excitement over seeing her and being free to go wherever he pleased. Nicholas looked toward the familiar sounding voice and smiled. Maëlle Moulard, was sitting behind the driver's seat and she looked damn good.

Nicholas knew in his heart that Maëlle was the other half that complimented him, neither one of them were perfect. Far from it. They were both capable of sinning against each other. They both had. But he knew his life wouldn't be nothing without Maëlle in it.

"Hello, my beautiful better half!" Nicholas whistled out getting into the passenger side of the car.

He let his eyes lovingly take in every inch of her. Maëlle had her hair braided in long braids parted in the middle and piled high on top of her head. The effect was mesmerizingly elegant, regal and made him compare her to an Egyptian queen.

Nicholas smiled with his thoughts and felt like the two of them were like fragmented pieces of a whole capable of living life separate and independent but always waiting for the other one to join them to make them whole. *"She looked good enough to eat,"* he thought, *"And he wasn't thinking about food.*

Maëlle watched him standing there and admired his deep bronze tan skin. She knew he'd been working out in the sun. The color was flattering on his over six-foot frame. His body was tight and toned in all the right places. "Nicholas, stop staring at me like a hungry savage!" Maëlle purred, getting out of the car and leaning in close to him and kissing him.

Nicholas hungrily kissed her back. "I am hungry, and sweetness you know I'm not hungry for food. But some of your good loving."

Maëlle giggled. "You better stop it Nicholas you are making me horny."

Nicholas planted a long kiss on her lips. "Good, because I was hoping we'd check into the first hotel we find up the road. I'm a man with an itch and I intend to get it scratched."

"Well, Big Poppa, I'm just the right Kitty cat to handle

that job and brother I just got my claws done," she giggled showing off her freshly polished nails. "Do you like the color?"

Nicholas took her hand and examined her nails. He noticed her ring finger she was wearing the ring he'd given her and felt a sense of relief their checkered past was behind them now. He regretted having jilted her at the alter and had contacted her days later expressing his regret and telling her he would call up every guest and apologize for what he'd done. But once he told Maëlle about the big trouble Dante Channing had got him in legally she put on the brave face he knew she would and had his back.

He knew how Maëlle got turned on when he used his Cajun drawl. Since he'd been in prison, he and Maëlle had become old pros at having phone sex a couple times a week. He cleared his throat and then he switched his voice and said. "Why honey cakes, I think this color makes your hands look exquisitely, beautiful. Now, Miss Maëlle, what is this color? It's awfully pretty. No wait don't tell me, let me guess. Would that their color be jungle red? No... No wait a minute I see the glitter in it, it's Ruby Red Slipper, right?"

"Yes, sweet daddy, why yes, it is," Maëlle let out a sweet sexy Southern drawl.

"Damn, sugar, you make me hot when you talk that way," Nicholas declared in a sexy hoarse voice.

She purred with a giggle and reached over and felt the bulge between his legs. "Whoa, Big Poppa! Me, thinks your dick is harder than Chinese Arithmetic."

"That's the point little darling, now how about you put that petal to the meddle and find us a hotel, motel or a Holiday Inn! Hell, I'd take an Extend Stay America if you find one of them first!"

"Sho nuf I will, Big Poppa!" Maëlle shrilled out loudly, gunning the gas pedal, as she made her way down the road and took the right turn when she saw the US 101 highway. She gunned the gas pedal as she glided onto the freeway.

Nicholas smiled all his senses honed in on his memories. He had a lot on his mind. But the first thing he was going to do was make slow passionate love to Maëlle for the next several days.

Then he was going to find Dante Channing, his misguided trust in Dante had taught him a harsh lesson. In the corporate world no matter how, efficient you were someone was always waiting to try and screw you. Since he'd been in prison, he'd had a lot of time to think and one thing he was clear on was that the corporate world wasn't any different than the swamps of Lake Pontchartrain. He remembered that as a boy his father Louis had taken him on a tour of the swamps of Lake Pontchartrain. He remembered that they'd camped out in Atchafalaya swamp, while there he'd watched a snapping turtle take a bite out a man's boot and bite his toe off. And each day he had to be on the lookout for cottonmouth snakes and American alligators any one of which could take a man's life in the blink of an eye.

Nicholas theorized long and hard and as far as he was concerned the corporate world was just like the swamp world and in the swamp world you never messed with a gator in the water.

Nicholas ran his hand across his face and tried his best to hide what he was thinking. One thing he was certain he and

Dante Channing had some unfinished business and he was planning to fight Dante, like a gator in the swamp and everyone knows you don't mess with a gator in the water.

15

Chapter 8

What's Important Kienan Egan...

A startling chill of cold air blast across Kienan's face and woke him out of a sound sleep. Startled awake he sat up in bed. He looked over and saw his wife, Lacey sound asleep. He checked the clock it was three o'clock in the early morning. Dawn wouldn't come for hours.

Kienan got out of bed and walked toward the bathroom. He finished taking a leak, washed his hands and headed back to the bedroom.

The darkened room felt surreal.

Immediately Kienan noticed the atmosphere felt strangely serene and calm. Instantly a cold air swept through the room. It started with a flash of light. It was pale and silvery and the air in front of him warped and twisted as shimmering pale light shifted.

At first it was no more than chill air shimmering like a diffuse mist. Then in an instant a man appeared before him.

He was dressed in a familiar old-fashioned vintage dogtooth tweed blazer, instantly Kienan recognized him.

Kienan stood there transfixed to the spot.

"What the —!" Kienan's voice choked out. "Louis La Cour!"

Kienan stood there transfixed to the spot. Around Louis' head a ring hung like a halo

"Yes, Kienan it is I. You should be used to seeing me like this, by now. You are not afraid, are you?"

"I'm not afraid," Kienan replied. "Having lived among the La Cour's all these years have prepared me for many things."

"Excellent, my son. For, I need your help," Louis's ghost replied, his voice sounding like a faraway fairy tale.

The moment was surreal Kienan thought as he stood there staring back at the ghost of Louis La Cour. For one thing he couldn't believe how regal Louis looked floating before him. *Maybe the dying thing wasn't so bad,* Kienan thought as he stared back it him.

As if the ghost of Louis La Cour was reading Kienan's mind his eyes captured Kienan's in a piercing fierce stare that held him spellbound.

"Don't worry Kienan, you've a long life ahead of you."

"Thanks for letting me know," Kienan replied. "Now why are you here?"

"You know I always considered you like a son to me," Louis' ghost spoke in a disembodied voice that carried on the air like a hollow wind in a cave. "A son who takes his responsibilities seriously."

"Uh oh!" Kienan joked. "I'm standing here talking to a ghost and that ghost sounds serious."

"Yes, I am serious," Louis' ghost replied. "I need you to look after Nicholas. He's hell bent on revenge against that Dante Channing character and if he's not stopped. Nicholas could be making the worst mistake of his life."

"What can I do? Nicholas is his own man," Kienan found himself saying, without a thought.

"Now, let's get one thing straight Kienan, you made me a promise!" Louis ghost stated. "And you promised me you would always be a man of your word."

Louis' ghost began pacing. "You have to see the big picture Kienan, if Nicholas accomplish his revenge. Ask me what will happen if my son, carries out his revenge?" He asked but didn't wait for a response before he began talking again. "I'll tell you what will happen., he will take a man's life and his life will be over. Because if he's lucky the police will catch him and then he'll just spend the rest of his life in prison. But that's not what I see. Being here on the other side. The dead has a twenty- four hour a day job watching the living, make one stupid mistake after another."

Louis' ghost paused and stared straight ahead as if he was observing something

"I see it clearly. My son will be successful in escaping and he will leave the country and he will become the unluckiest La Cour to ever live. Because, in the process he will be on the run, for the rest of his life. I see it all.Nicholas will run, looking behind his back at every turn. Not knowing who he can trust. Oh, he thinks he can figure it all out. But he'll just spend his time hiding. Undercover, in Mexico first, with the help of his brother Quinn, and then in Australia or wherever he can run. But he'll never be safe. And it's not what will happen to him, that I am worried about. The truth of the matter is the pain Nicholas will cause his family if he commits this murder will become so deeply embedded into their soul it will cause such deep and permanent anguish, and only God himself knows how it will affect their lives. Just think what it will do to his mother Pearl, Grand *mere* Catherine and you know how much Lacey loves her brother."

As if he was under a spell Kienan stood there listening to the anguish in Louis' voice and when he heard his wife's name included, he saw the big picture as Louis did and he understood.

"What do you want me to do Louis?"

"Kienan, I want you to protect Nicholas from himself."

"How?" Kienan asked begrudgingly.

"Talk to him, gain his confidence."

"Gain his confidence?" Kienan repeated. "But what if Nicholas won't open up to me? You know prison can change a person."

"If he doesn't then you find Dante Channing before my son does and turn Dante over to the police. He escaped the police. Let them deal with him," Louis' ghost insisted. "In fact, that should be the plan of action in the first place. You find Dante Channing!"

"How am I going to find Dante Channing?"

"Use your connections, Kienan!" Louis' ghost demanded. "Do what you have to do. Because if you don't, I'll be like a ghost in the closet of your mind clacking it's chains louder and louder until you do so."

"Oh, really? So, you going to haunt me like that ghost in that Christmas story huh?"

"I see you still got jokes, Kienan," Louis' ghost replied sarcastically. "I see somethings never change. But the point that ghost was making in that movie is still true today and it's the same as the one I'm presenting to you right now. Mankind should always be one's business. And in your case. It's your family and I know you are sentimental about all of them. It's what I've always admired about you."

Louis ghost floated toward the window, and gradually grew less visible. "Are you leaving now?" Kienan asked, standing there transfixed to the spot.

"Kienan... Kienan... Babe," Lacey's soft voice called. "Babe, what's the matter? Why are you standing there talking to yourself?"

Kienan's head jerked around at the sound of his wife's voice. He could tell she hadn't a clue her dead father had been speaking to him. If it was true the dead watch the living, then Louis was going to be shocked with what Kienan had in mind.

He wasted no time in hurrying back to their bed before he said. "I'm sorry sweetness, I didn't mean to wake you. I was talking out loud, I've got a couple ideas running through my head. Nothing that can't wait," he said sliding in bed and wrapping his arms around her and pulling her in close.

He drew in a deep breath at the touch of her skin next to his. He lowered his head and let his lips caressed down the side of her face until they nestled at her neck, as he kissed her softly. He felt her body quiver at his touch. "Mmmm, you taste so good and you feel so warm."

Lacey gasped as an electrifying pulse ran through her body. "Ohhhh! Mmm! Woooo! That feels so good," she softly moaned.

Louis' ghost cleared his throat. "I see you have things under control Kienan, I'll leave you now."

Kienan tilted his head and look toward the sound of Louis" ghostly voice. He watched as his pale apparition form slowly disintegrated into thin air.

Kienan knew Louis' ghost had departed when he felt the air in the room raise in temperature several degrees.

"Oh, Kienan, you're making me so hot stroking your fingers there," Lacey moaned.

Kienan let his fingers explore her body. His voice was mesmerizingly sexy when he asked. "Can I make love to you."

"Yes!" Lacey pleaded. "Your fingers are already working their magic."

"And yet, they can do so much more," he said as his fingers roamed down her body until they reached her thigh and slid to the inviting warm flesh in between her legs. "There is more magic to be made, if I touch you here."

Lacey felt deep spasms of pleasure rip through her body as Kienan's fingers worked their magic stroking her body into a fiery furnace.

Lacey moaned with intense pleasure and then said. "Kienan... I want to feel you inside me," she gasped as a bolt of pleasure shot through her body and then frantically yelled. "Now!"

Instantly, Kienan swooped on top of her as she spread her legs wide, he entered her with a deep thrust filling her as he rammed her fiercely like a wild animal.

Lacey threw back her head and moaned feeling the intense pleasure Kienan was given her.

Kienan didn't know what came over him as he rode his

wife, watching her face with earnest as he felt his manhood ramming her hard until they both shuddered and climaxed together.

16

Chapter 9

Brotherhood & Visions!

The Next Day...

Del Norte International airport in Mexico was a great distance behind him when Quinn Darnell Rosolado Rolandis looked out the window as his plane descendant into the San Jose International airport. When he heard that his half-brother Nicholas La Cour had been released from prison, his first thought was to head home to San Jose.

As his plane slowly touched down, Quinn closed his eyes and prayed to the god of his grandmother Ina Rosolado. He wasn't praying that the plane would land safely. He was praying that his brother Nicholas would receive him with open arms. He was worried because he didn't know how much his brother knew about the brief yet extended affair he'd had with his on again off again ex-fiancé and girlfriend Maëlle Moulard. It wasn't something that he was proud of. In fact, he wanted to confess his sins to his brother, but he'd never had the chance. There just never seemed to be the right time when they were growing up together. Not to mention he had caused the distance between them when he had tried to run his brother off the road and ended up in the hospital on death's door himself. As far as he was concerned there had never been a right time to tell his brother, at least that was what he kept telling himself. Now all he could do was pray that Maëlle was as embarrassed about the whole situation as he was and kept it a secret.

Quinn shook out of his thoughts when he realized he was standing at the desk of his rental car agency. He felt like he had been sleep walking.

The rental car agent interrupted his thoughts. "Sir here is the key to your M6 BMW, do you need a map of San Jose?"

"No, thank you. I used to live here. I know how to get around," Quinn said taking the key.

The rental car agent smiled softly. "Very well Mr. Rolandis, and thanks again for choosing *Luxury rentals*, enjoy your visit in San Jose, California."

Quinn nodded as he slipped inside his rental car and closed the door. He started the car, it roared softly with its powerful engine. He leaned back put the car in gear and smile as he drove off. He wasn't in a hurry as he headed to his hotel to freshen up.

***

Hours later, that evening the valet at the swanky hotel on North First street, had park his car directly in front as he'd paid them to do. The premier parking space came with a price and Quinn did not have a problem paying it.

Quinn headed North on First street and glazed at the shops and offices as they flashed by. San Jose had changed a lot since he'd last been there, he reflected with his thoughts as he eased his car onto Southbound highway 280. The traffic was thick for that time of day as he took the Alum Rock exit and headed east toward the foothills. Little by little the traffic scene changed as he descended into the foothills. Houses got bigger and the space between them widen, as he descended higher into the familiar hills. Suddenly spectacular views of the East San Jose hills known as Mount Hamilton came into view.

Slowly he could see the La Cour's family home crest in the distance. The home could be called a mansion. It sat on forty acres off of the road. The man he later learned was his father, Louis Antoine Nicolas Avoyelles La Cour, had purchased the land in the early 1970's. He remembered Louis fondly. During his childhood he had often heard the story from Louis about how he'd returned to his hometown Goldonna Louisiana and selected for marriage his childhood sweetheart, Pearl Fanay Andries.

Quinn smiled with his thoughts. His family had many secrets and Pearl and Louis had kept some of the biggest ones. His half-brother Nicholas was his stepmother Pearl's big secret. He wasn't even Louis' son. Even though Louis name was on Nicholas' birth certificate. But the even biggest secret of them all was that Louis La Cour, Pearls husband was Quinn's real biological father. That was why Louis had insisted Quinn was raised a round Nicholas and Lacey. He knew the real love triangle they were all involved in through the decisions that had been made by their parents.

He slowed at the familiar curve that turned into the private road. He remembered back to one of the last times he'd been there and met Horace Sherlock Bailey Garrison. Horace was another secret of Pearl's because he was his brother Nicholas biological father and Quinn was Louis La Cour's.

Quinn laughed to himself. His dysfunctional family had a lot of secrets and most of them had already been brought out into the open. All except his as Maëlle Moulard and as far as he was concerned that one will not be brought to light, he thought as he kept driving.

17

Chapter 10

All in the Family
& Grand mere' Catherine

Seeing the old road leading to his family's home-made Nicholas smile wide. Having been locked up in prison had made him appreciate the spectacular views the East San Jose hills afforded the eye.

The area was called Alum Rock, and was part of Mount Hamilton, the mountain range just above San Jose, California.

Nicholas knew the hills well. He'd grown up there and had traveled all the roads, and trails daily during his childhood.

The La Cour roomy family home could be called a mansion but to Nicholas it was home. It sat on forty acres off the road. His father, Louis Antoine Nicolas Avoyelles La Cour, had purchased the land in the early 1970's and Nicholas was sure glad he had, because the price of land in Santa Clara County, California, had skyrocketed over the years.

Nicholas looked over at Maëlle smiled at her and ran his

fingers across his head as his mind raced with the memories of his life. His father Louis had been long dead. Still he'd always thought his father has being the smartest man he'd ever known. His father had graduated from high school at the age of fourteen and obtained a full scholarship to the University of Santa Clara where he'd obtained his PhD. His father had had a love for science, math and mechanical engineering. His mother Pearl Fanay Andries La Cour, had been his father's childhood sweetheart.

Nicholas smiled with his thoughts; his mother Pearl wasn't no ordinary woman. In fact, his mother had been the childhood sweetheart of his biological father as well. Horace Sherlock Bailey Garrison was Nicholas' biological father.

Horace, his mother Pearl and the father who raised him, Louis La Cour, had kept a big secret from Nicholas for most of his life. The secret was that Horace and his mother Pearl were Nicholas' real biological parents.

Suddenly, Nicholas snapped out of his daydream and looked over at Maëlle Moulard and smiled at her. If he told the truth she was his sweetheart. Always was and always will be. The two of them understood each other, not to mentioned they'd been through a lot.

He still couldn't believe how lucky he was to have an amazing woman stick by his side.

At the familiar curve Maëlle slowed to make the turn onto the private road. A few minutes later, she pulled into the driveway and watched as Nicholas climbed out of the car and walked over and opened the door for her. He looked up and spotted his grandmother waiting by the side of the driveway.

Catherine Marie Rousseau-La Cour was affectionately and fearfully known as Grand *mere* Catherine.

"Nicholas, come and give your Grand *mere* a hug," Grand *mere* Catherine's gray eyes glistened with tears.

At the sound of the familiar distinct Cajun drawl Nicholas felt his head hanging with guilt, and shame for what he knew he had done to his family. He felt a sob breaking from his throat as he felt his grandmother's arm tenderly hold him in a loving embrace.

His voice shook as his chin quivered. "I'm sorry Grand *mere*..."

Grand *mere* Catherine's voice was tender and loving. "Hush up now *young-in*. Stop feeling sorry for yourself. Guilt and pity are two pieces of baggage a La Cour man ain't supposed to carry."

Nicholas kissed his grandmother on the forehead. He knew she knew exactly what to say. "Thank you, Grand *mere*."

"Besides we raised you to be a moral man. You've got nothing to be ashamed of," Grand *mere* Catherine said patting his back. "Now go on inside you know your mother Pearl is anxious to see her baby boy, and so is the rest of them."

"Rest of them?" Nicholas inquired.

"You know Lacey and Kienan are here. They even brought that nanny of theirs to watch the kids. Not that I'm complaining, I'm just so glad the house is of full of people since every bodies staying overnight."

"Staying the night," Nicholas repeated and before the words left his lips his eyes grew wide watching the entourage descending upon him.

"Nicky! Oh, Nicky! You're home!" Lacey voice was charged

with energy as she hurried and closed the distance between them.

Suddenly she jumped in her brother's arms. "Oh, Nicky! I'm so glad you are home, brother!"

"Nicholas, my baby," his mother Pearl's voice was laden with love as she rushed up behind her daughter and wrapped her arms around her children.

Instantly Nicholas' arms enfolded around them both hugging them close. He felt something strange. It was a most unusual feeling, and it hit him hard. He was home with people he loved most in the world.

Nicholas felt the tears roll down his face. The feeling was surreal and overwhelming. For the first time he really realized he was free. He no longer had to worry about living every day in a state of being prepared to handle violent confrontations, that each new day brought while he was in prison. Or the constant yelling among inmates, nor the daily instructions of being told what to do. Nor, most importantly, did he have to hear the blaring loud sounds of doors slamming and keys turning, locking your life away.

He was finally home with his family. He was free.

Minutes later, Nicholas' mother Pearl was the first to break their embrace.

"My son, it's so good to have you home. Come, let's go inside. I know you've got to be hungry," Pearl said.

Before Nicholas could answer his sister, Lacey said. "Mother, you know he is. Guess what Nicholas, we are having an old-fashioned Mardi Gras French Quarter Brunch in your honor!"

"Yes, we are Nicholas!" Pearl interjected. "And we're serving all your favorite breakfast foods. We've got Fresh French Quarter Beignets, New Orleans Style Cafe au Lait, Oeufs Poches, Eggs in Purgatory, Shrimp Remoulade, Baked Cheese Grits, Country Breakfast potatoes, Homemade Buttermilk Pancakes, Pain Perdu - Custardy French Toast, Cafeteria Yeast rolls, and Apple Cider Ham slices."

"Mmmm! That sounds so tasty," Nicholas moaned. "But what happened to my Speedy Breakfast Casserole?"

"I'm not sure if there's any of it left," Pearl shrugged with sadness in her voice. "You know it's my son-in-law's favorite too."

"I ate the whole dam casserole too, brother-in-law," Kienan yelled, closing the distance between them as he and Nicholas embraced.

"So, glad to see you home, Nicholas," Kienan smiled pulling out of their embrace and patting him on his back. "Sorry about the casserole."

"I don't know if I'm glad to be home, man," Nicholas joked. "You ate up all the Speedy Breakfast Casserole and I had my mouth all set to get me some."

"He didn't eat it all," Lacey injected. "You know I made one just for you Nicky, and Kienan has no idea where I hid it."

"Oh, Lord, betrayed by my treacherous wife," Kienan laughed out joking. "Woman have you no loyalty to your husband?"

"I have loyalty to making sure you maintain that buff body of yours," Lacey teased.

Pearl laced her arm with her son. "Come on Nicholas let's get you inside. I can hear that stomach of yours growling with hunger."

Nicholas looked over his shoulder looking for Maëlle. He was just about to open his mouth.

"Nicky, you go ahead with Mother, I'll get Maëlle."

"Thanks, Lacey," Nicholas said letting his Mother and brother-in-law lead him toward the house.

Lacey took the opportunity to walk over to her best friend. "Maëlle, are you coming?"

Yes... Of course, I am," Maëlle replied.

Instantly Grand *mere* Catherine reached out and grabbed her arm. "Maëlle, I was hoping to have a word with you," she stated.

"Sure, Grand *mere* Catherine," Maëlle replied as she turned and looked at her best friend. "Lacey, I'll see you inside later, alright?"

"Okay, no worries, I need to go get the extra Speedy Breakfast Casserole, out of its hiding place," Lacey replied and turn and headed for the house.

"Great! Lacey don't forget to save some for me too, Maëlle yelled as Lacey headed to the house.

"I will!" Lacey yelled back at them.

Grand *mere* Catherine watched as Lacey made it to the front door and walked inside. She turned and placed her attention on Maëlle. "Well, Miss Maëlle Moulard, I guess it's time I welcomed you to the family," she exhaled and said. "You are one pretty tough sister, sticking it out with my grandson after he left you at the altar. I need to give you your proper respect."

Perplexed Maëlle shrugged. "I don't know what to say, anyway, thanks, Grand *mere* Catherine."

"You are one hell of a tough lady. Now come and give your Grand *mere* Catherine a hug."

The two women awkwardly embraced.

With a smile and a small nod Grand *mere* Catherine pulled out of the embrace. "Well, now that we've got that out of the way. Are you open to suggestions on where you and Nicholas should go and get away from it all?"

Maëlle' heart skipped a beat. She thought she was going to be read the riot act for all her shenanigans while Nicholas had been away. Still she had always known Nicholas was the only one for her. "Sure," she smiled. "How did you know we were thinking about going away for a while?" She asked but didn't wait for a response. "Oh, I forgot you've got that clairvoyant thing going on."

Grand *mere* Catherine laughed. "Gal, I'm full of lots of surprises. Even without that clairvoyant thing."

"Surprises? Grand *mere* Cat, you're not up to something. I mean. Are you throwing Nicholas a welcome home party?"

"You sound funny calling me Grand *mere* Cat, like that. I haven't heard that name in years. I forgot you kids gave me that nickname. Anyway, child, yes, I am and that's why I wanted to talk to you. I'm trying to keep it all a surprise, from Nicholas."

"No, worries I won't tell Nicholas if you don't want me too."

"There, now I knew I could count on you, Maëlle girl. Lacey got some ideas I want you to go over with her she can fill you in on everything. As soon as my surprise is over you and Nicholas can go off on your little adventure, and I'll keep you posted on when it well be."

"Great, I'm glad I can help." Maëlle declared.

Grand *mere* Catherine took Maëlle by the hand. "Now, come on Maëlle, let's go inside. I've got a pitcher of strawberry margaritas and a pot of gator gumbo."

"Sounds, scrumptious!" Maëlle said letting her lead her toward the house. She wondered what the surprise could be. *Grand mere Cat* didn't say what it was that she was planning as a surprise for Nicholas. Over the years, she had learned never to put anything past her.

***

Later that same day, Quinn pulled the BMW into the driveway and brought it to a halt as he parked and turned off the engine. He gazed out at the well-kept park-like garden in the front of the massive home. A glint of water hitting sunlight sparkled and caught his eye as he turned and took in the large swimming pool in the distance. He smiled the old family home was like something off the cover of an Elegant Homes magazine, he thought as he got out of the car and closed the door.

"Quinn! Is that you?" Nicholas called out.

Quinn's heart thumped loudly in his chest and he felt like his knees were going to give away. He wasn't sure how his brother was going to receive him. Regret, fear and anxiousness twisted inside of him.

Slowly Nicholas took a few steps toward Quinn.

Quinn froze on the spot. He couldn't read Nicholas' expression. He took a step toward his brother as a mix of emotions churned inside of him and then puzzlement flooded him. "Nicholas... Man... I'm so sorry..." his voice choked.

Nicholas rushed forward and grabbed Quinn in a bear

hugged. His voice excited. "Man, you've got nothing to be sorry about! I'm the one who got myself sent to prison."

It was now clear to Quinn, that Maëlle Moulard had kept their secret. He could understand why he wanted too. But to him, secrets had no place between a couple. Still, all he could think of was that love and money was two of the most powerful emotions in the universe and Maëlle, he believed really did love his brother Nicholas.

"How are you doing, Quinn? Nicholas asked breaking the silence.

Quinn looked back at his brother he stood taller than he was. He knew Nicholas had to be over six-feet tall. He was dressed in a pair of jeans and a black and silver football jersey with a bold number 8 on the front and back of it.

"I'm good!" Quinn finally managed to say. "Oh, sweet Jesus, it's so good to see you man! You look good!"

"Man, you look good too. What brings you back to *dull-villa San Jose*? Nicholas asked sarcastically.

"I'm here for your welcome home dinner, party thing! I wouldn't have missed it for anything in this world."

Puzzled Nicholas cocked his head. "Welcome home dinner?"

"Wait, you didn't know?" Quinn asked cautiously. "Damn, no one told me it was supposed to be a surprise."

"So, I see you made it Quinn!" Grand *mere* Catherine's voice carried on the air, as she closed the distance between them.

Nicholas and Quinn looked at each other and shook their heads in unison. "Grand *mere* Catherine."

"When I saw you two brothers hugging each other a few

minutes ago, I almost cried. I know my son Louis is smiling down from heaven, seeing his sons hugging, in brotherhood," Grand *mere* Catherine said, closing the gap between them she pulled them all together into a bear hug.

The moment was silent, powerful and emotional.

Finally, Grand *mere* Catherine broke the silence and said. "Boys, the look on your face's is priceless. No, one can tell me what's important. I know what's important. It's brotherhood, that's what's important."

She held the two men close a few seconds longer and then pulled out of their embrace.

"Nicholas said. "Grand *mere* that Cajun twang of yours is coming out. You been up to something. You didn't plan anything big, right?"

"Nicky really? You know your Grand *mere* Catherine has to have just a few of her friends over to celebrate."

"Grand *mere*, please tell me you didn't invite the Bingo Queen," Nicholas moaned.

"Gabby Baptiste is only one of the bingo posse," Quinn interjected with laughter. "Brother you going to have some party."

"What's wrong with inviting my friends over to celebrate?" Grand *mere* Catherine asked, as her Cajun twang rang out loudly.

"Yeah, Nicholas, what's wrong with her inviting a few friends," Quinn joked. "The more the merrier, so we can have a good time! Right?"

Nicholas shook his head. "Sure, we are. Just as long as she didn't invite any of my ex-girlfriends, I guess it'll be alright."

"I don't understand you Nicky," Grand *mere* Catherine,

stated. "You know you can't have a great celebration unless you invite family, friends and all the exes," she laughed.

"Even the ones that climb out from under a rock," Nicholas joked. "Alright, Grand *mere* Catherine go ahead and have your celebration dinner. I'm ready for anything. Now when is this big event supposed to happen? Today?"

"Oh! No!" Grand *mere* Catherine declared. "Even I need time to prepare. Don't worry it will be fun."

Nicholas nodded. "Well, that's good. It gives me and Quinn a little time to catch up," he said out loud and then thought to himself. *"And it'll give me some much-needed time to just relax away from the family."*

"That's my Nicholas," Grand *mere* Catherine said as her hands went up to cup his cheeks. "You've made an old woman happy."

"Nicholas! I've been looking everywhere for you," Maëlle called out as she closed the distance between them.

"Uh oh! Here comes the old ball and chain," Nicholas joked. "Too late to make my escape," he stated nudging Quinn. "Hey Maëlle, look who's here."

"Quinn! What are you doing here?" At the sight of Quinn standing there Maëlle abruptly stopped.

Seeing Maëlle Moulard, took Quinn's breath away. *She was a beautiful sight*, he thought, all pretty and dressed up in a mustard colored off the shoulder flowy dress that made her skin glow.

"That's one pretty dress you are wearing Maëlle, it suits your skin color perfectly," Quinn humbly stated not realizing the words were rolling off his tongue.

His quick compliment caught Maëlle off guard. Seeing

Quinn standing there brought back memories of their last encounter back in Mexico while Nicholas was incarcerated. She prayed they hadn't discussed any of that. Then her eyes caught sight of Grand *mere* Catherine standing there. Quickly she woke out of her fog and said the first thought that came to mind. "Nicholas picked it out. He took me shopping."

"It looks like Nicholas did a fantastic job. You look amazing," Quinn said and then caught himself. "I hope I didn't upset you saying so."

"No... No, not at all," Maëlle nervously replied.

Obviously distracted by Quinn's presence Maëlle shifted her attention and turned to Nicholas. "Nicholas I was hoping we could talk."

"Ah, not right now Maëlle girl, Quinn and I was just going to make a run."

"That sounds excellent," Grand *mere* Catherine injected. "Because Maëlle I was just about to ask you to help me get a few last minutes details together for Nicholas home coming party."

"Sure! Looks like I have the time," Maëlle stated, letting Grand *mere* Catherine lead her back toward the house.

Nicholas grinned as he watched his grandmother and Maëlle make their exit.

"Nicholas!" Quinn said eyeing his brother suspiciously. He studied him for a few seconds and then nodded slowly. "You're up to something. I know that wicked gleam in your eye anywhere."

Rubbing his chin Nicholas make eye contact with Quinn. "I know what we should do."

Quinn grinned. "What you thinking we got time for a game of golf?"

"Naw!"

"Uh Oh!" Quinn laughed. "The Cajun drawl is coming out. This must be serious."

"Let's make a run and go and see Annie Mae!"

Nicholas saw Quinn freeze in his tracks at the sound of Annie Mae's name. Curiously he watched as his brother's brain processed the information.

"Gimme a break!" Quinn replied annoyed. "What you are thinking of adding a drug habit to your resume now?"

The smile on Nicholas's face was cynical.

"Uh... Uh!" He said shaking his head. "Think brother! You're not using your head everybody knows every drug dealer or user in Santa Clara County knows Madame Annie Mae."

"Don't we know it," Quinn agreed. "Not to mention she knows things. Information... Secrets..."

Nicholas watched as Quinn processed the information. Suddenly Quinn looked up.

"Now, you are thinking like I'm thinking! While I was in prison, I found out Madame Annie Mae is the most powerful person in Silicon Valley." Nicholas exclaimed. "If anybody can tell us where Dante might be hiding."

"Really" Quinn replied.

"Yeah, and I was thinking she might be able to tell you about Lucy Mondragon."

Quinn interest peaked. "Oh, yeah, maybe she will know what she did with our son," Quinn muttered out interrupting him and finishing his sentence. "Damn! Why hadn't I thought of that?"

"Don't get your hopes up to high. We first got to see if we can find her," Nicholas replied. "I see what you're thinking. I hate now that I even mentioned it. Annie Mae may not know anything about what happened to your son."

The smile on Quinn's face was cynical. "I know. Don't worry about me. I haven't had my hopes up for a long time," he hesitated. "Besides, we are going to see her to help with your problem, Dante, right?"

Nicholas reached over and patted Quinn on the back. "Never give up hope, brother."

Quinn looked back into Nicholas eyes. "Thanks for saying that. Now, we've only got one problem. Where to find Madam Annie Mae?"

Nicholas laughed. "That's easy too. I found out how to find her when I was in prison. All we have to do is go see Maëlle' Aunt Joan, you know she's the one with the *Magickal Enchanted Gift* shop on Murphy Avenue in Sunnyvale?"

At the mention of Maëlle' name Quinn froze dead in his tracks. "Oh?"

"Don't worry, I'm not inviting Maëlle to join us," he said out loud and then thought to himself. *"Hell, I need some space, right now."*

"You got a point there," Quinn agreed.

Nicholas grinned. "Yeah, she doesn't need to know what we're up to. Not to mention we don't need her yapping her mouth off trying to figure out what we are up too and besides, since you got this nice new BMW to style in. How about we take it for a drive?"

Quinn nodded. "Sounds like a plan. I've been dying to see what it can do"

"I'm in agreement, brother!" Nicholas replied, turning and strolling toward his BMW.

Quinn followed closed behind tossing the car keys in hand.

***

From her hiding place on the second-floor, above the driveway, Maëlle secretly listened and watched Nicholas and Quinn engrossed in their deep conversation. Hidden behind the curtain of the great room window s

he'd heard every word they said as she noticed that they looked happy together.

Still she worried. *Who was Madam Annie Mae?* She wondered and then turned her attention back to when she heard them mention her name. She had prayed her name would not be brought up, but when it was it wasn't as bad as she thought. In fact, all they mention was keeping her from joining them. Watching Quinn's BMW exit down the private road. She quietly closed the open window.

Just as she secured the window lock. She heard the voices coming down the hallway. It was Grand *mere* Catherine, Nicholas' mother Pearl and a man Pearl's love, Horace Sherlock Garrison. They were exchanging an animated conversation in Cajun, French and English, a mixture dialect she knew they had spoken while living in Louisiana. Maëlle recalled that the older generation loved to speak to each other in their old home language.

The second she heard them talking she rushed toward the bathroom. She knew it held a connecting door to the other bedroom, which would give her an easy exit to the back stairway. She entered the bathroom and looked around. It looked like a bathroom at a five-star hotel complete with marble counter tops, designer sinks and tub and a smoky glass window. She'd reached for the door handle of the connecting door and knew that if she hurried with any luck, she could reach her car and follow them. The door quickly gave as she pulled it.

"Oh! Maëlle! There you are! I've been looking all over for you," Lacey declared casually walking over and grabbing Maëlle's hand.

Instantly the vision flashed before Lacey's eyes.

Lacey felt a strangeness the moment her hand clasped around Maëlle. It was as if time had stood still. An eeriness and a chill swept around her.

Out of the corner of her eye Lacey saw the vision. It was vivid and intensely real as it flashed through her mind. She saw a man's naked body grinding on top of a woman. The woman was groaning and moaning thoroughly enjoying the passionate pleasure the man was giving her. All at once she glimpsed the man's face. It was Quinn. She could see his face clearly and he was enjoying what he was doing.

Lacey couldn't believe the scene that was playing out right before her eyes. She watched as Quinn leaned over and started licking and kissing the woman's face as his lips kissed down her neck to her chest and then his lips clasped around a nipple and sucked hard.

As Quinn body moved across the woman's the woman's face slowly shot into full view as she moaned out in pleasure as her face contort passionately in Lacey's full view.

Lacey felt her heart catch in her chest. The pain was excruciating. "Oh, Christ! She thought the woman looked like Maëlle... Maëlle! I see you," she yelled. "I see you making love with Quinn!"

Just as soon as she said her name the woman came clearly into view, she had blond hair and blue eyes. It wasn't Maëlle.

"What?" Maëlle declared, pulling her hand out of Lacey's. "Lacey what are you talking about?"

"I thought I saw you Maëlle! In my vision. You and Quinn where making love."

"You saw me and Quinn, in a vision," Maëlle repeated. "Since when did you start believing in that mumbo jumbo hocus pocus stuff that Grand *mere* Catherine does?"

"Don't try and change the subject Maëlle, I saw you and Quinn. Well I mean... I ... I ... I think it was you. I don't know how to explain it?"

The air around Maëlle felt thick. Of all the times for Lacey's clairvoyant powers to kick in it had to be now. Her thoughts raced wondering what she could say. She didn't want to tell Lacey the truth and she wondered if Lacey could see through any lies, she told. The she remembered Lacey had said. *"I think it was you."* She thought about it. Lacey wasn't sure of her vision. She saw an out and said the first thing that came to mind.

"I don't know where you're picking up that vibe from Lacey. But tell me, did the woman have dark hair like me?"

"No... I mean at first I thought she did, but then at the end the woman's hair was blond."

Maëlle let out a sigh of relief. "Oh, really blond hair, what color was her eyes?"

"Oh, I don't know. No, wait a minute. They... They were blue, at the end of my vision," Lacey replied."

"Well, all I can think of is that you must have been picking up some of Quinn and Nicholas' old cheating habits or vibrations or better yet, maybe you were picking up vibes when your brother Nicholas jilted me at the altar. I would have slept with anybody back then to get back at him. Maybe you were picking up on when we were teenagers and me and I told you about that time Quinn kissed me. We were all horny teenagers back then. Maybe you were picking up on that vibe and that time, long ago. I don't know," Maëlle replied with as must truthfulness as she could.

"Of course, I knew about you and Quinn back when you were teenagers. But in my vision, I saw the two of you together as adults, but by the end of my vision it changed. I don't know what was happening."

Maëlle stood there adamantly shaken her head. "I don't know what to tell you, Lacey! I don't know. I'm not inside of your head. You can't expect me to figure it out."

"Look Maëlle! I know what I saw! I saw you and Quinn as adults!"

"And then you said we disappeared and changed at the end of your vision. Why are you trying to make me admit something I know nothing about?" Maëlle declared raising her voice.

"And why are you trying to make me angry!" Lacey declared.

"Enough!" Grand-*mere* Catherine bellowed, as she walked into the room. "What are you two yelling and arguing about?"

Maëlle placed her hands on her hips. "Oh, Lacey's declares she seen me in a vision making out..."

"I did see you and you were an adult, not a teenager, like you're trying to get me to believe."

"Yes, but you said yourself that your vision started off with me and Quinn and then changed to a blond hair, blue eyed woman, am I right?"

"Yes!"

"Ah Hah! Maëlle declared. "See you yourself admit your vision was flawed."

Grand-*mere* Catherine knew her granddaughters Lacey had finally started coming into her gift of clairvoyant powers. But she also knew that gift didn't come with an instruction booklet and knowing when it was time to tell the full truth and time to tell a partial one. Whatever her granddaughter had seen she had no right to pass judgment on those she saw in her visions.

Grand *mere* Catherine decided to take control of the situation now as not the time for a round of let's be truthful. Not to mention, she needed to make Lacey aware somethings you were not to tell people. She took a deep breath and said. "Lacey, baby, you must learn not to assume everything you think you see in a vision is real."

She clasped her arms, linking one with Lacey and the other with Maëlle. "You too forget this is a wonderful happy occasion, we are celebrating Nicholas' coming home. Now stop that arguing."

Grand *mere* Catherine begin leading the two toward the house. "Besides Lacey I checked, and your nanny has gotten your children to sleep and she's has occupied herself with some class she's studying. I want the two of you to join us in a..."

"A game of contract rummy," Lacey and Maëlle said in unison.

"I was trying to tell Maëlle that when I came looking for her, "Lacey replied.

"Good! Good! You young ladies no how much I love to play...

"Contract rummy," Lacey and Maëlle said again in unison, as they stared between each other.

Grand *mere* Catherine laughed out. "See there I knew you two knew me well," she declared and stopped abruptly and made sure both Lacey and Maëlle were looking at her.

"Okay, ladies, now I need the two of you to promise me you won't bring up this vision nonsense and I'm begging you both not to say a word to Nicholas," she said making eye contact with the two of them. "Agreed?"

"Agreed!" Lacey and Maëlle said in unison.

"Good! Good! Besides, I'm sure Nicholas would forgive Maëlle anything, considering what he put her through." Grand *mere* Catherine replied giving them both a stern look.

Grand *mere* Catherine placed her hand on her hips. "Oh, and don't neither of you dare to tell Quinn either."

Lacey shrugged. "Quinn? Quinn?' He's..."

"Didn't Grand *mere* Catherine tell you Quinn was here?" Maëlle stated.

Lacey felt her heart pounding. "Quinn is here? But why didn't he come inside?"

From the moment she uttered Quinn's name, Maëlle regretted it. She could see the shock written all over her best friend's face.

Lacey pressed her lips together. "I guess I knew Nicholas getting released from prison would be big news. I'm actually glad Quinn decided to come and celebrate with us."

They stood there taking stock of each other. Finally, Maëlle spoke. "Look, Lacey, I don't know why Quinn didn't come inside, but I when I saw him and Nicholas talking, well I could tell..."

"Tell what?" Lacey interrupted.

"He and Nicholas were talking and then they headed for Quinn's car. I just thought someone ought to see where they were going, that's why you saw me heading for my car," Maëlle replied as her words trailed off. She realized how pathetic she sounded.

Maëlle opened her mouth to say something and then closed it once she realized she didn't want to explain to Lacey the real reason why she wanted to stay close to Nicholas and Quinn was to see if Quinn was going to spill the beans about her flying down to see him while Nicholas was incarcerated.

"Maëlle you're still trying to keep up with the boys," Lacey teased finally breaking the silence.

"Of course, she is," Grand *mere* Catherine declared. "You could learn a thing or two from Maëlle and learn to keep up with your husband."

Lacey gave her grandmother a puzzled look.

"Where's Kienan?" Grand *mere* Catherine asked but didn't wait for a response. "What did you do send him home?"

"Kienan had some business to take care of," Grand *mere*

Catherine. "He promised to check out a new restaurant with his old friend Thomas as they had some things to talk over."

"Now, stop trying to change the subject, you and I both know Grand *mere* Catherine. Somethings will never change. You know Maëlle still prefers hanging around Nicholas and Quinn rather than us ladies even after all of these years," Lacey stated.

"You are so right, Lacey," Grand *mere* Catherine declared with laughter.

"Whatever!" Maëlle stated sarcastically as she wrapped her arms defensively around herself.

"Look you two. We need you to play cards. Now you both know how much your Grand *mere* Catherine likes to play contract rummy."

"You mean Love to play Contract rummy?" Maëlle mumbled and then thought. *"No wonder Grand mere Catherine's been so nice to me. She's going to make me stay and play her old card game. I'll never get away to track what Nicholas and Quinn are doing."*

"Yes, we know how much you love the game, Grand *mere* Catherine," Lacey finally added.

"Oh, what fun we will have! Come let us go forth and play Contract rummy!" Maëlle sarcastically hissed out through clenched teeth.

"Come ladies, I'll lead the way!" Grand *mere* Catherine laughed out with glee. Clasping her arms with theirs as she led them to the family room, where their card game waited.

18

Chapter 11

That's what friends are for...

Hours later that same night, "Ahhhh! Something ain't right, Lacey La Cour-Egan. I can feel it in the air," Maëlle exclaimed.

"Uh-oh! You sound serious. You're calling me by my full name. What's up?"

"It is serious!" Maëlle declared. "That's the reason why I have to keep an eye on Nicholas." Even though Maëlle knew her real reason for keeping an eye on Nicholas and Quinn was purely for her own selfish reason. She didn't want her best friend to know she was stalling for time, she needed time to think of a good lie to keep Lacey from knowing the real reason she wanted to keep an eye on Nicholas and Quinn, was because she was scared. Quinn would tell Nicholas about their short brief affair while he was incarcerated. Her mind worked quickly, and she thought back to when she was little and was told "Little lies, can spiral and stream roll into big balls of evil."

Maëlle cleared her throat loudly and said. "You know like the story of that shepherd who had the little black sheep. You know the one who kept leaving the flock and going out exploring his big new world, only for me, it's Nicholas, as the little black sheep, it's the big bad world, and me, I'm the shepherd."

"Big bad world, huh? And you are the shepherd. Maëlle you are making a point, right? Or just trying to tell an old story in a new way?"

"Here's my point. Well Nicholas is the little black sheep that keeps leaving the herd and I'm the shepherd and I have to keep an eye on the little black sheep! I'm the only one who can save him. I'm the only one who really cares about Nicholas!"

Hearing her best friend say those words hit a nerve in Lacey's soul. The words left her mouth before she even had time to think about them.

"You, silly fool!" Lacey screamed at her! "I can't believe you said that!"

"Now wait one-minute Lacey!" Maëlle stated.

"No! Maëlle Moulard! You wait a minute. Not only was that story crazy but you are insane if you think you are the only one who cares about my brother!"

"But... Lacey?"

"Don't you but me, Maëlle! You weren't in that courtroom watching what happened to my brother, day in and day out! Where you?"

"Look Lacey calm down... Nicholas told me .."

Lacey screamed out. "Shut -up Maëlle! Don't you dare tell me to calm down! You weren't there! But I was and my mother and my grandmother!" She yelled staring off into space.

Maëlle could see Lacey was becoming hysterical. She watched as a flood of tears started streaming down her face. She had suspected the court hearing had been harsh, but seeing Lacey's anguish, she could only imagine how brutal it had been for her. She could tell her best friend's mind was back in that courtroom reliving every horrible detail.

Gently she reached out and touched her friend's shoulder. Her voice softened to a whisper. "Lacey, my dearest friend, who's more like a sister to me. I'm so sorry I wasn't there for you. I had no idea of what you were going through. I can't imagine what you endured. Please forgive me."

Her pleading voice jarred Lacey out of the vision running through her mind. As it did Lacey felt the weight, she had been carrying, worrying about her brother overtake her. Her voice trembled out. "Oh, Maëlle... Maëlle... It was so horrible! When they put the handcuffs on Nicholas and started to take him out of that courtroom without our saying goodbye. My heart broke watching it. Then when Grand *mere* Catherine jumped up and pleaded with the judge. I thought I would finally get to talk to my brother. But the judge would only let Grand *mere* Catherine and mother say their goodbyes. I felt so lost."

"I'm so sorry, Lacey," Maëlle softly spoke to Lacey tenderly, reassuring her as if she was a child. "Come, sit down Lacey," she said leading her over to the sofa.

Maëlle wrapped her arms around her best friend and cradle her like she was holding a baby.

Finally, Lacey murmured. "I'm so sorry I was angry at you Maëlle. I don't know what came over me."

"It's alright Lacey, this is the first time I heard you speak about what happened in that courtroom. You've been holding all of that in for far too long," Maëlle softly said. "Remember your grandmother used to tell us we needed to talk about things that unsettled us, or bother us so that they would not seem so big?"

"Yes, I remember," Lacey nodded her head. "She said it was the best way to keep things from bottling up inside of us and bothering us."

"So, talk to me Lacey. Tell me how you felt in that courtroom? I'm here to listen."

Lacey looked back at Maëlle's eyes and seeing the trust staring back at her. She hadn't meant to be so abrupt with her. She had known the feelings had always been there lurking, waiting. She hadn't felt at ease enough to talk about them.

She took a deep breath. "You are right Maëlle, maybe I do need to talk about it," her voice softened.

"Of course, you do. I'm here for you," Maëlle pleaded. "Please talk to me Lacey."

Lacey stood up and paced the floor, her fist clenched tight by her side and said. "I went through hell in that courtroom! Each day I had to look at my brother and hear all the vile things the witnesses were saying, and the news people were reporting... Day-in and day-out. It was like you were living in a nightmare. Each morning I got up, got dressed and went to court. Only it wasn't a courtroom, but a room filled with sharks, devils and monsters. All hell bent on crucifying my brother and killing our family a little bit more each and every day."

"Lacey... Lacey... I'm so sorry," Maëlle whispered. "I didn't know. You never told me."

Lacey hung her head. "How could I? I couldn't even put words to it then, myself. But you know Maëlle? That wasn't the worst of it. The worst day was the day he was found guilty. That was the worst day of my life. I stay there watching the bailiff handcuff my brother and drag him out of that courtroom. I've never cried so hard in all of my life."

Maëlle watched as the tears rolled down Lacey's face. She reached out and wrapped her arms around her. "My Lacey, I'm so sorry. I never once thought about your feelings. You so deserve to have a good cry!"

Lacey let out a sob as she leaned on Maëlle shoulder and cried hard.

***

An hour later, Lacey and Maëlle sat looking out the window.

"Thanks, Maëlle for letting me cry. I didn't know I needed to. Those tears had been pent up inside of me for so long."

"No, worries, that's what friends are for," Maëlle replied.

Lacey let out a sigh. "You do know that story you told about the lost Black Sheep was pretty crazy and wild."

"Naw, uh-huh, crazy and wild," Maëlle repeated. "Maybe it was. But really it was just a real story about a sheep who needs a shepherd to watch over him."

"Yes, it was a crazy wild story!" Lacey exclaimed.

Maëlle shook her head. "I don't think it's a wild and crazy

story. I think it shows how I feel. You see, I see Nicholas as the sheep who needs a shepherd watching over him."

Lacey turned and looked at her best friend. "I get it, Maëlle. I think I understand. Right now, you're just worrying about Nicholas, for goodness sake, let's find a movie on TV or something," she said, turning her focus, she looked across the extra-large family room, at the TV. "Where's that remote?"

Lacey could tell her best friend was in one of her moods. She hoped that it wouldn't last too long. Not while she had a few hours of leisure time while her children were with their nanny.

Laughter carried from down the hall.

Lacey and Maëlle both looked up at the sound of the laughter.

Maëlle was the first to speak. "The old folks are sure having a good time telling their old stories, I mean they are really into it."

"You mean their old distorted fudges on the truth," Lacey quickly interjected.

Maëlle snorted down a laugh. "You are telling the truth there. Those folks do know how to add to a story to make it bigger than life."

"Yeah, and it's a good thing they are way across the house, because we'd be catching a lot of attention from them right now if they heard the little black sheep story you just told me. I can just see it now, one of them would have said..."

"What kind of cockeyed story is that?" Both friends said in Unison, giggling with laughter.

Lacey nudged her friend, and gestured for her to follow

her lead as she got up and walked across the room to the large window a good distance away.

"You know Maëlle, that story you told me about the shepherd needing to watch his sheep? Well... I was thinking..."

"That story was the truth," Maëlle said, through clenched teeth. She rolled her eyes and gestured for her to follow her over to another window, farther away. She didn't want to start an argument with Lacey. Besides, she knew Lacey had been right. They didn't want to attract attention from the old folks.

Lacey quickly followed her over and leaned in close. "Suppose what you say is the truth. Then tell me how you, as this shepherd, who must protect the little black sheep... Well, how are you going to keep him safe, I mean your sheep, safe?"

"I don't know! I haven't thought it out that far ahead yet," Maëlle declared sighing heavily.

Silently the two friends stood at the window staring out.

The huge family room was really a typical great room combining a family room at the center of the home off the kitchen. With its raised ceiling and floor to ceiling windows that afforded excellent views of City of San Jose east foothills.

The two friends were still silently standing staring out the window just as Grand *mere* Catherine's laughter erupted down the hall. She was laughing at a joke Lacey's mother Pearl was telling. They could hear, Pearl's longtime fiance Horace Sherlock Garrison add his share to the joke. A chorus of laughter erupted down the hall.

"They are having way too much fun," Lacey replied.

"Yeah they are. Now back to my story. I thought of something. I think I got a plan and it was all in what I just told you."

"Really?" Lacey curiously tilted her head asking before adding. "Well, what is it?"

"I haven't thought it completely through just yet. But I think I have a place to start, to try and figure out just what I need to do or find someone to help."

With deep interest, Lacey glanced back at her best friend and saw the seriousness in her face. "You look sure about this. So, where are you going to start?"

"I am serious and I'm going to start by going to see my Aunt Joan."

A bewildered expression flashed quickly across Lacey's face before recognition registered. She had the answer to her unanswered question. "Of course, your Aunt Joan, hears all gossip, chitchat, secrets, every piece of news uttered about anyone in Silicon Valley. With her shop located right down the street from the Cal-train station. Somebody is always dropping into her shop, bringing news and information."

Maëlle played with a strand of her hair. "Don't you know it. It's the best gossip factory for miles around."

"Yes, it's even better then the local beauty parlor," Lacey nodded agreement. "That shop of hers is really an underground grapevine of information on all the good, bad and ugly that happens in Silicon Valley."

"Don't I know it," Maëlle declared. "And it's in the perfect location. Located right on Murphy street with all that foot traffic of people coming and going from that Cal-train station, I'm sure somebody would have stop in and give her some information, about Nicholas' case."

Maëlle rubbed her chin and started daydreaming about her Aunt Joan's shop. It was called the *Magickal Enchanted Gift* shop, located right on Murphy Avenue, in a rustic old building that looked like it could be sitting in the French Quarter in New Orleans instead of the downtown section of the good old the town of Sunnyvale, California. She thought to herself it was the perfect place to find out anything.

"So, when are we going to Aunt Joan's?"

Stunned out of her daydream by Lacey's words. Maëlle's words tumbled out. "What? You think it's a good idea? For me to go, I mean?"

"I think it's a great idea for us to go," Lacey corrected her.

"You want to go too?" Maëlle asked but didn't wait for a response. "But, what about your kids?"

"My children have a Nanny, remember? So, I'm free. Besides, I want to get out of this house as much as you do," Lacey declared, pulling out her cell phone and pressing speed dial. "Hi Maria, how are my babies? Still asleep? Good," she said. "Look, I'm going out for a while with Maëlle, call me if you need me."

Maëlle contemplated objecting but watched as Lacey hung up the phone. She realized she'd finally got what she wanted. "Come on Lacey let's get going."

"Follow me," Lacey replied. "We'll take the back hallway, they will never see us leaving."

19

Chapter 12

Murphy Street, Sunnyvale, California...

The "Magickal Enchanted Gift" shop was nestled in the heart of Murphy Street, where the architect had been erected to re-semble the heart of the French Quarter in New Orleans, complete with a replica street sign planted right in front that read *"Bourbon Street"* as well as a neon light Bourbon Street that flashed continuously twenty-four hours a day, in the front store window.

Quinn pulled the BMW up to the curb in from of the *"Magickal Enchanted Gift"* shop. He watched as Nicholas got out the car and walked over to the front window and stood underneath the neon sign flashing Bourbon Street.

"Somethings never change," Nicholas said, glancing back at Quinn. "This place still looks like it did when we were back in high school."

Quinn grinned as he walked over and patted Nicholas on the back. "Nicholas don't tell me you're now lumping us in the good old school gang already."

"My ass ain't old. Not yet, anyway," Nicholas joked.

"Hey, you know I wonder if she still has that Egyptian Book of the Dead?" Quinn inquired. "You know Maëlle always said that book was the real thing."

"If anyone would know Maëlle and her family would. Those Moulard's are one strange clan of people, stuff like that interest them. By the way why you interested in the Egyptian Book of the Dead?" Nicholas asked.

"The spells and stuff, why else. Their spells are fascinating and the real thing," Quinn declared, leaning over and playfully punching Nicholas' arm, then letting his hand linger on his upper arm.

Nicholas thought about it. "Yeah, you know those Egyptians knew their stuff. They had spells written in that book that spelled out what they were to do in the afterlife. They even had the information on embalming bodies and stuff."

"Handling dead bodies would gross me out," Quinn declared. "Just thinking about it makes my skin crawl."

Nicholas gave Quinn a strange look and glanced back at his arm. "Fascinating topic, but dude, we are about to go into a *Magickal* shop that I'm sure the owner dabbles in Hoodoo or that Voodoo crap, so let's stop that talk about that Egyptians stuff, and let go of my arm while you at it."

Quinn nervously chuckled. "I'm sorry man, your right," he said dropping his grip.

Nicholas gave Quinn a nudge "You know I know that Hoodoo stuff makes you nervous Quinn."

Nicholas thought back to when they were kids. He recalled how Quinn was uncomfortable around Hoodoo and magic stuff. Even though he always made it a point to show interest in some topics, his grandmother's strict catholic up-bringing had taken hold of him early.

He smiled and then said. "Quinn if you feel the need to hold my hand while we're inside, don't do it man. Man up! Man up! Be strong bro!"

Quinn frowned irritated by Nicholas joking. "Very funny! Come on let's go inside."

The soft tinkering of a bell chimed as they crossed the threshold.

A woman's loud cracking, hoarse deep laughter rose up and greeted them as they walked further into the store.

The woman's voice bellowed out with a deep Southern twang. "Oh, Lord have mercy, would that be little Nicholas and his sidekick the Mighty Quinn, I see coming into my store?"

The woman's laughter rose higher. "My goodness, you two are a sight for these old eyes. Maëlle, girl never told me that you were coming!"

"Hello Aunt Joan," Nicholas and Quinn said in unison.

Aunt Joan was a motherly looking plump woman with her kinky-frizzy gray hair piled high on the top of her head in a bun.

Aunt Joan made her way from behind the counter and lov-ingly hug the two of them. Her voice song out as if crying and laughing both at the same time. "My God has heard my prayers and that old root doctor did what I asked him too. Here you are Nicholas free and clear of the law."

Nicholas immediately noticed she was wearing a lavender scented perfume. He thought it must have been her favorite because she was wearing the same scent when he'd last seen her many years ago. "Well Aunt Joan you still look the same. You haven't aged a bit."

"She sure hasn't," Quinn added attempting to make small talk but seriously looking around the shop at the many quirky and unique items that it contained.

"What's that smell? Quinn blurted.

Nicholas nudged Quinn with his elbow trying to get his attention. Before he could whisper to him.

"You smell my tea! I'm brewing a fresh pot of red bulb beet tea," Aunt Joan stated. "And brewing right next to that on the stove out back is Neem Oil.

"Neem oil?" Quinn asked. "I've never heard of that."

Aunt Joan smiled and said. "Neem oil comes from the nut of the Neem tree, which originates in India, where it's been used for healing purposes for thousands of years."

"Tea... Right, that's the smell. By the way it smells wonderful," Nicholas replied.

"Oh, now Nicholas," she giggled. "I see you still Louis' son. With all them sweet words and sugary talk, trying to keep from saying the truth, it smells like shit, because it does."

"Now ain't that the truth!" Nicholas blurted out laughing.

Quinn let loose a snicker that instantly broke into loud laughter.

Aunt Joan joined in their laughter. It lasted for a few moments and then abruptly stopped in mid-laugh as she placed her hand on her hip. Her sweet face took on a stern expression when she said. "Now why did you and Quinn really pay me a visit today?"

"Looking for information?" Quinn quackingly interjected. "In fact, we're looking for a woman."

Aunt Joan chuckled at Quinn's statement. "Quinn, I always knew you never had any manners," she quickly injected. "Now, this ain't no whore house, but if you are looking for one. It's right down the street."

Nicholas coughed out a laugh.

"This isn't funny," Quinn exclaimed failing to see the humor. "We're serious. This isn't some kind of sick joke. She may be able to help me. I mean us."

"Steady now Quinn," Nicholas replied. "Watch your tongue. Aunt Joan was just having a laugh."

Nicholas reached over and placed his arm on Quinn's shoulder. He felt the motion calming him. He cleared his throat and said. "What Quinn means is, we were wondering if you could help us on a very serious matter."

"What you two bad boys playing at. You two ain't no detectives. Me, Aunt Joan. Me not some old woman you can pull a con game on. Now tell me what you are really up to."

Nicholas went into his practice speech. He hadn't told Quinn a thing about what he had planned to say to Aunt Joan.

He made eye contact with Aunt Joan before he began to speak slowly. "You're absolutely right Aunt Joan. We can't con you nor are we here to con you," Nicholas spoke to her clearly and plainly.

Aunt Joan shrugged. "Now here's a man who's speaking the truth. Go on Nicholas, I'm listening."

Nicholas let out a long sigh and said. "The truth of the matter is we were hoping you could help us find Annie Mae. You know the lady they called the angel."

"Ain't know call to it," Aunt Joan said matter of factly.

"That lady's an angel, alright. Now, what the two of you want her for?"

Determined to persuade Aunt Joan, Nicholas took over the conversation. "I read about her in the newspaper. There were several articles about her this year alone, talking about how she's been able to track down missing people using extrasensory perception that she's had since she was a child. I even read that it was a gift that she was born with."

He studied her face and watched his words set in. "I know she has a partiality to finding lost children and Quinn desperately wants to try and find his son."

"Yes, I do," Quinn quickly added. "My son's mother gave him away without my consent."

"Miss Annie Mae, ain't an easy Lady to find," Aunt Joan replied, just before letting out a big sneeze."

Instantly a piercing multisyllabic yowl whelmed out. The piercing sound sent a shock to the senses and demanded everyone in ear shot undivided attention. Then the loud crashing sound of metal hitting concrete filled the air.

"Cat! Is that you? What's going on?" Aunt Joan called in a deep southern twang, as she turned toward the back of her shop. With the sound of her voice the meowing of the cat stopped.

"Sounds like two cats were fighting," Nicholas replied.

"Naw, my cat is the best look-out cat there is. She's sounds like that when someone startles her. If she was fighting with another cat, she wouldn't have given up so easily."

"Really?" Quinn inquired. "You sure know the ways of your cat."

"Someone must be in the back alley," Aunt Joan turned

back around and said. "Cat doesn't usually scream that loud if it's just another cat."

'So, Aunt Joann," Nicholas stated trying to get their conversation back on track. "Do you think you can help us find the angel Annie Mae?"

Aunt Joan shrugged "You don't just find Annie Mae; she has to want to be found."

The soft tinkering of a bell chimed signaling someone had walked in. They heard footsteps coming from the direction of the door.

"Jesus! Have mercy!" Aunt Joan murmured startled. "What are you doing here?"

Nicholas and Quinn's head turned in the direction of the front door just as Aunt Joan voice turned into a hoarse whisper.

Nicholas let out a breath. "Who is that?"

"You mean what is that?" Quinn whispered leaning in close.

There was nothing good looking about the strange small framed man who wobbled toward them. His leathery wrinkled face smiling broadly, and he looked comfortable wearing odd color arrangements including a men's black and white houndstooth blazer over red cargo pocket shorts, with bright green and black checkered socks that stopped just under the door knocker looking kneecaps.

Slowly he closed the gap between them. Smiling wide as he did. His pointed looking teeth made his face looked demonic, and frightening.

A quirky voice screeched out. "Good day gentlemen. The name is Ghost Braveheart Bartholomeus," he said, with a proper British accent. "And who might you two gentlemen be?"

"Keep away from them Ghost!" Aunt Joan commanded. "I won't ask again. Why are you here?"

"My radiant lady," Ghost said in a distinct hoarse voice, taking a dramatic bow as if he was making the presence of the Queen of England. "I was missing seeing your charming smile."

"Liar!" Auntie Joan bellowed.

He raised up out of his deep bow and adjusted his coat and said. "I seem to be in need of your services, as I lost a small fortune on Ghost Rider in the tenth race."

"Ahh! You're coming from Golden Gate racetrack," Aunt Joan laughed. "I should have known. Why the hell did you bet on a horse called Ghost Rider?"

"Madame," Bartholomeus replied. "I had it on good word that Ghost Rider was a sure winner."

"I bet you did, no pun on words," Aunt Joan giggled.

Bartholomeus joined in her laughter.

All at once Aunt Joan shrugged. "Stop with your lying Bartholomeus!"

"I'm on the up and up Aunt Joan," Ghost replied. "In fact, I'm here to have you fix me up one of those good luck Gris-Gris bags of yours."

Aunt Joan looked flustered as she turned her attention to Nicholas and Quinn. "Nicholas and Quinn, you should head for home or wherever you were headed to," she stated. "If I hear anything, I leave a message with Grand *mere* Catherine."

She waited and watched as Nicholas and Quinn made

their exit and the tinkling of her doorbell stopped. Before she turned her attention back to Ghost. "You got money?"

"Of course, I do, beautiful lady," Ghost said, digging into his pocket and pulling out cash.

Aunt Joan walked over to a glass counter and started to open the cabinet.

"Oh, no! ... No! ... No! ..." Ghost stated. "I want a freshly made good luck Gris-Gris bags. Those things in the counter have lost their mojo juice."

Aunt Joan threw up her hands. "Whatever!" She declared turning and heading to the back.

Ghost waited until she was out of sight and then tip-toed to the front door and silently made his exit. He would pick the bag up later, right now he had important business.

He just made it to the curb and spotted Nicholas and Quinn getting into Quinn's BMW, quickly he stuck out his walking cane and gently tapped on the window.

Quinn rolled down the window. "Yes?"

"Gentlemen, I believe you are seeking the whereabouts of the Madame Annie Mae? Perhaps I can help you."

"How?" Nicholas asked.

Ghost reached into his pocket and pulled out a coin. He handed it to Nicholas. "Take this coin and meet me down at the House of the Southern Queen, in half an hour."

"The House of the Southern Queen? Where- ...?"

Ghost lean in close. "It's the house at the end of Murphy street. You can't miss it. It's a big old white house that looks like it should be in sitting in Down South, in Magnolia country. Hand the coin to the hostess, she'll know what to do."

Ghost patted the side of Quinn's BMW. "Nice car." He

smiled and turned and wobbled away from the curb heading back in the shop.

Nicholas rolled his window back up and turned to look at Quinn. He looked back at the coin he held in his hand. "Well Quinn what do you think?" He asked handing Quinn the coin.

Quinn took a look at the coin and flipped it over. It was a gold coin with an angel on the front and back of it. "Well, Nicholas, I think we going to have an interesting time at the Southern Queen. Come on, let's get over there."

20

Chapter 13

Master of Circumstance...

"Mercy! Mercy!" Aunt Joan declared with a Southern twang. "What the hell is going on around here?"

"Now Aunt Joan control yourself," Maëlle declared closing the distance between them.

"Hi Aunt Joan," Lacey said, walking across the threshold.

"Why am I being bombarded by all you bad children? Now, what are you up too?"

"We ain't children any more Aunt Joan," Maëlle declared. "Therefore, we ain't bad."

"Shut that tart mouth of yours niece! You ain't too grown for me to smack," Aunt Joan declared snapping her teeth. She looked back and forth between her niece Maëlle and her best friend Lacey. She studied them. While she did, she didn't say a word.

Finally, Maëlle broke the ice. "Auntie, are you going to stand there all night and stare us down?"

All at once Aunt Joan grabbed Lacey and gave her a hug.

"Lacey child forgive my manners. It's good to see you again," she said patting her back gently.

Aunt Joan held Lacey for a few seconds longer as she looked deep into her eyes and then released her.

Finally, she spoke and released her.

"Sit down Lacey... Sit down," she said and then walked over and reached and grabbed her niece.

"Maëlle! Maëlle! It's good to see you. Have you found a job yet?"

"Aunt Joan, I'm not looking for a job. Nicholas is home, remember," Maëlle declared trying to escape from her grasp.

"Of course! Why didn't I see it!" Aunt Joan declared with a nod her eyes intrigued n a cynical kind of way.

"Ahhhh, see what?" Lacey inquired.

"Your brothers Nicholas and Quinn were here earlier," Aunt Joan replied defensively as she stared between her niece and Lacey. Something was up, she was sure of it.

"Where they?" Maëlle answered with an innocent look on her face. Feeling the need to pretend like she wasn't aware of it.

"You know they were. Don't play innocent with me, niece. I used to change your stinky diapers. I know what you're thinking!"

"And don't we know it, Aunt Joan," Lacey declared. Feeling the need to take over the conversation. "So, Nicholas and Quinn were here earlier. Did you help them find what they were looking for?"

Maëlle saw what Lacey was doing and decided to join in. She'd heard Nicholas and Quinn talk about a woman. A woman they called Madame Annie Mae. "Did you tell them where they could find Madam Annie Mae."

The look on Aunt Joan's face mirrored an adult talking to a child who didn't understand. "Miss Annie Mae...She ain't no, damn, Madame. Why you want to call her that!"

Maëlle shuddered. "I ... I didn't mean. I mean..."

"But Maëlle," Lacey injected. "You must have heard Quinn and Nicholas call her a Madame and that's why you called her that."

"I did," Maëlle confirmed.

"You see, Aunt Joan, that's what Maëlle heard. Why does it matter if she is a Madame or not," Lacey replied?

"Oh, the paradoxes of life," Aunt Joan declared waving her hands in the air. "It matters because this world is full of half-truths and this earth God gave us is just his earth school. A university for learning and some folks has to go through the several classes of hard knocks before they even get a clue."

Aunt Joan shook her head and it looks like I've got a lesson I need to teach the two of you about truths and half-truths."

"Oh, Aunt Joan, we don't have time for no lesson. We need to find out where Nicholas and Quinn went."

Aunt Joan put her hands on her hips and gave her niece a commanding stare. "Maëlle child you trying to run and find Nicholas and Quinn and Nicholas and Quinn are out running around trying to find a woman named Annie Mae but who ain't no Madame. Have you stopped and asked yourself, why?"

Lacey shook her head. "My father Louis would say it sounds like this whole world is going crazy."

Aunt Joan laughed. "Your father Louis, always did have some great wise sayings and normally he was right."

Lacey touch Maëlle shoulder and leaned in close and said. "I think we should listen to Aunt Joan's lesson. I've got a feeling there is more to this Lady named Annie Mae, then either of us knows."

Aunt Joan waved her hand. "There now, niece. Lacey is full of knowledge; you'd best listen to her."

"Why does it matter?" Maëlle asked but didn't wait for an answer. She shook her head. "Okay, Aunt Joan let's get it over with. What is this lesson."

Aunt Joan rubbed her arms and walked over to the window. "It matters because the outer world is a mirror of our inner world. Nothing rests everything moves in circles, we are made up of cells of energy, of light."

Maëlle and Lacey exchanged glances and followed Aunt Joan over to the window.

"Aunt Joan, what are you looking at?" The two friends asked in Unison.

"It's a bad moon tonight, "Aunt Joan declared. "You can feel it, pushing like something leaning on the porch screen door trying to get in."

A chill filled the air.

Instantly a piercing multisyllabic yowl whelmed out. The piercing sound sent a shock to the senses and demanded everyone in ear shot, undivided attention. Then the loud crashing sound of metal hitting concrete filled the air.

"Cat! Is that you?" Aunt Joan asked but didn't wait for a response. "Of course, it's you cat trying to warn your mamma about that bad moon coming. Just like earlier when you were trying to tell me Ghost was near."

"Who's Ghost?" Lacey asked.

"His full name is Ghost Braveheart Bartholomeus," Maëlle stated. "He's an ugly looking little man with a leathery wrinkled face and a very proper British accent. Who I believe calls Rio Claro, Trinidad his home," she hesitated and glanced back at her Aunt? "Oh, and he has two loves in this life that I know of, one is playing the horses at Golden Gate Fields racetrack and the other is coming in here several times a week to make goo goo eyes at his love crush, Aunt Joan."

"Maëlle! It's not nice to call someone ugly," Aunt Joan declared. "Besides he's harmless."

"Well, harmless, he could be. But ugly is a defiant truth about that man," Maëlle declared and blurted out with a laugh. "And what kind of mother names her son, Ghost Braveheart Bartholomeus?"

"You have much to learn niece," Aunt Joan declared. "It's not nice to laugh at a mother's name for her child. His mother's intentions were well when she named him."

A sudden chill filled the air.

"Aunt Joan, do you have the air conditioner on?" Lacey asked, but didn't wait for an answer. "I feel a bad chill."

Aunt Joan held up her hands as if testing the air. "You see that niece, the signs are bad. I saw it when I looked at that moon. I suggest that you take heed. If you were sensitive at all you could feel it."

"What are you talking about?" Maëlle asked. "I don't feel anything."

"You're not trying to feel it. You need words to understand. Take for example spirit and matter it's one and the same. Just like love and hate are one and the same. They are just different degrees. Your lower self can become your higher self. This is the reality that not everyone can see with their eyes. You have to have an understanding in order to see the truths, otherwise, you can only see half-truths."

"The art of rising above, is that what you are talking about," Lacey inquired

"What? I don't get it," Maëlle declared.

"Yes, Lacey I am talking about the art of rising above, but I am also talking above the other laws of the universe," Aunt Joan paused.

She shifted her attention back to her niece. "Maëlle, what I'm trying to teach you is this just because you see a person with your eyes does not mean you know the person. You see, what I am trying to teach you is that some people have learned the art of rising above their circumstance in life."

Maëlle's eyes lit up. "Oh, this I know, it is the art of rising above your circumstances learning to operate in grace on a higher plane. Which means daily creating thoughts of love, strengthening your connection with spirit, God, and oneness."

"You've got that part right niece, Aunt Joan declared. "But ideally you also have to understand everything has to have a balance, you can't drag around the past. There's nothing you can do about it. It's gone. You must balance... Balance!"

"Everything has it's yin and yang." Lacey added. "This means that the person has rose above their circumstance in life, to a higher level."

"Yes," Aunt Joan declared. "The person that I speak of was once a victim and now..."

"They are a master of their circumstance," Maëlle added. "I get what you are trying to say Aunt Joan. Annie Mae was once a victim of her life, but now she has overcome the obstacles to become a master."

"Yes, you understand. Obstacles overcome, make you the master for obstacles are only illusions of life. You can create your own place in this world," Aunt Joan voice was low and slowly faded as she continued. "You can even change your name."

Maëlle shook her head. "I don't get it, why would they change their name? And who change their name?"

"The changing of a name is a tradition as old as time, in many cultures. Some people never change, so they never need a new name, and in other cultures, they change their name as often as the river flows to the ocean, many times over. Take for example, the Native American had a tradition that when a maiden or a warrior proved themselves and enrich their sense of identity then they could change their name in reverence of their new-found identity."

Lacey could see her best friend didn't get her Aunt's meaning. She knew Maëlle was smart but sometimes she needed a little help.

"Maëlle what your Aunt means is that once Annie Mae became in control of her lower self. Through rising up out of her circumstances. Well, she became an Angel, or rather she changed her name to, Angel, in fitting of her new-found grace," Lacey declared.

"How right you are Lacey," Aunt Joan declared. "But you see Annie Mae was so secure in both of her worlds and herself that she came to embrace both of her selves. How can I put this? When she was in her old life, many men did refer to her as Annie Mae the Angel stripper. And once she moved to her higher level of existence, she embraced her Angel side and became a real angel, though one walking on the face of this earth."

"Of all the paradoxes of life, you mean to tell me that Madame Annie Mae is really this Angel person, that Nicholas and Quinn are looking for?"

"Yes, Madame Annie Mae is the Angel both ways so to speak.," Aunt Joan stated walking over to a glass cabinet she opened the door and adjusted some knick knacks and placed a for sale half off sign in front of them.

"Wow, you know I'm starting to understand what you're saying Aunt," Maëlle sighed out.

Aunt Joan tilted her head towards Lacey and Maëlle and exhaled loudly. "Yes, of course I see it now. You see when Nicholas and Quinn came to see me, earlier today. I didn't have the talk with them that I had with the two of you two, and well. I never got to tell them what I told you about the real Annie Mae."

Lacey shot Maëlle a look and she could tell they were thinking a like.

Curiously Maëlle asked. "Aunt Joan, why is that important?"

"Well, I have a feeling Ghost somehow met up with them somewhere and he's sent them on a wild goose chase."

"A wild goose chase?" Lacey inquired.

"Yes, a wild goose chase, if I know Ghost as well as I do. He' put some nonsense into their heads and sent them off looking for God knows what, probably even a stripper or two."

Maëlle and Lacey exchanged glances. For once they could tell each was thinking the same thing.

"Aunt Joan," Maëlle said softly. "Where do you think, Ghost would send them?"

Aunt Joan shook her head. "Why, the House of the Southern Queen, of course. It's a bad... Bad place. Filled with strippers, illegal gambling, illegal prostitution, and a whole bunch of other illegal stuff they don't even have names for. They always have a lot of fighting going on over there. The police are always getting called. Still, it's Ghost's favorite place to take his meals. You know lunch and dinner."

Lacey shot Maëlle a glance. She knew they were both thinking the same thing.

Maëlle broke the ice. "Well Aunt Joan, Lacey and I need to get going. I just remembered I promised to drop Lacey off to check on something."

Mystified Lacey squinted her eyes at her best friend and then recognition stuck. She cleared her throat. "Oh, yes, Maëlle I almost forgot we have a stop to make."

"What kind of a stop do the two of you have to make at this time of night," Aunt Joan inquired.

Maëlle gave Lacey the look jolting her eyebrows with one of her you should have stopped talking before you opened your mouth looks.

"Ah..." Lacey said a prayer for forgiveness feeling the lie rolling off her tongue. "I promised to stop and pick up a black sheep costume. I found a little old grandmother on Craig's list who makes them. She lives over in Aviso and we promised to stop by there to pick it up tonight."

"Yeah, she really wants her money for making the costume, tonight," Lacey added, signaling her support.

"Yeah, that's right, she made it a point to say she had to have her payment, tonight, and we need to get going," Maëlle added, lifting her chin in determination, taking the lead in making their exit.

21

Chapter 14

Peppermint, Annie Mae, & Ghost...

Nicholas and Quinn grinned wide as they watched the heavy black and gold curtain rise on the theater stage of the House of the Southern Queen.

Scantily covered topless women dressed half-naked in sequins, feathers, and rhinestones in the glamour of a burlesques glitz show, sashayed and strode fiercely and provocatively across the stage. Their skin color in shades of cappuccino, ivory, caramel, mocha, cream, tan and every skin color imaginable. The ladies were radianted in a tantalizing erotic swirl of decadent pleasure across the stage as in their individualized strip teasing performance as their audience applauded and screamed for more. The girls strutted individually to the end of the stage accepting money and applause from the throng of men heaping them with praise.

"Damn, if this place doesn't remind me of old times," Nicholas declared, as his eyes beamed with excitement.

"Nicholas, I hear you man, this place is something else," Quinn replied. "But Nicholas…"

Quinn's words died on his tongue as his eyes captured the sight of a topless cappuccino skinned young woman as she walked right in front of them and lean over and clutched her breast between her hands.

Instantly Nicholas produced a twenty-dollar bill. His eyes looked hungry on the well proportion breast in front of him. He was sure the girl had to be a 40 EE cup, he thought as he pushed his twenty-dollar bill in between her waiting bosom.

"Thank you, mister" the young ladies soft spoken voice said, before moving out of distance.

"Quinn? Quinn? Quinn did you see that?" Nicholas words studdered out.

"Yeah! Couldn't miss them, had to be at least a 40 EE cup," Quinn muttered.

Quinn rubbed his face he needed to focus. He shook out his thoughts and said. "Say, Nicholas, I think we're getting off track regarding why we are here."

"Quinn, what's wrong with you? Normally, you're the one who enjoys this sort of thing," Nicholas let out a loud whistle over the loud laughter and whistles coming from the crowd of men eyeing the next young lady strutting half-naked across the stage.

Abruptly Nicholas stopped and glanced back at Quinn. "Hey Quinn, have you forgotten I was locked up?" He asked but didn't wait for a response. "The sexual neurons in my brain has been on empty!"

Just then another topless young woman approached their part of the stage. She skillfully executed a moon-walk dance as she backed her well-developed buttocks up to the end of the stage where Nicholas stood and erotically spread her legs wide and bent over.

Immediately, Nicholas slowly and securely placed a twenty-dollar bill on her black lace G-string.

"Damn! Can you feel that Quinn?" He asked but didn't wait for a response. "That's the sexual neurons in my brain firing up. They are coming to life! This place is feeding the sexual provocative neurons in my brain right now. I am being rewarded by the universe; it is giving me a fill up on my pleasuring dopamine neurotransmitters!"

Quinn ran his hand across his head. "Yeah, right Nicholas, that's just your body telling you, you are getting horny," Quinn declared. "Look Nicholas I'm going to go and see if I can find Ghost."

"Suit yourself, I'll be standing here enjoying the floor show," Nicholas declared as he glanced back at Quinn as he made a hasty exit. Before turning his attention back to the stage.

Quinn headed back toward the hostess desk. He'd figured she'd know where to find Ghost. "Hey, Miss, your name is Tanya, right?"

"It's Toya, what can I do for you?"

"Can you tell me where I can find Ghost?" Quinn replied.

"It's Ghost soup time," Toya replied. "He's right over there, by the entrance to the kitchen." Toya pointed. "He likes to sit by the window when he has his soup."

Quinn's eyes scanned the direction Toya pointed and his eyes focused when he caught sight of Ghost. "Thanks," he muttered back at Toya, as he headed over.

Ghost was having a bowl of soup just like Toya said. "Hey Ghost, can I talk to you?" Quinn called out.

"Have a seat Quinn, this is my favorite spot. I love sitting by the window and having my late-night supper," Ghost replied. "Best view in the building."

"Sir would you like for me to refresh your tea?" A waiter inquired.

"Yes," Ghost replied and glanced up. "Quinn., would you care for a bowl of soup? It's quite good."

"No, thank you," Quinn replied, taking a seat.

"What is it you want to talk about?" Ghost inquired.

"You said we would find the Madame Annie Mae here..."

"What made you think that?" Ghost's laughter filled the air interrupting him.

"You told us so," Quinn replied. "That's why we met you here, remember?"

"I did you and Nicholas a favor. You both said you were seeking Annie Mae and well, there's hundreds of Annie Mae's running amok around this place. Big ones, tall ones, black ones and white ones. Take your pick!"

Quinn could feel his anger rising. He was just about to respond.

"In fact, if none of the ones running around here suit you. Just look there," Ghost pointed out the window, "Quinn, here comes two new Annie Mae's for you to choose from."

Quinn's eyes darted out the window where Ghost pointed. Ghost was right it was the best spot in the house as he watched Lacey and Maëlle walking from the back-parking lot. "Oh, shit!" He muttered under his breath as he rose.

"What's that?" Ghost asked but didn't wait for a response

as he looked back out the window. "That young lady is Joan Moulard's niece, Maëlle Moulard, and she's with that La Cour girl, she's married, you know. I saw pictures of her wedding, Joan showed them to me. What on earth are they doing here?"

"I'll talk to you later, Ghost," Quinn said, rising quickly he dashed back to find Nicholas. He walked back the way he'd come. The place had filled up to the brim with more people then when he and Nicholas had arrived. He found the gigantic double doors entrance to the stage room and rushed in.

Frantically his eyes searched for Nicholas in the spot where he'd left him and for a minute, he'd thought he was out of luck. Then he saw Nicholas glance in his direction and caught his attention.

"Quinn, where the devil have you been? Man, you've missed one hell of a show!" Nicholas yelled. "By the way, I got the name of that girl with the 40 EE cup, her name is Peppermint, like the candy."

"That's great Nicholas! But we've got a problem," Quinn blew out a breath as he got closer. "I just saw your sister Lacey, and Maëlle coming into the premises from the window while I was sitting with Ghost. Man, we've got to get out of here before they spot us."

Nicholas turned his attention back to the crowd of people. "That shouldn't be a problem. But I don't like the idea of leaving Maëlle and Lacey alone up in here."

No sooner had the words rolled off Nicholas tongue, a turbulence rose up in the thong of people.

"Raid!" Someone yelled from the crowd above the clamor of music, and laughter. As people swarmed around like bees in a hive.

A shrill voice yelled. "The police are coming! The Police are coming!"

Frantically, people started yelling and running in all directions.

"Quinn did you hear that?" Nicholas blurted, stepping out of the way as people ran past him.

"Yes, I did," Quinn yelled. "Sounds like the police are raiding this place Come, we've got to find a way out of here!"

"You know Quinn, I know I may not have been what many would call a good person. In fact, I'll be the first to admit that you and I are heartless bastards sometime. But I don't think we can just leave them here.

"Look man, we both need to look for a way out of here.," Quinn declared.

Nicholas focused his eyes on Quinn. "We've got to find Maëlle and Lacey! Now!" Nicholas declared, dodging people as he and Quinn headed behind the stage.

"Damn! I was hoping you wasn't going to say that," Quinn stated.

"Let's get behind the stage then we can figure out how to reach the girls," Nicholas said as he led the way

Nicholas and Quinn pushed their way through the throng of people running wildly. They just darted behind the thick black stage curtain when Nicholas collided with a woman. It was Peppermint, the girl with 40 EE cup.

"Your name is Nicholas, right?" Peppermint asked but didn't wait for him to answer. "Ghost sent me to get you."

"Where the hell is Ghost?" Quinn demanded.

"He sent me to tell you he has Lacey and Maëlle safe. You

are to follow me, I'll take you to them," Peppermint said. "Hurry this way!"

Nicholas and Quinn followed Peppermint through a hidden door and into a narrow dark passageway.

Instantly a flashlight shown in Nicholas face. "Are you and Quinn looking for me!"

"Ghost!! Nicholas and Quinn called in Unison.

"Yes, it is I, Ghost and I have Lacey and Maëlle safe, follow me," Ghost said, waving his hand in his direction. "Thanks Peppermint, I knew I could count on you to find them for me. Do you need my help getting out of here?"

"I'm good Ghost," Peppermint replied, turning to leave. "You know I know my way around this place in the dark."

All at once Ghost pressed his hand on the wall behind him and it opened.

"Whoa! What's this a secret passageway?" Nicholas asked.

"Yes, it is. This old house has many of them," Ghost explained, as he led the way. "It's a carryover from the old prohibition days and before that these old passages ways took you to some of the best opium dens you could find this side of San Francisco."

"You're a regular walking encyclopedia. Tell me did you ever hear the legends of labyrinthine passages running beneath the streets and sidewalks of this fair city?" Nicholas inquired.

"How do you know about that?" Ghost asked and then said. "Never mind, I forget your friends with Joan's niece, Maëlle Moulard. Speaking of which. We'll find the ladies threw here."

Ghost, Nicholas and Quinn walked threw a narrow passageway and step into a small room.

Instantly, Maëlle leaped forward and slapped a tight embrace on the man in front of her. "Nicholas, I'm so glad to see you!"

Lacey followed her lead. "Nicholas, brother its so good to see you. She pulled back and turned and gave Quinn a hug.

Quinn stood there admiring the love Lacey was showering on Nicholas. But it was the feeling that swept over him seeing Maëlle in Nicholas arms that he hadn't expected. Still, it gave him time to admire her. Silently, he admired her a few moments longer. Enjoying her beauty without being caught. Her slender frame had just the right amount of thickness to her amble breast and curvy hips.

Ghost broke the silence. "Could we all keep walking. We got a little way to go. This way if you please," he commanded.

Nicholas and Maëlle fell in step behind Ghost.

Lacey took the opportunity to touch Quinn's arm. "Quinn, brother, I'd didn't mean to neglect you. It's good to see you too," Lacey said, giving him a hug.

"No worries, sister," Quinn replied, knowing time had quenched his desire for Lacey once he had finally accepted their blood lines did hold that they were real blood brother and sister. "And it's good to see you too, sister."

Maëlle's eyes swept over them as if assessing the attention Quinn was paying to Lacey. She felt a twinge deep within but didn't want to put a name on it. Finally, she found her voice and said.

"Nicholas, Aunt Joan told us you were asking her about Madame Annie Mae, earlier today."

"What - - !" Nicholas nearly cursed out loud. He caught himself and then shook his head. "Maëlle, what were you and Lacey at Aunt Joan's for? You two weren't following us? Were you?"

All at once Maëlle's words tumbled out. "Ghost sent the two of you on a wild goose chase. Aunt Joan told us so. And we know more than the two of you put together about Annie Mae, the Angel, you know that was the name! She's not a former stripper they now say is a Madame. She's an Angel!"

"Yeah, and she doesn't hang out at the House of the Southern Queen!" Lacey declared.

Nicholas and Quinn stopped abruptly and turned and looked at Ghost.

Ghost chuckled. "Well, now gentlemen, correct me if I am wrong. But as I recall you ask me the whereabouts of Madame Annie Mae. You did not however ask me the whereabouts of The Angel."

"We thought you understood us," Nicholas replied.

"Well now, I understood the two of you were looking for a good time and that's what I gave you. I didn't understand that what you meant was you wanted to see "The Angel" and therefore owing to the difference in circumstances I gave you what you asked for not what you meant. If you meant "The Angel" you should have said you wanted The Angel Annie Mae who serves the poor and honors Christ, it would have saved us all a whole lot of time. For she would never travel in my company."

Just at that moment Ghost stopped walking and turned and said. "Well we are here."

"Where is here?" Quinn inquired.

"If I still remember correctly. We're standing right under Aunt Joan's shop," Maëlle declared.

"Even I knew that," Lacey added.

"How do you know that?" Quinn asked.

"Let me show him," Maëlle said, reaching for Ghost's cane. "Ghost, let me borrow your cane for a moment," she said, taking it and pushing up on the circular looking contraption and demonstrating as she opened and closed it with Ghost's cane.

"This opening takes us straight behind Aunt Joan's shop. Watch and follow me," Maëlle said entering the opening.

"Nicholas you know how to do this. Follow me. I'm next," Lacey declared. As she walked over and crawled into the opening behind Maëlle. Instantly she disappeared just as Maëlle had done.

Nicholas touched Quinn's arm. "You go next Quinn, so I can make sure you don't get left behind. Don't worry about Ghost he's known about this way for years and I bet he doesn't want to face Aunt Joan right now," he said glancing back at Ghost.

Quickly, Quinn did as Nicholas instructed.

Nicholas waited patiently while Quinn maneuvered into the shaft. It gave him time to think. Ghost was a wealth of information. Maybe he could help Nicholas find the perfect place he could take Dante Channing once he found him.

Ghost closed the distance between him and Nicholas. He reached into his pocket and pulled out something and handed it to Nicholas.

"What's this?" Nicholas inquired.

"Take it, you'll need it," Ghost said, placing a gold coin with an angel on the front in his hand.

Nicholas looked at it. It was another coin like he gave him before.

"Don't worry, Nicholas. This one is the real thing," Ghost said. "Aunt Joan knows where to find "The Angel" or should I say she knows how to get in touch with *The real Angel*" and have her find you."

Nicholas studied Ghost face for a second longer. "Ghost could I ask you something?"

"Sure... Sure... What is it?" Ghost asked nodding his head.

"Are there any other old buildings like this around. I mean with hidden chambers and torture rooms, stuff like that?"

"Yes, Nicholas there is. In fact, one of the most famous old houses with a real torture chamber is the old abandon Sepulveda Monastery. Located in the Livermore hills," Ghost eyes flashed with excitement. "The torture room itself is located in the basement. It was built completely soundproof. You're not going to hear anyone screams of pain down there."

"Is that so?" Nicholas replied listening attentively. "You said it's been abandon?"

"Yes, but the building like the basement was very well built. It's abandoned but totally usable."

Then Nicholas maneuvered his body over the shaft. He paused for a second and look back at Ghost.

Ghost declared with a nod of his head. "By the way please accept my sincerest apology for I never could have introduced you to "The Angel" for she and I do not travel in the same company."

"No worries, Ghost, you been a big help," Nicholas replied reaching for the cover over the shafts.

"Oh, Nicholas, "Ghost said. "Do tell Aunt Joan, business called me away."

With Ghost's words carrying on the air. Nicholas let the circular opening carry him away.

22

Chapter 15

Land of the living...

The next day... "Brother-in-law, welcome back to the land of the living," Kienan said, patting Nicholas on the back as he watched him maneuver with the tray of food down the hallway.

Kienan and Nicholas had first met as children, their families had been the only neighbors for miles. As they grew and got to know each other they had become the brothers they never had. Once Kienan had married Nicholas' sister Lacey. Their family union was complete.

"I want to thank you for rescuing me from my mother and sister," Nicholas said with a bored tone in his voice.

"Ahhhh, I could see that the women folk was starting to rattle your nerves with all of that babying they were giving you," Kienan chuckled. "Besides, I want to thank you for grabbing a tray of food for us."

"You know I wasn't leaving out of there without substance," Nicholas grinned. "Besides didn't you see Grand *mere*

Catherine helping me, fill up this tray with enough sandwich fixings to feed an army? She knew I was at my wits end with those chatterboxes that don't stop talking, especially that wife of yours, I love my sister, but man she can baby a guy to no end."

"Lacey has been missing you, big time, Nicholas. And there's not a day that's gone by that she didn't bend my ear, worrying about you. I'm glad you are home and get to hear it for yourself."

"I knew you were going to say that Mr. Kindness," Nicholas joked. "But face it my sister's a nag. She thinks if she can keep track of my whereabouts at all time, I won't get in trouble, again."

"Your sister loves you she means well." Kienan replied, trying to gauge when it would be the right time to talk to Nicholas about Dante Channing. He was about to open his mouth when Nicholas interrupted him.

"I know! I know!" Nicholas replied. "Man, you never change."

For as long as he could remember Kienan Egan was a kind and gentle man. His tall height and broad shoulder gave the impression otherwise. But once you got to know him Kienan was the best friend you could ever have.

"I have to say it, "Nicholas shrugged. "You are starting to look like someone's daddy," he joked but then added. "Come to think of if how many kids do you have now, five, six?"

"Now you've got jokes," Kienan chuckled. "Well, if I did have six kids. I'd love them all and spoil them to death. But no, my joking brother-in-law. I've only got two. Wish I had more, but Lacey wants to make ago of her Tea Shop," Kienan said lumbering over and taking a seat on the sofa.

Nicholas placed the tray of food on the coffee table in front of them. He had filled the tray with a variety of sandwich fixings. Ciabatta rolls, rye bread, Genoa salami, Roast beef, ham, roast turkey pepper jack, provolone and Swiss cheese, lettuce tomatoes, pickles, bell peppers and onions. There was even a salad fixing platter and cans of soda.

Immediately Nicholas reached over and started making himself a sandwich. "Help yourself brother-in-law, I want to talk to you about something."

"That's why I'm here, have at it," Kienan said with an amazed tone, watching Nicholas making a sandwich piled too high to fit around his mouth. He couldn't wait to see what technique Nicholas was going to use to get the sandwich in his mouth.

He didn't have long to wait. He watched as Nicholas stuffed his mouth around as much of the sandwich as he could and then take a huge bite. It made him wonder if he really wanted to sit with Nicholas and watch him eat in a public restaurant.

As Nicholas chewed his sandwich, he knew talking to Kienan privately was the best thing. Kienan always had answers or knew where to find them. Still he could feel the butterflies taking flight in his stomach. He didn't know how Kienan would react if he knew his real motive. He swallowed hard as his thought raced, he wanted to say. *I heard Dante Channing's has disappeared.*" But he thought better of it and cleared his throat and said. "I was wondering if you still were in contact with that retired San Francisco detective. The one who takes private cases."

Kienan's brow went up as he started fixing a sandwich off the tray. Things were going better than he expected. He looked around the room and wondered if Louis' ghost was listening. "Yes, I'm still in contact with Thomas Holmes, and he's a fine private investigator, and he's excellent at keeping confidential things, confidential."

"A private investigator and he's confidential," Nicholas repeated, glancing at Kienan with interest. "Is he now? Does that mean he's any good?"

Kienan was silent. He knew Nicholas had been through a lot and he didn't want to judge him, in fact he wanted to help and to keep an eye on him just like he promised his dead father, Louis.

Kienan smiled with his thoughts thinking how just mornings ago, he'd been having a conversation with a ghost. He'd never held any preconceived ideas about life after death. There was wisdom and knowledge found from the dead as well as the living. Besides, he didn't want Nicholas getting himself in trouble and being sent back to jail, or worst what Louis' ghost had told him would happen, he could take another man's life.

Kienan's thoughts turned to Thomas. Thomas Holmes had retired from being a San Francisco detective many years ago and started his own private investigation business. Thomas was good at it and he could be trusted.

Kienan reached over and grabbed a can of soda and opened it and then said. "Yes, Thomas is one of the best in the business, if I do say so myself and from time to time, I still use him." he said taking a big gulp then swallowing. "Why the interest?"

"I was just curious," Nicholas replied.

"Is that the story you're going with?" Kienan said. "Now, Nicholas I've known you a long time and don't get me wrong, but I can see that brain of yours churning. I know you've heard about Dante Channing being on the run. But he's the police's problem."

"I know... I know," Nicholas replied.

"Look, Nicholas, you're a free man, you've got your whole life ahead of you," Kienan said with a tinge of worry in his voice.

"Yeah, I know," Nicholas said chewing his sandwich and swallowing hard. "I would just feel better if I could talk to your detective friend and see what the chances of them finding him, are. And in the same process, use your private investigator as my very own sort of a private shrink."

"Private shrink?" Kienan asked puzzled.

Nicholas shrugged. "Yeah, you know they sent me to one, while I was incarcerated, I learned that talking things out with a shrink was a great stress buster. So, I figured, rather than pay for a shrink and a private investigator. I just hire a private investigator and do a little whining, bitching, moaning, and complaining, at the same time. Without paying a real shrink and see if the guy can't find Dante in the process."

"Isn't that what family is for?" Kienan joked. "I mean, listening, whining and complaining?"

Nicholas thought to himself. "*Yes, but I may want to tell him some confidential stuff. Stuff I wouldn't want getting back to my family or friends.*"

He took a drink and swallowed hard. "If you're feeling uncomfortable by my asking, Kienan, it's okay. I can look one up myself.

"No, I'm not uncomfortable at all," Kienan stated. "In fact, I'll arrange for Thomas to meet you at his favorite restaurant, here in San Jose."

"Really?" Nicholas asked looking surprised. "The guy lives in San Francisco, the restaurant Capital of California and he likes a restaurant in San Jose?"

"Don't look so surprised. Sutter's Bistro on First Street in downtown San Jose has got some of the best steaks this side of the Rocky Mountains. They melt in your mouth, and the prime rib, has won numerous awards."

"Okay, sounds great. When can you hook us up?"

"Let me give Thomas a call, knowing him he'd like to make lunch at eleven thirty. He's an old fashion guy who likes to it a big meal at lunch," Kienan slipped his cell phone out and dialed the number.

He stood up and paced the floor as the number rang. Thomas Holmes.

"Hello Thomas, "Kienan barked into the phone. Quickly he told Thomas the reason for his call.

Just then Kienan turned and eyed Nicholas and said. "Just a second Thomas, I'll check with my brother in law and see if lunch tomorrow at eleven thirty works for him?"

Nicholas nodded an affirmative yes.

"Well, Thomas it looks like it does. Nicholas will meet you at Sutter's Bistro on First Street and East Santa Clara, thanks, Good-bye."

Kienan turned and smiled at Nicholas and said. "Okay

brother-in-law, you got your meeting and you might want to go online and check Sutter's Bistro lunch menu. Give yourself a heads up, and see what you want to order," he said with a laugh.

"Are you serious?" Nicholas curiously asked.

Kienan nodded. "Yes, Thomas, is serious about the steaks there. You can bet money he places his order the minute he walks through the door."

Nicholas nodded his gratitude and proceeded to take another bite of his sandwich and then he felt the guilt. Here he was asking his brother-in-law for a favor, knowing he'd just made it out of a bad situation by a hair, and to make things worst yet, his own sister was almost put in a bad situation too. He knew he had to come clean as he swallowed hard.

"Ah, Kienan, there's something I need to tell you, man. I need you to keep an open mind when I tell you this," Nicholas said composing himself. "You see, the other day, me and Quinn, went to a club on Murphy Street, and Lacey and Maëlle, kind of showed up. I mean they followed us and the place got raided, but luckily we all got out of there safe," he said telling his story and leaving out the fact that they had visited Maëlle's Aunt Joan, *Magickal Enchanted Gift*, and the fact that they had been looking for a lady.

Kienan lifted his brow as he stared back at Nicholas.

"Nothing happened, everything was cool, we all made it back home safe, " Nicholas assured him. "I just thought I should tell you, because it's not like when we were all just kids. Now, my sister Lacey is a mother and she's your wife. I'm sure if the shoe was on the other foot, you'd tell me, right?"

Kienan had a lot on his mind and he didn't want to answer

that question right away. Besides he had more important things to think about. Like why the four of them were on Murphy street. He was grateful his brother-in-law was telling him this, but he also was sure that there was more to this story. He also knew Murphy street was the home of Maëlle's Aunt Joan, *Magickal Enchanted Gift* and he was sure it wasn't a coincidence that this was the case. The first chance he got he was going to stop by and have a talk with Aunt Joan, privately. He thought long and hard and chose his words carefully.

"It sounds to me like the four of you had a mystical experience," Kienan said. "Glad to hear everything turned out alright."

"Magical experience," Nicholas repeated. "I guess you could call it that,"he replied, self-consciously. Hoping Kienan never discovered the truth.

***

Traffic was unusually heavy the next morning, when Nicholas made his way downtown and parked his car at the Metro Center across from the Fairmont Hotel. He walked the one block over to First and East Santa Clara Street and hustled into the restaurant and asked the maître d if a Thomas Holmes was waiting for him. The maître d took Nicholas to his table.

A stylish dressed well-built older man wearing a well-made black tweed jacket and a black mock cashmere turtleneck sweater rose just as Nicholas reached the table.

"Hello Nicholas La Cour, I'm Thomas Holmes," he said holding out his hand.

"Nice to meet you Mr. Holmes, "Nicholas greeted him. He

didn't look like a private detective to him. The man had an old-world class San Francisco sophisticated dress and manner style.

"You can call me, Thomas, if it's alright if I call you Nicholas."

"Sure thing," Nicholas assured him.

Thomas sat back down. "Nicholas you might want to hurry up and check the menu. I'm afraid I have a weakness for the steaks here at Sutter's Bistro and I've already placed my order."

Nicholas smiled glad Kienan had given him the heads up. "No worries, I checked their menu online last night and I already know what I want also."

Thomas motion for the waiter and he came right over and took Nicholas' order.

***

An hour later Nicholas couldn't believe how wonderful his grilled nine-ounce rib-eye steak with garlic butter mashed potatoes and caramelized onions had tasted. He also couldn't believe Thomas had devoured a one-inch thick sixteen-ounce Porter-house steak in one setting. The man was serious about his meal.

"Now, that's my idea of a steak," Thomas said pushing his empty plate away from him. "Do you mind if we talk serious business now, Nicholas?"

"Sure," Nicholas said perking up. "But...?" He hesitated.

Thomas chuckled. "I saw that look you gave me throughout lunch Nicholas," he said. "But you see I'm a firm believer that if a man eats his biggest meal for lunch, he has the rest of the day to work if off. Besides, I never have nothing for dinner but a blueberry smoothie.

"Really? Is that so?" Nicholas asked with a distracted tone.

"I noticed something else about you also during lunch Nicholas, you were thinking a lot of the time. And I think I know why you're here having lunch with me today."

"Is that so?" Nicholas asked with a curiously glean in his eyes as he leaned back in his chair and said. "What is that?"

"You want me to find something or someone," he said pulling a pen and pad out of his pocket.

"Yes, I do," Nicholas said enthusiastically. "But what I was really thinking during lunch was that you don't look nor act like a private detective to me. I mean you're well-dressed and you give off an old-world class sophistication that makes me wonder if you, can handle what I need."

Thomas smiled. "Let me be frank with you Nicholas. I read the newspapers. You had some serious charges dismissed against you and got yourself released from prison. Now the guy, who put your there, your ex-best friend, has gone missing and you want to find him so that you can see justice served, am I right?"

"Ahhhh," Nicholas replied with a shy smirk. "Not even close," he shook his head, and leaned back in his chair.

Thomas started to speak but notice Nicholas was thinking hard. He decided to wait. Patiently he waited and watched Nicholas. He looked like a man with a lot on his mind and he looked like he was ready to unload. After several minutes he said. "I'm a good listener, Nicholas, if you want to tell your story."

Thomas' sincere voice brought Nicholas back to the present moment. He took an extra moment and then said. "If you find Dante that's icing on the cake. For me it's more than that. You see I feel that the system failed me. Just as it has many other people. I know it can be incompetent."

"Yes... Yes, the system can be incompetent but it's the best we have," Thomas nodded. "We have to believe that eventually will do the right thing."

Nicholas nodded. "Sure, it will do the right thing but only if it can find Dante."

Thomas voice was filled with conviction. "You have to understand something Nicholas, the system needs time, time to find Dante and I believe, in time, that it will."

"But what if I want to help the system find Dante, pay for what no tax dollars can?"

"Why? Why do you want to spend hard earned money to find Dante?" Thomas asked but didn't wait for his response. "Is it so that you can have revenge? For God's sake don't you know what that will do to your Mother? Your family?"

Nicholas looked up and prayed Thomas couldn't read his mind. He was sure his brother-in-law Kienan must have put the idea of revenge in his head, still Nicholas knew his family was worried about him. "I have no intentions of causing my family anymore pain. All I want is for Dante to be turned into the authorities and face what I went through."

"Are you sure about that Nicholas? Are you sure you're not harboring some guilty secret?" Thomas asked. "I've can't take any chances that you have an ulterior motive, like a deep desire to see Dante dead?"

Nicholas leaned back in his chair and let out a deep breath. "No! I don't want to see Dante dead. I want to find

Dante to get back the ten million dollars he personally stole from me!"

Thomas let out a long whistle. He knew his questions had provided him with the results he needed. But he still wasn't sure if Nicholas was telling him the truth that he only wanted to find Dante to turn him in to the authorities and get his money back. But he decided to keep his thoughts to himself.

"Whew. Nicholas, that's a lot of *dinero*," he stated. "I'll do the best I can, but I need to know more of the story," he said getting Nicholas' full attention. "You know who Dante Channing was, some basic about your business, that sort of thing."

Nicholas stared curiously back at Thomas and blinked rapidly before nodding agreement. He then took a deep breath and said. "First of all, we were registered with the Secretary of Corporation, for the State of California. I know because I did the paperwork and I hired the CPA firm of Anderson, San Filippo, and Scott to make sure everything was done right. Anderson, San Filippo, and Scott are the most respected CPA in Northern California. All our banking was done through the most trusted bank on the west coast, Golden California Bank and Trust. Everything I did was on the up and up. But I'm sure you know all of this stuff already," he said as his voice trailed off.

Thomas nodded. "I wanted to see if you would be truthful with me and you have. I discovered the basic stuff about your company already. What I really want to know is any information you have on Dante Channing," he blurted out. "I mean everything, like how you met? Who was his friends, family, and other girlfriends besides the one in the newspaper How well did you know him? Where he was from? What was he like?"

"I get the picture," Nicholas nodded, playing with his glass of water for a few seconds and letting it all sink in. He could tell Thomas had done his homework. He knew Thomas wasn't the type to try and pull the wool over his eyes. He was sure Thomas had already checked out Dante's background.

Their waiter brought over the check.

Nicholas seized the opportunity. "I'll take care of the check now," he said, glancing a the check and reaching for his wallet and then counting out one-hundred and sixty-dollars including the tip.

"Thanks for lunch Nicholas," Thomas said.

"No problem," Nicholas replied and then took a deep breath. "Let me finish the rest the story, about Dante," he blurted and then told him everything he knew about Dante even the part about having introduced him to the blue-eyed Russian woman named, Yanni Smirnov.

"Yanni Smirnov name was in the news. She had been in the prostitution business for a while, I found out when I checked on her," Thomas replied.

Nicholas nodded. "Dante got himself in a mess if he thought he could double cross her on a deal. Anyway, I know Yanni had several girls in her posse she used to let Dante use from time to time. Yanni is where you want to start. Up until her. Dante wasn't seeing any action in the love department if you know what I mean."

Their waiter walked over with a fresh pot of coffee. "Would you like for me to freshen your coffee?"

"Yes, I would love another cup," Thomas stated.

"I'll take a refill too," Nicholas agreed.

"They do have excellent coffee here."

"Yes, they do," Thomas agreed and waited for their waiter to move out of earshot. "Anyway, Dante got himself into a load of trouble when he double crossed Yanni Smirnov."

"Yes, she is not someone you want as an enemy. I'm sure you know most of the story about Dante Channing, already, I mean, if you read the newspaper lately," Nicolas finally said. "Oh, and if you read the rumors, they say that I introduced him to a life a vice. Well, Dante was from a strict catholic up-bringing, complete with the guilt-trip thing about no sex before marriage. And at Dante's insistence I did introduce him to the vice of having sex at a brothel or two. It's where he met Yanni Smirnov."

Nicholas paused for a moment his mind was racing with so many thoughts. "So, at any rate I might have introduced him to a life of sex and debauchery. But it was Dante himself who felt the need to jump in hook line and sinker."

Thomas cleared his throat and said. "Thanks for being truthful with me, Nicholas. You're right I knew most of this stuff. But Yanni, is someone I will talk to."

He noticed Nicholas mind seemed to wonder off again. It was apparent he was wrapped up in his thoughts.

Thomas sighed loudly before he began to speak. "I don't think you had a clue that while you were handling the business end Dante was aggressively pitching his investment style enabling him to scam not only his business partner but other investors and consumers while stealing millions of dollars."

Thomas watched as Nicholas just sat there shaking his head. He was amazed at how often people didn't really know the people they went into business with. He cleared his throat and said. "There's one more thing, Nicholas. Dante Channing picked up another bad habit along the way and since you didn't mention it when you were telling your story, so I don't think you knew anything about it."

"Oh? And what is it?" Nicholas curiously inquired.

"He has a drug habit," Thomas said, letting the words sink in.

Nicholas sat there stunned by what he just heard. His thought went back to working with Dante. He remembered his strange behavior then. He wondered why he hadn't suspected. Silently he played with his water glass.

When Nicholas didn't respond Thomas finally spoke. "If you can Nicholas, I'll need for you to get me the account number for the Golden California Bank and Trust doing so will make it easier for me to get started checking all of the transactions to try and trace the money flow."

Nicholas shifted in his seat and then reached into his jacket pocket. He felt the data stick for just a second and then let his fingers rest on the piece of paper in his pocket. He pulled it out and handed it to Thomas. "I thought you might ask me for the account number. I took the liberty of writing it down."

Thomas took the paper and looked it over he then pulled out some client forms he needed for Nicholas to sign.

Nicholas looked them over and then began to read them. Finally, he pulled out a pen and signed his name before passing them back to Thomas.

Thomas took the papers. "Well, Nicholas it looks like you've hired me. If you don't mind, I want to leave and go and get started. There's a contact of mine, I want to talk to, that is in Redwood City, if I leave now, I can beat the traffic on highway 101."

"Sure, no problem and thanks Thomas for taking my case," Nicholas said rising and shaking Thomas' hand. "Oh and keep me posted."

Nicholas watched as Thomas made his exit, he smiled with his thought, daydreaming about the day Thomas would find Dante Channing for him. It would be the happiest day of his life. He was sure of it. Now he just needed to start looking for that special place. A place where he could take Dante Channing, and no one could hear his screams.

He let out a deep sigh enjoying his daydream. He wondered how long it would take him to kill Dante. Then he thought about whether he should do it quick and swift or have Dante linger and take his time.

His waiter walked over to his table holding the coffee pot. "Sir, I have a fresh pot of coffee, would you care for a refill?"

Nicholas smiled wide. "Yes, I'll have another cup of your excellent coffee," he replied feeling content that his plans for revenge where taking hold.

23

Chapter 16

Kienan Egan...

The next day across town, Kienan watched as Thomas Holmes cross the street at the corner light. He'd been circling the block looking for a parking space when he'd spotted Thomas just as a parking space had opened in front of the new Brazilian Steak House.

He stepped out of the car just as Thomas reached him. "Greetings Thomas," Kienan said.

"Kienan, so good to see you," Thomas replied closing the gap between them and shaking his hand.

Thomas Holmes was a retired, former police detective, who had started his own private investigation business. Kienan had used Thomas' services many times over the years.

"I hope you brought a good appetite," Kienan said as they strolled into the upscale restaurant.

"This place is supposed to have some of the best steaks in town," Thomas replied.

"So, I've heard," Kienan said. "I knew I could count on a man of your distinction picking a great place."

An impeccably dressed waiter introduces himself as Salvador as he showed them to their table.

They sat down and looked over their menu. "So, what are you going to have?" Kienan inquired studying the menu.

"I'm going to start with the seared pork belly with maple glaze I hear it's the best appetizer on the menu," Thomas added.

Kienan chuckled. "I'm sure you know. But what kind of steak? The 35-day dry aged boneless Angus beef rib eye or the 60-day aged one? Aren't you interested in ordering one of those?"

Thomas flashed him a smile. "Oh, yes! I want the 60-day dry aged boneless Angus rib eye, with scalloped potatoes, grilled asparagus and roasted Brussels sprouts."

Just then Kienan glanced up at their waiter. "Hey Sal, you're back, right on time. My friend Thomas will have the oldest 60-day dry aged rib eye you can find, scalloped potatoes, grilled asparagus and roasted Brussels sprout and I'll take the 30-day one with the same side dishes."

"Yes, sir! Right away. I'll bring the seared pork belly with maple glaze appetizer right out."

"It's alright if it arrives with the meals," Thomas declared.

Their waiter nodded his agreement and made his exit.

Kienan watched as their waiter walked out of distance before glancing up. He turned and glanced back at Thomas. He'd always had a great respect for Thomas. He knew he gave any job he took his undivided attention. When Thomas had called him and suggested they meet. He knew he'd gotten some information. "So, Thomas let's talk. First thanks for meeting with my brother-in-law."

"No, problem, glad to help," Thomas replied. "Besides Nicholas gave me some good information about Yanni."

"Did you find Yanni Smirnov?"

"Yes, I did. I got a lead on her form an old friend I know in the Fraud Detection Unit in the San Francisco City office. It seems Dante Channing didn't just rip off a few wealthy citizens in Santa Clara County. But he took advantage of a few citizens of San Francisco China town. He used a Chinese guy named Ace Kong, as his inside man."

"Sounds like, Dante was an equal opportunity rip off artist," Kienan added.

"That he was," Thomas chuckled. "Anyway, Dante had Ace Kong keep him in a steady supply of fresh new investors to keep funding their prior investors, so no one would find out it was a sophisticated pyramid scheme."

Just then their waiter returned and placed the hot food in front of them.

"Man, would you look at that rib-eye? Oh goodness! Doesn't that seared pork belly with maple glaze appetizer look delicious?" Thomas said before cutting a chunk off of the seared pork belly appetizer and stuffing it in his mouth.

Kienan watched Thomas with interest. "Looks like that seared pork belly with maple glaze appetizer is worth waiting for?"

"Yes, it is. The taste is exploding on my tongue. You've got to try it Kienan!"

Kienan looked at the appetizer plate loaded with succulent looking seared pork belly smothered with running eggs, oozing with the maple glaze. He reached over and cut off a chuck of egg, and pork belly making sure to load his fork with some of the bread pudding accompanying the dish. He than placed his fork full in his mouth and chewed. The experience was so good it was almost earth shattering.

"Hmm... MMM, you are so right Thomas this seared pork belly with maple glaze appetizer is deliciously scrumptious!"

Thomas silently continued to devour his food as he nodded his head in agreement as their waiter watched them.

"Everything taste great," Kienan added before nodding his satisfaction to the waiter and watching him leave.

Kienan turned his attention back to Thomas just as he was lifting another bite of rib-eye in his mouth. He went to cut his steak and said. "So, Thomas how does Yanni Smirnov play into this?"

"Glad you asked," Thomas said between swallows. "Besides what you may have heard in the news. Yanni and Dante were what you would call silent partners. She knew all about what he and Ace Kong were doing, and she was fine with it until Dante cut her out of her share of the action. And of course, she knew a few other things. But it wasn't until she thought she was going to face charges and the fact that he roughed her up pretty bad even breaking her arm, that she decided to cooperate with the authorities. She shared with them the story about how Dante set Nicholas up to take the fall for all his shenanigans, so that they would give her immunity."

Kienan nodded with confidence. "I'm glad she did, otherwise my brother-in-law would still be in Lompoc prison." He chewed a piece of his steak and swallowed. "I just wished Yanni had more to give us She didn't know the bank accounts, but Nicholas gave me a number I got my tech support guy researching it now, trying to see what we can find."

"Really, that's a good place to start. So, Yanni has no idea where Dante might be hiding? Doesn't sound like visiting her was any good."

Thomas hesitated and put his fork down and leaned across the table. "Well it just so happens my visit to Yanni was worth it. You see at the end of our little heart to heart conversation she gave me a personal tip on where I should start looking for Dante."

Kienan leaned in close. "Really? Where?"

Thomas reached into his coat pocket and pulled out what looked like a playing card. He placed it on the table and pushed it toward Kienan.

"Bingo! Behold the Jack of Spades." Thomas blurted. "This will lead us to Dante."

Kienan took the card and laughed. "A playing card is going to lead us to Dante?"

"It sure will," Thomas nodded. "You see that card has the address of a church called Angels of Mercy, that's run by a bunch of nuns who feed the homeless every day in West Oakland and I've been told I will find Jack of Spades there."

Kienan took a sip of his drink. "And who's the Jack of Spades?"

"Ace Kong's baby brother."

"That sounds easy. When can we go and see him?"

Thomas glanced over at Kienan and just laughed. "We ain't going. I am. You remember you paid me to do a job?"

"Oh, yeah." Kienan laughed and said. "It just sounds like something interesting to do. You know when you said a bunch of nuns run the place, I figured it would be kind of fun to go there."

"Well, I'll let you know just how interesting and fun a place it is, once I go and see them. Besides I wasn't promised Jack would be there. Just told that it was a place the he frequents."

Kienan nodded understanding exactly what Thomas was saying. Still he knew it was a lead. And if it was a good lead than that would be a start in the right direction. He turned his attention back to the plate in front of him. He was neglecting his rib eye. He cut a piece of meat and put it in his mouth and chewed. "Damn this is an excellent piece of meat. I should have known you knew, that this was a great place to eat!"

"Mmmm! You got that right," Thomas said with a look of utter pleasure on his face as he nodded agreement as he shoved another chunk of meat into his mouth and chewed.

24

❦

Chapter 17

The Jack of Spade ...

West Oakland is a neighborhood situated in the north-western corner of Oakland, California. The Angels of Mercy Nunnery was located in an old thatch roofed adobe built over hundreds of years ago during California's mission frontier days. It was attached to nine other buildings including the chapel, cafeteria, residential complex for the priest, sisters, and housing for the homeless population it served in the West Oakland community.

Thomas Holmes cross the street at West Grand with a determine glide in his step as he walked up to the front of the mission and studied the directory on the wall of the building. An arrow pointed the way. He was to walk straight a head past the adobe building and the chapel. There he'd find the cafeteria.

It didn't take him long to do so. Thomas opened the door of the cafeteria and walked up to the first person he saw. The nun looked to be well into her seventies with a full head of gray hair and wearing a silver and black apron with a giant Oakland Raiders logo on the front of it. She was walking down the rows of tables with an oven mitt on one hand holding a tong clasping a biscuit and holding a basket, with the other hand.

"Sir, would you care for a biscuit?" The nun asked a man. "They are fresh just made this morning."

Thomas closed the distance between them. "Good morning Sister? May I ask your help?"

The nun stopped what she was doing and turned and studied the man who asked her for help.

"You don't look like a man in need," she said. "By the way, my name is Sister Elizabeth and you are?"

"My name is Thomas Holmes."

"Well, Thomas I have to say, my instincts tell me you look like a cop," Sister Elizabeth stated. "What kind of help do you need?"

"You have good instincts, I used to work for the San Francisco Police department. I'm a private investigator now. I need your help to find a man. A man called Jack. Jack of spades?"

"We only call him Jack, you'll find him in the kitchen, in the back. It's down that hallway," she pointed with a biscuit in her hand. "Here, take a biscuit. They are fresh just made today. Oh, by the way, try not to keep Jack too long. He's got soup duty today for our dinner meal. Today is Pho noodle soup day. It always draws a big crowd," she said, placing the biscuit in Thomas' hand.

Thomas took a bite out of the biscuit. It tastes pretty good.

Good and fresh just like Sister Elizabeth had said. He kept eating it as he walked.

The kitchen was right where Sister Elizabeth said he would find it down the hallway in the back. Out of view of the public, it served up front. As soon as Thomas crossed the threshold, he couldn't believe the change in temperature. The temperature felt like it was a hundred and ten degrees.

Thomas finished off his biscuit and took a look around. Big commercial mixers where just to the right of him. He was sure that's where the batch of biscuits had been mixed up.

He walked over to several commercial ovens and could feel the heat radiating off them. No wonder the kitchen was hot.

A young woman who couldn't have been more than fifteen walked up to him. "Excuse me sir, but I need to get past you. Sister Elizabeth needs more biscuits."

"Sure, sorry I'm in your way," Thomas replied. "Oh, can you tell me where I can find Jack?"

The young girl skillfully removed the hot biscuits from the oven and then yelled at the top of her lungs. "Hey Jack, you've got a visitor over at the ovens."

"Tell my visitor I'm at the chopping station by the window! And I ain't moving from this spot, so you better come on over," Jack yelled back.

Thomas followed the voice. It didn't take him long to spot Jack, standing right in front of an open window.

"You ever work in kitchen before mister?" Jack asked, with a distinct Asian accent.

"No, can't say I have." Thomas said.

"Kitchen loud, hot, hectic dangerous place mister. People

can get burned, cut, or worse all the time. So, you stay there where I can see you."

He watched as Jack walked from the chopping table over to fill a huge stock pot, on the stove with what looked like beef bones, mounds of chopped onions, and mounds of carrots from the chopping table.

Jack took his time walking back and forth from the chopping table to the stock pot on the stove.

"That's the base of the soup," Jack finally said, in broken English with an Asian accent, studying Thomas face as he watched him. "You have to do it right the first time so the soup tastes just right."

Jack walked over and picked up a big wooden spoon and a step ladder and walked back over to the stove. He stepped up on the ladder and stuck the spoon in the pot and begin stirring, "There's garlic, star anise, cloves, ginger, cinnamon stick and fish sauce in that pot too. Pretty soon the broth will marry with all the ingredients and you'll have the best soup for pho noodle."

"I'll take your word for it, Jack," Thomas replied.

"So, what you are looking for Jack for Mister...?"

"The name is Thomas. Thomas Holmes, and are you Jack? The Jack of Spade?"

Jack laughed and stepped down off the step ladder. "I only go by Jack when I here. But when I'm in San Francisco China town my friends call me Jack of Spade."

"I hope you don't mind, but if you want to talk come over by the open window. This place is hot all the time, but there is a nice breeze coming in by the window."

Thomas followed Jack over to the window. "Well Jack, I'm

really looking for your brother Ace. Do you know where I can find him?"

"What you need my brother for?" Jack asked but didn't wait for a response. "You lose money in one of his Ponzi schemes?"

"You know about them?"

"My brother Ace isn't a nice fellow. You sure you want to find him?"

Thomas studied him. He looked like a chef deeply in love with what he was preparing. "That's why I'm here. I gather that you're not a big fan of your big brother?"

"What younger brother who lives in his brother's shadow is?" Jack asked.

"Tell me, what was your brother Ace like growing up?"

"My brother was your typical smart-ass Asian kid. You know the kind your tiger mother puts all her faith into, because she believes he will lift the family and be the next coming success king, make everybody rich."

"Tell me more about the family genius. Sounds like he's the kind of son who makes his mother proud."

"Made my mother proud? Hump!" Jack declared with a laugh. "My brother was a showoff, a pompous ass who thought he was the smarter person in the room and sad to say he thought I was just your average dumb-ass bunkum too and if that wasn't bad enough. He thought our mother was too."

"You don't say, no love lost between you and your brother." Thomas replied as he thought about what he said about their mother.

"No love lost..." Jack mumbled in a lunatic stare. "My brother has always given me a bad time. When I was seven, my brother Ace beat me up in front of his friends, just to show them how tough he was. So, I guess you can say we ain't that close."

Thomas was glad Jack was spilling the family secrets. But his thoughts kept going back to what Jack had said about his mother. "So, there's no love lost between you and your brother. But what about your mother does he stay in contact with her?"

"Ace got our mother involved in one of his Ponzi schemes. He owes her money. If you'd been here a few days ago, you would have seen her in here screaming at me to get her money back. I'm sure as far as mother's feelings go for their favorite son, she still loves him, but she loves getting her money back even more!"

"So, your mother came to you to ask you to help her get her money back. Did you help her?" Thomas inquired.

"Nope! How can I help her?" Jack shrugged. "My mother is broke now from investing with my brother. Even though she's broke. She doesn't want me to go to the police, to ask them for help to catch my brother. But you..." Jack paused and rubbed his chin.

Thomas watched while Jack's mind seemed to be running in overdrive as he studied him.

Finally, Jack leaned in close and stared straight into Thomas' eyes. "Sir, are you a cop?"

"You've got it almost right, "Thomas replied. "I'm a former cop turned private detective and I have a client who is on a mission to get his money back too."

Thomas let his words sink in and turned and faced the

window. "You're right there is a real nice breeze coming in this window. Are you going to help me Jack?"

"I was thinking about asking you the same thing Thomas."

"What?" Thomas asked, turning to look at Jack.

"What will you do for me if I help you find my brother Ace?"

"What do you want?"

Jack exhaled and then shook his head. "Everybody in this world is working their asses off trying to get somewhere. If they ain't, they're working trying to get something they want."

"Meaning?" Thomas asked.

"Meaning if I help you find my brother then I want you to help me get my mother's money back!" Jack declared.

"Now, about getting the money back," Thomas replied. "I'm working for a man who is on a mission to get his money back also. So, I'll do what I can."

"So, you were a cop, which means you got cop connection, right?" Jack asked.

"Sort of, I've a few old close police friends, but like I said. I'm a private investigator."

"That's not a problem," Jack replied. "In fact, it's sounds to me like a good thing."

His voice grew low as he leaned in close. "My brother has a storage pod over in Alameda. I'm thinking maybe you can use your police connections to get us access into his pod. There has to be some information in there to help us."

Thomas nodded but he was deep inside his head coming up with a contact to it them access to the storage unit. A plan was forming.

25

Chapter 18

Maëlle, Lacey & the come upping ...

"What kind of brother are you Nicholas?" Lacey screamed at the top of her lungs as she crossed the room and stood in front of her brother and pointed her finger in his face.

He was wearing a cream-colored fedora with a black ban with a black tailored jacket.

Lacey blinked hard confused and then shifted her finger at the hat on top of his head. "What's with this get-up Nicky?" She asked but didn't wait for a response. "This hat you're wearing does not make you a gangster. Stop acting like you are the Godfather!"

Nicholas rubbed his face and then started mumbling in non-coherent son sequitur niceties like Al Pacino in the God-father. Finally, he cleared his throat and said. "Insolent woman! This ain't no Godfather hat. You must respect the hat!"

Lacey wondered with Nicholas was playing at. "If you're not playing the Godfather, then what's with this get-up

Nicky? Do you think you're playing detective?" She paused looking confused. "With me?"

"Detective, selective! It's all just rhyming words to me," Nicholas shrugged. "I'm just trying to get my point across to you. Woman! Stay home with your children where it's safe!"

Nicholas adjusted his hat and then took it off and looked at it, before putting it back on. "I look good in the hat, huh?" He nodded. "It does have a detective quality to it."

Lacey shook her head. "Sometimes you don't make sense, Nicholas," she said closing the distance between them and removing his hat. "You sir are inside. You don't wear hats inside. And by the way," she replied as she pointed her finger to stress her point. "I'll have you know I'm a grown woman and the mother of two children. I am responsible enough to take care of them and myself."

She eyed Maëlle sitting across the room refusing to make eye contact with her. What a coward Lacey thought shaking her head.

"Then act like it!" Nicholas blurted back at her.

"Nicholas, why are you making this only about me? Maëlle was there too."

"Ah... Ah...Excuse me!" Maëlle went to interject.

"I got this Maëlle!" Nicholas declared, patting her hand. His eyes pleading with her. "Okay, babe you promised me..."

"Dah... Oh! Yeah, right, Nicholas. Okay." Maëlle slowly muttered before glancing back at her best friend frowning and making an invisible zipper motion over her lips.

Lacey responded by rolling her eyes at Maëlle' gesturing silently with her mouth. *"You coward."*

Maëlle rolled her eyes.

"You two cut it out!" Nicholas yelled. "You both could have been hurt or worst killed or something and God knows what mother Pearl or Grand *mere* Catherine would have done to me if I'd let something happen to you two."

'Yeah, well thank goodness you didn't tell mother or Grand *mere* Catherine!" Lacey exhaled. "But, why did you have to tell Kienan that I was there!"

Frustrated Nicholas rubbed his brow. "Look, Lacey, I had too, alright!"

"You had too? Really?" Lacey rolled her eyes and yelled. "You told my husband for Christ sake! I'm furious with you for doing that Nicky!"

"Look baby sister you have to understand it was a man's honor thing. I couldn't have my brother-in-law mad at me for not looking out for his woman, my sister."

"Yeah, well I would have rather you'd told mother Pearl and Grand *mere* Catherine."

"I know… I know… Because those two would have accepted any poor excuse you and Maëlle thought up," Nicholas replied.

"That's because they would have understood Maëlle and I was only out there to help you and Quinn. We didn't want to see you two hurt. That's why we were there!"

"Oh, that's your reason!" Nicholas yelled with a surprise look on his face. "You were there to help me and Quinn? Really? Is that the only answer you can come up with or are you just trying to emasculate me?"

"Hey, you forgot to include me, in that emasculation, Nicholas, brother?" Quinn laughed.

He turned and looked across the room. "So, Lacey you

think Nicholas and I can't defend ourselves! Why you've got a lot of nerve, woman!"

The moment was playful, neither Quinn nor Nicholas could hold back their laughter.

Nicholas watch the expressions on his sister's face change repeatedly. He decided to take it up a notch, since he'd been in prison, he'd had plenty of time to prefect his gangster image.

Nicholas adjusted his body into his best James Cagney stance. "Woman, do you know who I am! Now, look here you, little new Momma chick! You, new breed of dames forgot it's us men who wear the pants around the house. You just stick to doing what you know best! Taking care of my niece and nephew and handling them pots and pans in the kitchen. You got what I'm saying, sister? Now accept this little bit of being in your face for what it is. Your come upping, for being in the wrong place at the wrong time!" He paused to drive home his point. "And take it like a man! Man, up little woman!"

Quinn whistled loudly. "Here! Here! Preach it brother! Preach it!"

Filled with frustration and rage Lacey yelled. "Nicky! Whoa! First of all, who are you calling a... Mommy chick! I ought to slap the James Cagney Sh**!"

Kienan's voice carried over the room, interrupting her, as he walked in. "Don't forget to tell her she needs to stick to satisfying her husband in the bedroom! When you give my wife, her come upping! Give her the full course! The full Monty!"

A chorus of laughter filled the air as Kienan Egan's broad-shouldered over six-foot frame filled the room.

"Well, look who's here!" Nicholas declared. "Kienan Egan,

the man himself. So, I scored points with you brother-in-law, for laying down the law to my sister, your wife?"

"Yes, I would say you handle my wife well, brother-in-law," Kienan's gray eyes winked at Nicholas.

Immediately his arms encircled his wife, Lacey pulling her close against his shoulder and hiding her face from the silent laugh he was sharing with his brother-in-law.

Finally, Kienan spoke. "Are the bad guys giving my wifey a hard time?" his voice caringly asked Lacey.

"Gosh you look so handsome today hubby," Lacey softly said. "I always love the nerdish bad boy quality you ooze when you wear your black turtleneck and leather jacket combo," her eyes batted back at him.

"And that's why I wore it today, so that you can bat those pretty gray eyes of yours just like you are doing right now, wifey," he teased and then turned and said.

"Speaking of wearing stuff, Nicholas what's with you and the fedora, looks like you're playing detective."

"Him thinks he's the Godfather!" Lacey joked.

"I sort of have been," Nicholas replied.

"Have been what?" Lacey curiously asked.

"Ah, wifey, leave it alone," Kienan said, as he released his wife.

He leaned over and whisper. "Huh, Nicholas, there's something I want to talk to you about later, privately."

Nicholas nodded agreement. "Sure, thing."

Kienan then turned and said. "How is everyone?"

"I'm good," Quinn said. "Good to see you again, Kienan."

"Same here," Nicholas chimed in, as he walked over and sat down next to Maëlle.

Maëlle rose slowly and walked over lowering her eyes as she drew close. She patted his arm. "I'm so sorry, Kienan for talking Lacey into going to the House of the Southern Queen with me that night. I wasn't thinking about how unsafe it could be, please forgive me. By the way, I helped Lacey prepare your favorite for dinner today."

Kienan grinned. "You and Lacey made macaroni and cheese. The way..."

"The way Grand *mere* Catherine makes it! Because that's the way you like it." Maëlle interrupted.

Lacey walked over to Maëlle and nudged her best friend and got her attention. "You're a bad actress Maëlle! All I can say is you'll never get nominated for an academy award with that sad performance".

"What?" Maëlle countered. "What's the difference between my performance and Nicholas' poor rendition of James Cagney? Or was it Al Pacino?"

Everyone laughed.

Lacey gave her best friend a quick hug and linked her arm with hers. "Come on, Maëlle let's get dinner on the table. It looks like the guys are having a private conversation."

Maëlle glanced back at the fellas they looked like they were deep into their conversation. She noticed Kienan turned and asked Lacey something and it took her away from their task. She wondered what they were talking about.

Maëlle's eyes fell on Quinn, for just a second.

Instantly, his eyes captured hers and held them before Maëlle quickly looked away.

She hoped no one had noticed their glances as she lowered her head and headed for the kitchen she turned abruptly just as she walked past the kitchen door and instantly, she collided with Lacey.

"Maëlle! Watch where you are going."

"Sorry! I didn't see you standing there," Maëlle smiled, benignly.

"Oh yeah Maëlle before I forget. I promised mother and Grand *mere* Catherine, I'd stop by on Thursday and help with the planning of Nicholas' party. If you are free stop by and join us."

"Sure... Sure, if I'm free I will, Maëlle replied.

"Lacey darling," Kienan called out. "I need you to help me reason with your brother.".

"Can you handle things without me for a while Maëlle?"

"Sure, Lacey, I got this. Go and see what your hubby wants," Maëlle replied as she watched Lacey take her leave.

Maëlle turned and looked back and saw Lacey standing with her husband Kienan as he began talking to Nicholas, while Quinn sat next to him.

The spot afforded a perfect view of where Nicholas and Quinn were sitting. She let her eyes wander over to them. Her eyes focused on Quinn sitting there listening to their conversation. For a second, they were all talking at once and then just for a second Quinn looked across the room. She could have sworn he was staring back at her.

Quickly Maëlle looked away as her thoughts raced. She looked back to see if Lacey had noticed her staring, but Lacey was still in deep conversation with Kienan and Nicholas.

All at once Nicholas' cell phone rang and he looked down and checked the number. 'I need to take this," he said, glancing back at his sister, Kienan and Quinn. He quickly made his exit the room looking for privacy.

Quinn's eyes darted secretly back to Maëlle just in time to see her enter the kitchen. He cleared his throat nervously and wave. "Excuse me, seems I need to make a stop at the bathroom."

Lacey and Kienan hardly gave Quinn any notice as they sat together in a huddle whispering to each other.

In the kitchen, Maëlle walked over to the refrigerator determined to give it her full attention as she reached inside to retrieve a pitcher of fresh iced tea.

"Here let me give you a hand."

Maëlle stiffened at the sound of Quinn's voice. She hadn't heard him walk in. She turned and faced him.

Quinn stood there watching her.

"Oh, Quinn, I didn't see you standing there, thank you for your help, but I can manage," she nervously said, letting her eyes dart back at the family room.

"It's alright, Nicholas had to take a call, and Lacey and Kienan are so wrapped up in their private conversation, they won't notice a thing," Quinn said taking the pitcher from her hand.

"I... I can manage Quinn, I don't need your help," Maëlle found herself saying without knowing why.

"I think you want more than my help," Quinn replied, letting his eyes capture hers.

"Excuse, me?" Maëlle replied, standing there shocked that she and Quinn were standing there alone together.

"Let me put it another way," Quinn said leaning in close. "I think you and I both know that we need to talk, privately," he hesitated and looked toward the other room. "But not here."

Nervously Maëlle walked over and retrieve a tray. She placed the tray in front of Quinn.

Maëlle slowly nodded her head. "Yes, Quinn, I believe you're right."

"Good, let's meet, since Nicholas' home coming party is this weekend. Let's shoot for that Monday after, say one thirty at the Black Orchid Restaurant, I'll be sitting in the lounge area waiting for you," Quinn stated as he placed the pitcher of tea on the platter, Maëlle had placed in front of him. He picked up the tray. "Oh, I'll take the iced tea in for you. You should wait a few minutes before you return..."

"I get it Quinn... No, problem," Maëlle replied. "Besides, I was thinking the same thing. I need to get the dessert and some fresh plates," she said turning around and looking busy. She walked over to the cabinet to locate the plates. She knew it would keep her mind from over thinking what just happened.

***

Down the hallway Nicholas, sequestered himself in a back bedroom and closed the door tight. He knew the number didn't look familiar.

"Hello," Nicholas replied. A quirky voice screeched out at him with a quirky proper British accent.

"Ghost?"

Hello, Nicholas, I bet you didn't think you'd be hearing from me," Ghost declared.

"No...Ghost, I didn't," Nicholas replied. "What is this about?"

"I found her." Ghost replied excitedly. "Or should I say she found me."

"Found who?" Nicholas asked in a totally innocent voice.

"*The Angel,* Annie Mae, of course, unless you're not interested in still meeting her."

Nicholas let out a heavy whistle. Then he noticed the other end of the phone sounded quiet. "Ghost? Ghost? Are you still there?"

"Yes, Nicholas I'm still here," Ghost replied. "So, what will it be, Nicholas? Do you still want to meet with *The Angel,* Annie Mae?"

"Of course, I do."

"Good... Good," Ghost replied. "Meet me, on Monday afternoon, at the old Victorian house called Shenanigans, it's on the corner of Third street and Plum, right by the alley, you can't miss it it's right across from Kelly Park, in Downtown San Jose," he paused. "Make it three o'clock sharp Monday afternoon."

"Okay, sounds like a plan, see you on Monday at three o'clock" Nicholas replied.

"Oh, and Nicholas, do come alone. Don't bring that posse of hanging-on friends you like to travel with. *The Angel,* Miss Annie Mae is just doing me a big favor meeting you."

"Sure, no problem," Nicholas grinned.

"Good, then I'll see Monday afternoon, goodbye," Ghost stated hanging up

Nicholas was filled with excitement he was finally going to meet Annie Mae. She was supposed to know everything. She would tell him where he could find Dante.

All at once the smile on his face died when he thought he

had to keep his visit from Quinn. Quinn desired to ask *The Angel,* Annie Mae some questions too. He rubbed his chin and exhaled deeply as his thoughts raced. He knew Quinn wanted to find his son, maybe he could ask *The Angel,* Annie Mae if she could help Quinn, too. Maybe *The Angel,* Annie Mae would allow Nicholas only one question. His mind raced trying to think of what to do because he finally decided it was a waste of time trying to out guess what *The Angel,* Annie Mae would do.

The first thing he needed to do was slip back into the family room and try to figure out a way to cut out of there early. He thought about the second thing he needed to do. Finding the perfect place to take Dante Channing once he found him, to take his revenge. He stood there frozen in his spot letting his mind wander.

All at once Nicholas let out a deep breath. He did not have to meet with Ghost until Monday afternoon this would give him plenty of time, tomorrow, he thought to himself as his vision came into focus.

Nicholas smiled with his thoughts and nodded. Thinking that the secret passageway was soundproof, and it led to several places. All he had to do was find the perfect spot in the passageway. He could check it out in the morning and then think of a plan to take Dante there.

Finally, he made up his mind. The first thing he needed to do was go and get a better look at that place he was thinking of to use for his revenge.

Nicholas knew he had a full day tomorrow and needed to get some rest. Because he needed to get up real early for what he had in mind. Making sure the place he was thinking of was the perfect place to take his revenge on Dante Channing.

26

Chapter 19

Perfect place ...

Nicholas thought, the Southern Queen looked different at the break of dawn. The huge house glistening majestically as the soft rays of the rising sun cascade over it reminded him of the old plantation mansions done in the antebellum mansions style he used to see as a boy when he visited New Orleans Louisiana, to see his father's relatives.

Nicholas was about to make his way around to the back when his cell phone rang. He answered it.

"Hello?"

"Good morning Nicholas, it's me, Maëlle. What are you up too?"

"Excuse me? What do you mean by that?"

"Oh, nothing, I just meant you're up bright and early, I thought maybe you had made some special plans," Maëlle replied.

Nicholas was silent for a moment when he realized he had spoken abruptly. Maëlle wasn't checking up on him. Quickly he thought of something to say. "No... No... No special plans," he nervously replied. "I just wanted to get up early today and walk around and see what it felt like, that's all."

Silence lingered between them. Their conversation was strained.

Nicholas decided to change the subject. Besides he didn't want Maëlle to start asking him a bunch of questions he didn't want to answer. "Hey, did you see the sunrise this morning?

"Yes, I did see it. You're right it was beautiful," Maëlle replied with a smile in her voice.

Making the effort to put an extra dose of care in his voice Nicholas soften his voice and tenderly and softly he asked. "Do you need me for anything? Is everything alright?"

"Oh, yes, everything is okay. I didn't want anything really, Nicholas. I was just calling to remind you everyone is dropping by Lacey and Kienan's place tonight, remember?"

Nicholas smiled he knew his soft tone had diffused any questions she might have had. "Oh, that, I'm glad you called to remind me. I had completely forgot. I'm sure glad I have you to remind me of things like that Maëlle, I don't know what I'd do without you."

Maëlle's voice detected that she was blushing. "Ahhhh shucks, Nicholas that was so sweet of you to say," she said. "Well, Nicholas I won't keep you. See you tonight, goodbye."

"Goodbye, "Nicholas said before hanging up the phone.

Nicholas turned and focused his attention as he made his way around to the back. He found it was easy to gain entrance when he maneuvered over and join a team of service and delivery workers entering through the back door.

Once inside he quickly separated himself from the workers and silently strolled down several corridors. He concentrated with each step as he made his way to the stage part of the huge house. He walked up the steps leading to the stage and went behind the curtains heading for the door that led to the basement.

As he walked into the darken space, his thoughts wandered as he cautiously made his way. There was just enough light to see as he walked the dark corridor. In the darkened space he remembered what Ghost had said about the secret passageways and the old passageway leading to the secret *torture room in the basement.*

Quietly he made his way down a dusty corridor, the place looked ancient. He was sure he was in the right place. When he spotted the rusty door, his hands trembled as he reached to turn the knob. The door opened and he stepped across the threshold and his eyes adjusted to the room, as he scanned it.

Nicholas' mind flashed back to that day Ghost had told him about the torture room located in the basement. He remembered how his mind had snapped into focus thinking about what he could do in that room. Ghost had been right. The room was *the real McCoy*, he thought as he surveyed the room.

A butcher looking meat cleaver hung against a wall along with chains, belts and other instruments that had been used to inflict deliberate, systematic, cruel pain. He walked over to the wall and touched the meat cleaver. It didn't look rusty. It looked usable. That was when he noticed the walls. The walls were so thick, he knew the design principles that had been used. They had been designed with acoustics in mind. The kind of acoustics that muffled the piercing screams and cries of the victims who had been unfortunate to be a guest in this room, which was a torture chamber.

Nicholas couldn't believe what he was looking at. The room was the perfect place to have his revenge against Dante Channing.

Nicholas felt the corners of his lips curl up into a sinister grin as he nodded his head happily. All at once laughter erupted from his lips as he realized he was getting close to having his revenge.

27

Chapter 20

A Favor...

Later that same evening, Maëlle was amazed at the spread of food she and Lacey had sat out on the table. A casserole bowl filled with piping hot creamy macaroni and cheese, oven roasted Brussels sprouts with bacon, baked sweet potatoes, sliced pickles, tomatoes, sautéed bell peppers and onions with grilled steak, along with piping hot hoagie rolls for making Philly steak sandwiches and a ton of sandwich fixings.

"What do we have to drink?" Nicholas asked.

"Sweet Ice-Tea, lemonade, coffee and water," Maëlle replied.

"Non-alcoholic drinks, really?" Quinn stated rather than asked.

"The drinks were by special request," Maëlle stated. "So, sorry but no one checked on your order, Quinn."

"I did!" Nicholas declared, pulling out a cooler, he'd hid early.

"You got Tsingtao!"

"Ice cold and ready," Nicholas said with a smile on his face. "I'll grab us a couple."

"Grab a couple for me two," Kienan blared. "I'm going to work up a big thirst after I have a couple of glasses of sweet tea."

***

Hours later, their meal finished. Kienan leaned back in his chair and looked around at everyone at the table.

It was funny he thought, it seemed like yesterday, he had been in elementary school with Nicholas and Quinn. The three of them had been friends for as long as he could remember. His eyes took in his wife Lacey. Who would have thought old man Louis La Cour would take a secret to his grave, that Lacey, Nicholas and Quinn were all three his children. But old man Louis was special.

He smiled with his thoughts thinking about old man Louis. He remembered a conversation he'd had with Louis one day. Kienan remembered it faithfully because it was the day of his eighteenth birthday. He recalled how he'd been at the La Cour's family home that day. Grand *mere* Catherine had made him a cake and after everyone had been served cake and ice cream, Louis had walked over to him. He still couldn't believe what Louis had said.

Kienan's thoughts felt vivid and real as that day took hold in his mind.

"Kienan, I bet I know what your birthday wish was?" Louis had stated more than asked.

"I know you are very smart Mr. La Cour, but I don't recall you're having the ability to read minds," he'd jokingly laughed.

"Kienan, you forget I was born in the grand old state of

Louisiana and come from a long line of mystic, physics, mediums and good fairies," Louis laughed. "Therefore, my son, I possess many powers."

"Ok, Mr. La Cour, I'll play along. What does your crystal ball tell you? What was my wish?"

As soon as the words left his mouth Louis' eyes had fasten on his and then his eyes narrowed slightly, and he looked as if in a trance. "You wished to marry my Lacey, someday."

Kienan's eyes widen in shock. "How... How did you know that?"

"As I said my son, I come from a Louisiana family rich in the knowledge of things not of this world. Just be glad that I'm not Marie Laveau."

"Why?"

"Because if I were, I'd expect you to come to my grave tomb and place an "x" on it and leave an offering for my granting you your wish." Louis smiled. "But I do expect some form of payment for my daughters' hand in marriage."

"Oh, really and what would that be?" Kienan had asked.

"I expect you to look out for all three of them," Louis had said.

"Three of them? But there's only Lacey and Nicholas."

"Don't forget Quinn," Louis nodded. "He makes three."

From that moment on Kienan had felt responsible for looking out for all three of them. Nicholas, Lacey and Quinn.

Kienan shot back to reality feeling a soft hand touched his brow.

"Earth to Kienan... A penny for your thoughts," Lacey's soft voice woke him out of his trance, as she patted his hand.

Kienan looked up at her and kissed her hand. "Looks like

I'm daydreaming in the middle of our guest and their lively conversation."

Lacey exhaled. "You tired? I'm good if you're ready for everyone to leave. We've both had a long day."

"Naw, I'm good. Besides, we invited everyone to spend the night, remember?"

"Yeah," Lacey said. "I remember, but if you're tired. I'm sure they would understand."

Kienan shrugged. "I'm good. Could you help me grab some ice cream and bowls out of the kitchen?" Kienan asked.

Lacey rose and followed. "Looks like you want to ask me something in private," she said as soon as they were out of earshot of being overheard.

Kienan walked into the kitchen and headed for the refrigerator and opened the freezer. "First of all, I noticed you didn't sleep well last night wifey. What's going on in that clairvoyant mind of yours? Are you worried about Nicholas?"

"Oh, maybe just a little," Lacey said.

"I think it's a lot. Care to tell me about the dream you were having? Or should I say, nightmare?" Kienan countered.

Lacey smiled at his truth. "Well, hubby there's no way I can get around telling you the truth. I mean, I've been having these reoccurring dreams about Nicholas wanting to take revenge against Dante Channing."

"Really, do you care to share any more detail?"

"Well, sometimes it's as if Nicholas is defending himself from Dante and so the dream of revenge seems more like self-defense and then there are other times when Nicholas' acts of revenge on Dante are so fiercely merciless, and filled with bitterness, loathing and despair that I... I," she paused. "Let me just come out and say it. It's so bad I feel for Nicholas soul. Because what he does to Dante is nothing more than cold cruel murder."

"Wow! That's deep," Kienan declared. "Well, I did ask for you to tell me and now I ask that you stop worrying about Nicholas and try to relax more. Do your meditation stuff, or whatever it takes to get your mind off Nicholas."

Lacey smiled. "It felt good telling you about my dreams. I feel better already. Now, hubby how about we change the subject?"

"Agreed!" Kienan declared looking across the way at Nicholas, Maëlle and Quinn. "What's up with all three of them getting along, so well."

Lacey glanced back at her brother, Nicholas, sitting at the table, Maëlle was leaning in close next to him while Nicholas was in an animated conversation with Quinn.

"I don't understand?" Lacey asked.

"You know, what I'm talking about. I know you're trying to protect those you love. But there's a love triangle sitting over there talking, all nice. And yes, by all appearances they are getting along right now. But I worry.I don't get it?"

"You were young, wild and in love once upon a time yourself Kienan and you did somethings you weren't proud of," Lacey said. "That's the thing about being young and being wild you don't realize the things you're doing can hurt other people. You don't know the effects that get left behind."

Lacey grabbed some spoons and added them to the bowls she had collected. "The three of them are getting along now. "Maybe they've changed. Besides, what's there to worry about?"

Kienan put the ice cream, bowls and spoons on a tray. "For one thing, the three of them are playing detective and I don't know why. That's got me worried."

Lacey paused and then grabbed some napkins and placed them on the tray. "So, what are you going to do"

"First off, I've got to look out from my most precious assets," he locked eyes with Lacey. "And if you don't know who or what they are, wife?"he paused as his eyes held hers spellbound. "Then let me explain. My most precious assets are first you, and then my children." Lacey exhaled as she moved in close her arms circled around his waist. "Uh, oh, I know that look."

Kienan looked back at the three people sitting at the table. He took a deep breath. "I think it's time I play inquisitor," he reached for the tray

"Alright, husband," Lacey smiled. "But are you sure you want to do that tonight? I mean ..."

"I know... I know... Everyone is getting along right now. Is that what you were going to say?" Kienan interrupted her teasing.

"Yes, I was going to say that, and that your being an inquisitor might spoil your appetite and mine," she laughed. "And spoil the evening since everyone is getting along so well, Mr. Know it all."

Kienan laughed. "Ok, I'll tell you what. I won't put all three of them on the spot tonight. I think I'll wait and talk to each one, alone. Unless a situation presents itself. But I need you to do me a favor."

"What's your favor?"

"Don't you go following Maëlle, off, on one of her hair

brained schemes trying to help Nicholas or Quinn. Things could get dangerous. I'm not sure what your brother Nicholas is up too."

Lacey saw the worried look on Kienan's face. "This has really got your nerves up."

"Yes, Lacey darling it has. That's why I always have to know where you are at, and that you're safe."

"Okay, I understand. But how about we finish out the night with bowls of ice cream and everyone turn in for the night. That way everyone gets a good night sleep and bright and early tomorrow you can be the master inquisitor."

"Hmmm… That sounds like an even better plan," Kienan smiled. "Good thing you thought of it."

"Actually, as I recall you mentioned you wanted to invite Nicholas and Quinn to spend a few days with us, so I had already suggested everyone consider spending the night."

Kienan leaned over and kissed her lips softly. "Oh, yeah wifey, I meant to tell you., But it sort of slipped my mind."

Lacey kissed him back and laughed. "Huh, hum. Don't start getting old and senile on me."

"Senile, huh. We'll see just how senile I'm getting later tonight," he teased, nibbling her bottom lip.

Kienan abruptly stopped kissing her and took a deep breath. "If we don't stop that ice cream is going to melt."

He turned and walked over and lifted the tray.

Lacey watched as Kienan turned and walk back into the dining room. He stopped abruptly and turned and looked at her.

"You coming Lacey?

"Yes, Master inquisitor, I'm right behind you."

There was as loud burst of laughter coming from Nicholas, Quinn and Maëlle, when they walked in.

"Quinn, I've heard you tell that joke a million times. It's still stupid, but funny as hell," Nicholas laughed as he looked.

"Hey brother-in-law you need a hand?" Nicholas asked but didn't wait for an answer, rising and closing the gap between them.

"Sure thing," Kienan said steering them to the buffet table.

Kienan looked Nicholas right in the eye and said. "One scoop or two Nicholas?"

Nicholas saw the look in Kienan's eye and looked around the room to find his sister. Lacey had commandeered Maëlle and Quinn's attention. He could tell it had been on purpose. That meant he was supposed to be alone with his brother-in-law. He could also tell by that look in Kienan's face it was serious. "You want to speak to me in private, right? Nicholas asked."

"You bet I do, Kienan scooped out the ice cream and said. "Why are you playing detective?"

"What? I don't know what you mean," Nicholas replied a bit too fast and regretted it as soon as the words left his mouth.

"Didn't you hire Thomas Holmes?" Kienan demanded.

"What? I mean, yeah. Why?"

"Why did you stop by Aunt Joan's shop in Sunnyvale?"

"Oh , you know about that? Of course, I should have known. What did Aunt Joan tell you?" Nicholas didn't want to say much. He wasn't sure what Aunt Joan had told Kienan.

"Aunt Joan, guess you and Quinn were playing at detective. Other than that she didn't tell me much," Kienan paused.

"Look Nicholas, you hired Thomas to do a job. Let him do the job. If you don't want to do it for yourself then do it for your sister and Maëlle. You don't want them to get hurt."

Nicholas looked back at the table and his eyes caught sight of Maëlle. His sister and Maëlle had followed them. What if something had happened? He'd never forgive himself.

"I was just trying to help Thomas find Dante, faster. I mean... I wasn't trying to get anyone hurt."

Kienan watched as Nicholas stood there looking forlornly.

"I see what you're thinking Nicholas," Kienan stated. "In fact, none of us start out trying to hurt, anybody. But it doesn't matter what our good intentions are. It only takes a split second for something to go wrong and someone ends up hurt. Or worst killed. What if something had happened to my wife, your sister or Maëlle."

Kienan studied Nicholas' face as his words sat in. The tight squint of his eyes let him know his words made a difference. He figured it was best to drive home his point and make sure his meaning was clear to his brother-in-law. "I don't know Nicholas, perhaps I got it wrong. But I thought you and Maëlle had gotten serious."

"Serious," Nicholas breathe out with a smirk. "Come on, Kienan are you being funny? Are you for real?"

"Yes, serious," Kienan replied. "For the last several months all I've heard Lacey talk about is Maëlle driving out to visit you and how wonderful you two were getting along. I don't know, maybe I got it wrong. I thought you had feelings for her," he shrugged.

Growing up Kienan always knew Nicholas cared about what Quinn thought. He quickly thought about how he could make Nicholas remember Quinn used to have a crush on Maëlle. He took his time and choose his words carefully and then said. "Oh well, all I know is that ever since Quinn got here, all you do is spend your time with him. I guess maybe someone should suggest Quinn take Maëlle out, a time or two so she won't feel left out. You know a woman can get awful lonely being left alone a lot."

At just at moment, across the room, Maëlle laughed out loud and bellowed. "Quinn! Stop it! I can honestly say that was the stupidest joke, I've ever heard wasn't it, Lacey?"

Lacey tried to hide her giggles. "Quinn! You know that joke was stupid. Funny, but stupid."

"Yeah, it was but I won. Now where's my ice cream," Quinn said and then turned and yelled. "Kienan and Nicholas what's taken you two so long? I won the bet! I get my ice cream first!"

Kienan glanced at Nicholas and then nudge him and placed a bowl in his free hand. "Here Nicholas you should take Quinn his ice cream. Sounds like he won the bet. You don't want to keep the winner waiting," he said with a curious glint in his eye.

Nicholas grabbed the bowl of ice cream Kienan handed him and rolled his eyes. He was still fuming about what Kienan had said. As he got closer to Quinn his eyes studied him. He didn't like the way Quinn was looking at Maëlle.

Nicholas thrust Quinn's bowl of ice cream in his hands. "Here!"

"Thanks," Quinn said. "Maëlle looks like Nicholas forgot to be chivalrous, do you want my ice cream?"

"What?" Nicholas interrupted.

"Nothing Nicholas, come and sit beside me," Maëlle injected reassuring Nicholas everything was alright.

She then turned her attention to Quinn. "It's alright Quinn," she replied. "Kienan made those manly size portions for you and Nicholas. He knows not to give me and Lacey that much ice cream."

"Don't I know it," Kienan said, walking over and handing Maëlle a much smaller portion. "Lacey and Maëlle will waste good ice cream if you let them."

"We don't waste it, we just know how much of it we can eat and still keep our figures," Lacey replied.

Nicholas scooted in beside Maëlle on the sofa and leaned in close and asked. "So, what was so funny? That had you guys laughing a while ago?" he asked and shoved a big spoon full of ice cream in his mouth.

Guilty Lacey looked at Kienan, Maëlle looked at Lacey. Quinn looked puzzled back at Kienan, Lacey and then Maëlle.

"Ah... "Quinn finally said and shrugged his shoulders. "I don't remember."

"You don't remember what?" Nicholas demanded.

Lacey could see her brother was riled up. She wasn't sure why, but she knew Kienan had said something to stroke his anger. She knew she needed to defuse the situation and said the first thing that came to mind. "Oh, hell! Let's just tell him," Lacey replied. "I told mother just saying we were giving Nicholas a welcome home party was silly. It needed a theme, right Kienan?"

Kienan looked at his wife. "Lacey, my name is Bennett and I ain't in it."

Chaotic laughter erupted all around.

"Oh, be quiet, Kienan!" Lacey laughed playfully.

"It's a theme party, Nicholas," Maëlle said.

"Theme party? What kind?" Nicholas asked.

"I think it's a costume party," Maëlle replied.

Quinn looked puzzled. "Costume? What kind of costume?"

Maëlle interrupted. "Any costume, silly. Just as long as it has a Mardi Gras theme. But I don't recall Grand *mere* Catherine saying to wear an actual costume."

Chaotic chitchat erupted regarding costumes.

"Oh, my goodness," Maëlle said. "None of us ever thought to think about a costume. Can you rent a costume?"

"What the hell!" Quinn blurted. "I don't want to wear a costume someone else wore."

"Mmmm! Nicholas, Quinn just gave me an idea for your costume," Kienan smiled mischievously. "How about a Devil costume, for you."

"Hell no!" Nicholas declared. "I ain't wearing no devil costume, I don't want to offend Quinn, he's been one for years. Besides, Quinn might think I'm trying to take over his territory."

Hysterical laughter erupted all around.

"Watch it Nicholas," Quinn declared. "And let us thank the Lord, I ain't what I used to be. I'm a reformed sinner of a man, now."

The room filled with laughter again.

Bewildered Nicholas pull an empty spoon out of his mouth and said. "Lacey, what kind of party is your grandmother throwing, for real?"

Lacey stopped laughing and said. "Your home coming celebration is a Mardi Gras themed party."

"Ain't a Mardi Gras themed party a costume party?" Quinn asked.

"Not always," Maëlle declared.

"It would be hilarious if it was," Kienan added. "Can't you just imagine, what costumes Grand *mere* Catherine's bingo posse would wear?" He asked but didn't wait for a response. "I remember that time, your father, Louis had a costume party fund raiser for his Elite men's group and the Bingo posse all wore old wild west saloon girls."

"I remember that, Grand *mere* Catherine and Gabby Baptiste got dressed at our house," Lacey declare. "When they came out to show off their costumes, several of Dad's Elite men's group were there. Do you remember that Nicholas?"

"Yes, I do, I remember some of the Elite men's names too. Let see. There was Andre Pascal, Mathew Henson, Hugo Toussaint, Russ Jackson and Jean Baptiste."

"And don't forget Armand Manteau," Lacey replied. "Remember he was the one who was sweet on Grand *mere* Catherine."

"Oh, yes! I remember, Dad said Gabby Baptiste and Grand *mere* Catherine looked like a couple of Old Wild West Saloon girl hookers," Nicholas blurted.

"Yeah, but Grand *mere* Catherine corrected Dad and said she was Mae West and then she did a sexy sashay strut up to Armand Manteau and said..."

"Is that a pistol in your pocket or are you just happy to see me, Big Boy?" Lacey and Nicholas laughed in unison.

Nicholas blurted with laughter. "Oh, yeah, I remember

that, old man Armand Manteau, held out his arm and told Grand mere Catherine he was escorting her to the fundraiser!"

"And he did. Not to mention Mr. Manteau, came by our house every week for almost a year, taking Grand *mere* Catherine out on dates."

"Until Dad chased him away when he found out old man Armand Manteau, was a two-timing snake!" Nicholas declared.

"He wasn't two-timing Grand mere Catherine. I heard Grand *mere* Catherine tell Momma that Mr. Manteau was smothering her, because some special male friend of hers had returned to town and she wanted to go out with him, but Mr. Manteau was monopolizing all her time. Mother Pearl and Grand *mere* Catherine cooked up that plan to tell Dad, Mr. Manteau was two-timing her. So, Dad could run him away."

"What scandalous ratchet women!" Quinn declared. "No, wonder I lived a life of debauchery. I got it naturally from my father's mother."

"Whew!" Lacey blurted. "If Grand *mere* Catherine heard you say that, Quinn, she would beat you..."

"With her broom!" Nicholas declared.

Hysterical laughter erupted all around.

Finally, Lacey interrupted their laughter. "I hate to spoil all the fun that everyone is having over what costume to wear, but I believe Grand *mere* Catherine, has already settled the issue of wearing costumes. It is a black-tie affair, men in black suits or tuxedos, women in evening gowns. Oh, yeah, she is requiring everyone to wear a Mardi Gras eye mask only, so re-

ally it's a formal Mardi Gras Masquerade Party, and not a costume party."

"Of course, it is," Kienan said. "You all know how much
Grand *mere* Catherine, hates folks wearing scary costumes."

"Don't I know it!" Nicholas declared, with laughter.
"Quinn and I, scared Grand *mere* Catherine fiercely bad one
year at Halloween and she got so mad at us she almost talked
Dad into banning us from wearing costumes, forever!"

"I remember that time!" Quinn declared. "We created this
garbage can monster costume. We each had one."

Kienan injected with laughter. "So, you two stinky shanks
scared Grand *mere* Catherine, by smelling like some old dead
cheese?"

"Naw, man we used a very clean new garbage can inside,
where we were hiding. But the outside look like a normal
everyday garbage can, complete with dents and dirt,"
Nicholas replied.

"In fact, it looked so normal outside, all roughed up and
old looking, you couldn't tell the difference," Quinn added.

"Yeah, but inside were we were hiding, in the can was
clean.," Nicholas interrupted. "However, we were wearing
some really scary mask, over some all black furry costumes
that were, complete with claw hands and bulging eyes. It was
really hideously monstrous."

"Yes, it was," Quinn interrupt. "Inside Nicholas and I were
made up so hideously no one could tell it was us."

Nicholas laughed. "And then we put our garbage can selves
right where the regular garbage cans sat in the driveway and
waited for Grand *mere* Catherine to empty the trash."

Lacey exhaled. "And then you two nincompoops jumped

out and scared Grand *mere* Catherine half to death," she injected. "You two should be ashamed of yourselves for scaring an old woman half to death."

"Dawg, huh! Made me afraid to go near a broom for years. She beat me and Quinn with her broom that day," Nicholas added.

"And I'm still traumatized from that beating," Quinn added. "Every time I see an old woman with a broom in her hand, I have flash backs to that day."

"Ha! Ha! Ha! You both got what you deserved," Lacey stated.

"Yes, they did. Poor Grand *mere* Catherine, being frightened out of her wits like that by the two of you," Maëlle replied. "That's so shameful."

Lacey stared back at her brother. "You know Nicholas, you should think of making it up to Grand *mere* Catherine at this party she's throwing in your honor."

Nicholas shrugged. "What? I'm going to be there, ain't that enough? Besides, I let her put my baby picture on that blanket she keeps on her bed for the whole world to see."

Lacey shook her head. "Nicky...That's so cruel. You should be ashamed..."

"Alright!" Nicholas interrupted her. "What choice do I have?"

"I see what you're thinking Lacey," Maëlle replied. "Nicholas should do something extra nice... Like... Like? Oh darn, I can't think of a thing."

Lacey stared back at her brother curiously. "I was thinking Nicholas that you could brush up on your waltz shuffle dance skills and do a special dance with Grand *mere* Catherine and mother too," she stopped talking letting her words sink in.

Lacey saw understanding flash instantly across her brother's face.

"I get it Lacey," Nicholas replied. "You think I should do something special for them since I cheated them both out of dancing with me at my wedding, his words trailed off as his eyes capture Maëlle. He saw the sadness in her eyes. "I guess I need to do something to make you happy too, huh Maëlle?" He asked but didn't wait for her response. "Looks like this so-called welcome home party, that's being thrown in my honor, is getting to be a what can Nicholas do for everybody party."

Maëlle exhaled aware she'd been holding her breath. Silently she bit her lip. "Nicholas... I... I didn't..."

Nicholas got up and began pacing the floor. Realizing he'd been place on the spot. "Damn! Damn! Damn!"

Kienan quickly got control of the room and walked over and took Nicholas' bowl out of his hand. "I think it's about time we all turned in for the night. Don't worry about the dishes," he turned and looked at his wife. Lacey do you think you could show everyone to their rooms. I'll collect the dishes and take them to the kitchen."

"Sure, no problem." Lacey said. "Besides it'll give me a chance to talk to Maëlle in private."

Maëlle close the distance between her and Lacey and followed her as she led them from the room. All at once she reached out and touched Lacey's arm and glanced up at her with a puzzle expression. "What do you want to talk to me about?"

"Maëlle," Lacey leaned in close and whispered. "You know

we need to make arrangements to do lunch and talk about the details Grand *mere* Catherine mentioned," she said with a wink.

"Oh, yeah. Your right, Lacey it completely slipped my mind. Do me a favor and call me to remind me, to set that up."

"Sure, thing," Lacey declared as she opened the door to their room. "Are you alright with sharing a bathroom with my brother? This is the Jack and Jill bedroom that shares a bath. If not, I have another bedroom down the hallway."

"Of course, she is alright with it, Lacey," Nicholas declared as he walked past her and slapped Maëlle on the butt. "You know Maëlle and I could both be angry at you for the Jack and Jill bedroom thing. But you know we ain't going to sleep in but one bed. Right Maëlle baby?"

Maëlle assuredly patted Lacey's arm and gave her a knowingly wink as she turned and walked across the threshold. "You, got that right, Sugar Daddy, we don't need two beds."

Lacey rolled her eyes in annoyance at their outward display of affection. "You too are just too syrupy sweet with that sweet talk. Goodnight."

***

Hours later that night, Maëlle lingered in the bathtub enjoying the warm water as it calmed the tension.

Even though she had told Lacey they would share one bedroom, she had lied to save Nicholas from any embarrassment in front of his sister. In fact, the minute Nicholas had upset her earlier she had decided she wasn't sleeping with him that night. She was too angry to do so.

For over an hour, she had waited, patiently and listened

attentively until Nicholas had finished his shower and exited the bathroom into his bedroom. Now more than ever she was grateful they shared the Jack and Jill style bedrooms and bathroom, in his sister's home.

She'd been sure Nicholas had fallen asleep before she'd slow crept into the bathroom and filled the tub. She knew she had been angry at Nicholas for the tension he'd caused her at the end of their evening together.

Everything had been going fine until Lacey suggested Nicholas make amends to mother and grandmother, by doing a special dance with them at the party they were having in his honor. It brought back the painful memories of Nicholas leaving her at the altar.

Maëlle thought it was the stream from the warm water that was making her eyes mist up. Until the first tear drops rolled down her face and a soft sob escaped her lips.

She hadn't realized she was making a sound until the bathroom door opened.

"Maëlle... Maëlle! Are you alright?" Nicholas stood at the entry of his bathroom door.

Suddenly Maëlle's anger flared up. "What do you care?" She yelled in a voice so harsh she could hardly recognize it was her speaking.

Nicholas paused a moment before taking in the sad look on Maëlle's face. In one long stride he made his way over to the side of the bathtub and then he kneeled down beside it. "Look, I know what this is all about. I hurt you, leaving you at the altar like I did," he reached out and cupped her face tenderly. "And tonight, I saw the look on your face and the pain in your eyes., just like it is right now. All I can think of it taking your pain away.

Tenderly his fingers caressed her face and his eyes took in her beautiful body. "Damn, Maëlle! I'm a weak man, when it comes to you baby. Damn! You smell so good!"

"You smell good too, Nicholas, I heard you showering earlier."

"I was hoping you'd come in while I was showering," his voice was low and husky.

Shhhhh," she interrupted her. "No words, we're both here now. Just kiss me, Nicholas. I 'm so lonely without you."

Nicholas gave her a long lingering kiss and then pulled out of their embrace.

"Nicholas, what are you doing?"

"I'm getting you a towel so I can get you out of that bathtub. I don't think both of us can fit together in it. So, what say I dry you off?"

Nicholas reached for a towel and then held it open for Maëlle.

Quickly Maëlle stood and raised her arms as Nicholas began gently drying her off. He stopped abruptly and stood there staring at her naked and then slowly kissed her neck.

"Maëlle, I'll do anything you want."

Instantly Maëlle moved in close. She let her naked body lean in close to him. So, close she could feel his penis throb next to her body.

Slowly Nicholas moved his body against hers. Tell me what I want to hear Maëlle.

Instantly Maëlle wrapped her arms around his neck.

"Nicholas, sugar," she cooed and purred in ha sexy hoarse Southern drawl. "I want you inside me Big Poppa!"

Nicholas scooped Maëlle into his arms and carried her to his bed. "The Lady gets, what the lady wants."

28

Chapter 21

Mardi Gras Masquerade Ball

Welcome Home Party for Nicholas...

Nicholas could barely breathe in the bear hug; his father Horace was giving him. He didn't mind. He knew how happy Horace had been when he got released from prison. He turned his head to the side and saw his mother smiling proudly at him and then finally she tapped Horace on the shoulder.

"Horace, you and Nicholas are going to wrinkle your tuxedos from all that hugging stuff. Let the boy breathe."

"Alright Pearl, I'm just so happy today," Horace replied squeezing Nicholas harder.

Horace Sherlock Bailey Garrison, or Horace as he liked to be called pushed out of the embrace with his son and stood next to the love of his life, and mother of his only child, Pearl La Cour.

Horace was in his late fifties, tall, over six feet two inches, he had an imposing figure, with slightly graying hair and warm tanned skin he owed to his mixed race ancestry that he could trace back to the legacy of his Irish Jamaican roots. His middle name Bailey was a result of his White Irish Great-Great Grandmother, who had also been the reason why he had some of the deepest vivid green eyes anyone had ever seen.

Whenever Nicholas got a chance to look at Horace, without his noticing, he was amazed at just how much he looked like him. Once he'd learned Horace was his biological father everything that he remembered from his childhood, when Horace was around, had all made sense.

"You good Pops?" Nicholas teased and grinned. "You need a Kleenex or something? Maybe a paper towel to catch all those *man tears,* thing you are doing?"

"You know son, I never get tired of hearing you call me Pops, and I'm not ashamed to show I'm happy that my son is home and free," Horace voice choked.

"Ah! Come on Pops, I was just kidding about that paper towel thing," Nicholas declared, watching his father tear up with happiness again.

Nicholas turned and eyed Horace. This was his heritage. This was his real father.

The love, concern, care and happiness, in Horace's face was real. "Do you need me to get you a drink or a cup of tea or something?"

"Maybe we should go and get you that drink, Horace," Pearl said. "Besides, I think we're holding up things, there's a line of people waiting to greet our son."

"Okay Pearl," Horace replied and turned and glanced at Nicholas. "I'm so glad you're home safe, son," his voice choked.

"I'm going to let your mother take me to get a drink so you can say hi to the rest of the folks who came out to see you," he said patting his son on the back.

Nicholas stood there and watched his parents make their exit.

"Congratulations, Nicholas for getting your case dismissed."

Nicholas' eyes widen as he looked up in surprise at the familiar voice of Xavier Newhouse.

"Xavier! Man, it's good to see you."

"Your buddy Quinn hooked me up with your grandmother and got me on the invite list," Xavier declared, casting his eyes in the direction of a young woman standing a few feet away. "There sure is some good-looking ladies up in here and now that you're out, we need to start hosting some of those happening parties, we all used to go too. Nothing like finding you some happiness to make up for that time you were in jail, you know what I mean?"

Nicholas chuckled as he eyed Xavier's pearly white teeth and mischief smile. He knew exactly what kind of happiness, Xavier wanted to get into. "Why don't you check with Quinn and see when he's free, maybe we could all hang out together. I'm not sure what Quinn's schedule is, but you can check with him and tell him I'm free anytime, just let me know the date and place."

"Now that sounds like a plan," Xavier replied looking around the room.

Nicholas watched as Xavier caught sight of a young woman well-endowed in the breast department as she sashayed in a fog of perfume, near them.

"Hump! That's Chanel Number Five, my favorite! And boy does she wear it well," Xavier declared as he watched the woman walk by.

"The perfume or that skintight dress she's wearing?" Nicholas asked, when he noticed Xavier was still looking at the woman. "Earth to Xavier!"

"Right! Right! Right! My bad, Nicholas I forgot you were standing there. Where were we? Oh yeah. That's sound like a plan. I'll hook up with Quinn and we will make some arrangements and he'll pass on the information, to you."

Xavier adjusted his tuxedo. "Would you look at the time, Nicholas, sorry man but I need to get going."

Nicholas nodded and chuckled as Xavier took off in the direction of the young woman swimming in Chanel Number Five with the huge breasts.

Nicholas didn't have long to savor his newfound freedom when he saw his half-brother Quinn Rolandis escorting his grandmother Ina Rosolado on one arm and a very beautiful exotic young woman on his other arm.

"Hello brother, Quinn called. "My grandmother Ina Rosolado, has been wanting to talk to you?"

Nicholas stretched his arms wide to pull her into his embrace. "Grandmother Ina, it's so good to see you. I'm so glad you could come."

"Nicky, I would not have missed your home coming party for anything," Ina whispered in Nicholas' ear. "What do you think of the date I got for my Quinn for this evening? Her name is Abril Navarro?"

Nicholas whispered back. "She's very good looking. Now

what does Quinn think about your matchmaking, Grandmother Ina?"

Grandmother Ina smiled mischievously. "I ambushed him,
he didn't have a chance to respond," she whispered.

Grandmother Ina laughed loudly and led him over to
Quinn and Abril. "Quinn aren't you going to introduce your
date?"

"Sure, Grandmother," he said glazing back at Abril. "Ms.
Abril Navarro, this is my brother Nicholas La Cour."

"Nice to meet you, Nicholas," Abril said with a heavy
Spanish accent.

'I'm please to meet you, Abril, and may I add that gown
you're wearing is beautiful. I've never seen a so vivid color in
royal blue before, and the design looks like an original."

"Thank you, I selected the color and fabric myself and the
dress is an original. I designed it myself."

"Ina! Ina! You finally made it!" Grand *mere* Catherine bellowed as she strolled over closing the distance between them.
"Oh! My goodness, Ina. Your dress is beautiful. Where did you
get it?"

Ina embraced Grand *mere* Catherine. "Oh, Catherine, I'm
sorry we were late. But I refused to allow Quinn to drive fast.
Anyway, my dress is one of Abril designs. She made it for me.
This is Abril, right here."

Grand *mere* Catherine looked at Abril and smiled. "Abril
you and I will have to talk. If you made that dress for Ina, I
want one just like it only in a soft sky blue color and with
a sweetheart neckline, and I do believe I should have you do
one in a deep red."

"Grand *mere* Catherine. Abril is Quinn's date, they just got here," Nicholas interrupted her.

Instantly a familiar female voice pierced the air. "Nicholas, I've been looking for you!"

Nicholas turned his head at the sound of the familiar voice. For an instant their eyes locked. The voice that came out of his mouth was almost a whisper. "Maëlle, damn you look! Look! Sensational!"

Nicholas stood there staring spellbound at the black gown Maëlle was wearing. It showed off her beauty seductively in a regal manner, but it was the way her black Mardi Gras eye mask, adored with pearls and with an array of well-placed feathers, gave her an alluring mysterious quality that was igniting sinful as she slowly sashayed over. "Hello everyone, please forgive me for taking my time, walking over. But, I'm not used to wearing heels this tall," Maëlle stated.

"Gosh, Maëlle, look at you all fancied up," Grand *mere* Catherine exclaimed. "Don't you look beautiful?"

"Yes, you do look beautiful!" Ina declared.

"Thank you, Grand *mere* Catherine and Grandmother Ina, I appreciate your compliments," Maëlle said giving both women air hugs.

"Gosh, Maëlle you look magnificent!" Quinn declared.

"Yes, you do. May I say the designer of your dress really understood how to make your gown, personally your own," Abril declared.

"Thank you also, may I say you have exquisite taste. Ms.... Ms.?

"My name is Abril Navarro and I should have exquisite taste; I am a fashion designer."

"Really?" Maëlle replied. "Are you here with Grandmother Ina?"

"Yes and no, Maëlle, she's Quinn's date," Nicholas declared.

Nicholas turned and looked at his grandmother. "By the way they just arrived and haven't had a chance to make the rounds and find out where everything is."

Grand *mere* Catherine saw a chance to be useful. "Nicholas why didn't you say so," she stated. "Come along Ina, Quinn and Abril, let me show you were the appetizer buffet station is. We've got a wet bar too, if you fancy a cocktail., and let me tell you about our dinner menu for tonight."

Quinn turned and looked at Maëlle and exhaled. "That sure is a beautiful dress you're wearing, Maëlle."

"Quinn, if you keep complimenting me like that and then I'll have to save you a dance," Maëlle said. "That is if Abril doesn't mind."

"Yes... Yes... Huh." Quinn nodded and cleared his throat and leaned over and patted Nicholas arm. "Well Nicky, looks like I'll hook up with you later after I get Grandmother Ina and Abril, squared away."

Nicholas nodded. "No problem. I'll probably be stuck here, playing greeter for a while longer. Grand *mere* Catherine wants me to welcome all my guest before I can roam around the ballroom."

Quinn nodded and let Abril take his hand and lead him away.

Nicholas and Maëlle watched and waited until Quinn was out of ear shot.

"Nicholas, you really have to hang around here and greet people?"

"Yeah Maëlle, I promised Grand *mere* Catherine and mother I'd be the hello greeter for the first hour or so and I think I still owe them a half hour or so."

"Darn that's no fun. I thought I was going to get priority treatment tonight?"

"You did. Don't you remember I spent the first thirty- or forty-minutes walking with you, arm and arm, talking."

Maëlle looked conflicted. "Yes, I do. But no one was here then. We got here early I want to dance."

"I'm not stopping you from dancing. I just can't go with you for at least another half hour or so," Nicholas replied. "Go on, go have some fun."

"You mean it?"

Nicholas gave her a soft kiss. "Yes, I mean it. If I leave my post my grandmother will be furious."

"Yes, your grandmother would be furious if you left your post before greeting her best friends," a loud shrill voice called. "Is that your girlfriend Maëlle Moulard."

Maëlle froze at the sound of her name and looked back at Nicholas. "Nicholas look who has arrived?"

Nicholas knew who the familiar voice belonged to without Maëlle saying her name, it was the Bingo Queen herself, Gabby Baptiste.

"Hi, Ms. Gabby, I'm so happy you could make my welcome home party!"

"I'm so glad to be here Nicholas," she said turning her attention to Maëlle. "Ms. Maëlle Moulard don't you look fabulous in that dress."

"Thank you, Ms. Gabby, it's so nice to see you," Maëlle declared, swapping air kisses with Gabby.

"You both remember some of Louis' dear friends," Gabby said turning and introducing the three-gentleman standing behind her.

"That's Mr. Andre Pascal, Mr. Hugo Toussaint, and Mr. Armand Manteau."

"How do you do, gentlemen," Nicholas and Maëlle said in unison as their eyes looked between each other recalling they had been talking about the three men days before.

"So, where is your grandmother?" Gabby asked. "I promised her I'd bring along some single eligible bachelors and let me tell you I did not disappoint."

"She just left to show Quinn's Grandmother, Ina, where the appetizers buffet and bar were set up," Nicholas replied. "In fact, Maëlle was just about to head in that direction."

"Yes, I was," Maëlle declared. "The dance floor is that way too, and I wouldn't mind taking you to Grand *mere* Catherine."

"That's an excellent idea," Grabby exclaimed. Grabby turned and addressed the men with her. "Come gentleman, food and the dance floor is this way."

Maëlle touched Nicholas' shoulder. "I'll catch up with you later."

"No worries," Nicholas replied watching her lead the small party away.

Almost an hour later the Ballroom was crowded with all the familiar friends and family of the La Cour family. The atmosphere took on an aura glowing as in a dream-like state with men dressed fashionably in black tuxedos and ladies in spectacular glistening evening gowns.

Nicholas stood off from the dance floor between two huge

gold fleurs-de-lis concrete columns that stood as an entry way to the massive dance floor. He gazed around spellbound as he watched the couples sashaying mesmerizing as they danced about on the dance floor. He estimated there had to be well over three-hundred people in attendance at his welcome home party.

Nicholas watched as his mother Pearl, descended down the curved formal grand staircase, as the hanging massive rock crystal chandelier shot cascading brilliant light accenting the beautiful deep green evening gown she was wearing. He watched as she held her matching Mardi Gras eye mask as if it was her royal scepter.

Pearl La Cour was a slim woman with delicate features and a delicate bone structure that gave her a regal bearing that made her appear taller than she was. She had soft dawn-gray eyes just like his sister, Lacey.

"Wow! Mom you look fantastic! I see you've changed." Nicholas declared as his mother drew close. "That gown makes you look like royalty especially when you carry your eye mask like a scepter, nice touch."

"Why thank you son," Pearl replied kissing Nicholas on the cheek. "And you look resplendent yourself! Where's Maëlle?"

"She's somewhere walking around," Nicholas replied.

"Nicholas, why did you let her wander about alone in that beautiful gown she's wearing? Gosh, it makes her breast look sinfully alluring, Nicholas aren't you jealous when men stare at her in that dress?"

"No, Mother," Nicholas softly replied. "Maëlle knows she belongs to me."

"Wow! Don't you sound like Mr. Controlling, tonight,

Nicholas. Please don't sound like that. when Father Perez, Senior gets here."

"The Father Perez Senior of the Church of the Good Shepherd? I can't believe it. Is he still alive?" Nicholas repeated astounded that he'd been invited.

"Yes, Nicholas, he is still alive, kicking breathing and blessing lost souls," Pearl declared sarcastically and annoyed. "He's the original. Father Perez Senior, and he was invited. So, get over it."

Anxiously annoyed Nicholas licked his lips and said. "You can't be serious! Father Perez Senior is really coming? Who invited him?"

Pearl gave Nicholas a stern look. "Your Grandmother insisted he'd be invited. She wants him to bless the food."

"More like she wants him to bless me and keep me out of jail," Nicholas added.

"Nicholas, why on earth would you say that. Your grandmother means well, you know how much she is in awe of that man. Now, Nicholas, when Father Perez gets here, please don't antagonize him, be kind."

"Alright! Alright! If you insist," Nicholas declared. "Let me go and look for Maëlle, at least I can let her flaunt her alluring breasts in front of Father Perez and distract him from holding a conversation with me. I'm sure they will inspire a lecture on virtue and other high moral standards, for her!"

Pearl laughed. "Gosh, Nicholas you are so wicked. Please don't do that to Father Perez. Besides, you won't have time to find Maëlle, because here comes the good father now," she said nodding in his direction.

Nicholas eyes searched in the direction his mother was looking. The priest did not look like time had aged him at all.

Father Perez Senior was a slim small man who had a regal bearing that made him appear taller than he was. He wore the traditional cleric uniform robe that bellowed around him as he walked in a dreamy flowing way. His robe uniform had a black sash tied neatly around his waist.

"Nicholas! Nicholas! My son it is so good to see you!" Father Perez said as he embraced him. "I prayed for you each day you were in that prison."

"Thanks, Father Perez," Nicholas replied as he let himself be bear hugged by the old priest.

Father Perez Senior pulled out of his embrace and turned and placed his attention on Pearl. "Pearl do forgive me; I was just so happy to see Nicholas again."

"No worries, Father, I understand, in fact, I'll leave you and Nicholas alone. I need to go see what Horace is up to."

Father Perez Senior and Nicholas watched as Pearl made her exit.

"Nicholas, did you know that band your grandmother found plays a variety of music? And they take request too. They played *Dream Away* for me, it's an old Frank Sinatra song."

"Naw, I didn't know that. They sound good though," Nicholas added.

"Yes... Yes, they do, and they did an excellent job with that song," Father Perez Senior said, smiling. "Have you ever heard the song *Dream Away* by Frank Sinatra?"

"No...," Nicholas paused. "Wait a minute. Yes, I have. It's

one of Grand *mere* Catherine's favorite Frank Sinatra songs. She used to play it all the time."

"Yes! Yes! It is!" Father Perez Senior replied taking a deep breath and then saying. "Nicholas speaking of your grandmother. I suppose you know she wanted me to speak with you?"

Nicholas shrugged. "I kind of figured as much. And I bet my mother did too?"

"Yes, Nicholas she did and so did Horace, you don't mind if I say, your biological father's name?"

"You know about that too? Horace, being my real father, I mean?" Nicholas inquired. "But how?"

Father Perez Senior looked back at Nicholas. "The how answer is rather complicated, as you young folks are fond of saying. Anyway, just know that I know all about Pearl and Horace and your situation. You should know they all love you and want the best for you."

Nicholas stared off into the sea of people walking around the ballroom. "Why do I get the feeling your really hear to teach me a lesson?"

"Well, Nicholas I would say you're having that feeling because God has placed it on your heart to have that feeling and to know and remember that we are all instruments of God. Take for example your grandmother and parents coming to me to pray for your release from prison and to keep you safe while you were there. We were all instruments praying to God our Lord for help and he heard us. Don't you see?"

Nicholas nodded. "Yes, I see. So, what is the lesson?"

Father Perez Senior placed a sympathetic hand on Nicholas shoulder. "The lesson is what the Lord says about vengeance. The Lord says vengeance is mine, right Nicholas? You learned that in Sunday school, remember?"

Silently Nicholas studied the old priest face. He saw the real caring and love Father Perez Senior had for everyone including himself. One thing he knew for sure is Father Perez Senior was the real thing. He figured Father Perez Senior and Mother Teresa must have both been truly touched by God in their lives.

Finally, Nicholas nodded his head in understanding and said. "Yes, Father, I know that the Lord has said vengeance is mine and I believe this to be true," he said out loud. *But internally Nicholas thoughts were telling him, if we are all instruments of God and God answered his prayer, setting him free, it must be God's will that I carry out vengeance against Dante Channing for what he did to me.*

Silently Nicholas stood there staring off into space as his thoughts drifted.

Father Perez Senior sighed heavily and said. "You know Nicholas, I've been thinking. That song Dream Away has the real lesson to teach us about life, you know."

"How is that Father?" Nicholas asked.

"Because like the song says we carry our greatest wounds inside ourselves. Well, really we hide them deep within where they never show and when there is no room left to live inside ourselves, we dream away."

"Really? That song says all that?"

Father Perez Senior nodded. "You should ask the band to play the song for you, Nicholas and listen to the lyrics. Or better yet, you got one of those new cell phones, don't you?"

He asked but didn't wait for a response. "You can probably play it on YouTube or one of those music apps."

Nicholas smiled to himself it looked like Father Perez Senior was hip to all the latest technology devices.

"Yeah, Father, I do have one of those cellphones," Nicholas replied.

"Well, there you have it. Take a listen when you have a chance, Nicholas. By the way, I need to get going. I promised Quinn's grandmother Ina Rosolado, I'd pop over to her table. I'm sure she thinks I got lost. Nicholas could I ask you a favor?"

"Sure, Father Perez Senior, what is it?"

"Nicholas, please come by the church and talk to me, anytime you feel like it. I promised your father Louis before he passed away, I would let you know I'm always available to talk to, okay?"

"I will father," Nicholas assured him as he watched Father Perez Senior make his exit.

Nicholas watched politely staring around the ballroom as people continued to socialize. He heard the fierce beat of dance music coming from one of the small ballrooms off the main one. He knew everyone in there were getting their groove on.

All at once Nicholas looked up and saw Maëlle hurrying over to him.

"Nicholas! Quinn only danced with that woman he brought with him, tonight? Can You believe it?"

"Huh? Well that woman is his date."

"Quinn having a date with him never stopped him from dancing with me before," Maëlle ranted.

"So, you're in a panic Maëlle because you didn't get a chance to dance tonight?"

"Oh, no I'm not in a panic and I did get a chance to dance. I danced. But you know how well Quinn dances. I was forced to dance with every left foot Leroy out on the dance floor. Quinn would only dance with his date Abril and that dress she's wearing is just...Just! Plain old spectacular in a sexy slutty kind of way."

"Yeah, that dress does cling in all the right places, but I don't think she looks slutty. Sexy, yes. But not slutty," he paused. "You know Maëlle, someone told me your breast looked very alluring in that dress you're wearing, tonight?"

"Really? Do tell. Who was it? Was it Quinn?"

"No, Maëlle it wasn't Quinn," Nicholas chuckled. "I don't think I'll tell you who told me that. I don't want it going to your head."

Instantly Maëlle close the distance between her and Nicholas. "I can't believe Grandmother Ina, hooked Quinn up with that woman!"

"Hey Nicholas and Maëlle!" Quinn's voice carried on the air.

Nicholas and Maëlle both looked in the direction of Quinn's voice. He was standing at the top of the staircase.

"Stay where you are, we are coming down," Quinn yelled as he took Abril's arm as they made their way to the bottom of the staircase.

Quinn was grinning wide as he approached them. "I'm so glad I caught the two of you together." Instantly he hugged Maëlle. "Maëlle, I'm so sorry I forgot to ask you to dance. I hope you forgive me."

Maëlle bashfully smiled. "No worries. I didn't even notice."

Quinn voice was excited. "I was just telling Abril how you and I used to makeup all kinds of crazy dance steps, when we used to dance together."

"That we did, Quinn," Maëlle replied. "I'm sure Abril noticed what a great dancer you are."

Abril smiled. "Yes, I did. Quinn makes me want to take lessons."

Quinn looked at Nicholas. "Hey Nicholas, I have another party I need to run to and make an appearance and I want to show off Abril. We will just make an appearance. We'll come right back to your party," he said. "You don't mind, if I leave and come back? Do you?" He asked but didn't wait for a response. "Besides, I have to come back, I have to pick up Grandmother Ina."

"No worries, Quinn. I don't mind. I got Maëlle to keep me company," Nicholas replied.

"Thanks Brother," Quinn declared. "Come on Abril, we've got to get going."

Nicholas and Maëlle stood there silently watching Quinn and Abril make their exit as Maëlle rolled her eyes.

"I can't believe the nerve of Quinn. He was so rude. Nicholas you should have never let him leave your party."

'Excuse me? Quinn is a grown man. I'm not the boss of him. Why you got attitude, Maëlle?"

"Because, now I don't have anyone to dance with me. You hate dancing, Nicholas. I was counting on Quinn being my dance partner tonight."

"Oh yeah, I forgot. You could always get Quinn out on the dance floor. But you know something Maëlle?"

"What?" she asked.

"I don't hate dancing. I just always let you and Quinn dance together because the two of you could always think of some unique dance moves to capture everyone's attention. But what you didn't know is, Quinn always came to me to show him how to do the latest dance moves, I bet you didn't know that, did you?"

"No, I didn't," she said looking curious. "Are you serious, Nicholas?"

"Only one way to find out, I guess you have to dance with me to see, how about right now?""

"Really Nicholas? You mean it?" Maëlle asked.

"Yeah, come on."

Maëlle smiled as Nicholas took her hand and led her to the ballroom with the blaring dance music. She forced a smile on her face. But inside she knew the truth. She wasn't angry that Quinn wasn't there to dance with, she was angry because Quinn came with that beautiful woman, named Abril.

One thing was for sure Maëlle thought, she was definitely going to have a talk with Quinn about Ms. Abril, when they met for lunch.

29

❦

Chapter 22

Secrets, Chocolate Cake, & The Devil...

That Monday afternoon, Maëlle drove her car to old Market Street just off San Pedro Square in the old section of downtown San Jose. She felt lucky finding the parking space just on the corner from the restaurant.

The Black Orchid restaurant was one of San Jose's oldest establishments in downtown San Jose and had a long pride of being a discreet place where business both public and private could be done without the prying eyes and ears of everyone.

Maëlle's eyes flashed in anticipation, as she recalled the numerous times she dined at the Black Orchid restaurant. It had always been one of her favorites.

Maëlle found the entranced and walked into the dark lounge and found Quinn exactly where he'd said he would be.

"Hello Quinn."

"Good to see you Maëlle," Quinn replied rising to give her a hug. "Won't you have a seat? Unless of course you prefer a table in a private booth.?"

Maëlle cautiously looked around. "No, this is good, Quinn. I don't think we have to worry about spies or secret agents."

"Or newspaper people," Quinn chuckled and added.

At the mention of the newspaper Maëlle's eyes swept around the room. "Perhaps a private room would be best."

"Suit yourself," Quinn shrugged and turned and motioned the waiter.

"Ah... Waiter, the lady and I would like a private booth after all."

"I have it ready," the waiter replied. "Right this way."

Quinn rose and beckoned for Maëlle to follow their waiter.

They'd just rounded a corner when a man yelled. "Maëlle... Maëlle Moulard! Is that you?"

Instantly Maëlle recognized the voice. It was Paul Lombardi a half Italian half African American policeman she'd had a brief torrid affair with, and he wasn't alone. He was standing next to a very beautiful African American woman who also looked familiar, she knew the woman. She'd went to high school with both of them.

After her panic anxiety attack melted Maëlle nervously cleared her throat. "Paul it's been a long time. You remember Quinn from high school," she said but didn't allow him to respond. "And I see you're with Dominique Bledsoe. I didn't know the two of you were an item."

"Whoa! Wait a minute, Paul and I are just old friends, and I live in Denver, but work here several times a month. I'm just here now for a work conference and I promised Paul several months ago, I'd take him out to lunch to celebrate his promotion to lieutenant," Dominique declared.

Paul nodded. "Yes, Dominique is correct. Besides Dominique has been in a long-term relationship with Lawrence McCready, you remember he was a star football player on our high school team, who went on to play for the Raiders?"

"Yeah, I remember Lawrence, he was a couple of years older than Kienan. In fact, he was a senior when Nicholas and I got to high school. Wow, that's right I heard he is a defense coach for Denver," Quinn pointed out.

"That's my man!" Dominique replied. "Now you see why I had to correct the record. I don't want to get the gossip columns racing, my Lawrence would have a fit."

"Well, it is so nice to see both of you again and congratulation on your promotion, Paul, I'm sure you earned it," Maëlle declared. "I'm sure you won't mind if we both continue with our lunch."

Paul nodded his agreement. He could tell by the flash of fire in Maëlle's eyes, she was nervous being seen out with Quinn.

"Thanks, Maëlle," Paul cleared his throat. "Yes, we are pressed for time for lunch, Dominique and I both are on our lunch breaks, she should be getting back to her conference soon," he replied. "Well it was really good to see you again, Maëlle... And Quinn."

"Likewise," Maëlle assured him as she took Quinn by the arm and led him away.

"Now that was an awkward moment," Quinn declared turning to locate their waiter.

Their waiter was waiting for them at the end of the corridor, where he stood by a door. He quickly showed them to their private dining room and within seconds the two were seated.

"Oh, waiter, you can bring the food now."

"Yes, sir," the waiter replied taking his leave.

Quinn waited until their waiter was out of earshot. "I hope you don't mind Maëlle, but I had anticipated your wanting a private room and I took the liberty of ordering.

"Let me guess, you order me the braised beef medallions and mini Cobb salad?" she asked.

"Of course, I believe it's your favorite," Quinn replied. "A long with the house specialty."

For the first time Maëlle smiled. "Yes, the braised beef medallions are both our favorites, as I recall. Not to mention they make some of the best homemade fettuccine noodles. Only you always get the twice baked potato," she chuckled and then paused.

"Yes, and of course we always shared the house salmon specialty," Quinn added.

"Hmmm...," she said. "I wonder are you serving a rich meal before bad news or what?"

Quinn shook his head. "No, I figured it was the other way around. I figured I should feed you before you tell me whatever it is that I saw flash across your face the other day."

"Well, was it upon my seeing you with Abril Navarro, at Nicholas' homecoming party or dinner at Kienan and Lacey's house?"

Quinn didn't really know what to say about his date that night. He did find her intriguing, but he didn't think talking with Maëlle about her was the right thing to do. He cleared his throat and said. "Well, Abril Navarro, was just a blind date my grandmother matched me up with. She will be lucky if she ever hears from me again."

"Now, that sounds like the Quinn I know," Maëlle declared. "So, I guess it would be the looks we were giving each other at Kienan and Lacey's house."

Their waiter gently knocked on their door, and then push it open bringing in their meal.

Maëlle watched as their waiter placed their braised beef medallions before them along with her mini Cobb salad, salmon with herbs, and freshly made fettuccine in an Alfredo sauce.

She then waited while he poured glasses of red wine for the two of them.

The aromas of food made Maëlle's mouth water. She waited until their waiter closed the door.

"Look thanks for doing all of this Quinn," she said taking a fork full of braised beef medallions and placing it in her mouth. She chewed slowly and then said. "So, you did notice my staring at you the other day."

"I couldn't miss it, now, where were we?" Quinn inquired.

Maëlle lifted her wine glass and studied it. She took a deep breath as her thoughts raced. "What you saw running across my face the other day was fear. Pure and simple."

She took a sip of her wine and savored it as she studied Quinn. She noticed he didn't even raise an eyebrow.

"Oh, really!" Quinn declared. "Are you going to tell me why? Or should I guess?"

Maëlle let her eyes search across his face. She wondered if Quinn really had no idea. Or if he was just toying with her. She took another sip of her wine finding it was giving her the courage she desperately needed. Finally, she said. "You see Quinn. I've been afraid you were going to tell Nicholas about, my short visit to see you in Mexico."

Quinn finished chewing. He took his time before he said. "I would never do that. Nicholas is my brother and what happened between us in the past is over. Besides if I ever mentioned it to him or if he ever found out, it would hurt him, and I have no intentions of hurting my brother," he paused. "Not to mention I'm sure it would hurt you too and I couldn't live with myself if I hurt you like that again."

At the sound of sadness in Quinn's voice, Maëlle glanced up and saw the spark of affection Quinn had for her in his eyes. She was just about to open her mouth when Quinn interrupted her.

"Yes, Maëlle maybe I do still have feelings for you," Quinn softly replied almost in a whisper. "Just like I know you still have some for me. But our time together is over, it's the past."

At that rare moment Maëlle's eyes met his and they both knew the truth. The moment was powerful. She went to open her mouth to speak.

"Don't say it Maëlle," Quinn declared. "I know what you're thinking. But when you came to me in Mexico it was only because you felt hurt because my brother had jilted you. That's all it was... And that's all it can be."

Maëlle hung her head. "But Quinn..."

"You know I'm right, Maëlle girl. Don't. Please don't let's just enjoy this wonderful lunch."

"Our last lunch together, it would seem," Maëlle whispered exhaling. "Oh, Quinn. I know you're right. But I didn't ..."

"We're doing the right thing Maëlle, keeping it our secret," he said giving her a smile.

"Our secret," Maëlle repeated. "Our dirty little secret."

"And a damn good dirty little secret it is! Every last lustful sinful bite of it! Just like a decadent scrumptious piece of Chocolate Cake. You remember how we loved our Chocolate Cake together, Maëlle," Quinn declared with raunchy laughter.

His humor made Maëlle laugh.

Immediately, Quinn raised his glass of wine and leaned over. "Here's to us both keeping our dirty little secret," he said waiting and watching Maëlle.

Slowly Maëlle lifted her glass and toasted with Quinn as she silently said a prayer as her eyes watched his and prayed that there was honor among liars, and cheaters, such as the two of them.

Instantly, a soft knock sounded on their door, as their waiter appeared holding a silver covered dish he carefully placed in the center of their table.

"What's that?" Maëlle inquired.

"It's our famously Sinful Sinners Devil's Food Chocolate Cake," their waiter said. "Compliments of our chef."

Instantly, Maëlle eyes sought out Quinn's just as he choked on his glass of wine and said. "Damn that Devil! He's always poking about in Grown folk's business! Just stirring up shit!"

He then laughed out loud.

Maëlle joined Quinn laughing out loud at Quinn's shenanigans.

"Damn, that Devil!" Maëlle declared. "That son-of-a-bitch

loves his chocolate cake too," she roared with laughter as Quinn joined in.

"Here's to the Devil, his love for chocolate cake and keeping dirty secrets too," Quinn laughed out.

***

An hour later, Maëlle made her way back to her car, she just reached the corner where she parked it when she heard a familiar voice slice the air.

"Maëlle why didn't you tell me you were having lunch at the Black Orchid today? You know it's my favorite restaurant too," Lacey said in a huff.

Instantly Maëlle froze feeling her tension building before she abruptly tilted her head just in time to see Lacey crossing the street. "Lacey? Where the hell are you..."

"On why way to have lunch of course," Lacey declared interrupting her.

Maëlle looked back at her best friend and breathed out a sigh of relief when she realized the direction Lacey was walking from. It was clear to her that Lacey was on her way to thee Black Orchid restaurant and not coming from it.

"Of course, I knew that," she snapped feeling the tension in the words she spoken let her know she needed to calm down? She took a deep breath and said. "I didn't mean to sound so harsh. I just meant I didn't make any advance plans or anything to have lunch at the Black Orchid today. It was just a spur of the moment thing, or I would have mentioned it to you. Of, course I would have invited, you."

Lacey noticed Maëlle' abrupt tone and manner for a moment and then shook out her thoughts thinking maybe she had imagined it. She stood froze to the spot in front of her best friend for a moment longer before the words rolled off her tongue. "Why are you so... So... I don't know, nervously tense or something, today, Maëlle?"

"I'm not tense," Maëlle interrupted her. "Look I'm just in a hurry. I'm late... "She paused, trying to think of a convincing lie to tell. "I'm just late. I have a very important appointment that I have to keep, and standing here chitchatting with you is making me later," she declared opening her car door and getting in.

Maëlle rolled down her window. "Look Lacey, I'm so sorry but I have to run. Why don't you give me a call later and we can chat, okay?"

"Sure," Lacey replied rolling her eyes as she watched her best friend's car pull away from the curb. She thought, Maëlle was acting nervously strange, she didn't have long to think about it when her cell phone rang.

"Hi Mrs. French, I'm here at the restaurant."

"Good, I'm waiting inside by the door," Mrs. French replied. "See you in a flash," she replied hanging up.

Lacey shook off Maëlle's slight turned and headed for the front door of the restaurant. She reached for the door handle just as someone was pushing from the inside. The two people collided.

"Oh, my! I'm so sorry!" A male voice declared as the two crashed into each other.

"Quinn?" Lacey called out instantly recognizing the voice, as she pulled out of his embrace.

"Lacey? What are you doing here?"

"I'm having lunch with my cooking instructor," Lacey rapidly replied.

Lacey looked into Quinn's face and watched as he diverted his eyes. She was just about to open her mouth to ask what he was doing there.

"Lacey, they have our table waiting," Mrs. French called out. "I don't know about you but I'm starving."

Lacey turned and looked at Quinn and gave him a fake smile. "It's good seeing you Quinn, as you see I had a prior engagement and lunch calls."

"No, problem Lacey, I need to get going myself," Quinn replied." Enjoy your lunch he said turning and making a quick exit.

Lacey followed Mrs. French to their table not listening to a word she was saying her mind was racing rapidly with so many thoughts that kept bringing her back to an obvious possibility. A possibility that she didn't want to believe as her gut began twisting in knots as she tried to make sense of what just happened.

Frantically, Lacey shook out her thoughts determined to enjoy her lunch with her teaching instructor Mrs. French.

30

Chapter 23

Ghost, Nicholas, & The Angel Annie Mae...

Promptly at three o'clock pm, that afternoon. Nicholas walked down Plum street heading for the corner of Third street and Plum. He exhaled and stopped walking when the old Victorian house, on the corner, came into view. It was impressive, just then his cell phone rang. He checked the caller-ID, it was Quinn. He picked it up.

Nicholas laughed. "Hey Quinn, what's up, man?"

"Nicholas, my brother. Can you talk?"

"Ahhhh, I was kind of in the middle of something, important. Can I call you back?"

"Sure, no problem."

"Ok, cool. Goodbye," Nicholas said hanging up the phone. He had no intentions of calling Quinn back. He was a busy man.

Nicholas turned and let his eyes take in the massive old Victorian mansion, across the street. It was located right where Ghost had said it would be on the corner of Third street and Plum right by the alley.

The massive Mansion had a gingerbread look to its exterior, complete with fake giant size candy canes standing regally at its entrance. The name Shenanigans hung on an old wood rustic looking sign, like the kind you'd find in an old west town.

Nicholas stood across the street and studied the building. He noticed no one was entering or leaving the front entrance of Shenanigans, it gave the place an eerie feeling. Out of nowhere a cold breeze whipped up and blew around him. He listened as the wind began singing an uneasy strange song. A song he'd never heard before.

"Yo hoo, Nicholas I'm over here." Ghost's oddly quirky voice screeched out, over the wind.

"Ghost!" Nicholas declared, walking across the street and closing the gap between them.

"Come along Nicholas," Ghost declared steering him quickly inside and down a long corridor.

Ghost seemed to be walking as fast as his feet could carry him. He tilted his head back at Nicholas and said. "Hurry, we must not keep Angel waiting."

Nicholas kept pace with Ghost strive and before he knew it Ghost stopped in front of a shiny black door and knocked hard three times.

A sweet-sounding woman's voice called out and said, "You may enter."

Ghost thrust open the door and crossed the threshold. Quickly followed by Nicholas.

"Greetings Ghost, is this the man named Nicholas La Cour you told me about?"

Nicholas felt his jaw dropped wide open when he beheld the woman standing before him. The woman looked and sounded just like an Angel. He couldn't believe his eyes was looking on an earthly being who radiated a presence not of this world. Nicholas couldn't believe it, he felt like crying as she was so beautiful to be hold. "Oh, my... I've never seen an Angel before; this may sound geeky, but you are beautiful beyond words. Are you really an Angel?"

Angel's clear radiant eyes focused on Nicholas. "Yes, angels are real Nicholas, there are sent to earth by God to perform various tasks and have been sent for thousands upon thousands of years. Traditions tells us that angels are messengers of God. Now tell me Nicholas, why are you seeking me?"

Nervously Nicholas grinned. "Well, first I really need to thank Ghost for setting up this meeting with you, I have something to ask of you."

Angel's eyes didn't appear human as they seemed to flicker brightly back at him, Nicholas thought.

Nicholas squinted hard trying to make out the color of them. For a second the color looked a bright violet and then sparkle like a ray of light. and her words sounded like music on the wind. "Let me set the record straight Nicholas, Ghost did not set up this meeting with me, he was just a means to the end."

Astounded Nicholas stared back at her. "He didn't?"

Angel didn't respond to Nicholas' question instead she turned and settled her gaze on Ghost.

"Ghost Braveheart Bartholomeus, may I please speak with Nicholas in private?"

"Sure... Sure. Just call if you need me, I am at your service," Ghost said in his proper English voice and turned and made his exit.

Nicholas watched as the door closed behind Ghost. All at once he felt Angels eyes upon him. It was uncanny how he could feel her benevolent presence.

Angel's caring eyes stared back at Nicholas. "I'm sorry for dismissing Ghost Braveheart Bartholomeus from the Room Nicholas, but sometimes I cannot tolerant his, malevolent spirit around me."

"I'm sorry, malevolent. Ghost is malevolent?" Nicholas stated rather than asked, looking back at her puzzled.

"There is good and bad in everyone and everything Nicholas. As there are far greater things in the unseen world that interact within this earthly world," Angel cautioned. "Besides I didn't think you'd want Ghost to hear who really summoned me."

"I don't understand," Nicholas replied.

"Your deceased father Louis is the one who contacted me. He sent me to speak to you, Nicholas."

Nicholas looked back at her sharply, he didn't want her to know his hearing, his deceased father had contacted her, made him a little scared knowing what he'd came there for and what he intended to do if she didn't help him.

All at once he felt Angel's piercing gaze silently studying him. Nicholas looked up and saw that she was amused watching him think.

He rubbed his jaw and tried to think of what his dead father had said to Angel.

Nicholas shook out his thoughts and said. "I don't understand, my father Louis he's dead. Why would he contact you?"

"Your father is a watcher who watches you from the other side. Still very much dead, but the dead do watch the living. You are seeking the whereabouts of Dante Channing your old business partner, correct?"

"Yes, yes of course. That's why I wanted to see you..."

"The bible is specific on committing sins, Nicholas," The Angel interrupted him.

"Say what is this? I didn't come to you for a bible reading..."

Angel's eyes focused in on Nicholas like a radar gun in the hands of a police officer issuing tickets. "And your purpose for seeking Dante Channing's whereabouts Nicholas, isn't it for the purpose of revenge?"

"So, what of it, God gives every man the right to choose. Dante chose to backstab me and betray me! I have a right to choose what revenge I want to wreak on him, you know like it says in the bible an eye for an eye," Nicholas replied.

Immediately Angel said. "But you do not take the full meaning Nicholas, in Matthew chapter five verse thirty-eight through forty-two it reads in the New Testament, Jesus repudiates even that notion of self-revenge and he says..."*Ye have heard that it hath been said, An eye for an eye, and a tooth for a tooth: But I say unto you, That ye resist not evil: but whosoever shall smite thee on thy right cheek, turn to him the other cheek also.*"

"That still doesn't apply to me," Nicholas held his position.

Angel locked gazes with Nicholas as her eyes pleaded. "Even if it is written do not take revenge my dear ones but leave room for God's wrath for it is written God says I will repay. Why do you have no mercy, Nicholas?"

"I don't know you tell me," Nicholas said shaking his head.

"There are some theories Nicholas, on the subject of forgiveness and revenge that research has suggested the tendency to seek vengeance and to forgive are related characteristics. Highly forgiving individuals were said not to be containing narcissism tendencies on a high level."

"What the hell does that have to do with me!" Nicholas demanded.

"All I'm saying Nicholas I feel your aura your soul essence, you are not a vengeful being."

"Look Angel, you don't know what I'm capable of. I've been locked up from society, remember?"

Angel opened her mouth. "But ..."

"But nothing," Nicholas interrupted. "Look Angel I didn't come her to have a conversation with you about the bible. I came to you to ask you for help because I was told you know everything. Now are you going to help me, tell me where I can find Dante?"

Angel shook her head. "No, Nicholas, I will not freely become a part of that which makes you become corrupt. There is goodness in you."

Before Angel could finish speaking Nicholas closed the distance between them and halted right in front of Angel. "You know Angel, darling, I so hate to rudely interrupt you. But I've read the bible too, and there is a passage in the bible that I believe wills you to help me. Now who was that..."

Nicholas tilted his head. "Oh yeah, that was the story of Jacob and his struggle with the Angel, and guess what Jacob did?"

Angel didn't answer keeping her focus on Nicholas. The moment was tense.

Nicholas didn't wait for a response as he instantly reached out and grabbed Angel with both of his hands holding her tight.

"Nicholas let me go!" Angel struggled trying to break loose from his hold.

Nicholas, laughed. "Nothing doing sister, I mean Angel. I ain't letting you go until you bless me to find Dante just like I read in the bible, when Jacob held and wrestled the angel and said... I will not release you until you bless me. And I want my blessing to be that I find Dante Channing pronto!"

"Very well, Nicholas, as you wish. Please check your hand," Angel said calmly.

"You're trying to trick me into letting you go!" Nicholas blurted.

"No, I am not. You don't have to release me to feel what is in the palm of your right hand," Angel declared.

Instantly Nicholas felt something cold and round in his right palm. It felt like a coin. Slowly he relaxed his grip, on his right-hand holding Angel and opened the palm of his hand. An ancient looking gold coin was nestled in the palm of his hand.

Dumbfounded Nicholas studied the coin in his hand.

Slowly Nicholas' rage subsided as he released his hold, Angel, with both of his hands, he glanced back at her.

"You should seek out Yanni Smirnov. She can lead you to Dante."

"Yanni Smirnov. I don't know how to find Yanni," he said her name as if he was in a trance.

"Yanni goes to Brunch every Sunday at the Russian Tea Room over in Los Gatos," Angel said calmly and matter of factly. "She never misses. She takes her mother, it's her mother's favorite place to go."

"Wow! Thanks," Nicholas replied, in awe of the presence standing across from him.

Angel stepped away from him. "You should get there early Nicholas, Yanni's mother likes to get there early, when they first set out the food for brunch, she like to eat everything fresh."

She then strolled away quickly putting a great distance between them. She walked over to a door stopped, paused and said. "Oh, and Nicholas, you know loneliness is a strange companion. You know kind of like you and your woman Maëlle's relationship. You should spend more time with her. You know being more attentive to your woman, Maëlle. Just because you have sex with her doesn't mean she's not lonely. Sex ain't companionship, and loneliness can be a motive for some to seek the companionship of others. I'd just thought I'd share that with you in case you didn't know," Angel said taking a deep breath. "Anyway, I'll leave you with this. Just so you know, the dead are always watching you," she said before a strange fog slowly descended around her.

Nicholas stood there staring his eyes transfixed on her, as if time had stood still.

All at once Angel was gone. The moment felt surreal. Nicholas couldn't explain it. He could not say for sure he ever saw the door open. But Angel was gone. He shook his head trying to clear his thoughts.

"This can't be real, Angel, you didn't open that door and walk through it, but you're gone," Nicholas said out loud to no one but himself.

The room felt strangely warm and Nicholas felt like his eyes were being made to look at something on the floor where Angel had last stood. It felt like something was pulling him to the spot as he made his way over, to something white, laying on the floor where Angel had last stood, by the closed door. He walked over stooped down to pick it up.

Nicholas picked it up and exhaled. "What the —!" It was a fluffy white feather. He was flabbergasted.

31

❧

Chapter 24

Jack of Spade and Queen Mary of Hong Kong

That same afternoon, Thomas Holmes took the Doolittle exit off Interstate 880 heading into the City of Alameda. Alameda was really an island in San Francisco Bay. He stayed in the right lane and drove just passed the golf course and headed for the bridge. He knew once he crossed it the storage unit facility was located down the road heading for the wharf.

Thomas drove to the front of the building and parked his Jeep Cherokee right in front. He was just about to get out of his jeep when someone approached the side of his vehicle.

"So, glad you made it here Thomas! I wished you'd drove faster."

Thomas looked up into the stressed-out face of Jack of Spade.

"Hey Jack, you look like you could use a good night's rest," Thomas said greeting him.

"If you had to spend time picking up the Queen Mary and take her from Chinatown in San Francisco to Treasure Island all in one morning. You'd looked like you could use a million years of sleep too," he declared. "I'm the Jack of Spade but Queen Mary treats me like I'm her servant."

"Queen Mary? Who's that?" Thomas asked closing his car door.

A slender frame elegant looking gray-haired Asian woman walked slowly over and stood right next to, Jack of Spade, a cloud of perfume floated around her.

"Hi, I am Queen Mary Chan of Hong Kong. All my friends call me Queen Mary of Hong Kong," she said in a heavy Mandarin accent. "I am the daughter of a famous Hong Kong dancer. My mother was the first one in our village to go to Ballerina training school in Hong Kong."

"Nice to meet you, Queen Mary," Thomas said.

"Careful Thomas don't let her sweet smile fool you. My mother is fiercely competitive," Jack cautioned.

Thomas smiled back at her. He said the first thing that that popped in his head. "I was wondering are you called Queen Mary of Hong Kong, because you were a great dancer, like your mother?"

"No, my friends call me Queen Mary of Hong Kong because I whoop their arse in Zi pai," she patted her chest symbolically with hands. "I am the reigning Queen of Zi pai, in my women's group. I win all the time."

"Thomas, see what I mean, my mother is fiercely competitive," Jack declared. "That's why brother and I called her Queen Tiger mom."

"I always have been, competitive and I always will be. Where you think you learn to be good in cards, Jack of

Spades," Queen Mary boasted. "My DNA give my sons that ability. But I still think my sons jealous of my fighting spirit."

"Well, Thomas, see what I mean. You've met my mother, Queen Mary and oh by the way, let me tell you before I forget. She thinks she's royalty too."

"Yes, I am royalty and this Queen is tired of waiting. Let's get started."

Thomas looked around and smiled benignly. "I was supposed to me a contact here, but I'm afraid he hasn't made it here yet."

"What we need him for?" Queen Mary asked.

"He's the one who is supposed to help us get inside your sons storage pod," Thomas replied.

"We don't need him to get inside storage pod," Queen Mary replied.

"Why would you say something like that?" Thomas inquired.

"Because, I have the keys," Queen Mary said thrusting a ring of keys in front of him and shaking them.

"Ahhhh! Mommy!" Jack yelled. "Why didn't you tell me?"

Queen Mary slapped her son on his back. "Son, you never asked me if I have keys," she said. "Look here the storage number is on the key, C247."

Instantly Jack stared to speak in the complex tones of Mandarin Chinese. Thomas knew the sound of the language well since he'd spent quite a bit of time eating lunch in San Francisco China Town.

Soon Hong Kong Mary joined in the loud conversation and Thomas quickly intervened between the two family members. "Now that we have the keys, don't you think we should get started to see what is inside?"

His words did the trick as the three headed inside the huge storage warehouse.

"C247, should be this way," Thomas gestured with a wave of his hand.

They quickly located the corridor they were looking for and a few doors down they located Ace's storage pod number.

"Here it is, C247," Jack declared. "Mommy use your key."

"Here son, you take the key ring," Queen Mary replied. "I don't have my glasses with me, the key is marked C247."

Jack did as he was told and soon the metal door slowly cranked open and rolled up like a garage door. The storage unit was filled to capacity with rows and rows of boxes, a high-tech looking desk, chairs, file cabinets, bed headboard, mattress and some expensive looking leather sectional furniture.

Jack of spade looked like he was going to cry. "Oh, goodness where should we look first?"

"Stop whining! Whining boy," Queen Mary declared. "You need to think like your brother, Ace. Now, hop to it!"

"My brother Ace..." Jack mumbled under his breath and walked over to a row of boxes and begin opening the first one he reached for."

Over an hour passed.

Thomas walked further into the storage unit. He checked his watch. He couldn't believe over an hour had passed since they'd been there.

The storage unit was a good size, he thought. He pressed his lips together thinking about what Queen Mary had told her son Jack, earlier. He turned his head and watched Jack busy opening another box. He turned his gaze and looked for Queen Mary. He studied her as she went over to a box marked clothes and began rummaging through it.

Thomas thought about what Queen Mary had told Jack. *Think like your brother Ace.* As he walked around the storage unit and randomly opened one box after the next and looked inside.

Where would a genius like Ace want to hide something, he didn't want anyone else to find. Then some boxes caught his eye across the room in a corner.

"Will, you look at this!" Mary's shrill voice carried on the air.

"Ma! What is it?" Jack inquired as he hurried over.

Thomas watched as Jack hurried over and helped Mary finish opening a box. He knew he needed to keep them both occupied if he wanted to check out the boxes across the room without their help. Quickly he walked over and picked up an unopened box marked Oakland.

Jack shook his head dubiously "Wow! This box has all the Christmas presents I gave to Ace over the years!"

Mary's face contorted with anger. "Not, just yours, mine are there too," she exclaimed. "My son Ace is one ungrateful bastard!"

Thomas opened the box marked Oakland. He found a bunch of brand-new Oakland sports merchandise. There were Oakland A's jerseys and Warriors caps and Raiders jerseys. "Say, there a lot of great sport stuff here that just going to waste sitting in a storage unit," he said pushing the open box in front of Mary.

Jack whistled loudly. "Well, will you look here. There's brand new Oakland A's sports stuff, here."

"That's my Oakland A's sweatshirt I gave him, and it's still got the store tags on it," Mary declared.

"This stuff is worth big money," Thomas said, as his eyes caught the attention the tall boxes across the room again. "After we're done going through everything. You might want to think about what you want to do with all this stuff. You know maybe get a truck and haul things away," he said, as he turned and walked over to the tall boxes.

"Good idea," Jack replied. "This stuff, I can sell at the Berryessa Flea market."

"Huh! Too far! I like the Oakland Flea market," Mary declared.

I'll sell my stuff at the Berryessa Flea market," Jack stated. "We'll see who gets the best price."

Thomas listened to Jack and Mary's friendly badgering and felt a knowing in the pit of his stomach as he walked in closer to the tall boxes on the other side of the room.

Silently he stood in front of them studying them.

The tall boxes were clustered together and marked plants. But one box stood out. The box had the words *water weekly* written in small black letters, in the top right-hand corner.

Curiosity got the best of him as he wondered why anyone would put live plants inside boxes in a storage unit.

He turned and checked to see where Mary and Jack were. Both, where totally absorbed in their tasks at hand to take notice of him.

Slowly his hands caressed the box and before he knew it. He pulled out a box cutter knife and cut opened the top.

Instantly, a deep vivid green Ficus Benjamin branch poked out the box eager to be free. The healthy looking deep green leaves on the branch looked so inviting, Thomas couldn't believe the plant was thriving inside a box in a storage unit.

From a distance, Thomas watched as Mary and Jack began sorting through the next box. He knew the task at hand would keep the two occupied as he turned his attention back to the tall boxes in front of him.

Reactively his hand reached out and touched a leaf, it was artificial. Why would someone mark that an artificial silk plant needed water? He wondered as he reached his hand inside and pulled out the whole plant and stood it in front of him.

The plant was at almost six-foot high and in immaculate condition right down to the base. Thomas studied the base and then tapped it and studied the plant again as he smiled. He reached his hand down and felt the moss covering on top of the base and then took his box cutter knife and cut the top open. It held a secret compartment he pressed his hand further inside and felt his hand clasp around a soft velvet feeling bag and pulled it out and gently opened the bag. The bag held several data sticks. The kind used to store information from a computer. The bag also held something else. Several old collectible match boxes. All had the same name written on them, *The Jade Room, China Town, San Francisco,* and a strange looking key. He studied the key in his hand. There were no markings on it. He'd found a lead. Like any good detective he knew that the lead he just found would probably lead him to another one and so was the life of a detective. He thought about telling Mary and Jack. And then looked at his watch. It was getting late. He hadn't realized they'd been there for hours.

Jack was standing by his mother Mary. They both looked content going through his brother's belongings. Each of them had selected items they each wanted. They were each wearing some and stacking piles of stuff in front of them.

Mary was wearing an Oakland A's baseball hat and sweatshirt. Thomas smiled hearing Mary's voice.

"Look here, this is the Raiders' jersey he begged me to buy for his birthday," Mary yelled. "It still has store tags attached to it. He never wears it. That ungrateful bastard! This is mine, now."

Thomas closed the distance between them and then loudly cleared his throat getting their attention. "It's getting late. We've been at this for hours and it doesn't look like we've found anything."

"Speak for yourself," Mary blurted. "I found lots of unused gifts; I gave to my ungrateful son."

"That she brought at Costco and probably still has the receipts for," Jack interrupted. "Do you know what that means, Thomas?"

"No," Thomas replied shaking his head.

"It means my Tiger mom is going to take back Aces gifts she gave him to Costco and get a full refund."

"What's wrong with that?" Mary asked with a bewildered look on her face. "It's the American way."

Thomas muffled a chuckle watching the two of them was comical.

"Ace's leather furniture, and high tech-toys is top of the line," Jack declared. "We'll get good money for all this stuff.

Didn't you say you were going to sell stuff, at Berryessa Flea market."

"I have a better idea," Mary declared. "I know a guy in China town who pay top dollar for this stuff."

Thomas knew this conversation could go on and on. He cleared his throat. "Look, it's getting late and I need to get going. If you two find anything interesting. Jack you have my number. Just give me a call."

"Sure thing, Thomas," Jack replied.

Thomas turned and made his way toward the exit. He was just about to close the door behind him when his ears perked up when he heard Hong Kong Mary's voice fill the air.

"Jack, my son, I'll treat you to dinner at your favorite restaurant, tonight. If you help me take these things back to Costco, first. What you say?"

"Texas Roadhouse, here we come. Tiger Mom, It's a deal!"

Thomas smiled with his thoughts he'd helped two people find their happiness living off the material gains of a treacherous relative.

32

❧

Chapter 25

After Nicholas met with Angel, that night his mind had been racing back and forth with what she'd said about people being lonely and sex not being companionship. He'd felt a tickle of uneasiness thinking about how he'd been neglecting Maëlle. While he'd been in prison, he'd known what loneliness felt like for him it had been like a dull knife just cutting away at his spirit.

Nicholas knew that Maëlle had stuck by him, she'd been loyal, and he also knew he kept her tucked away safely in his heart in a special place. He knew he could act like a jerk sometimes and he knew that was the reason why he called her the night before and arranged a surprise. He was taking her out to dinner today at her favorite restaurant.

Nicholas pulled his car into the valet parking right in front and said. "Stay put Maëlle I'll come around and open your car door for you and don't remove that blindfold."

Before Nicholas could reach the passenger side his cellphone rang. He picked it up without thinking. "Hello?"

"Hey Nicholas, it's me Quinn, long time no hear."

Nicholas almost cursed out loud. "Quinn! How are you?" He asked but didn't wait for a response. "Man, you caught me at a bad time. I'm on a date with Maëlle. I'm just about to help her out the car. That's why I haven't called you back. I been trying to rekindle that couple love thing," he lied and prayed Maëlle couldn't hear him in the car.

"Really? Quinn stated. "Sounds like you and Maëlle are really doing the couple thing."

"Yeah, we are. Look, I'm sorry Quinn, but I really have to go, goodbye," Nicholas said abruptly hanging up the phone.

Quickly Nicholas opened Maëlle's car door reached in and grabbed her hand helping her out of the car.

"Nicholas did I hear you talking to Quinn?" Maëlle asked.

Nervously Nicholas thought of something to say. "Yes, I told him I couldn't talk. I was taking you out. I'll call him back later," he said as he handed the valet his keys and led her to the front of the restaurant.

"Okay Maëlle, I'm going to remove your blindfold," Nicholas said.

"Ta Da! Your favorite restaurant awaits you my dear!"

Maëlle looked up at the Black Orchid restaurant, and her mouth dropped opened in shock. She was conflicted with a heavy heart. She stood there for several seconds in silence before she finally said nervously, "Wow! Nicholas, I don't know what to say. This is a surprise. I'm speechless."

"Come on they have our table waiting," Nicholas said reaching for her hand.

Maëlle clasp her hand in his she was speechless, but not for the reasons Nicholas thought of her being happy to eat at her favorite restaurant. That was the farthest thing from her mind. Her thoughts were that she'd only recently had lunch there with Quinn. She wondered if Quinn had told Nicholas about their lunch date. Quickly she shook her thoughts of Quinn from her mind.

Maëlle put on her best smile as she let Nicholas lead her to their table and hold her chair for her. He then sat down and pulled his chair over close to hers.

"Hello, I'm Juan, I'll be your waiter today, can I start you off with some cocktails or a glass of wine?"

"Yes," Maëlle declared, glad she didn't recognize their waiter. "I'll have a white wine spritzer."

"Give me a Jack Daniels on the rocks," Nicholas replied.

"Coming right up," their waiter said.

Maëlle scanned the room trying to see if she recognized anyone from the other times she'd been there.

Nicholas relax back in his seat and said. "You look exceptionally beautiful today Maëlle, I'm loving the blinged out dark denim skinny jean with matching jacket ensemble you're wearing. It's looks very chic on you. In fact, you look stunning."

Maëlle felt her stomach flutter at the sound of the compliments rolling off Nicholas' tongue. Before she could respond their waiter returned with their drinks.

"Here you are, a white wine spritzer for the lady and a Jack Daniels on the rocks for the gentleman. Would you like some more time to decide what to order?"

"No, I think were' ready," Nicholas said as he looked at Maëlle.

"Maëlle I bet I know what you want to order," Nicholas

said. "How about we have the braised beef medallions, and salmon with herbs? Their your favorite."

Maëlle almost choked on her white wine spritzer. "Oh, yes they are but you're forgetting..."

"You also want the mini Cobb salad," Nicholas finished her sentence. "Babe, you are still so predictable."

"Yes... Yes... I guess, I still am," Maëlle replied with a raised brow. "How about we get the garlic mashed potatoes, to share, I remember they are your favorite."

"Thanks, Maëlle, your right," Nicholas smiled. "Well waiter that's our order."

"Thank you, sir, I'll bring your salad and some bread shortly," their waiter replied as he turned to leave.

Nicholas let out a sigh as he reached over and took Maëlle's hand. "I'm glad our waiter left, now I can get down to taking care of business."

"What?" Maëlle nervously laughed as she felt the heat from Nicholas skin as it touched hers.

Nicholas leaned in real close. He let his leg touch hers under their table. "Maëlle did you know that you have soul eyes?"

"Nicholas what are you talking about?" she muttered feeling the room getting hotter as she felt the heat rising from Nicholas' body with his leg pressed so close to hers.

"I'm telling you; you have soul eyes. It's like staring into your soul, when I look into your eyes."

Maëlle let out a girly giggle and licked her lips. She was getting turned on from Nicholas being so close to her. "Really? Tell me what you see in them?"

Nicholas let his fingertips caress her arm. "Do you know what I'm doing right now?"

She giggled. "No, what?"

"I'm mentally undressing you right now, right here in this restaurant."

"Really?" Maëlle asked. "Why pray tell are you doing that?"

"Because seeing you in those skintight jeans has my mind wandering to dangerous places as I watch lust lingering deep inside your eyes, sending pleasurable shock waves through my body," Nicholas said letting his tongue slowly lick the top of his lip.

As if he could read her mind. Nicholas' eyes captured hers as he placed a tender hand on hers and then started to gently caress her skin as he leaned over close as his lips were about to touch hers. The moment was sensual and electrifying as the two sat close together.

Maëlle swallowed hard and took a deep breath before she could say a word. She knew Nicholas was about to kiss her.

"Ah Huh!" The waiter loudly cleared his voice. "Your food is ready," he barked.

"I... Err... Sorry, babe, the food's here," Nicholas said. Instantly stopping his caressing her. "It smells good doesn't it?"

Maëlle laughed a dry laugh, as she fanned herself. Nicholas' come on was making her hot. "Yeah... Ah... Yes, the food does smell good."

Maëlle nearly jumped out of her skin, yanked from her romantic slutty daydream at the sound of the waiter's voice.

Instantly Nicholas let go of her hand and turned and placed his napkin on his lap as he changed the subject. "Wow! Doesn't this food look good Maëlle?"

Maëlle stared back at Nicholas wondering what had come over him. The man had stroked up a fierce fire in her that needed to be dealt with, she thought as the aroma of delicious food overtook her. Slowly she shook her head. "Yes, babe everything looks and smells like a dream."

An hour later, after a leisurely dinner, Nicholas paid their check and grabbed Maëlle's hand. "Hold up! You're not getting away from me. We've got to go and finish what you started," he laughed.

Maëlle gasped. "Finish what I started... You were the instigator."

Nicholas pulled her close and kissed her passionately.

Maëlle groaned out a moan and muttered. "What the hell did I start."

"You got me horny, and deliciously full," Nicholas declared leading her to the front of the restaurant.

"Say, Nicholas, do I have time to run to the little girl's room, those white wine spritzers I had with dinner are running through me."

"Sure, babe, don't take too long.," he paused for a second. "You know I think I should do the same, the little boy's room... I mean the bathroom."

Maëlle brushed a kiss on Nicholas' lips. "Okay, see you back at the car lickety split!"

Minutes later, after using the bathroom and washing her hands. Maëlle made her way back the way she'd came, heading to the front of the restaurant.

Muscular arms reached out pulling her into them. Thinking it was Nicholas she said.

"Nicholas, you are one horny bastard," she giggled.

"I'm not Nicholas but I am horny," a deep familiar masculine voice replied.

Instantly Maëlle froze, when she realized it wasn't Nicholas. She knew the voice. It belonged to, Paul Lombardi a half Italian half African American, full blooded male, she known since middle school and whom she'd had a brief affair with.

Maëlle swallowed hard. Her words stumbled out. "Paul... What are you doing here?" She asked with a nervous trace in her voice.

Paul paused for a moment and let his eyes roam up and down her body. Before he drew in a deep breath and said. "And hello to you, Ms. Maëlle, My! My! You're looking exceptionally well. I see you still got a thing for those La Cour brothers. Didn't I see you here a couple of weeks ago with Quinn?"

Maëlle was bewildered. "What? How?"

Paul smiled. "How did I know you had a thing for Nicholas and Quinn, or how did I know that they were brothers?"

Maëlle looked around hoping to spot Nicholas praying he'd come to her rescue.

Paul watched her with interest. It was obvious he knew she was nervous. "Don't worry, Nicholas is occupied. Seems he has a small problem, his car was backed into by one of the valets, they got him filling out one of their reports."

The way he was looking at her was making Maëlle nervous.

Finally, Maëlle found her voice. "Look Paul, I don't care how you know about Nicholas and Quinn being brothers, I don't care," she hesitated. "And I think you've got some misunderstanding about..."

"About you and your twisted love-triangle with Nicholas and Quinn? Sorry, I'm not mixed up about that. I saw the way Quinn was looking at you the other day. And just a while ago, I saw the way Nicholas was looking at you today. But what you failed to realize is that I'm not completely over you and our little fling."

"Mercy!" Maëlle groan, as her brain grasped what she just heard. She looked up at him, staring trying to read his mind. She wondered if he was serious or if he was just playing games.

"Look Paul the last time I saw you wasn't you with Dominique Bledsoe? By the way I saw the way Dominique was looking at you and it wasn't as a friend. More like a decadent dessert she couldn't wait to have."

Paul laughed Dominique Bledsoe means nothing to me and she's married. But you on the other hand do. He leaned in close. "You know what I'm thinking about Maëlle? I sure miss sucking your nipples and watching them get hard. And I miss feeling your hands rub up and down my manhood making it hard, remember Maëlle? We were good together."

"Knock it off, Paul. You can't be serious," she said staring back into his eyes. "Your serious?"

Paul leaned in close his voice was almost a whisper. "Yes, Maëlle I'm serious," he paused letting his words sink in. "What if I told you I'd tell Nicholas you and Quinn where here together a couple weeks ago, or worse yet, what if I tell Nicholas about you and me?

"You wouldn't dare!" Maëlle hissed.

"Maybe I will, if you don't agree to meet me someplace private? What do you say? Huh, Maëlle?"

"If you tell Nicholas, I'll... I'll ... I will go to your superiors at the police force and tell them about your cousin Ham. You remember Hamilton, don't you Paul? I'm sure if they knew about all the times you've helped a man who stole a baby and sold him to the highest bidder."

Recognition hit Paul like a ton of bricks. He wanted Maëlle, but he also knew he hadn't been a clean cop all of his life, especially when it came to his cousin Hamilton. He wasn't even thinking when the words rolled off of his tongue.

"Ham, didn't sell that baby, he found a wealthy family to adopt him."

"I knew you, knew where that baby was!" Maëlle declared. "Who has him? Where is he at?"

Paul regretted the words that left his mouth the minute he said them. "Stop with the questions, Maëlle!" He murmured. "Look, I don't know where the child is. I only know that the people were wealthy."

"Damn! Paul that's just totally fucked up."

"Gosh, Maëlle I've never known you to curse so much, what's gotten into you."

Maëlle rubbed her face with her fingers. "Get use to it! I can't believe you have the nerve to try and blackmail me into seeing you. I can't believe this is happening."

"Look, Maëlle don't be scared I'm not an idiot. I got enough sense not to get in the way of any of the La Cour's, he shrugged. "I was just trying to get to see you again, that's all. I won't be telling Nicholas anything. Not to mention, I don't want to mess up my promotion."

"Wow! That's a relief," Maëlle replied.

Paul shook his head looking apologetic. "I'm sorry for upsetting you Maëlle. You want to know something else? I'm a very patient man. I'm willing to wait for something that I want. You tell Nicholas I said he'd better treat you right! I mean, it. By the way, here comes your Romeo, now."

Paul walked around Maëlle and blurted. "Hey, Nicholas good to see you again. You have a nice rest of your night," he yelled as he walked past him.

"Did you see Paul, Maëlle?" Nicholas declared. "That guy still looks like he did back in school. You know he caught some guy in the parking lot hitting my car? Did you know he made lieutenant on the Police force?"

Nicholas noticed Maëlle looked distant. "Babe, are you alright?"

"Yes, I'm fine. What did you say about your car?"

"Oh, yeah, Paul was pulling in when he caught some guy backing into my car. He made sure the valet took care of the paperwork, so that my insurance won't get charged. It was the other guys fault."

"Nicholas is your car okay? I mean can we drive home?"

"Yes," he replied.

She rubbed the back of her neck as she drew in a breath. Trying to cool down her thoughts. After what Paul Lombardi had said to her. She was now really horny. "Good, I could sure use a hot shower."

Nicholas walked up and stood behind her. He reached up and placed his hands on her shoulders and massaged her neck. "You look tense, how does that feel," he said letting his hands brush her hair from her neck as he gently massages her shoulders.

"Ahhhh, yes, that feels nice. Nicholas, I think we should leave."

"Come on Babe, I agree, and I know just the place we can go," Nicholas replied kissing her neck before leading her to his car.

A half hour later, Maëlle stood at the back elevators of the De'Anza Plaza Hotel, in downtown San Jose waiting for Nicholas. They were given a suite on the nineteenth floor and Maëlle thought her heart would burst from anticipation.

From the minute she entered their suite that overlooked Mount Hamilton Maëlle felt like the moment was magical as her eyes looked in awe at the luxurious extravaganza of the room.

Everything delighted her from the breathtaking jaw dropping views she'd ever beheld to the sophisticated glamorous flamboyant designs of the wallpaper, to bellowing flowing heavy drapes and colorful murals and coromandel Lacquer furniture.

"It feels like magic," she gushed in astonishment.

"And you look perfect," Nicholas declared.

Maëlle turned and looked at Nicholas feeling his eyes roam over her body.

Instantly Maëlle recognized the look on Nicholas' face. Their hunger had built into a great need that had to be satisfied.

Nicholas closed the distance between them as his hands went to work loosening her clothes and dropping them to the floor.

Instantly, Maëlle began performing the same ritual on

Nicholas until their clothes laid piled in a heap on the floor beside them.

Hungerly and passionately Nicholas kissed her lips, as he gently glided her over to the bed.

Maëlle sat down on the edge of the bed just as Nicholas begin letting his tongue slide down to the pulse of her neck.

Maëlle quickened and moaned unable to control her feelings of pleasure.

Nicholas' mouth kissed its way down her breastbone as his hands stroked the soft flesh of her breasts, ash they swirled toward her erect nipples.

Then his lips were on her nipple, nibbling and then sucking hard.

Maëlle moaned and closed her eyes, as she felt shafts of electricity sear through her with sensation after sensations. "Stop wasting time, Nicholas, just fuck me!"

"Damn, Maëlle girl, you are so impatient," Nicholas grinned. "I'm a man who wants to take his time pleasuring his lady," he replied, as he kneeled down before her between her legs, and spread them wide, as his fingers stimulated her clitoris, slowly at first and then harder and firmer with more urgency.

Intense pleasure pierced Maëlle's body until she couldn't stand it any longer and opened her eyes and looked down and saw Nicholas watching her.

With one hand he was caressing and teasing her clitoris over and over again and then his mouth found her swollen clit and sucked it as one of his fingers entered her.

Maëlle couldn't stand it as she felt a shaft of intense pleasure pierce her body and made her moan with delight.

Then she felt Nicholas erect cock move to the mound between her legs. In a husky voice he said. "Is this what you want?"

Maëlle help guide him in. "Oh, yes," she moaned. "Damn, that feels good."

"Do, you want more," Nicholas asked teasingly.

"Yes... Yes... Yes!" She moaned out in a soft yell. "I want more. I want you deep inside me," she murmured moving rhythmically in time with Nicholas.

She wrapped her arms tight around him as she felt him grabbing her buttocks. She knew he was ready to come when he shuddered as he held her tight, they both climaxed together and ended with their arms locked together.

33

Chapter 26

Nicholas & Yanni Smirnov ...

That Sunday morning, Nicholas found the Russian Tea House, filled with mouthwatering aromas as he stood before the window housing the eye-catching array of comfort food.

Quickly he walked into the Buffet room and felt the warm cozy ambiance as he made his way around many tables filled with food. His eyes spotted plates filled with Norwegian salmon with a sprig of dill, smoked salmon, Piroschki, marinated herring, along with Traditional Russian Beef Borsch, Traditional Russian beet and vegetable soup, eggplant caviar, classic Russian salads of potatoes, carrots, peas, dill pickles, cucumbers and apples, along with Russian cheesecake, bliny, crepes and more were spread out over several tables around him. The place was a well-stocked haven of classic Russian food.

Just as Nicholas decided he wanted to eat and was about to enter the crowded dining room and look for a waiter to seat him, his cell phone rang. He checked caller ID. It was

Quinn, he ignored the call. As he wondered when Quinn was going to get the message, that he had no intentions of calling him back.

Nicholas's eyes searched the crowded room and found the waiter. He was just about to get the waiter's attention and ask him to find him a seat, when he saw her across the room. It was Yanni Smirnov sitting with her mother.

He turned and headed for her table and was surprised when Yanni spotted him.

As soon as, Yanni Smirnov spotted Nicholas La Cour, she waved to him, as he came over to her table. Immediately she leaned in close and said something to her mother in Russian before she rose and hurried over to intercept Nicholas before he reached her table.

"Nicholas, my old friend, I'm so happy to see you. Please let me apologize for all the bad deeds our once friend Dante Channing did to you. I am deeply sorry for all your troubles," Yanni nervously smiled.

"I don't hold any grudges against you Yanni, you had nothing to do with Dante's betrayal."

Yanni exhaled. "Thank you, my friend. You don't know how glad I am to hear you say this," she said. She sauntered over and slipped her hand in his before placing her arm in his. "Please walk with me to the garden outside."

"With an invitation like that, how can I refuse," Nicholas replied. "Lead the way."

"This way, please. The gardens are really beautiful this time of year," Yanni replied with a nervous edge to her voice.

The first thing Nicholas noticed about Yanni was that she was shaking, as if she was afraid. Immediately his hand patted her arm reassuringly as they walked through the doorway leading into the garden.

Yanni steered them over to a dangling grape-like flower cluster vine, growing along the trellis of the garden.

"This is the Chinese Wisteria isn't it beautiful? It pretty much blooms year-round here in California."

"Yanni, I didn't expect to get a lesson about blooming plants, today."

"And I didn't expect to see you today, Nicholas," Yanni replied. "What do you want Nicholas?"

"I'll cut right to the chase," Nicholas replied. "I'm looking for Dante Channing, your old boyfriend, remember?"

Frowning as she looked around. "I'm not," Yanni barked in a nervous voice as she looked around cautiously. "And if you knew what I know about Dante, you wouldn't be looking for him, either. You're free now Nicholas why don't you just live your life and enjoy your freedom?"

"What gives, Yanni? You seem a little paranoid, or something."

Yanni's eyes sternly looked back at him. "I am and you should be too. Seeing you here today. All I could think of was that I hope you weren't being followed," she said.

"I'm a big boy, Yanni. I can look out for myself. Anyway, I wasn't being followed.

"Listen, Nicholas. You're not the only one looking for Dante. A private investigator came to see me. He was looking for Dante too. And he hasn't found Dante and neither will you."

"What was the private investigator's name?" Nicholas asked.

"I believe it was Thomas, why?" Yanni asked.

Nicholas silently stared back at her.

"The investigator was working for you? Wasn't he Nicholas?"

"Maybe..."

Yanni shook her head. "He was working for you I can see it in your eyes. I gave him the name of someone who knew one of Dante's friends. And since you are here, I can tell your private investigator had no luck. Don't you see, Nicholas? Dante can't be found."

"You're wrong, Yanni. We are still looking and we will find him!" Nicholas declared.

"Dante isn't a very nice person. You don't know what he's capable of. In fact, if you really want my opinion, Dante is a sick piece of work. A real-life deviant sexual sociopath."

"Really? Do tell."

Nervously her eyes swept around as if making sure that they were alone. "Look, Nicholas, I'm serious. You don't know what kind of monster Dante is. I'm not a shrink but I know what a deviant is. He's a sexual deviant, capable of rape, torture ... Maybe... Maybe even murder."

"Murder?"

"Yes, murder, Nicholas. After I started to see Dante for what he was, after he double crossed me. I distance myself from him. But a few of our mutual friends kept tabs on him for me. I heard that he had taken up with a young woman. I heard that she was a real young prostitute he picked up while cruising through Oakland. They said the girl was desperate to change her life and she thought Dante was the way to do it.

But instead of changing her life her friends fear that Dante took her life."

"Are you saying he killed this young girl?"

Yanni focused her eyes on him and shook her head. "I only know what I heard. All I know is that her friends think he did. They haven't seen her since she took up with Dante and they all believe that she is dead."

Birds twittered in the branches of the trees above the hanging Chinese Wisteria. Soft music was playing all around them.

Nicholas took a deep breath. "You wouldn't by chance know the girls name?"

Yanni spoke very softly. "Yes, I do. Her name was... I mean, if she is still alive," she hesitated. "Her name is Molly Chen."

Nicholas shoved his hands in his pockets as he said the name over and over in his mind. Finally, he took a deep breath and said. "Tell you what Yanni, why don't you tell me where I can find Dante and I'll leave and let you and your mother enjoy the rest of this beautiful day."

Slowly Yanni shook her head. "Dante is a sick piece of work and I don't know where he is, and I don't want to know. I'm glad he's out of my life," she took a deep breath.

"I don't believe you. You got to know someone who knows how to find him."

"No...No!" She protested and then instantly stopped. "Hold on! Wait a minute, Vodka Joe might know how to find him!" She declared.

"Vodka Joe," Nicholas repeated shaking his head. "But I thought Vodka Joe was..."

"Dead?" Yanni answered for him. "The liquor hasn't killed him yet. By the way stop in at Houlihan!"

"Houlihan's?"

"Stop repeating yourself, Nicholas. If you determine to find him, Dante go to Houlihan's', the old one-off Winchester and Stevens Creek. Vodka Joe likes to hang out there. Besides Dante and the owner, Carlos Goldstein, went to grade school together, who knows maybe he's been dropping in and out of there. But be careful," she warned with a serious tone in her voice. "The owner is a rat, just like Dante. They are two of a kind."

Nicholas checked his watch and then glanced up at Yanni, he smiled, and she smiled back at him.

"Thanks, for the information, Yanni, I'll leave you so you and your mother can enjoy your brunch!" Nicholas declared turning to leave.

Yanni watched Nicholas head for the exit in the garden. Silently she prayed he would heed her warning. Without a thought she took a deep breath and didn't hear the words until they left her lips. "God help us all."

34

Chapter 27

Girlfriend let's go to lunch...

The next day, Lacey was glad she had been determined to get a hold of Maëlle for lunch days before. It had paid off she was on her way to meet Maëlle.

A petite blond middle-aged woman with a velvety voice greeted her. "Hello Miss, are you meeting someone for lunch today?"

"My name is Lacey La Cour-Egan, I made reservations for two."

"Yes, I have your reservation, right this way, please."

Fifteen minutes later...

Now, Lacey sat waiting for Maëlle, as she looked around the familiar restaurant. She was glad she had their waiter bring her a glass of Pinot Noir, when she'd first sat down. Her hand lifted the glass of wine and she studied it as her hand swirled the wine around in the glass. She thought back on how Maëlle had been hesitant when she had suggested they have lunch at the Black Orchid. It was only after she had told

Maëlle, she didn't understand why she was hesitant, when she had always thought the Black Orchid was her favorite restaurant. In the end, Maëlle had agreed to meet her there.

Lacey loved coming to the Black Orchid restaurant. She thought back to the last time she had been there. It had been when she was having lunch with her Culinary cooking instructor, Mrs. French.

Suddenly a thought popped in her mind. She recalled she had thought it was strange seeing Maëlle that day down the street from the Black Orchid restaurant. That had also been the day she'd ran into Quinn leaving the Black Orchid restaurant just as she was entering it.

Lacey was completely engrossed in her thoughts when Maëlle's voice broke into her daydream.

"Lacey, you haven't been waiting for me too long, have you?" Maëlle asked as she approached their table.

Lacey looked up and saw their greeter the petite blond-middle age woman bringing Maëlle over to their table.

"Maëlle, girl, so glad you made it," Lacey declared. "No, I haven't been sitting her long."

Maëlle looked up at Lacey just in time to see her sipping on a glass of Pinot Noir. She watched as Lacey went to put her glass down to stand up to greet her.

"Don't get up Lacey, I can see you are enjoying your glass of wine," Maëlle declared greeting her with air kisses before she sat down and grab her menu. "I'm starving she said looking over her menu."

A strong floral scent filled the air. Lacey looked around her trying to determine where the strange scent had come from. She was sure it hadn't come from Maëlle, as she could smell her perfume when she gave her an air kiss. She shook out her thoughts and said. "Oh, does that mean you will be ordering your regular braised beef medallions with mini Cobb salad."

"That does sound good, but you know Lacey, I believe I'd like a change today. I have a taste for their chicken breast sautéed with herbs, and freshly made fettuccine in an Alfredo sauce."

"Oh, then I'll have your regular braised beef medallions with mini Cobb salad," Lacey declared.

"Good, then we can share and enjoy both meals," Maëlle declared, summoning their waiter. "Just like the old days."

"Yes, I agree," Lacey replied. "Now, let's get down to girl talk. Tell me what did you think about Nicholas' welcome home party?"

"It was kind of fun I guess," Maëlle floppily replied.

"Oh, wow! You don't sound enthused! Care to tell me why?"

"Of course, it was a very lovely party and the food was delicious. But did you see that Avril, what's her name girl, who came with Quinn?"

"Her name was Abril Navarro," Lacey declared. "I did see her she was nice enough to me, when Quinn introduced us."

"Will, maybe she was nice to you," Maëlle replied.

"I don't know why you don't like her. You know, she's a clothes designer and pretty good at it from what I've seen of her work."

"Lacey, you've seen her work. When?"

"Grand mere Catherine had her over to the house, and

Grandmother Ina came with her. They were both having her make them a couple of new dresses."

"Really? Did you see any of her designs?" Maëlle inquired.

"Yes, and her designs are unique and very fashionable. I don't know if I should tell you. But Grand mere Catherine picked out some dress designs she could wear to a wedding?"

"What do you mean you don't think you should tell me? What's Grand mere Catherine picking out dresses for a wedding got to do with me?"

"Okay... Okay," Lacey blurted shaking her head. "Grand *mere* Catherine was talking with Grandmother Ina as if she thinks you and Nicholas might be getting married sometime in the future and that's why she wanted Abril to make her some dresses."

"For real?" Maëlle exclaimed.

"Yes!" Lacey exclaimed with wide eyes.

"Wow!... Wow!" Maëlle stammered speechless.

"You got to see the pictures of wedding dresses; Abril has done. I think one of them will be perfect for you," Lacey declared as she rummaged through her purse and pulled out several pictures. She thrust the photos in front of Maëlle.

A sexy thigh-high split front Marilyn Monroe satin styled off the shoulder white wedding dress with a sweeping train, was thrust in front of Maëlle.

"Wow! Would you look at that, this gown is beautiful. But look at this one Lacey, I love the plunging neckline, and it's on a wedding dress."

"Look at this dress here Maëlle."

Lacey threw out a picture of a gold sequin evening gown with a bustier top. This dress is called *Illusion*. It has a fine mesh fabric underneath the sequence that gives the illusion you are naked underneath and covered in sparkles."

"That's not a wedding dress," Maëlle declared.

"No, it's not. I like this one for me," Lacey said.

"Lacey, I don't think Kienan is going to let you wear that dress. It shows to much cleavage and it's damn near see through. You are the mother of his children for Christ sake. Woman have you no shame?" Maëlle replied.

"Whatever!" Lacey declared and thrust another photo in front of her. "What about this one?"

"That's another you lost your damn mind dress, Lacey, Kienan ain't going to ever let you wear that one."

Lacey held up her hands. "Gosh, your brain has gone soft, Maëlle," Lacey declared. "I was thinking that dress would be perfect for you. Abril said she could easily do this dress in white and change the gold lace and gold beads to white lace and white beaded sequined, trumpet-mermaid styled, off-the-shoulder floor-length gold chiffon evening dress, see here's a photo in all white."

Maëlle looked at the photograph of the dress. She was right it would be perfect for her. Abril Navarro was a master with her designs. The gold color of it would accent her coloring and the gold color in the trumpet-mermaid bottom was fantasy meet reality.

Finally, Maëlle spoke. "You are right, Lacey, Abril Navarro is a master designer. I love this dress in white lace and white sequin and beads. I think the gold color accenting on white in the trumpet-mermaid styled at the bottom would be exquisite."

A moment of excited silence lingered between them until

finally Maëlle cleared her throat. "I can't believe it. This dress is so, perfect."

Just then their waiter brought over their food. Lacey and Maëlle were silent while their food was placed in front of them.

Lacey waited until their waiter left. "I knew you'd love that dress Maëlle, now let's bless this food and eat."

***

Forty-five minutes later Maëlle and Lacey were just finishing lunch. They had caught up on old times and went over ideas and laughed and talked a lot as their conversation turned to easy chitchat.

"I'm so glad you invited me to lunch today Lacey. I really enjoyed it.

"Yes, I did too," Lacey agreed. "But most of all it felt like old times with me and you. I missed you so much old friend. We must do this again, real soon."

"I missed you too, my friend," Maëlle declared.

All at once Lacey reached out and grabbed Maëlle's hand. A surreal burst of energy pulsed through Lacey's fingertips as she held Maëlle's hand.

What's up? Are you thinking of when we should have lunch again?" Maëlle inquired.

"I was thinking today is as good as any, to make another lunch date, when are you next available?"

"Depends?"

"On what?" Lacey inquired.

"On where you want to go for lunch.," Maëlle declared.

"I thought the Black Orchid restaurant, was your favorite."

Maëlle grew silent. She was conflicted with a heavy heart.

The Black Orchid was her favorite restaurant. But it held secrets for her. She was afraid to say no, because she didn't want to have to explain to Lacey why she'd didn't want to eat there. The next thing she knew the words rolled off her tongue.

"I just think we should go someplace different sometimes. Maybe you can pick the next place."

"Me pick the next place. Are you sure?"

Maëlle giggle. "There she goes, Miss can run a household like a boss, but can't pick a different place to go to lunch. Yes, I'm sure, Lacey you pick."

Lacey laughed. "What did you call me? Miss can run a household, like a boss, you got jokes today."

"Now, you know that name fit you like a glove," Maëlle laughed out.

Both friends laughed out in happiness together in unison.

Instantly the strange floral scent filled the air and as Lacey felt a bolt of cold air race across the back of her neck as a loud evil hollow voice echoed all around her.

Quickly Lacey looked around as the ghastly sound assailed her ears. It sounded like rushing wind carrying the voice of thousands wailing and crying out in despair. Whose voice was it.

Instantly recognition hit Lacey fast. It was her brother Nicholas. No longer was she having a dream of him taking revenge, in her sleep. Now it was playing out in the daytime.

Then she heard it. Nicholas' voice. Carrying on the air all around her. It sounded sinisterly crazed.

She knew what she was seeing and feeling. It was her clairvoyant gift, the gift of sight.

Suddenly a white light flashed and seared cross her vision

and then she heard Nicholas voice again laughing gutturally all the while his voice began mocking, demeaning and talking to someone. She knew who it was. It was Nicholas' victim. It was Dante Channing, just like in her dreams at night. It was then she noticed it. She saw it. She flinched in pain when her vision turned into a vivid real-life motion picture right in front of her eyes. She blinked several times to see if it would stop. To see if she could make herself wake up. But it didn't, there was her brother Nicholas standing over Dante Channing knee-deep in blood and guts, laughing hysterically.

Maëlle studied Lacey she could tell her friend was in some kind of trance. She tried to think back to something her Aunt Joan may have taught her. All at once she spoke. "Lacey... Lacey! Breathe. Take a deep breath!"

Lacey took in a deep breath and gasped out loud in shock and fear. "Oh, my God Maëlle! It was awful!"

"What is it?" Maëlle inquired.

All at once Lacey reached out and grabbed Maëlle's hand. A surreal burst of energy pulsed through Lacey's fingertips as she held Maëlle's hand.

It was another vision and it came fast. In this vision the images flashed through her head like a movie on a big screen projector, stuck on fast forward.

Out of nowhere she heard an evil laugh again only this time it wasn't accompanied by images of blood and guts but of the bold intense colors of naked flesh. Naked skin in the raw touching naked skin, sensually and seductively. It was two bodies locked in the thongs of heated raw sexual pleasure.

With a passion so deep and powerful she felt herself being pulled in by the explosive energy it generated.

All sounds ceased.

It was then Lacey saw their faces as clear as day. It was Maëlle and Quinn making love. Her voice was a stern whisper. "Oh, my god! Maëlle you slept with Quinn! You slept with Quinn!"

Maëlle gasp out in shock as she pulled her hand from Lacey's. "Stop bugging Lacey," she nervously declared. "What's wrong with you? How can you say that?"

Lacey froze shocked to her spot. She knew what she seen was the truth. She was overtaken by a flash of vengeance.

She looked back at Maëlle and knew she needed to calm herself to make sure her point was made. But first, she needed to state the fact of what she saw, was the truth. She took a deep breath and said. "Don't lie to me Maëlle! You know my gift has been getting stronger and stronger every day! I had a vision, just now! I saw you in Quinn's arms, you were both naked. You were having sex!"

"You bitch! How dare you!" Maëlle yelled at her.

"I got your bitch," Lacey declared through gritted teeth. "All I do is help you all the time and look what you do to me. You've got your nerve calling me a bitch! At least I wasn't a low life sleazy heifer sleeping with my fiancé's brother!"

"Half-brother," Maëlle declared in her defense.

"Look heifer, do you think his being half, makes any difference? It still speaks volumes to your level of morals, values and loyalty! Or rather your lack of them!"

"Ouch! That was raw, Lacey. Do you have to be so cruel?"

The moment was tense.

Lacey's word stung Maëlle like one-hundred needles pressed into her skin at one time, Maëlle thought as she picked up her wine glass and took a sip to calm herself. She studied Lacey and realized becoming a mother had made Lacey grow up. She was a lot tougher than the old Lacey. Then there was the fact that they weren't kids anymore. Actions had consequences. She was living proof of that.

Then Maëlle remembered who she was talking too. Lacey always had been there for her. "Look Lacey I was wrong for calling you a bitch. I'm sorry."

There was a moment of awkward silence.

"Oh Lacey!" A soft sob escaped Maëlle's lips. "It's just that I feel so ashamed! Please don't tell Nicholas!"

Maëlle's tears caught Lacey off guard. She hadn't come there that day to fight with her. She saw tears running down her face and took a deep breath. She knew her emotions and remorse were real. She could feel the vibe.

Lacey softened her voice and said. "Okay, Maëlle, I apologize for calling you a heifer. What do you mean don't tell Nicholas? Nicholas has a right to know!"

"Lacey you're just being petty! You're trying to ruin my life!" Maëlle blurted out in a sob.

"Ruin your life! You did that when you slept with Quinn!"

Maëlle's throat was dry. She was scared her world could come crumbling down at any moment. Her voice pleaded as she choked out. "Lacey, you don't know what happened to me, when Nicholas left me at the altar. Something happened," her words rambled out. "I fell into this darkness. I was so low. I was hurting really bad. I didn't care what happened to me anymore."

Lacey's heart was breaking sitting in front of her was her best friend with a powerful secret that could tear the world of the people she loved apart. She exhaled and softly said. "Please help me to understand why Maëlle. Was it because Nicholas broke off your engagement...? I mean wedding?"

"Yes, that's when it started. I went downhill fast from there. I felt so ashamed standing at that altar all alone. I wasn't even good enough for him to stay and marry me. The depression, the darkness. I thought I didn't have any reason to live." Maëlle replied.

"Why didn't you tell me?"

"Lacey, I couldn't," her voice choked.

"Was that when you wouldn't return my calls?" Lacey asked

"Yes, it was," Maëlle swallowed hard and wiped the tears from her face. "After Nicholas left me standing at the altar alone," she choked out a sob and continued. "I was standing there alone, embarrassed in front of all of our family and friends. I felt like I was nothing. I would never be nothing but a loser! Lacey I was so depressed over what Nicholas had done to me. I felt like killing myself. And then Quinn's grandmother contacted me out of the blue and brought me a ticket to Mexico to go and cheer up Quinn and I thought... I thought... I thought... I thought I was finally going to be made whole again. That I matter." she choked out sobs.

Lacey got up and walked over and sat beside Maëlle. She remembered what Maëlle had looked like standing at the altar all alone. She knew Maëlle had been devastated. Her voice was gentle.

"Shhhhh...Stop crying. I know what Nicholas put you through and I know you thought Quinn would right the wrong Nicholas' had done to you.Oh, how 1 I wished you would have let me in to help you during that difficult time. I could have saved you the trouble of sleeping with Quinn. If it's one thing I do know, Nicholas and Quinn won't hurt the other one when it comes to the love, they have for each other."

"I know that now," Maëlle declared. "Quinn told me he would never hurt Nicholas by marrying me."

There was an awkward silence between them. Then Maëlle looked up at Lacey for reassurance. "Lacey I really love Nicholas, he's my world. When I slept with Quinn, I was hurt, stupid, reckless and immature. I would never hurt Nicholas again. You have to believe me. Please don't tell Nicholas!"

Lacey stared back into the eyes of her best friend. She remembered Grand *mere* Catherine had told her that her gift came with a lot of responsibilities for other people's lives. She exhaled and said. "Maëlle your secret is safe with me. I won't tell Nicholas. But... You have to promise me."

"What? What is it Lacey?"

"Promise me you'll never sleep with Quinn again."

"Oh! Lacey! "She mumbled almost like a whisper. "Of course, I promise you that. Lacey, I swear!" Maëlle declared.

Lacey stared back into Maëlle's face and saw the anxiety and panic she'd seen earlier disappear. She had a horrible feeling about not telling her brother what Maëlle had done. But she knew she'd made her a promise and she kept her promises. "Alright, Maëlle, that's all I ask."

Maëlle sat in silence reflecting on everything that had been said. As much as she wanted to convince herself she wasn't to blame for what had happened between her and Quinn. She was forced to take a look back on her life and the thing she had done. She exhaled studying her best friend she knew she needed to make things right between them, she thought as she sat there with a heart filled with regret.

***

After Maëlle and Lacey left the Black Orchid Restaurant, Maëlle got into her car and drove down San Pedro Square and head over to highway 87 and took the exit for San Francisco merging her way on to highway 280 and looked for the sign that told her the highway's name changed to Junipero Serra freeway. She leaned back and enjoyed the lush green scenery as it flashed by. Soon her exit came into view and she took Edgewood Road and headed to Canada Road and made the right. The historical house loomed into view. It had become a state park and a place Maëlle had added to her favorite places to go, when she wanted to be a lone. She drove all the way to the end to the last parking lot. This was her favorite area. Not many people knew there were park benches hidden among the many California pepper trees scattered about. She quickly found a parking space and grabbed her tissue box, and blanket and then went looking for her favorite bench as a soft smile crossed her face when she realized she had her spot all to herself.

Maëlle wrapped her blanket around her and sat down. She was all alone. She stared off at the beautiful park like setting for several seconds and let her mind wander back to that day her life had changed. It was the day Nicholas had left her at the altar.

Instantly her mind was transformed, and she was standing in her beautifully embellished white bridal gown smiling. The one she had paid almost five thousand dollars for. All at once the noise of the crowd standing up looking at her became overwhelming. And then she heard what they were saying.She'd been stood up. Her groom wasn't coming. Nicholas had stood her up.

A flood gate of tears overwhelmed her as Maëlle sat on the bench and pulled her blanket tight and sobbed out loud. As if on cue her mind flashed to the day in court when Nicholas had been convicted and mandated over to jail. What Nicholas hadn't known was that Maëlle had been there all along. Even though he had told her not to attend. She had dressed up in a blonde wig disguise and a lot of theater make-up to watch the man that she loved be sentence for a crime she'd known all alone he hadn't committed. And then her mind flashed to her best friend Lacey discovering her secret.

The feeling of fierce misery was so powerfully overwhelming Maëlle's cries of anguish rose up and out of her and floated among the California Pepper trees, she sat among.

As she sat there a feeling of being in the world, she pulled her blanket securely around him, praying it would give her comfort. She was all alone in the world, with no one she could count on, a feeling of utter misery engulfed her as she cried harder, crying her heart out.

35

Chapter 28

The Jade Room,
China Town, San Francisco...

That night, Thomas drove his car through the heart of downtown San Francisco, thankful it was the end of rush hour traffic as he headed for Jackson avenue. He knew where he was going, Ross Alley, in the heart of San Francisco, China Town.

Navigating the streets of San Francisco came easy to him since he had been a regular cop for several years before he left the force and became a private investigator. Not to mention he had frequently had lunch at several of the local restaurants, on Ross Alley and he knew all about the Jade Room, and its reputation.

The Jade Room had been named after the most prized gemstone of China, and it made proud it's royal name. Once you walked through its slatted ornate double door entrance you found yourself surrounded in a world of golden brocade of the imperial royals with its elegant stone carvings, conveying China's history, romance and love for the color of jade.

From its vaulted high ceilings, to stained glass doors in jade green, to gold floral stenciled jade green and gold wallpaper, the inside of the Jade Room eluded a striking influence of the club's namesake, pure China Jade. The imposing classic crystal chandelier lent a sophisticated charm to the place.

Thomas wasted no time as he made his way to the back of the Jade Room. He knew where he was going, to see a man who had all the answers. The man he'd left a message with a few days before. That same man had called him that morning and told him he had something he wanted him to see.

Thomas made eye contact with a bartender as he walked around the counter. The bartender nodded and pulled back a velvet heavy curtain, as Thomas walked through the curtain and opened the door.

Vic Chung was the man Thomas had come to see. Vic was sitting at his desk surrounded by numerous monitor screens, when Thomas entered. He turned around and stared at Thomas and beckoned him to come closer.

Vic Chung was a short middle age Asian man of Chinese and Japanese descent. He'd spent five years in the US Air Force IT department before working for five years with the San Francisco Police department's computer unit and had an expertise in computer surveillance that was unmatched on the west coast. He was also the baby brother of the Tommy Chung, the man who ran The Jade Room.

"Thanks for your help," Thomas declared as he sat down in a seat Vic had pointed to.

"No problem," Vic declared. "I think I found the man you've been looking for."

"Really?" Thomas declared. "Is he here right now?"

"Sorry, no. I was scanning video footage from a week ago. We had some patrons complain they thought there was cheating going on in the poker game last week and I took a look and found your guy. Take a look."

Thomas leaned in close and watched the monitor as Vic brought the screen into focus as he panned in close and blew up the face of a man sitting at the poker table.

Thomas scanned the video again, but nothing stood out. He pressed the rewind button and played the video a second time.

Then Vic piped in. "Use your detective skills Thomas, I remember you were really good with your skills. Now look past the cheap plastic nose job and bad dyed hair. Whoever did their plastic surgery wasn't very good."

All at once, Thomas let out a whistle. "That's him. Its Dante Channing and sitting right next to him is Ace Kong. You are right it does look like the two of them had a bad plastic surgery nose job."

"Yup! It's the worst nose jobs I've ever seen," Vic declared. "I don't think they went to the best beauty salon for their hair dye jobs either."

"Do you recognize the other guys?" Thomas asked.

"Yes, and they are sitting right next to Roscoe Jones, he's a famous poker player and coach out of Hunters Point, and the guy next to him is Miami Max and the guy next to him is City Sax. They call him that because he plays the saxophone in a quartet that regularly plays at the Fairmont hotel on Nob Hill."

"I need to check out City Sax," Thomas declared.

Vic nodded agreement. "Bingo! He's the one I would pick. So, you good. You found your guy, right?"

"Maybe, maybe not. What other information do you have?" Thomas inquired.

Vic shrugged. "Nothing out of the ordinary. Ain't like folks stop in to play poker and tell you their home address."

"Can you tell me anything?" Thomas asked.

"Yeah, if I had to guess. I'd put my bet on the saxophone player. I'd say you should question City Sax, if not at least follow him. Looks like every time City Sax has been here, his two buddies, Ace and Dante have been with him. He might lead you to what you're looking for."

"Too bad you left the force Vic," Thomas said. "You're good. Thanks for your help."

Thomas rose and made his exit. Next stop, the Fairmont Hotel. He had a saxophone player he needed to find.

***

The Tonga room, at the Fairmont Hotel was alive with music once Thomas arrived and walked to the bar and ordered a fog cutter. The Tonga room was not for the quiet wall flowers. If you were the type who were looking for a quiet romantic place to have a gourmet meal, you would find the gourmet meal, but the quiet place was another story.

Thomas loved the ambiance of the place; it was upbeat and filled with energy. The band playing was the quartet he was looking for and they were sitting nestled inside of a boat that looked like it was floating in the middle of the dance floor.

Thomas sat at the bar and spent a few moments enjoying his drink, the music and surveying the place. He was glad he had a number of contacts and he was pretty sure he could find a couple in the Tonga room. He didn't have long to wait when a man walked over and sat beside him.

"Hey Thomas, what brings you here?"

The man greeting Thomas was tall and muscular with dirty blonde hair styled impeccably, like a Hollywood movie star with intensely deep green eyes that didn't look real.

"How are you doing Brett, I see you've changed your eye color."

To look at Brett Goodman, he looked like the perfect man. His smile was soft with a hint of femininity, his strong bone structure was all male. But in the Gay community of San Francisco Brett was considered a wolf. In in the eyes of those who got to know him he was a lone wolf. A lone wolf who had once taken a chance on love only to lose it through no fault of his own. Eight years before his husband had been killed in a freak plane crash on its way to Lake Tahoe. Brett had been single ever since and everyone who knew him called him the lone wolf.

"Yes, I did Thomas, you know I liked it better when you used to ask me what's a nice guy like you hanging around in a place like this."

"Yeah, well I didn't want you to think I was one of those white males who never notice anything. So, pretty boy tell me. What happened you got tired of wearing that baby blue contact lens color?"

"Yes, I did. Blue eyes ain't popular anymore. Thomas besides there too many blonde hair, blue eye men running around trying to find the love of their life, like me. I decided I needed to be different. What's up with you? Are you working on a case?"

"Maybe, maybe not... If I am..." Thomas hesitated. He knew this was a game to Brett who spent his days writing articles for a local detective magazine. Thomas didn't care what Brett did for a living he only wanted the answer to one question at the moment. He cleared his throat and asked. What do you know about the saxophone player?"

"If you are working on a case, I want the regular cut for information," Brett declared, as his eyes looked around anxiously.

"You got it!" Thomas said.

Brett glanced at the band in the boat. "City Sax is cool. He's a straight heterosexual. If you want to know any more about him. Meet me outside in five minutes, by the garbage gate in the alley. I don't want to be seen leaving the room with you. You never know who's watching."

Five minutes later, Thomas made his way to the alley as Brett had instructed. He found Brett waiting for him.

"Okay Thomas, what is it you want to know?"

"What does City Sax like to do in his spare time? Who are his people he hangs with? His hangouts? His..."

"Looks like you want the works?" Brett declared interrupting him.

"Yeah, you can say that," Thomas said.

"Well, every Monday night, City Sax loves to play poker with a few rich buddies over on Potrero Hill. The rest of time he hangs out playing video games at an adult store right down the street, on Washington Street," Brett replied.

"What days of the week does he hang out there?" Thomas asked.

"Any day he's not working here. They always have Mondays off. That's when City Sax plays poker over on Potrero Hill. Most of the time it's Monday night only. But sometimes they give the band a rest and use a DJ. When they do, they post a notice in the lobby letting everyone know it's the band's night off."

"What about where he lives?"

"Some people would say he lives at an adult store, he's always there except when he plays here or playing poker on Monday nights."

Thomas nodded stiffly pondering what he was hearing. "Where's this adult video store."

"That's easy, right down the street, on the corner of Washington Street and Grant," Brett replied. "It's one of those classic old Victorian houses."

"Really," Thomas declared. "What's the name of the adult store?"

"Look for a sign that reads Hard Cock Candy Store."

"Hard Rock Candy Store?" Thomas said.

"No, Hard Cock Candy Store, it's a play on words. You can't miss it, it's the bright yellow building on the corner. There's a lollipop with a bite out of it where the "c" should be in the word cock, if you get my meaning."

"Poker every Monday night, huh? Got anything else?"

"Yeah, City Sax got himself a side hustle," Brett replied.

Thomas couldn't believe what he was hearing, his old pal Brett was a wealth of information. He almost felt like yelling out bingo for all the information he had given him. He decided why stop asking questions now. He had one more question Brett just might have the answer to. "Ah, Brett, you wouldn't by chance know what that side hustle was?"

"Sure do, City Sax has a very rich doctor brother. He's one of those plastic surgery doctors. Fixes noses, faces you know that sort of thing."

"Really?"

"Yeah, and he pay's City Sax for every client he refers to him. Once the show ends every night, City Sax passes out his brother's business cards and tell them his brother will hook them up with a discount, all they have to do is mention his name."

Deep in the recesses of his mind Thomas silently yelled *"Bingo."*

"Ah, Brett one more thing, you wouldn't by chance know where I could get one of those business cards?"

"Yup! Got you covered, I happened to have a couple," Brett said pulling out his wallet and handing him the card.

Thomas took the card and then reached into his jacket pocket and pulled out twenty, twenty-dollar bills he had neatly folded. He reached to shake Brett's hand. "Thanks, Brett, goodnight. Don't stay out too late."

Instantly Brett scooped the money out of his hand and patted him on the back at the same time. To anyone watching it just looked like to old friends was saying goodnight.

Thomas turned and headed back the way he came. Careful to observe his surroundings as he walked. He was pretty sure the doctor on this card had probably performed the bad plastic surgery on Dante Channing's nose job. There was no reason to go back inside of the Fairmont he had all the information he needed, he thought as he headed for his car.

36

Chapter 29

The Hard Cock Candy Store...

Later, that Monday night, after parking his car. Thomas walked the distance to the corner of Washington and Grant Street.

A big yellow building loomed in front of him on the corner, just like Brett had said.

Thomas walked along the side of the building to the alley to check it out before he walked back to the front entrance and went in. He was determined to cover every inch of the space that occupied the store to see what clues he could find.

The Hard Cock Candy Store was an X-rated Adult Store complete with a room filled with provocative video arcade.

Thomas wasn't the least bit surprised when he walked into the darken arcade and found numerous private booths where patrons could be alone with their video fantasies.

He walked a little further and found his lips lighting-up into a smile when he walked past a private video booth that boasted it was an X-Rated Paradise. That Promised a Raucous Steamy Hot Good Time!

Careful to observe his surroundings as he walked around exploring and he came across another sign that read. *"Our food service establishment is also your kinky space; health code must be followed. Genitals and feet must be covered at all times."*

"Talk about modern times," he thought as he continued walking and found another video arcade in the back. This one looked different from the one he'd seen earlier. He looked around and found a strange Gothic looking tapestry wall covering and it piqued his curiosity, as he walked over.

Standing right in front of the tapestry was a double wide Vintage photo booth complete with a strange black curation hanging in front of it. Written in bold white letters on a black board was the words "Employees Only".

Thomas casually strolled over and looked in. The booth didn't have a camera in it but contained a small rectangle window that looked out of place where it had been placed. There was something odd about the way the room was made. He walked inside and stood under the "Employees Only" sign as his hand reached out and ran across the wall. He wondered if the wall was an illusion.

Before he could explore the room any further a man cleared his throat loudly. "Mister this room is for employees only."

"Huh, sorry?" Thomas shrugged, taking a couple steps out of range of the man.

With his head bowed low he studied the suit the man was wearing from the waist down. The suit was expensive for someone employed by an adult video store and he was carrying a bag of take-out food, from the Gold Dragon Chinese Restaurant.

He was thankful the man didn't show much interest in him. He figured that the man must have encounter people looking at the sign in the room before, because he didn't pay him much interest.

For a quick second Thomas took a glance back at the man's face. The man looked familiar. It was City Sax. He pretended, he was interested in a video game next to the booth and slanted his eyes to see what was happening.

City Sax tapped once than three times on the rectangle window. Then suddenly a hidden door opened, revealing complete darkness. He walked across the threshold and disappeared into the darkness.

Thomas stood frozen in place spellbound. His mind raced trying to figure out what was happening behind that hidden door. He had to find out because it was obvious to him none of the employees, he saw walking around the store ever went into the room with the vintage photo booth and the sign marked for "Employees Only."

Thomas looked around and decided to play the video game he was standing in front of. He pulled out a couple of one-dollar bills and sat down at the machine. He put a couple dollars into his machine with little interest before he looked down at it and realized it was a video poker game with naked women.

Thomas played the video game with interest. He needed to kill time. He didn't want to make a mistake and attempt to enter the door too soon after seeing City Sax enter.

He didn't have long to wait, in the next moment when he looked up, he saw City Sax walked out of the secret door.

Thomas rose up out of his seat and watched to see where City Sax was going. His eyes trailing him as he watched him leave through the front entrance.

All at once a clerk walked over holding a well stock tray of bottled water, and other snacks and goodies.

"Sir, would you care for a bottle water, candy, gum, or chips?" The clerk asked. "The bottle water is free, but the candy, gum and chips is five dollars each. I got beef jerky sticks, two for five dollars too."

"No, thank you," Thomas declared as he watched the clerk walk away. He watched as the clerk was distracted by a man who was yelling his machine had malfunctioned. It was the perfect time to see what was behind the hidden door.

Walking into the darken booth he tapped on the window just as he'd seen City Sax do. Instantly the door opened, and he walked through the door under the sign, *"Employees Only,"* the first thing he notice was that it was totally dark.

Instantly the door closed behind him and he used his cellphone as a flashlight to see his way around. He was glad he did as a stairway came into view and he made his way down to the bottom.

There was a large open room at the bottom of the stairway. Numerous card tables were scattered around the room.

He snooped around the room. There was a large stone fireplace on a wall It looked peculiar being in a basement. The wall next to the fireplace was covered in neatly cut round shaped wood. The too neat precise cut wood caught Thomas' attention as he walked over.

The first thing he noticed was that the fireplace was fake. It didn't burn real wood it was gas. The next thing he noticed was the *too neat stacks of a wall of wood* could be hiding something. He was sure of it as he let his fingertips explore the out edge of the too neat precise cut wall of wood.

When his fingertip found the lever, he almost yelled out in glee. Instantly the wall of wood became ajarred. It was just as he thought, it was a hidden room. A bedroom large enough to hold a full-size bed to be exact as his eyes took in a clump of rumpled sheets lying in the middle of the bed. It looked like someone had been sleeping in it earlier.

Thomas close the wood wall. The room with the bed was too small to snoop around. He wondered if the person who had slept in it earlier was still around.

Right next to the wall of wood was a half-opened door. He peeked inside and found a nasty bathroom in need of a good cleaning, but it was large enough to walk inside. He walked further in looking down and then he saw it. It was a trap door hidden by a fake wood cabinet that had been opened. The cabinet was tall enough for a man to walk inside. He snooped around further inside the trap door there was a ladder that went down into the dark.

Thomas stuck his head in and felt a cold gush of air. He cursed under his breath and went down the ladder to find himself in a dank musty tunnel underneath Chinatown.

He exhaled he had heard rumors of their being tunnels lying beneath Chinatown. Some said they went ten miles in all directions. It was said that the tunnels had been built in the 1900's to hide Chinese women rescued from indentured servitude and human trafficking.

Thomas had an eerie feeling. The tunnels where huge, and mysterious. With a surreal feeling all its own, like a strangle hold deep in the bowels of a gutter.

He felt a strange chill run up his spine before his nose made contact with a smell. It was a strange smell like someone smoking a cigarette. A strange smelling cigarette that wasn't marijuana.

Thomas heard a strange noise just as the cigarette smoke drifted in real close as he heard footsteps coming his way. He pushed his body back into the shadows and felt his back press up against cold metal, as he sucked in a deep breath.

37

Chapter 30

Nicky why you got to be so mean...

Lacey was determined to talk to Nicholas and find out what was going on with him. Since that day she had lunch with Maëlle and saw images of Nicholas covered in blood and guts. She knew she had to let him know she had no intentions of letting her brother take revenge on Dante Channing.

Conflicted and with a heavy heart she pulled into the driveway of her childhood home and parked her car right next to her brother Nicholas' shiny black custom BMW M6 with a panoramic sunroof.

"Gosh, I'd love to drive that car down to the ocean in Monterey, with the wind in my hair and my hubby by my side," Lacey said out loud thinking no one would hear her.

"Huh! What you gonna do with those sticky finger crumb snatchers of yours? They ain't getting in my car!"

"Nicky, I didn't see you. By the way my children are not crumb snatchers!" Lacey snarled. "Besides, I figured you would want to build a relationship with your niece and nephew and say babysit."

"Hell no!"

"Nicky why you got to be so mean?" Lacey declared.

"I ain't being mean, there's plenty of time for me to babysit after your little one is potty trained. Remember," Nicholas stated holding up his hands. "These hands do not change diapers. Now repeat after me, Lacey one more time. My brother, does not change do... Do diapers."

Lacey blurted out laughing. "Stop it Nicky, you are making me laugh!"

"Laughter is good medicine," Nicholas declared. "It looks good on you."

Lacey stopped laughing and said. "Well, I need to get a grip. There's something important I need to talk about."

"Uh, oh! I need to get out of your way. Looks like you need to get inside and talk to Mom, or Grand *mere* Catherine," Nicholas replied.

"Actually, Nicky I was hoping to speak to you in private," she said as she touched his arm.

Nicholas stood there silent for a moment. "Well, from that look on your face, I can see it can't wait. So, what's on your mind little sister?"

"Well, Nicholas, I guess I have to just come out and say it. I've been having some bad juju lately. It's been coming in my dreams, both day and night," Lacey hesitated and glanced up at her brother. "There's just something I have to ... I mean... Can I ask you something?" She asked but didn't wait for a response. "Nicky, are you happy?"

Nicholas looked disoriented for a moment. "What?

Happy? I... I guess I never remember being happy. Maybe miserable when I was locked up in prison."

Nicholas paused and studied his sister wondering where this conversation was going. What was Lacey up to, he wondered if she was trying to put some kind of head trip on him.

"Look, Lacey I don't know where you going to with this. First you start off saying you been feeling some kind of *juju*. Now this, head trip. Either you tell me the real reason why we're having this crazy conversation or I'm out of here."

"Okay... Okay! Look, Nicholas, I been waking up with these terrible nightmares where you're covered with blood and standing over..."

"Covered with blood?" Nicholas repeated.

"Yes, Nicholas, you are covered with blood and standing... Standing over..." Lacey paused not being able to say his name. She let her eyes capture her brother's. "Nicholas, I'm scared. This is serious. I just have this really bad feeling that you been formulating some plan for revenge against Dante Channing and that's wrong. Really... Really ...!"

"What the hell Lacey?' Nicholas interrupted her in mid-sentence. "You don't have a right to tell me what I should do! Besides, it ain't none of your business anyway!"

"It is my business Nicholas! You're my brother for God's sake!"

"Don't judge me Lacey, you ain't God! If I have a desire to hurt that bastard who set me up and sent me to prison that's my business! Not yours!"

"What about our family?" Lacey snapped back at him. "Can't you see what this will do to mother and Grand *mere*

Catherine? Nicholas you don't want to do that! You don't need to do that," she pleaded.

Before Nicholas could respond back to her, his cell phone rang out loudly piercing the air. Instantly Maëlle's face flashed across the screen.

Nicholas cell phone rang out a second time and Lacey eyes captured the face of her friend Maëlle.

"Maëlle," she whispered as Maëlle's face smile back at her, and then she saw the chance to turn the conversation around in her favor and said. "Nicholas, aren't you going to pick up the phone, it's Maëlle?"

"Hell Naw!" Nicholas grunted and declared. "I got one crazy female yelling at me. That's enough for today!"

At first Lacey was shocked by his outburst and then his lack of respect for her feelings not to mention the way he thought he could just wave her off with another insult. But then she had an idea. Maybe she could appeal to his feelings for Maëlle when she said "What about Maëlle, Nicholas? Are you so gun ho on having your revenge against Dante that you destroy your chance at happiness with Maëlle?"

"Fuck Maëlle!" Nicholas declared angrily. "In the first place, I ain't sure that bitch loves me, and in the second place, I ain't sure if I love her. Hell, if the truth be told, ever since that time back in high-school, when I caught Quinn checking her out, all I'm really sure of, is that I think, all I ever did was want her just because I knew Quinn would envy me, because I got her and he didn't."

Lacey frowned. "Envy you? Are you joking? Do you mean to tell me you and Quinn were playing some stupid game with Maëlle's feelings?"

"Why are you asking me?" Nicholas shrugged.

Lacey was caught off guard. "I mean... Don't you ever care about Maëlle's...," she hesitated. "I mean Quinn and Maëlle's feelings?"

"Maëlle doesn't count as far as it goes. You probably know more about Maëlle's feelings than I do. I don't know what she's thinking half the time. And how the hell am I supposed to know, what Quinn is thinking or playing at? You have to ask him. Are you done with your holier than thou ranting now?"

Lacey exhaled loudly at her brother's truthfulness. Then she said. "You know Nicholas if I were you... I would pay attention to MMMaa ... I mean...I... I would..." She mumbled and Instantly she froze overtaken by a flash of seeing Quinn and Maëlle making love in her vision. She quickly shook out her thoughts. Now was not the time to talk to Nicholas about that. Not that she would, since she'd promised Maëlle, she would not.

Nicholas felt strange as he stared back at his sister. He had a weird feeling she was just about to tell him something, important. He felt the words roll of his tongue while his thoughts were racing. "What is up with you Lacey? You gonna finish that sentence?"

Lacey regained her composure. "Naw, Naw! Look, Nicholas, I mean... It wasn't important..." she said, shaking her head as she realized his revelation startled her into complete silence. Funny how life works she thought standing there staring back at her brother dumbfounded. She thought about the promise she made to Maëlle not to tell Nicholas about her and Quinn. She realized at that moment; she no longer had a desire too. After listening to her brother, she knew Maëlle had bigger problems than she knew about.

Lacey stood there looking off in the distance as she realized it was getting late. The sun had long ago set for the day. She was tired. She wanted to go home to her family.

Finally, Lacey found her voice as she broke the silence. "I can't believe you would do this to our family Nicholas! I am so ashamed of you..."

Nicholas rudely interrupted her. "I don't give a damn about your feeling ashamed at me! Hell, you can write it on a t-shirt a walk around and advertise it for all I care! I don't give a shit!"

"Fuck you Nicholas!" Lacey spat out as she stormed away walking over to her car. She opened her car door paused and glanced back at him. Then got into her car and started the engine and drove off.

Nicholas stood there staring back at his sister realizing he'd really pissed her off. He thought back for a moment and he was sure now, that there had been a moment, when she was going to tell him something important. He wondered what it had been, he thought to himself.

Instantly his cell phone rang, and he checked the caller-Id. It was Quinn. He slammed his cell phone shut, as he turned and walked up the driveway toward their family home.

***

Across town, Quinn looked at his cell phone, he'd lost count at the number of times Nicholas hadn't answered his phone. This was the last time; he wanted some answers. He was on his way to see Father Perez Senior. He remembered seeing Nicholas and Father Perez Senior talking at his welcome home party. He was sure Father Perez Senior could give him some answers as to what was going on with his brother.

Quinn checked the time and realized it was getting late. But he knew that the time of day didn't matter with Father Perez Senior, if you were in need of talking to him, all you had to do was say so. Quickly, Quinn made a U-turn and headed his car in the direction of the Church of the Good Shepherd, determined to talk to Father Perez Senior.

38

Chapter 31

Narrow Escape ...

Thomas quickly climbed up the cold steel ladder and felt the temperature change with each step he took. He knew it was taking him up to the street above, he could hear the sounds of city traffic. His hands hit the manhole before he knew it and he pushed up on the manhole cover above his head and was surprise when it easily gave away.

Thomas felt his body shaking with relief when his face made contact with the cold crisp San Francisco air. His experience in the tunnel had him questioning if what he just experienced was real. Right here in the middle of this city was a whole other world lying deep underground.

A gush of cold air crept up and covered his body. The chill air shook him to his core. But he knew he wasn't shivering from the air but from the unreal feeling he had minutes ago, while he was deep below this great city.

Once he cleared the manhole his eyes looked up into the black navy-blue sky and let out a sigh of relief. The lights of the stars were fuzzy as he tried to focus his eyes and realized a thick blanket of fog was obstructing his view. His body was starting to miss the warmth of the manhole. He checked his watch it was almost two o'clock a.m., in the morning. He looked around him and realized that he was a no where near the Hard Cock Candy Store. In fact, the building across the street from him was a huge storage unit facility and directly across the street from it on the corner was old St. Mary's Cathedral. He turned and looked for a street marker and found one. It read Sacramento Street. He was a good distance from where he'd started on Washington and Grant Street.

Taking a deep breath, he decided the first thing he needed was a good strong cup of coffee to calm his nerves.

At the Corner of Sacramento and Quincy street he spotted a twenty-four-hour coffee shop. The bright lights beckoned him as he strolled across the street and walked in.

The first thing he thought was, the place was neat and clean, as he found a seat at the counter and sat down.

A soft brown-eyed petite waitress with blond ends and black roots, wearing a 1930's style waitress uniform in a dull yellow color, hurried over. "Good morning to you sir. Would you like some coffee?"

"Yes, and keep it coming strong and black!"

"Sure thing!" His waitress answered, filling the empty mug in front of him. "Would you like to order we have our early morning breakfast special three eggs your way, toast, hash browns ..."

"Yes, I'll take that," Thomas interrupted her in mid-sentence. "Make the eggs scrambled soft, with sausages, patties."

"Do you want any toast?"

Thomas nodded. "Yes, sourdough."

"Coming right up," his waitress declared hurrying away.

Thomas wrapped both his hands around his hot mug and let the warmth of his cup calm his nerves and took a sip.

Thomas thought back to the tunnels. He was sure someone was hiding down there, and he believe it could be Dante, but he wasn't sure. He was hesitant about going back down there. The tunnels where huge, and mysterious. *With a surreal feeling all of its own, like a strangle hold deep in the bowels of a gutter,* he thought as he took a sip of hot coffee. His mind wandered thinking about how dangerous it was down in the tunnels. He wasn't sure if it was a good thing to go back down. Not to mention he wasn't sure he would find Dante Channing. In fact, he wasn't sure what else was hiding down there.

After several minutes of beating up on himself, he realized that he was being paid to do a job. He had no choice, he had to go back into the tunnels. He needed to be sure it was or wasn't Dante Channing living down there. But first, he needed a plan. He racked his brain and then the thought hit him. *"Motion sensing night vision,"* he mumbled as he took another sip of his hot coffee.

"That's it!" Thomas declared just as his waitress returned placing his food in front of him.

"Wow! Looks like you're ready for this meal," his waitress said thinking he was talking about the food she placed in front of him.

Thomas smiled back at his waitress and nodded as she walked away. He didn't have the heart to tell her what he had really discovered was the perfect way to determine how to tell if it was Dante Channing he had discovered in the tunnels.

He took a bite of his food. "Mmmm, these eggs are perfect," he declared out loud to no one but himself as he took another bite. The tasty food was bringing him back to life, he could feel his energy grow and give him strength as he worked out his plan. He knew what he needed, night vision cameras, maybe a pair of night vision goggles too.

39

Chapter 32

Kienan & Lacey

That night Lacey made it a point to put her children to bed early. She just finished reading their favorite story, Dr Seuss Sleep Book, when she listened attentively and realized they were both sound asleep. Slowly she crept out of the room they shared together and softly closed their bedroom door.

Earlier that day, after visiting with her brother Nicholas, she had thought about having their nanny spend the night but decided against it when she knew she was dogged determined to talk to her husband Kienan, alone without any interruptions.

Lacey thought back to earlier in the day, when she'd gone to see her brother, Nicholas. Their conversation hadn't ended as well as she'd planned. She'd voiced her concerns to him about her dreams of his seeking revenge against Dante Channing, but Nicholas had shrugged her off, in fact he had been downright rude. Now she was determined to tell her husband Kienan.

Walking down the hallway she glanced at the door of the last room and notice the crack of light at the bottom of the door. She knew Kienan was still in his office. Good, she thought it gave her a chance to stop by their master bedroom and fill the tub, for a bath.

Quickly she entered their master bedroom and walked through to their bathroom. She glided over to their huge tub and turned on the water. The jerky motion of the nozzle starting the flow of water, calmed her senses. Soon the sound of water in motion with its cascading roar filled the air. She retrieved her homemade bath salts, bubble bath and oils and poured them into the swirling water.

Lacey began stripping out of her clothes and tossing them on to the floor, as the water poured. After removing her blouse, jeans, bra and panties she went to reach for her most seductive robe, before walking back over and turning off the water. She then walked over to her full-length mirror and holding up the long sheer black lace fluffy chandelle boa feather trimmed lingerie robe, in front of the mirror before she put it on. This was the robe her mother Pearl had given her for her wedding night. Her mother Pearl had said the robe had magical powers to make a man do anything that a woman wanted.

Lacey ran her hands across the fluffy chandelle boa feather trimmed and said without thinking. "Christ! This is overkill, I'm taking this off."

"Oh, hell no! You ain't taking that off! I'm loving the view from here!"

With a shriek of annoyance Lacey screamed out. "Kienan!

You scared the hell out of me! I didn't know you were standing there watching me!"

"Why do you want to take that off, it's a man's eye candy and I'm loving what my eyes are seeing right now."

Lacey glanced back at Kienan. "Yeah, well, I need you to take me serious and I don't think this wickedly sexy lingerie robe is going to do that for me."

"Uh, oh! What's wrong? Are my most precious assets sound asleep as their mother wanted?" Kienan's voice took on a British accent. "Or did the little crumb snatchers give their mother a hard time?"

Lacey looked up at her husband. An annoyed glare frozen on her face. "You know Kienan, when my brother calls my children crumb snatchers, I want to beat him senseless," a soft smile warmed her face. "But when their father talks to me in that British accent, and calls his children crumb snatchers, Momma can't resist him. Come to Momma Big Daddy," she declared flinging her arms wide closing the distance between them.

"Whoa! Looks like Big Daddy is going to be well taken care of by Little Mamma tonight," he replied pulling her into his embrace and kissing her passionately.

"Huh, uh!Wait a minute. I knew I needed to change." Lacey declared pulling out of his embrace. "First things first. We need to talk, and I think I need to put back on some clothes."

"Uh, no. The robe is fine. Leave it on. I can tell this is serious! Because you sound really serious. So, what's wrong?"

"It's my brother, Nicholas," Lacey declared. "I went to see him earlier today."

"Thank God, I thought I was in trouble," Kienan interrupted, breathing out a sigh of relief. "What pray-tell has brother-in-law done now?"

"For goodness sake, Kienan, let me sit down so that I can tell you," she said walking over to her vanity chair in their bedroom, and sitting down.

Quickly Lacey told Kienan about seeing Nicholas earlier and their conversation.

Lacey was just finishing up on her meeting with her brother when she finally said. "I even told him I had been waking up with these terrible nightmares where he's covered with blood and standing over Dante getting his revenge and all he can tell me is that I have no right to judge him. Can you believe him?"

Kienan rolled his eyes and shrugged listening attentively. "Now, Lacey, get a hold of yourself. You know how Nicholas is. He doesn't want his baby sister fighting his battles."

Lacey voice rose a pitch. "You know I had a good mind to tell him that Maëlle and Quinn had an affair while he was in prison."

"What? Lacey, are you crazy?" Kienan declared. "I mean, serious?"

"Nope! I mean. Why do you think it's crazy? Oh, are you saying I'm crazy?" Lacey asked giving him a harsh stare.

"No, look, I didn't mean to say it like that. It was just so unbelievable," he replied looking flabbergasted. "I meant, how did you know Maëlle and Quinn had an affair? Did you dream it?"

Lacey glared back at Kienan for a moment and then slant her eyes as if studying. She took a deep breath and said. "You know, I have that clairvoyant thing."

Kienan shifted uncomfortably. "So, it's that clairvoyant thing of yours. It just came out and told you they were having an affair, huh, right?"

"Yes, it did. You know that my little family gift just keeps getting stronger and stronger."

Kienan laughed and then said. "Yeah, do I ever know about that little gift your family has. It makes me think of Grand *mere* Catherine and her rather big gift," he stared off into the distance. "You know, it makes me think," he repeated.

"Say are you going to listen to me tell you what happened between me and Maëlle? Or are you going to sit there daydreaming about my grandmother?"

"I'm sorry, sweetness. Of course, I want to hear what happened between you and Maëlle. Go on."

"Well, if you insist," Lacey declared. "So, all I did was sort of touch Maëlle's hand, friendly like, we used to do when we were kids and then puff! My clairvoyant gift worked, just like that. I saw the two of them naked, together."

Kienan cleared his throat and asked. "You mean to tell me you just clasped hands with Maëlle's, and you saw her having an affair... With Quinn?"

"Well, yeah!" Lacey declared. "Look, it was maybe a little more in depth than that. All I know is that when I was having lunch with Maëlle the other day, we clasped hands for a moment and in that moment... I had this vision. It was so vivid and real! I saw her and Quinn naked doing the wild thing and yet they were consenting adults and not teenagers, so I knew it had to be recent," she let out a deep breath. "And when I told Maëlle what I saw in my vision. She didn't deny it. In fact, she confirmed it."

"Really?" Kienan declared in utter surprise.

Lacey stood up and began pacing around the room. Her flowing sheer wickedly sexy lingerie robe cascading and bellowing around her as she paced. "Yes, she did, and she told me it was when she went to visit him in Mexico, while Nicholas was in prison. The next thing I knew somehow she got our conversation into making it about her and getting me, to of course, agree not to tell Nicholas," her voice grew soft as she rattled on telling Kienan more about her conversation with Maëlle.

Kienan sat there staring off into space as if he was under a spell. He knew his wife was pacing around naked with a sheer robe on and he couldn't focus his eyes on her. It was surreal. He heard Lacey talking but couldn't focus on what she was saying. He couldn't believe it Lacey's gift was now something very real. He'd known the gift ran in her family, but he had always assumed it had skipped Lacey. Now he wondered if she knew he'd seen her father Louis, that night. He sat there blinking hard several times lost in his thoughts.

"Kienan! Kienan! Did you hear a word I said? What's the matter with you?" Lacey inquired and then noticed he wasn't listening to her.

Instantly Lacey closed the distance between them and clasped his hands. "Kienan, are you alright?"

From out of nowhere, Lacey heard soft music carrying gently on the air, as the music hummed the air, the melodies of the song came to her. *"Remember dear each word divine..."* she knew the song; it was until I waltz again with you. It was her father's favorite.

Suddenly a light seared across her vision as she held her

husband's hand. The vision hit her hard just as she heard the faint familiar music and saw the room. It was completely dark, but it felt familiar. Instantly recognition hit. It was her bedroom. She saw it clearly, Kienan was standing in their bedroom and he was talking to a man. The music sounded again, as she focused and the man standing there with Kienan came into view. It was her dead father, Louis.

She heard him say. *"Kienan, I want you to protect Nicholas from himself, keep him from finding Dante Channing first!"* Louis' ghost insisted.

Lacey's vision faded out as the music died out. She couldn't see anything more, but the room she was standing in when she said.

"Oh my God! Kienan, did you have a dream about my father, Louis!"

"Damn! Your gift is fascinating!" Kienan declared giving her a wide-eyed look as he shook his head. "But I don't think it was a dream. In fact, I believe I was wide awake at the time, it happened," he nodded. "Believe me when I tell you, it was real. Very real!"

"Don't you see how important your seeing my dead father is?"

"Yes, I did then, and I still do, now. In fact, I know he meant every word he said to me. I am to find Dante Channing before your brother does and I am trying my best to do just that."

"Thank you... Thank you, Kienan, I am so happy to hear you see how important this is. I wished I came to you sooner. It would have saved me so much worry."

Kienan let out a deep breath. "Do me a favor and remind me never to cheat on you or my goose is cooked."

Lacey shook her head as she smiled back at him. "I can't believe that is the only thing you can think of."

"No, it isn't the only thing I am thinking of," Kienan said with a serious tone in his voice. "In fact, I think the two of us should go and tell Grand *mere* Catherine, about your vision and mine too. This is bigger than the two of us and I don't want to take any chances Nicholas might do something he'll regret."

"I see what you're saying, Kienan, and I agree. I believe you're right. Telling Grand *mere* Catherine is the best thing we can do. Maybe she can help us keep Nicholas from seeking revenge against Dante."

"Good, first thing tomorrow you and I will pay Grand *mere* Catherine a visit," Kienan said as he walked across the room over to a cabinet and opened it to reveal a small refrigerator. "In the meantime, I got some chilled Merlot; would you care for a glass, my dear?"

"Yes, I'll have a glass. You know, Grand *mere* Catherine said my gift won't always tell me when my loved one close to me is chea...," she caught herself and stopped and grew silent. Telling him she wouldn't be able to tell if he had been cheating on her, was something she decided to keep to herself. "Oh, never mind. Kienan why didn't you tell me you saw my father's ghost?"

Surprise and embarrassment ran a swift race across Kienan's face as he walked back over with two glasses. "Here," he said handing her a glass of wine. "It looks, like we're both guilty of keeping things from each other."

Lacey sighed and closed her eyes briefly. "Yeah, well. Looks like you and my dead father have some kind of special connection," she said taking a sip of her wine.

"Your father wants me to find Dante Channing before Nicholas does. I guess you're having vision of Nicholas standing over Dante covered in blood is our warning to hurry up and do so."

Lacey touched her wine glass to Kienan's. "On, that husband, we both agree. Now tell me, how can we go about finding Dante before Nicholas does?"

"I already got my investigator Thomas looking into it and come to think of it. I haven't heard from him in a while. I think the second thing I need to do tomorrow is to give him a call and see what the status is."

"Excellent!" Lacey declared as she downed the rest of her glass of wine. "Sounds like a plan. First, we go and see Grand *mere* Catherine and then you will call the investigator Thomas for a status update. Now the first thing we need to do tonight involves the two of us, taking a long relaxing bath," she declared, putting down her empty glass as she moved in close and wrapped her arms around his waist.

Kienan drowned in tenderness as he held her close. "Gosh, you feel good."

"Kienan, do you think you can scrub my back, this time? And maybe give me a little neck massage?"

Kienan leaned back from their embrace looking back at her, as his eyes held a peculiar excitement. With her holding him tight he let his hands slip up and down the curve of her hips. "You know sweetness we could try that position again, this time you sit on the side of the tub and I go down on you.

"Ou! Wow! Yes!" Lacey cooed and moaned shuddering letting her hands unbutton his shirt and watched as Kienan tossed it aside.

"No offense wife but you're moving a bit to slow for my taste," he said unfastening his jeans and dropping them to the floor.

His arms circled her waist as he led her over to the tub and in his best British accent said. "Your bath awaits milady."

"Now you are talking, my good and soon to be very hard man," she giggled and moaned seductively with a wicked smile as she purred out sensually. "When you are done serving me, I can service you and get our penis good and hard, right before I straddle you and ride you to a sweet orgasm!"

Kienan gave his wife a crooked wicked smile as he helped her step into their bathtub.

His eyes took in every inch of her body as he watched as she slowly and seductively lowered her body and submerged into the warm bubbly swirling water.

Lacey looked up into his face and felt mesmerized by the look she saw staring back at her.

She moaned as Kienan slicked his hands up and down her wet body.

Instantly his mouth found hers and his tongue explored the soft cavity of her mouth before plunging deeper into a dual with her tongue as his thumb began to massage her sensitive clitoris, slowly at first and then firmer.

He stopped abruptly letting his hands help his wife position herself on the side of their tub, as he promised.

Lacey watched him with her eyes dutifully. She knew what

was coming next as she spread her legs wide and watched as Kienan lowered himself and knelt between her legs.

Kienan let out a heavy sigh as he pushed his head between her legs as his lips started sucking, he moaned. "Oh! Sweetness."

Lacey moaned and moving in rhythm with Kienan as she felt her body shudder with pleasure as she felt her body tighten, tremble as it slowly built up a fire that she knew only Kienan could quench.

40

Chapter 33

Nicholas...

Just past eleven thirty that night Nicholas pushed open the darken front door of Houlihan's bar. It was located off the main strip of Stevens Creek and Winchester Boulevard, on a noisy busy street corner. He was amazed at how much the once little sleepy town of San Jose was starting to look, feel and sound like its big sister city of San Francisco just up the bay.

From the minute he walked through the front door, Nicholas knew he was a man on a mission. He had forgotten that Houlihan's was one of Dante Channing's favorite hang-out spots and he hoped he might find him there or find someone who had seen him.

Nicholas sat down at the bar and ordered a beer.

Seconds later his burly armed bartender brought over his beer and placed it in front of him. Then placing a delicious smelling barbecue tri-tip sandwich in front of the patron sitting next to him. He had forgotten Houlihan's was famous for having some of the best barbecue tri-tip in town.

Yearning hungrily gazing at the man sitting next to him, watching him wolf down his tri-tip, made Nicholas' mouth water. He quickly down his beer and he was just about to place his own order when his eyes caught sight of a familiar face walking past. The man was heading for the billiard room in the back.

Instantly Nicholas rose and followed the man. A flashing red neon sign of a cue stick hitting an eight-ball hung above the doorway the man entered. It was the billiard room locals called Goldstein's Mortuary. The relaxing sound of soft blues being played by a live band filled the air above the jarring noise of men and women waving money in the air and putting bets down on pool games.

Nicholas pushed through the crowd and made his way over to where the man had walked over to an empty table and picked up a cue stick.

The man standing at the table was in his early forties but looked older with his deeply wrinkled forehead on a shiny bald head. He couldn't have been more than five feet seven inches tall with unusual bubble eyes, like a fish.

"Well, hello Vodka Joe, long time no see."

The man called Vodka Joe, slowly looked up and laughed. He kept his eyes glued to Nicholas as he closed the distance between them. "Well, if it isn't Nicholas La Cour, fancy seeing you in Goldstein's Mortuary. I heard you got out. And I bet I know who you are looking for?"

Nicholas shrugged. "If you know who I'm looking for, have you seen him?"

Vodka Joe laughed. "Now wait a minute. You want to talk business and I being a gentleman and all and I be a teeny-weeny bit parched, can't do so, without a drink," he declared licking his lips. "You know you ain't even offered to buy me a drink," he let out a sinister chuckle.

"Alright, Vodka Joe, I'll buy you that drink," Nicholas declared raising his arm and then yelling. "Hey waitress we need drinks over here."

At his signal a scrawny Asian looking waitress with purple hair walked over and asked in a heavy accent. "What you having?"

"I'll have a Corona," Nicholas declared and give him whatever he wants."

"That'll be a Black Russian with a shot of vodka on the side, right, Vodka Joe?" The waitress asked.

"Peggy Sue gal, you know me so well," Vodka Joe laughed. "This gentleman will be paying for my drinks just so you know."

"I know... I know. You ain't never paid for your drinks on your own before," Peggy Sue declared in broken English as she hurried away.

"Mind if I hit a couple shots while we wait for our drinks, Nicholas?"

"No, problem," Nicholas said.

Vodka Joe raised his pool stick and knocked several balls around the table. He was just going to knock in the last one when their waitress returned and placed the drinks on a small table by the pool sticks.

Instantly Vodka Joe, grabbed his shot glass and down it

before picking up his Black Russian and taking a big gulp. "Hey, get me another one Peggy Sue!"

Peggy Sue took a look at Nicholas. "You still paying for Vodka Joe's drinks, Mister?"

Nicholas nodded. "Go ahead and get him another one. I'm good."

"You heard the man," Vodka Joe declared. "Get going!"

"Okay, okay," Peggy Sue replied, as she headed toward the bar.

Nicholas studied vodka Joe as he kept shaking his glass and taking another sip. He wondered if he was hiding something. He seemed nervous.

As quick as a Cheetah, chasing his prey, Peggy Sue returned with the second drink.

"Here you go, Vodka Joe," Peggy Sue said, placing the drinks down and turning and facing Nicholas looking for payment.

Nicholas reached into his pocket and pulled out a fifty-dollar bill and handed it to her.

Both men watched while Peggy Sue rumbled through a glass on her tray filled with dollar bills trying to make change.

"Keep, the change," Nicholas declared.

"Mister are you sure, I owe you change from a fifty. I sure I got enough in here to make change," Peggy Sue replied in broken English.

"Tell the man thank you and get lost Peggy Sue, now!" Vodka Joe cursed, taking a big gulp of his Black Russian.

"Darn Vodka Joe, you don't have to sound so mean, a girl's got feelings you know," Peggy Sue replied shaking her head as she stomped her feet walking a short distance away.

"You pissed her off real good. I don't think she'll be back to take any more drink orders," Nicholas said.

"Who Peg? She's got a thick skin, she'll get over it," Vodka Joe answered gruffly, then took a gulp of his drink. "Besides do you want to talk business, or do you want to call Peggy Sue back and talk shit?"

"Yes, I want to talk business," Nicholas answered.

Vodka Joe sinister laugh filled the air. "You still a dumb ass, Nicholas La Cour, do you think I would tell you where to find Dante Channing?" His laughter filled the air.

Angry and flushed Nicholas froze and then realized he'd been a fool, Vodka Joe was always loyal to Dante, he should have known better than to think he would help him find him. He went to turn around to leave.

"Mister look out!" Peggy Sue screamed.

Nicholas looked over his shoulder and saw Vodka Joe raise the pool stick at just the moment he dived and rolled out the way.

Instantly two big burly and hairy club bouncers appeared out of nowhere. One of them grab Vodka Joe from behind securing his arms while the other one yanked the pool stick out of his hands.

"Let me go!" Vodka Joe grunted as the bouncers led him away.

Peggy Sue walked over and helped Nicholas get up off the floor. "Mister are you alright?"

Nicholas dusted off his pants and said. "Thanks for warning me, I was trying to leave I didn't want to cause any trouble."

"You're not the trouble, Vodka Joe is. That one has a bad

temper when he gets drunk. You brought him two drinks but what you didn't know is he'd been drinking all evening. He should have been sent home a long time ago."

"Thanks, for your help Peggy Sue."

Peggy Sue helped Nicholas finish dusting off his clothes when she leaned in close as her voice cracked in a whisper. "I overheard you and Vodka Joe talking. You're looking for Dante Channing, aren't you?"

"Yeah, I am."

Peggy Sue glanced around making sure they were alone. "I get off in a half hour, meet me in front of the Old Winchester House on the corner by the big walnut nut tree at the benches there."

***

A half hour later, Peggy Sue was sitting on the bench just as she said she would be when Nicholas walked over.

Peggy Sue stood up as Nicholas closed the distance between them. "Sorry we have to meet like a couple of thieves, but you never know who's listening Goldstein's Mortuary, I mean Houlihan's. That place is full of spies," she said revealing a smile filled with perfect little teeth.

"Have you been waiting long?" Nicholas inquired.

"Not too long," she said. "You wouldn't by chance have any more of those fifty dollars bills you paid me with earlier? I mean, if my information is good. You'll pay me, right?"

"Sure, I willing to pay, if the information is good," Nicholas said.

"My brother worked a job for a catering company that provided food at a big mansion over in Japan Town in San Jose. The house was owned by an old Japanese actor named

Jack Nakahara. Apparently, he known for hosting a big illegal poker party that bring in a lot of big money and ever bigger people. My brother says Jack Nakahara has his butler pick up young prostitutes from Chinatown, to service the men playing poker. My brother said he saw Dante Channing there, a couple of times."

"When was that party?"

"The last one was about a month ago."

"That's a long time ago. I don't think it'll help me," Nicholas replied shaking his head.

"I'm not finished," Peggy Sue declared. "My brother overheard Dante talking to a guy and mentioning that he frequents a poker game that's held in China Town every week."

Nicholas looked confused. "China Town? In San Jose? San Jose doesn't have a ..."

"I didn't say in San Jose," Peggy Sue interrupted him. "Everyone knows San Jose doesn't have a real China Town. But..."

"San Francisco does," Nicholas said finishing her sentence.

"Yeah that's right, and Jack the actor butler's picks the girls up somewhere off Ross Alley. I know that because my brother made extra money several nights, when he rode with butler to pick up girls at Ross Alley. They asked my brother to go, because he speaks Cantonese and Mandarin."

A big smile formed on Nicholas face. I'll give you an extra hundred dollars if you have a contact name in San Francisco for the girls."

"Shop girl," Peggy Sue replied. "Really she's a shop madam but everyone calls her the Shop Girl. She works at the fortune cookie factory."

Nicholas shook his head. "Sounds promising. A fortune cookie factory, are you sure?"

"Yes, I'm sure," Peggy Sue thought for a moment and then said. "But I'm not sure she works at the fortune cookie factory. My brother said they'd walk up to the factory and she'd be there."

"What was that street name again, where you said I could find her?"

"You can find her on Ross Alley, in San Francisco."

"Ross Alley," Nicholas muttered under his breath. As his mind repeated Shop Girl, over and over again. His thoughts raced. He knew that area. A big smile rose across Nicholas' face.

Finally, Nicholas spoke. "Is there anything you brother might have, I don't know, been told about what kind of prostitute, he should look for," he hesitated. "I mean, did he receive any specific instructions to ask for when he pick up the girls."

"Now that you mention it, he did. My brother was told he had to make sure the girls weren't squeamish when it came to being asked to perform some kinky freakish sex acts. The girls had to be okay with the whole the bondage, blindfold rough sex thing and they had to be okay with licking his asshole."

"Whoa that's a tall order, sounds like you earned a bonus." Nicholas said as he reached into his pocket and pulled out ten fifty-dollar bills and then a one-hundred-dollar bill and handed them all to Peggy Sue.

Peggy Sue wrapped her hands around the money and looked back into Nicholas' face. "Thanks. Thank you very much," she said rising and walking down the block to her parked car.

Nicholas stood there staring after her. Finally, he had a lead worth following and he found the information all by himself. If the actor Jack picked up prostitutes from Chinatown, some of them might still be walking the streets of Chinatown. He smiled thinking how *"Thomas the great detective hadn't manage to find anything,* "he thought as he headed toward his car.

Chapter 34

Grand mere Catherine...

When Kienan gotten up early that morning, something told him that day was the perfect day to make the drive to see his wife's grandmother, Grand *mere* Catherine.

Days before, Kienan had promised his wife Lacey they'd go and visit her, but something just kept coming up. He couldn't put it off any longer. His gut feeling was telling him so.

It was a gusty and blustery morning as he drove the twisting road, he said in his thoughts as he made his way on the old county road leading to his wife's family's home. The old road provided some spectacular views of the Alum Rock hills of the Mount Hamilton mountain range high in the mountains above San Jose, California.

Kienan pulled into the driveway and watched as Grand *mere* Catherine stood off to the side waving happily.

"Kienan and Lacey it so good to see the two of you. But I am a little upset you left my grand-young ins with their nanny," Grand m*ere* Catherine declared as she hugged the two of them.

"I told you Grand *mere* Catherine, Kienan and I wanted to speak with you about something important, in private," Lacey declared.

"I know... I know...But I can still complain, it's part of my being a great grandmother," Grand *mere* Catherine said leading them into the huge warm comfortable kitchen. "I made gator gumbo, with blue crab sandwiches, my famous macaroni and cheese for Kienan and Ham and Swiss cheese sandwiches on sourdough bread."

"Sounds delicious," Lacey smiled softly. "Grand *mere* Catherine, can we eat after, we tell you why we are here," she hesitated. "And after you've done a card reading for us?"

With a puzzled expression, Grand *mere* Catherine said. "A reading? You've come to me for a reading? Why?"

Kienan and Lacey glanced between each other. They had agreed before their visit not to say too much about what they knew about her brother, Nicholas. They had decided it was just best to tell Grand *mere* Catherine, that they were concerned for Nicholas' safety.

Finally, Kienan spoke and broke the ice. "Lacey and I are worried about Nicholas. We wanted a reading done to see what we should do to protect him."

Grand *mere* Catherine froze at his words an turned and stared between Kienan and Lacey. "This sounds serious. Sit down at the table. I'll get my cards."

A few minutes later, Kienan and Lacey watched, fascinated as Grand *mere* Catherine spread her cards on the kitchen table and concentrated.

A small pot of incense burned in the center of the table.

"The stars in the cosmos are aligned and masterful," Grand *mere* Catherine declared out loud to no one in particular. As her soft gray eyes smiled lovingly back at her granddaughter.

Time ticked by slowly until finally Grand *mere* Catherine said again. "The stars decree and so it will be," she studied the cards and moved them around. "All ever knowing light bring to your surface the truth, about my grandson Nicholas, make the future clear that we may read it."

Kienan glance at Lacey and made a face as she wiggled her nose and shook her head at him, mouthing the words. *"Behave!"*

"The temple of the Zodiac, bring to the surface the truth about my grandson, Nicholas, make the future clear that we may read it," she said moving the ornate bright colored cards around the table she began stacking various picture cards together.

Kienan watched her attentively and noticed several strange cards. One was a Sun card, another was a Lovers card, and Kienan knew both of their meaning. Then she laid down a card with a rope on it. He reached to pick it up. "Is that a hang-man's noose? Is that a bad sign? Should I fear the cards?"

"Don't take the cards out of order, Kienan," Grand *mere* Catherine scolded. "And no, the hang-man's noose in most traditional Tarot card decks is meant to represent self-sacrifice more so than it does corporal punishment or death," attentively she adjusted the cards and said. "Do not be afraid of the Tarot cards, Kienan. Someone once said that the tarot cards are only cards that tell a story of life. Just like in any storybook of life, it shows us all of life's greatest human accomplishments, but it also shows us human's ugliest side because it can show us, all the bad, we are each capable of."

"So, I take it that the Lovers card mean what it says," Kienan inquired. "That two people are in love?"

Grand *mere* Catherine's soft gray eyes looked up sternly. "Don't you see that the *Lovers* are in reverse? Upside down?"

Kienan tilted his head. "Upside down? Really? That's not good, I take it?"

"No! It's not good," Grand *mere* Catherine declared.

At the sound of her words Lacey's eyes locked with Kienan's. They stared between each other for several seconds, Lacey was thinking about the conversation she'd had with her husband about Nicholas and Maëlle. She could tell Kienan was thinking the same thing.

Lacey swallowed hard and felt a knot twist in her stomach. "Grand *mere* Catherine, I thought the Lovers represented balance and finding your kindred spirit in your soul mate?"

"Yes, in a proper placement of the card that is what it means," she said. "However, you see the Lovers are in reverse, this isn't good. In fact, it means the lovers are in disharmony, imbalance, misalignment in their values to one another. But let us take a look at the cards that come next."

Kienan and Lacey watched spellbound as Grand *mere* Catherine laid down the next card. It was the Queen of Wands.

"The Queen of Wands is represented by the crow. It signifies paying attention to how you live your life," she said as she pulled out the next card and laid it beside it.

"The serpent!"

Lacey gasped out loudly. "Oh, Christ!"

Kienan reached over and clasped his wife's hand.

Grand *mere* Catherine glanced up at her. "Remember Lacey, in many cultures, the serpent is strongly tied to not just death, but the cycle of life, and rebirth," she paused and closed her eyes.

Out of nowhere a cold breeze whipped up and seized the room. Instantly a strange floral scent filled the air.

"Kienan did you feel that?" Lacey whispered.

"I felt something like a bolt of ice run across the back of my neck," he whispered back.

"That's what I felt too," Lacey whispered.

All at once, Grand *mere* Catherine took several deep breaths before she exhaled and said. "Something is not right here," she opened her eyes. "I'm worried, I have an overwhelming feeling that there is great danger all around."

The air in the room was tense as the three of them glanced between each other.

Lacey broke the silence. "Do you think we should stop?"

"No, we should continue," Grand *mere* Catherine declared. "Right, Kienan? Do you agree?"

"Agreed, we have to see where this goes," Kienan replied.

Grand *mere* Catherine nodded and then spoke. "All ever knowing light bring to your surface the truth, about my grandson Nicholas, make the future clear that we may read it," she pulled the next card.

"It's the Owl," she said and then flipped it over there was the Ten of Swords."

Kienan leaned in close. "Ten swords are good right? Like some kind of protection?"

"I heard that the Owl means choice to be reborn," Lacey added.

Grand *mere* Catherine's gray eyes looked between them before she focused her gaze and said softly, "It is true the Owl gives you a choice to be reborn within your physical body or to return home beyond the veil. Either way, things cannot stay the same. Some say the Owl helps people see an alternative way of life. But in the Ten of Swords Tarot Card the Owl Spirit signifies endings, it is the announcer of Death! And sometimes death just means death."

Lacey and Kienan gasped out loud and shuddered and stared between them as the room went deathly quiet.

Finally Lacey spoke. "Grand mere Catherine didn't you tell me once that — William Shakespeare said. "It is not in the stars to hold our destiny but in ourselves."

"I am sure I have said many things over the years but that's not a concern to me right now, Lacey," Grand mere Catherine focused her stern gaze on the two of them.

"Kienan and Lacey tell me the truth!" Grand *mere* Catherine hoarsely whispered out.

"You tell me you are worried for my grandson, yet you do not tell me why and now I have pulled the death card," she said as something unreadable flashed across her face.

Grand mere Catherine took a deep breath and said. "You know Lacey I do remember saying that William Shakespeare quote and right now I believe it fits this circumstance perfectly. If we each hold our destiny within ourselves— Then this doesn't look good." She cleared her throat"Someone or something is going to die, I hope I'm wrong, but ... But...," she paused and took a deep breath and looked between them.

"The owl card here signifies death! And simply put right here and right now, it only means just that. Someone is going to die!"

42

Chapter 35

China Town, San Francisco, CA...

From the balcony of the five-star hotel restaurant he'd just had dinner, Nicholas had a great view of China town. It had been a bright sunny chilly day when he had arrived hours earlier. Now the temperature had dropped even more. He was glad he had dressed conservatively and warmly for dinner at the fancy San Francisco Hotel. He wore a black cashmere V-neck sweater, under his houndstooth blazer and black jeans. He was glad he'd paired them up with his Black Converse All-Stars suede sneakers, because he'd known he'd have to do a lot of walking.

His eyes looked out on the two major streets of Chinatown, Grant and Stockton Avenue.

His eyes searched down Grant Avenue; he was looking for Ross Alley. He knew Ross Alley was one block west of Grant Avenue, finally he spotted the street sign and gauged how far it was. He checked his watch it was a few minutes after eleven o'clock p.m. It was just about the right time of nigh for the bad girls to take to the streets and go walking. He wanted to make the most out of that time, so he started walking in the direction of Ross Alley. He was on a mission to find the woman called *Shop Girl*.

As Nicholas walked down Ross Alley, he felt like he was discovering the diamond hidden away in Chinatown, it was a gem of a fun street with the sights and smells all working to grab his attention. The place felt like some secret society hidden right in front of you.

Nicholas soon found the fortune cookie factory located right next door to a barbershop. He walked over and open the door. He stood at the threshold and stared all around him. A nice little old lady beckoned for Nicholas to walk further in. He did as he was told.

"Are you Shop Girl?" Nicholas asked.

"How do you do sir," the old woman said in broken English with a heavy Chinese accent. "You want to buy fortune cookies?"

"No, I'm looking for Shop Girl?"

The little old woman wasn't pushy. "You look around," she said walking over holding a bag. "Put your hand in here?"

Nicholas looked down at the bag she thrust in front of him. It was filled with fortune cookies. He took one.

"Cash only, please." The old woman stated.

"You don't understand, I'm looking for Shop Girl," Nicholas said speaking slower than he had at first trying to get her to understand.

"I understand," the old woman declared. "Shop Girl is on her way. Like I said cash for cookies, please."

No sooner had she said this then a strikingly beautiful

young woman opened a hidden door and beckoned for Nicholas to follow her through the door.

Curious, Nicholas did as he was told and walked behind the woman through a narrow passageway that looked really old and made him think of a time tunnel. They walked up to a door that seemed to open on its own, as the beautiful woman sashayed in and Nicholas followed.

The room they entered looked like it was the size of a penthouse suite complete with a lush décor that was totally far East. To look at the room they'd entered it was hard to believe it was there. It looked like something out of a harem scene in a movie of the far East, complete with an abundance of Oriental rugs, silk pillows Chinese style motifs from Asian to Zen complete with beautiful girls in every size imaginable.

"You pick girl and she will show you to your room."

Nicholas nervously smiled and said. "But I wanted to talk to the woman named Shop Girl."

"Shop Girl not here right now. You pick girl and wait for Shop Girl to return."

At just that moment a young woman walked up to him. "Hey mister, lips, hips, or fingertips."

Nicholas mind flashed back at the sound of the young woman's voice. He'd heard that voice before, he took a good look at the young girl. She wasn't as young as he thought, but her face looked familiar.

The woman smiled and Nicholas could have sworn she winked at him. But it was her voice he thought and then recognition hit him.

"You want to follow me sir," the young woman asked.

Nicholas nodded. "Yes... Yes, I'll follow you."

Arm in Arm Nicholas and the young woman walked until they reached her room. He stood there silently and watched as she closed the door and closed the distance between them.

"You remember me, mister? Because I remember you. You're a friend what a guy named Quinn; you came to a house party in the Oakland hills a long time ago to pick him up."

"Of, course, you'll the girl... I mean young woman who met me at the door," Nicholas replied.

"And I serviced you well, did I not, Mr. ... Mr. Nicholas, right?"

Nicholas nodded. "You've got a good memory, you remember my name."

"Why you looking for Shop Girl?"

Nicholas rubbed his hands through his hair. "I'm hoping to get some information from her about a party she sent some young ladies too."

"You paying for information?" She asked in broken English.

"Why?" Nicholas asked.

"Because maybe I can help you, and make me a few extra dollars too," the young woman eagerly replied.

Nicholas thought on what she said for a few moments and figured what did he have to lose when he finally spoke and said. "I'm looking for Shop Girl to see if she remembers sending any young girls to a house party in Japan town in San Jose. The house was owned by an old Japanese actor named Jack Nakahara."

"Jack Nakahara," the young woman repeated his name. "You're lucky, I know about his parties; He's known for giving some big-time poker games for some very rich men."

"You do, good," Nicholas said. "I'm trying to talk to some of the young women attending those parties. I'm even willing to pay money for that information."

"You have excellent luck Nicholas; I was there," she shrugged. "I mean I've been to several of his parties., and I'd be willing to tell you anything you want to know if..."

"The price is right," Nicholas replied finishing her sentence.

"You got it! My information will be worth your while. Go ahead ask me what you want to know," she declared.

Nicholas reached into his jacket pocket and pulled out a photograph. "Did you see this man at those party?"

"This guy is normally always at his parties. But not with that nose and hair color. I think he had a nose job. But it's the same man. I think his name is Dan, Daniel or something. He plays poker there regularly."

"That was too easy," Nicholas replied. "You wouldn't by chance know anything else about this guy, do you?"

"There's a big illegal poker party that some guys throw over on Potrero Hill, that guy hires girls for his parties too. I think he plays there too," she hesitated. "You know I just remember the guy's name. It's Dante. He's a bad guy. I don't think you want to mess with him."

Nicholas froze at the sound of her words. "Why? Why would you say that?"

"Because I had a friend... Let's just say an associate, who used to work the streets over in Oakland Chinatown, she doesn't anymore. She hooked up with Dante thinking he was going to give her a good life. She hasn't been seen since she started hanging out with Dante. They say he used to beat her."

"Damn!" Nicholas muttered. Now he'd heard that same story from two different people. It had to be true. She'd given him some valuable information, but he needed an address to go on for the house in Potrero Hill. A thought occurred to him and then he reached into his pocket for his money. He pulled out four hundred-dollar bills and thrust them at the young woman.

"Will this do?"

"Sure," she said, taking the money.

Nicholas held up two more hundred-dollar bills. "I've got extra if you can tell me two more things. First, do you know the address of the house on Potrero Hill? And second do you have the name of anyone who attends the poker party over on Potrero Hill?"

"I don't know the house number but it's right on the corner of Arkansas street across from the rec center. It's a big Victorian house, you can't miss it," she paused. "One of the guys who attends the poker game plays in a band over at the Tonga room, at the Fairmont Hotel the one on Nob Hill."

"Got a name?"

"City Sax. He plays the saxophone. He's a real popular guy."

Nicholas went to hand the girl the money and then paused. He had forgotten to ask one more question. "Oh, by the way. You wouldn't by chance remember the name of the girl… I mean your friend who took up with Dante Channing, would you?"

The girl's eyes swept up to meet him. "Yes, I do remember my friend's name. Her name is Molly Chen."

"Molly Chen," Nicholas repeated back to her as he handed her the three bills turned and headed for the door.

"Mister Nicholas!"

Nicholas stopped abruptly and turned a round. "If you find my friend Molly, tell her to come and see me, I've been worried about her."

Nicholas' eyes captured the young woman's eyes and before he knew it. He nodded and said. "If I find her, I will tell her what you said," he assured her before turning and walking out the door and closing it behind him.

43

Chapter 36

Who Watches The Watcher...

Nicholas walked out the side door of the Fortune Cookie factory and back down Ross Alley the way he came. He was still stunned by the name of the girl's friend.

The busy bustling street was filled with sights, sounds, and smells that assured him he was still deep in the heart of San Francisco, China Town.

He just walked a few buildings down from the Fortune Cookie factory when an old woman called out to him and said. "Hey Mister! Hey Mister! You are very close to finding what you seek! The key is near," she waved her hand, summoning him to come over. "You are on the right path. I know what your future has in store for you!"

Dazed and confused Nicholas couldn't believe what he just heard. "Excuse me! What did you just say?"

"You are on the right path! The key is near," The old woman repeated. "Come! Come into my shop and I will tell you more!" The old woman shouted.

Nicholas stood there staring at the old woman, who was wearing the traditional Chinese form fitting long tunic with pants in a black color with red circle designs all over it. It seemed like he stood there a lifetime he thought before he slowly walked toward her and stepped across the threshold while she held the door for him.

The room he stepped into looked like something from a time far away in ancient China. It resembled an Oriental tent, in the deepest darkest color of red he had ever seen. Gold tassels hung from the ceiling along with hanging plants, gold fans ornate fans hanging on the walls and ceilings. Flowing red and gold color drapes were hanging all around. With numerous comfortable pillows thrown around the room. Thick incense burned intensely throughout the air.

"Come sit here," she said, leading him over to a table with some chairs.

Nicholas eyes locked with a strange fringe of what looked like old Spanish coins hanging from a gold colored rope. He felt it was strange because it was the only thing in the room that wasn't Oriental.

"I see you are fascinated by my rope of charms," the old woman said. "Most of them, are Gypsy charms to ward off evil spirits. Some of them are Chinese charms; each of the Chinese charms, have Chinese character inscriptions on them to identify their meaning. I am only part Chinese the rest of me is pure Gypsy. I read the runes, and the crystal ball," she said without pausing. "Runes are an ancient form of divination that dates back to the druids. To me they are more accurate in foretelling good luck, good fortune, good health, success, etc., etc."

Nicholas got comfortable in his seat. "I'm afraid I'm not much of a believer, all the hocus pocus stuff can't be accurate."

"You know that the best psychics for centuries have drawn answers from the universe. They've used tea leaves, coffee grounds, crystals, Tarot cards, Angel cards, and even playing cards. All of these provide answers to life questions, and deeper insights into a person's true purpose."

"How much do you charge?"

"It is not about the money. We won't speak of that now; we must let the runes do their work first. There is something you should know. I could feel it as soon as I saw you," she declared.

The old woman threw out the stones and concentrated. Her eyes glassed over as she stared focused on the stones.

Curiously Nicholas watched her, and in an instant, he was reminded of his grandmother, Grand mere Catherine. He'd seen her go into a trance like state many times. Instantly, he regretted telling the old woman he didn't believe. He wondered if she could read mines.

"Yes... Yes...," Finally, the old woman spoke. "You had a happy childhood. You've always had it easy. But things changed you went away to a big house with bars on the windows. You were in prison."

Nicholas gasped. "Whoa! You saw that?"

"Don't be frightened dear, it's nothing to be ashamed of. I saw it hanging around you like a big cloud when I first saw you. I know you were innocent. You were framed. Now be quiet, I see something."

Nicholas nodded and sat in silence, he was in awe of her, how did she know he had been incarcerated, he wondered and then thought better of it when he remembered his grand-mother.

"Yes... Yes... I see it. I see it," the old woman blurted. "You are close to finding what you are looking for, the Sacred river will vomit up the key you have been looking for," her voice changed and sounded like it was from another world. "The key, the key look for the key."

"Key? You mean like a real key? And what's the Sacred river?" Puzzled Nicholas asked with a baffled tone in his voice.

"Shhhhh! I see more! I must caution you. You are coming to a crossroad. There will be danger! You will be tested. You will have to make a choice. A choice about what kind of man you would like to be. Look for the key! Look for the key!"

The old woman started trembling and her eyes shut tight. Her breathing quickened. "I can't breathe! I can't breathe! It's getting dark!"

Startled Nicholas blurted. "Miss... Miss are you alright?"

The old woman's body trembled as she spoke. "Four, Seven, One," she blurted. "Four, Seven, One," she blurted a second time speaking in a trance induced voice. "You must remember Four, Seven, One! You must remember four, seven, one!"

Nicholas started to pat her hand. He thought it would help her to wake up. "Are you alright?"

Finally the old woman exhaled. "Yes, I'm alright! I'm afraid a storm is coming to you! A dark cloud is all around you! You will need to seek the advice of she who *Watches the Watcher!*" She declared.

Puzzled he asked. "I'm sorry, who is *she who Watches the*

Watcher, and what does the numbers Four, Seven, One, mean?"

The old woman tilted her head and let her eyes focus on Nicholas, as she stared puzzled. She stared back at him intensely as if she was trying to make recognition, as she sat there rocking back and forth. It was obvious she had no understanding as to who he was or why he was there.

Silence hung all around them.

Nicholas was baffled from all that had happened as he sat there in silence. His mind was racing from the long day and what he'd just heard. He was tired and he wanted to go home. He watched the old woman until her body finally stopped trembling and rocking.

Finally, he spoke. "Ahh… Miss you just told me three numbers; do you remember? I don't know what they meant. And you said I should seek the advice of she who *Watches the Watcher,* do you remember any of that?"

The old woman shook her head. "Sorry, no."

Nicholas took a deep breath and realized he wasn't going to get any answers. He reached into his pocket and pulled out his money and peeled off two-hundred-dollar bill. "Here something for your trouble," he said rising and heading for the door.

Once outside, Nicholas looked back at the shop. He was certain the old woman had been crazy. Still, he wondered how she knew about his being in prison and then shook the thought from his mind and headed for the parking lot where he'd left his car. He was tired and he wanted to go home.

For a brief moment he thought of Maëlle. He wondered what she was doing. After the rude way he'd been treating her he didn't think she'd pick up if he called, he thought as he got into his car.

Minutes later Nicholas exit the parking lot and took Bryant Street northbound toward the US-101. The southbound exit for San Jose, came into view and he quickly took it heading home. Soon the pagoda-titled roofs of San Francisco Chinatown were a distant memory.

44

Chapter 37

Nicholas...

At eight o'clock the next morning Nicholas woke up to the sound of what he thought was his cell phone ringing. "Hello," he mumbled into the phone before he realized the ringing was coming from the alarm clock he had set before going to sleep. Immediately he turned it off and reached for the TV remote and turned it on as he rose to get out of bed.

Yawning and sighing, Nicholas walked to his bathroom and quickly took a shower. The warm spray of the shower nozzle helped him to clear his thoughts. He reflected about meeting the old fortune teller he'd seen the day before. The woman had to be as looney as a cartoon he thought, as he dried himself off then reached for the lotion bottle. Since being released from prison he'd come to appreciate little things like rubbing lotion all over your body. He laughed thinking how if his old friends in prison could see him now. He reached for his deodorant and rubbed it on, then leaving his bathroom he walked back into the bedroom before walking to his dresser and opening the top drawer and grabbing his underwear, before heading for the closet and looking for some jeans, a shirt and his favorite All-Stars converse sneakers.

Suddenly a soft knock sounded on his bedroom door.

"Nicholas, you dressed?" Grand mere Catherine called. "I heard your shower going."

Nicholas exhaled. He'd been avoiding his grandmother, mother, heck pretty much everyone in his family for days. He knew he had to face them sooner or later.

"Yes, Grand mere Catherine, I'm dressed. The door is unlocked."

"How's my favorite Grandson this morning," Grand mere Catherine said, entering his room. "I got some fresh coffee made and I made you a couple of sausage biscuits, they are waiting back in the kitchen."

"Only a couple, I can eat more than two sausage biscuits, Grand mere Catherine, I'll head down to the kitchen in a few minutes, I wanted to listen to the news before I came down."

"Well, don't mind me I just stopped in to see if your dirty clothes hamper is full."

"You don't have to do my laundry," Nicholas said.

"I know I don't but it's no bother, that's why I got you one of those rubber-maid hampers with the wheels on it. I just roll it down to the laundry room. It gives me something to do. Besides I thought you like my doing your laundry?"

"Of, course my lazy behind does," Nicholas joked. "Tell you what as soon as the news go off, I'll wheel my dirty clothes hamper down to you. That'll free you up to go back to the kitchen and make me at least three more sausage biscuits."

"Five sausage biscuits! Boy that's too many carbs! Nicholas you ought to be ashamed."

"Ah! Grand mere Catherine please!"

"Boy, you lucky I'm a soft-hearted grandmother," she said throwing up her hands in defeat and walking out the door.

Nicholas watched as she closed the door behind her and ran his hands down his shirt making sure he'd closed all the buttons as he stepped out of the closet and heard the television. He reached for the remote and turned the television volume up.

The television sounded loudly as it penetrated the air.

"This is Action News in Silicon Valley, here's the latest news at the top of the hour, the body of Molly Chen, a young prostitute known for working the streets of Oakland California historic China Town was pulled from the Sacramento river where it flows into the Sacred River in South Sacramento County. Her body was found by fishermen late yesterday afternoon."

Instantly Nicholas froze at the words he just heard on the television as his mind raced thinking back to what the old woman had said. He turned the volume up on the television and then he heard the announcer say. "Police are looking for possible suspect Dante Channing in the connection of Molly Chen's murder. Police learned Molly had been living with Dante Channing, before she disappeared. Apparently, Molly's family and friends had filed a missing person on her months ago... Molly's body will be taken to Sacramento County Coroner's office for an autopsy."

Nicholas mind was working a mile a minute as he thought back to the old fortune teller prediction. She had been right;

the Sacred river vomit up the girl. Then he closed his eyes remembering what else the fortune teller had said. He remembered she said to look for a key and the numbers, four seven and one. The key had to be on the girl's body, he thought. He rubbed his chin as he tried to think of how he could get inside the coroner's office to see her body.

"Damn!" Nicholas blurted out loud. "I need to talk to Thomas," he said to himself. "Yeah, Thomas is a private investigator he should be able to get me into the Sacramento Coroner's office."

Quickly. Nicholas looked for his cell phone. He found it beside the bed where he'd left it and quickly dialed Thomas' number.

The phone rang.

"Hello, Thomas, this is Nicholas."

"Hi there Nicholas," Thomas replied. "You sound excited."

"Yeah, I am. I need to ask you a favor," Nicholas said. "You see I went to see this..." Nicholas stopped abruptly thinking it wouldn't be a good idea to tell Thomas what an old fortune teller had said. He cleared his throat and said. "I mean, I think I found some helpful information, but I need your help."

"Oh, I see," Thomas replied. "What kind of favor?"

"Can you get me into the Sacramento County Coroner's office?" Nicholas asked.

"Yes, sure, that can be arranged. Do you want to tell me why you need to go to the Sacramento County Coroner's office?"

Nicholas was silent for a moment. "I'll tell you this Thomas, if I find anything, I think will help you find Dante Channing I'll tell you the whole story, deal?"

"No Deal!" Thomas declared. "I've got to have more to go on."

Nicholas was silent for a moment. He wasn't sure he could trust Thomas with the information he'd received from a fortune teller. Finally, he thought better and sighed heavily. "Well, alright, but you're not going to believe this. You see I've discovered some good information that there is a body in that morgue that I need to take a look at."

"You mean the body of the girl they pulled out of the Sacred river? The one who was dating Dante Channing before her disappearance?"

"Yes, that's the one."

"Look Nicholas, I don't think that's such a good idea. I mean. The proper authorities will be looking into this and with your having once been connected with Dante Channing, I don't think it's a good idea."

"Yeah, well I do, Thomas," Nicholas boldly declared. "This girl's body may have some clues as to where Dante Channing is hiding! Look, I have to get in there and see that body!"

Thomas took a deep breath. He could tell Nicholas was serious even though he didn't think it was a good idea, at least if he was with Nicholas, he could be in a position to monitor his every move and make sure he didn't get into any trouble.

Finally, Thomas spoke. "Okay you have a deal. But Nicholas you have to let me in on what it is you think you might find on the dead girl. And I mean everything, deal?

"Deal!" Nicholas declared. "How soon can we go to Sacramento County Coroner's office?" Nicholas asked.

"Well, are you in San Jose?"

"Yes," Nicholas answered.

Thomas wanted to make sure he put into place some controls on Nicholas without his knowing. "I'm in San Francisco today, but I could meet you at the Old Nut Tree Plaza in Vacaville. There's a Starbucks there we could leave one of our cars and drive into Sacramento County together."

"Great, that sounds like a plan. What time should I meet you there?

"Let's shoot for 11:00 a.m., that way we can catch some lunch before we head up there. I don't think you'll have an appetite after," Thomas replied.

"Excellent, I'll see you then," Nicholas declared. "Thanks, Thomas."

"You are welcome, Nicholas, goodbye," Thomas declared hanging up the phone.

Nicholas went into the bathroom and grabbed his rolling dirty clothes hamper with a smile on his face as he headed for the kitchen.

***

At one o'clock p.m. that afternoon Nicholas watched the scenery flash by on highway I-80, as he sat in the passenger side of Thomas' jeep as they headed toward Sacramento. He watched as Thomas took the US-50-E.

"We're almost there Nicholas," Thomas said taking the Broadway exit at 59th street and turning into the parking lot.

The county morgue was located in the basement of the County Government Hall of Justice building on Broadway of 59th street in Sacramento.

A few minutes later, Nicholas shook hands with Fred Longhorn, after Thomas introduced him, as they walked the long corridor leading to where they kept the bodies.

"I assigned Al Johnson to do the report on the body of the girl," Fred stated. "The police ran a thorough background her prints were ran through the State Department of Correction and the California DMV. Her prints were matched to several arrest for prostitution in Oakland, California when she was underage. The funny thing after she turned eighteen there'd been no new arrest. We figured she must have become a high-priced call girl. The girls' full name on her birth certificate is Molly Tameka Chen-Jones; she was half-Chinese and African American. It appears, Jones is her biological father's name, his name was on her birth certificate. But all of her adult identification records, she dropped the last name "Jones.""

"Does she have any relatives?" Thomas asked.

Fred nodded. "Yes, her mother lives in East Palo Alto. She is planning on claiming the body when it's released and her biological father, is a Mr. Leroy Jones, he lives in Oakland."

"Burial?" Thomas inquired.

"No, cremation, Fred stated.

Fred opened the door and held it. "Well, fella's welcome to the county morgue," he said walking over to a large box containing latex gloves. He pulled on a pair of gloves and then held out a pair for Thomas and Nicholas.

The first thing Nicholas noticed when he entered the room was the coldness of the room. The next thing he noticed was there was a body with a sheet draped over it laying on a table. He wondered if it was Molly Chen. He didn't have long to wonder when he watched Fred walk over to the table.

"Well, here she is," Fred said, as he pulled off the drape.

Molly Chen's body laid uncovered on the table. She'd been cut entirely opened and her body organs had been removed.

You could see where the incisions had been made on her body and where she had been sewn up.

In a flash, Nicholas face contorted into shock and disbelief at the gruesomeness he saw lying there. He gave a horrifying glance at Fred.

"It's not a pretty sight, is it son," Fred said looking at the expression that appeared on Nicholas' face. Go ahead son, check the body over.

Nicholas didn't think he could move his legs. He felt frozen to the spot.

Lucky for him Thomas made the first move, inspecting her body.

Nicholas swallowed hard, in a fierce determination he willed his body to move forward and inspect her body. Finally, he took a step forward, walked over and stood next to Thomas.

Silently Thomas and Nicholas looked over her body. They noticed she had several fresh bruises and an old scar that look like she had been cut with a knife.

Nicholas looked her over. He was looking for tattoos. She was lying on her back and the part of her body that was exposed didn't show any tattoos.

Nicholas lifted each of her arms and inspected them for tattoos. He thought back to what the old fortune teller had said about the numbers, but he didn't find any. Carefully he inspected the front of her body. He was looking for numbers. Silently and thoroughly he searched.

"What were Al's findings," Thomas inquired.

Fred's hands reached out and pointed. "She had a blow to her head, that's what killed her. But she was strangled first.

See the bruise marks on her neck? In addition, Al believe she was killed at a different location and her body was dumped in the Sacred river."

"That's interesting. How long do you think her body had been in the river," Thomas asked?"

"A few days, possibly a week at the most," Fred replied.

"I see," Thomas declared. "And what was her cause of death?"

Fred rubbed his chin. "Well, now based on the visible injuries, even though she'd been strangled, it didn't kill her. We believe she may have been beaten to death."

"Doesn't look like she had any tattoos or birthmarks," Nicholas said.

"Now that you mention it, she did have a tattoo," Fred replied. "You know one of those tramp stamps girls like to tattoo, on their backs, in the middle of their buttocks."

Nicholas tried not to look excited. "Really, most women want flower tattoos. What is it a red rose, or something?"

"Yes and no," Fred said shaking his head. "The tattoo is some kind of Asian symbol, with a red rose wrapped around it. See for yourself."

Nicholas and Thomas watched as Fred turned over her body. There was an Asian symbol, right where he said. It read ??.

"Yes, that's Chinese alphabet alright," Thomas declared. "I've lived in San Francisco and eaten in China town long enough to know what the alphabet looks like."

"What does it mean?" Nicholas asked, but didn't want to say he could read Chinese. He knew what the letters meant. They read; she was Dante's woman.

"Al looked it up in the Chinese simplified translator," Fred said. "He found it's a name, Dàn ding, in English we call the name or person Dante. We figured it's the name of a boyfriend or lover."

Thomas registered understanding as his eyes sought Nicholas". They stared back at each other for several seconds.

Slowly Nicholas shook his head confirming silently with his eyes that the dead woman had been Dante Channing's girlfriend.

Thomas swallowed hard now he knew why Nicholas wanted to see the body. He cleared his throat. "Fred where are her belongings and personal effects."

"They are over there," Fred said, walking over to a table. I don't think you will be interested in what's in the other bags."

"Why?"

"Oh, they just contain her organs and stuff," Fred said looking for the bag.

Thomas continued looking over the body, and Nicholas watched him as he did.

"Hump! That's funny," Fred finally declared. "The bag with her personal belongings isn't here."

A telephone on the wall rung out.

"Excuse me," Fred said walking over and answering the phone. "Hello, Sacramento Corner's office. Al? Yes, I forgot about the meeting. I was just about to call you. Do you have any idea where the bag with the belongings for Molly Chen is?"

Seconds later Fred said. "You got it? Great I'll be right over to get it."

Fred got off the phone and walked back over. "Hey

Thomas, good news and bad news. I located the bag with Molly Chen's belongings. If you want to see what's in it, you have to come with me, now, I can take you to it. Bad news, I can't bring it back to you because I'm supposed to be in a meeting."

"No, problem, Fred. I can go with you and check through it.'

Thomas turned and glanced at Nicholas will you be alright if I leave you alone for a minute or two?"

Nicholas nodded. "Sure," he replied watching the two men make their exit.

Nicholas waited until the door closed and hurried over to the bags Fred had said contained her organs. He quickly looked through them. There were several bags each holding a different part of her body organs and then he saw it. It was a bag marked "stomach contents." Slowly he lifted the bag and prepared to open it and then he saw it. A clear bag holding a key. The small bag had been taped to the bigger bag holding her stomach. On the small bag was written the words "key found in Molly Tameka Chen's stomach."

The room felt surreal. Nicholas could see the old fortune teller. He thought he was looking through a glass mirror. He heard the old fortune teller's voice as it said. "The Sacred river will vomit up the key you have been looking for. Look for the key!"

Instantly Nicholas looked into his hand. He was holding the key from the bag. He flipped it over in his hand. He was looking for the numbers she had told him. The key had been filed smooth on both sides, removing any markings it might have had.

Slowly Nicholas placed the key back in the bag as he looked around. Then he pushed the clear bag into his pants pocket and walked back through the doors he'd came in, earlier with Thomas and Fred. He stood there waiting for Thomas to return and thought of what he would tell him, for one thing he was sure he would not tell him about the key. He didn't have long to wait.

"Nicholas, what are you doing standing out in the hall-way," Thomas asked as he drew near.

"Ah, you know," Nicholas shrugged. "Being around dead bodies like that gives me the creeps."

Thomas grinned. "I know what you mean. Come on let's head to my car."

The two men walked side by side as they made their way back the way they'd came.

"So, tell me, Thomas did you find anything interesting," he paused. "In Molly's belongings, I mean."

Thomas shook his head. "No, she was wearing the standard, expensive slut for hire uniform. A black dress too short to be a dress, a pair of thigh high black leather boots with a three-inch heel, and an expensive short leather jacket with a real fur collar and cuffs. I'm surprised the PETA people weren't looking for her," he shook his head. "Oh yeah, did I mention she wasn't wearing any underwear?"

Nicholas rubbed his brow. "Interesting. Her whole ensemble sounds expensive."

"Yes, it was. Our girl Molly Tameka Chen wasn't the kind of call girl who walked the streets. She was being well kept by someone with some big money," Thomas declared. "I forgot to mention, the reason why Al didn't leave her possession bag down in the morgue. Is because she had been wearing an eighteen-karat gold, three karat diamond Tiffany bracelets with a matching necklace, along with a pair of diamond stud earrings, a karat each. Which tells me whoever killed her wasn't killing her to rob her. Because they left all of her jewelry on her," he said as he opened his car door and got in.

Nicholas heard Thomas releasing the lock on his car door, for the passenger side. He could feel the plastic bag with the key in it, press into his skin as he slowly got into the car.

His thoughts raced as he thought about the brutal way Dante had killed Molly Chen. No one had to tell him Dante had done it. Somewhere deep inside himself he just knew.

For some strange reason he felt sad for Molly Chen, she didn't deserve to lose her life. He thought back to the girl he'd met at that party years ago and how she'd told him Molly had been her friend. For some reason it made him think of his sister Lacey. If any man had done Lacey like that, he would have killed him with his bare hands. All at once Nicholas looked at his hands.

"Are you alright Nicholas?" Thomas asked.

Nicholas let out a pained sigh. "Yeah, I'm alright," he exhaled and took a deep breath before shaking his head. "You know Thomas seeing Molly Chen laying in that morgue dead, did something to me."

Nicholas stared blankly out the window for what seemed like a long time before he finally spoke and said. "Thomas, I promised you I'd tell you what I knew about Molly Chen. The fact is, I don't know any more than you do. I was hoping Molly Chen, could point me in the direction of where to find Dante Channing," his voice was low as he let out a sigh.

"But with her being dead. I realize how powerless I am in the scheme of things; you know what I'm talking about Thomas?" He asked but didn't wait for a response. "Back there in the morgue I felt terrified beyond belief looking at her dead body. In the grand scheme of things, we are all truly powerless in the face of death. Just look at Molly, in the end there was nothing she could do, to save herself."

Thomas cleared his throat. "You know you're experiencing trauma right now, don't you Nicholas?"

"Maybe," he hesitated. "I guess so," he said with a ring of sadness in his voice. "All I know is you're my last hope."

Thomas heard the hopelessness in Nicholas' voice and he didn't respond. He knew Nicholas had been effective by what he'd seen back at the morgue. Finally, Thomas spoke. "Nicholas just like you thought you were staring death in the face back there in the morgue. The truth is we might be staring finding Dante right in the face and we just don't know it yet. Let's give it a few days and see what happens."

Nicholas stared out the window and pondered as he thought about the key in his pants pocket. He knew it was going to be a quit ride back to his car. His brain was running around in circles flashing with photos of the dead girl Molly, his sister Lacey and his girl Maëlle.

Nicholas knew that Maëlle had stuck by him, she'd been loyal. For some reason that made her special to him, no matter how bad he'd been treating her. He needed to see Maëlle and he needed to see her badly.

***

An hour later Nicholas got in his car and watched as

Thomas drove his jeep out of distance before he quickly dialed the number.

Maëlle's phone rang. She checked caller ID; it was Nicholas. She looked at the clock it was almost four in the afternoon. The TV was loud, so she found the remote and turned it down, before she picked up her phone. "Hello?"

"Hey, it's me, Nicholas, what are you doing?"

"None of your damn business mister I haven't heard from you, in like forever."

"Look, Maëlle, I'm sorry, I know I've been a jerk! I just been going through a lot of stuff. But I really miss that cute funny face of yours and your sunny disposition."

Maëlle heard the sadness in his voice. She knew something was wrong. "What happened Nicholas? What's going on?"

He took a deep breath and then let the story roll out. "I saw a dead body at the morgue today. It was a girl who used to date Dante Channing, in fact, she used to live with him," his voice shook. "I... I... I think Dante killed her, Maëlle! It was awful seeing her lying on that morgue slab dead."

Maëlle didn't speak she was thinking too hard. She'd been angry with Nicholas he'd been ignoring her calls. But hearing the sadness in his voice melted her heart. She couldn't stay mad at him.

"Maëlle? Maëlle? Are you still there?"

"Yes, Nicholas, I'm still here. How did you get to see the body?"

"Thomas took me."

"So, did Thomas find Dante?" Maëlle asked.

"No, not yet. But he's still looking for him"

"Nicholas where are you now? Are you alright? Are you safe?"

"I'm met Thomas in Vacaville. He drove me to see the body. He brought me back to my car and I'm getting on the freeway, right now, heading for San Jose, I was hoping you would let me come by and spend the night."

Maëlle exhaled. "Of course, baby. I don't have a thing to eat in the house, but it'll take you at least a couple hours or more to get back to San Jose with all that rush hour traffic you're going to run into. That will give me time to run to the store and buy some groceries and fix us something to eat."

"That sounds like a plan," Nicholas replied. "That's my Maëlle girl, I'll see you soon, goodbye."

Maëlle softly smile hearing Nicholas call her Maëlle girl warmed her heart. He used to call her that all the time when they were younger.

***

It was just past seven thirty, that evening when Nicholas pulled his car in front of Maëlle's townhouse and walked to her front door and knocked.

"Who's there?" Maëlle called.

"It's me, Nicholas."

Maëlle opened the door with a big smile on her face and jumped into Nicholas' arms.

"Damn you smell good!" Nicholas exclaimed, closing the door behind him, leaning over and kissing her. "But the aroma coming from the kitchen smells scrumptiously delicious! What are you cooking?"

"Just my take on Grand mere Catherine's Gator gumbo, only I use chicken, shrimp, and crab," she joked.

"Well it smells wonderful. How soon is dinner?"

"Dinner's in fifteen minutes, you've got time for a quick wash up in the bathroom while I get you an ice-cold Tsingtao."

"Did you get plenty of Tsingtao?"

"Nicholas, you know I did. I know what my man loves to drink. I got you a case and if that ain't enough, I figured after seeing that dead girl's body, you might want to take a ride on the Jack Daniels train."

Nicholas grinned wickedly. "You got Jack Daniels too?"

"Yes, baby. Mamma got your Jack Daniels too."

"You really do know your man," Nicholas arm circled around her waist. "Baby come close so your man can kiss those sweet tasty lips of yours."

Maëlle playfully giggled and purred, as Nicholas placed kisses down her neck. "Woooo Nicholas you need to stop that so we can eat first and work on getting drunk."

"Well, I'll let you go so I can go and freshen up," Nicholas said releasing her and heading for the bathroom.

***

An hour later, Nicholas poured himself a third straight Jack Daniels over ice and then made Maëlle a third glass of what she called a Jack Daniels cocktail. A mix of Jack Daniels, ginger ale, and lime juice over ice. "I'm a lucky man to have a woman whose Gator Gumbo tastes as good, no better than my Grandmother's," he replied handing her another drink. "Now, don't you ever tell Grand mere Catherine I said that."

Maëlle giggled. "Nicholas, I know that, I ain't stupid and I ain't crazy either. Only a totally insane person would tell your grandmother she can't make gator gumbo."

Nicholas laughed. "You forgot they'd have to be insane and ready to die and meet their maker."

Maëlle laughed. "You sho nuf right! Mmmm Nicholas, you make the best Jack Daniels ginger ale cocktail. This drink is delicious."

"Thank you little darling, are you drunk yet?"

"I'm working on it, this is my third one," Maëlle laughed in a hoarse sexy voice. "But I don't need to be drunk to give my man what he needs."

At the sound of Maëlle's sexy voice Nicholas felt a tidal wave build to an explosive level inside of him. "Damn I want you, Maëlle," Nicholas said kissing her. "But if you're not ready yet. I won't rush you."

"Sweet Daddy, I'm ready just pick up the tempo and let's do this thing. I don't know about you but I'm feeling me some Jack Daniels! And in a minute when I get your pants off, I'm going to be feeling me some you and your good cock! Good and hard!"

"Talk dirty to me baby!" Nicholas declared with a big grin on his face as he began helping Maëlle get his pants off and then started to do the same with her clothes.

Nicholas pulled her sweater over her head and then unloosen the clasp holding her bra and freeing the twins. Her breast perked at the stroke of his touch. He kissed her lips and then worked his way down to her nipples, devouring each one with his mouth.

"Oh, Nicholas," she moaned, looking at him with dreamy eyes. "That feels so good. Why am I so weak for you?"

Maëlle reached down her hand and squeezed his cock.

It was hard already. She moaned softly and purred. "Damn, Nicholas, feels like you're ready for Momma!"

"Not yet, I owe Momma her due," he said in a sexy hoarse voice as he moved down her body between her legs. He spread them wide as his tongue found what he was looking for and licked.

His tong was stroking her clit and Maëlle's body tremble with pleasure. "Oh, yes! Sweet Daddy!"

"Do you want more?" Nicholas teased.

"Yes, baby! Yes!" She yelled pulling his face harder against the aching throbbing sweet spot between her legs, as a shaft of intense pleasure pierced her body.

The next thing Maëlle knew Nicholas leaned her body down on the bed, as his hands grasped her hips and his hard cock found her slippery opening and he drove in.

"Oh, Sweet Jesus!" Maëlle moaned as Nicholas hooked her legs over his arms and thrust firmly.

"We're going for a fast ride!" Nicholas commanded.

"Sweet Nicholas, let's go for that ride, Sugar Daddy!" Maëlle moaned and purred out, as she moved rhythmically to his motion, softly moaning and purring every stroke he made until they both climaxed together, naked and sweating lying together overwhelmed by the intensity of what had just occurred, they fell asleep in each other's arms.

45

Chapter 38

The Visitor...

Thomas didn't know why he couldn't sleep that night. Normally after a long day of driving he fell asleep fast. For some reason he just couldn't quiet his thoughts.

There was no reason for him to keep lying in bed trying to force sleep to come, finally he got out of bed and walked back into his living room where he kept his liquor cabinet.

A thought occurred to him maybe he should play a round of solitaire, normally when he did, he found sleep with creep upon him. He took a deep breath and thought for a moment. He didn't really feel like playing cards. He reached for the Brandy bottle and poured himself a snifter of brandy and took a sip. It felt warm going down his throat.

He thought back to the day earlier at the morgue. Was there something he was missing he wondered. Molly Chen's body hadn't been long in the Sacred river. This meant that whoever killed her had done so recently. Before he knew it, he'd finished his brandy and headed back to bed.

A short time later, the liquor did the trick, he thought as he felt himself drifting off to sleep.

Soon bellowing white clouds surround him as he looked up at the sky and notice how clear and clean the blue sky looked above him. Instantly, he realized he was dreaming. The blue sky was the most vivid one he'd ever seen, he thought as it shined with ethereal brightness. The skies seemed like a movie screen as a sudden rush of memories flooded his mind, then the dream hit him hard. It was vivid and real. Instantly a man appeared in his dream right before him. He was dressed in a vintage old-fashioned dogtooth tweed blazer.

Thomas thought the old man said his name. Thomas... Thomas wake up. You must remember."

"Hmmm," Thomas mouthed out in a groggy muffled voice. "Who are you?"

"Never mind who I am. You remember Old St. Mary's Cathedral and the key."

Groggy Thomas tried to wake up. "Key? What key?"

"Remember Thomas, you found a key. Oh, for heaven sake. Just call Kienan Egan."

"Kienan Egan? How do you know him?" Thomas asked trying to force his eyes open. He just knew he couldn't be dreaming. The moment was surreal he thought as he stood there staring back at the ghost of a man standing beside his bed."

"What the H...!"

"I'm not from there Thomas, now just remember what I told you," the man said before he slowly disappeared.

Thomas reached over to the nightstand beside his bed and turned on the light and looked at the clock. It was three o'clock in the morning, "My mother was right, there is a bewitching hour," he said to himself and then turned off the light and went back to sleep.

46

Chapter 39

Father Perez Senior...

Early that morning Nicholas woke up with three thoughts on his mind, as he kissed a sleeping Maëlle and got out of bed.

First, he knew what the first thing he wanted to do was for that day, was. And second, he knew where it was, that he needed to go, in the third place he knew he'd better leave Maëlle a note telling her he was sorry for having to leave so early.

Nicholas knew that both the first two things had to do with Father Perez Senior, he thought as he quietly slipped out of the bedroom and made his way to the bathroom to take a shower.

An hour later, Nicholas pulled his car into the parking lot of the Church of the Good Shepherd. The old historic church was located in the East End Foothills of San Jose. It was a beautiful old church built in the old mission design with a beautiful fragrant garden surrounding it.

Nicholas sat in his car and called his favorite florist, Marlowe's in Milpitas. He quickly placed an order for three dozen red roses."Look, be sure you attach a card that says, *"These deep red roses cannot compare to the love I have for you in my soul, sign it Sweet Daddy, Nicholas."* You got that?"

"Yes, sir. I got that," the lady at the flower shop said. "Will that be all sir?"

"Oh, and add a box of chocolates?" Nicholas said.

"Sir, would you like that to be nuts and chews are all soft chocolates?"

"Make it nuts and chews, Maëlle hates soft chocolates. You got my credit card number, right? And can you make sure it gets there today?"

"Yes, Mr. La Cour," the florist said. "It'll be delivered before one o'clock. Will that be all?"

"Yes."

"Thank you, sir, Goodbye."

Nicholas hung up the phone and got out of his car and walked through the ancient double doors of the nave entrance heading into the sanctuary, main church.

He walked up to the candle altar and lit a candle and stood there for a moment with his eyes closed for several seconds.

Finally, Nicholas walked to the back of the church where the small closet-like rooms for confession stood. He didn't stop there but headed out the back door to the living area in the back across the garden, where he knew Father Perez Senior would be.

Father Perez Senior saw Nicholas marching across the garden as he got up from the chair he was sitting in on the front porch of his living area, to greet him.

Father Perez could tell from the look on his face, that Nicholas was deeply trouble.

"Nicholas! Nicholas! I am so glad to see you came to visit me," Father Perez Senior called out to him, as he welcomed him with open arms."

Like a lost child Nicholas walked into Father Perez Senior arms and did his best not to start crying.

"Sit down here, Nicholas," Father Perez said, patting him on the arm. "Even though I have a view of the back-parking lot on one side. I still think this is the most perfect spot, in the garden. Because it looks out over the garden, so that you can see all the flowers in bloom, and with the view of the parking lot you can be alerted on who's coming."

The old priest laughed.

"You always amaze me, Father Perez," Nicholas said. "You find humor in everything," Nicholas declared.

"One must I believe," Father Perez said. "Just as I believe one must find a peaceful place for clear thinking and I have found this to be a wonderful place for clear thinking."

Nicholas glanced around and sat down. He cleared his throat. "I see what you mean, you can see all around the garden from here. It's beautiful and tranquil with all the flowers blooming."

"I could start by saying what bothers you my son, unless of course you prefer to have a conversation in a private old stuffy confession box, today, would you?"

No, Father Perez, I do not want to sit in a confession box," Nicholas said. "This spot is calming just like you said."

"So, what is it you wish to talk to me about?" Father Perez Senior asked.

"I'm conflicted and confused right now Father," Nicholas replied. "When I got out of prison I had only one thing on my mind. Finding Dante and having my revenge!" He paused and glanced at Father Perez. "I think you already knew that about me Father."

"Yes, I suspected as much when I talked with you at your welcome home party, and I could see you were conflicted then, just as you are now, Father Perez said. "Have you had a change of heart?"

"I don't know if I'd call it a change of heart. But I have done some thinking. I don't know if you've seen the news lately, but there was a dead girl pulled out of the Sacred river, he exhaled. "Because I believed she had been dating Dante Channing before her death and I thought maybe if I went to see her body, I might find something that could lead me to him."

Father Perez nodded understanding and waved his hand encouraging Nicholas to continue.

Nicholas glanced around the garden for several seconds and then said. "So, I went to the morgue in Sacramento County, to see the body.'

"But!" Nicholas' started to open his mouth to talk and his voice choked. "I... I... I never seen a body cut up for an autopsy before. It was an awful sight," he gasped for breath.

Father Perez patted Nicholas hand. "Are you alright?"

"I'm fine Father. I just sometimes can't understand why God let's bad things happen to good people. Here was this girl who only wanted Dante to love her and what does he do to her? He killed her," He paused letting his words sink in. "Then I thought about me and Dante. There I was, working beside Dante day in and day out. Trusting Dante and all I ever wanted to do was be his friend and what did Dante do to me? He betrayed me and stabbed me in the back by framing me and sending me to prison. Then I ask myself where was God during all of this? Why, was God off hiding in some cloud somewhere? Where was his promises, to me?"

"So, is that what you believe, about God, Nicholas?" Father Perez asked.

Nicholas shrugged but didn't answer he just tilted his head and focused on Father Perez. "You know father, when I was little, you said we must always have faith in God. But how can I have faith in God when everywhere I look, I see nothing to have faith in?"

Father Perez shrugged. "Today Nicholas, I am only here to listen. Today is not a lesson my son, for you have been taught many lessons by God and by myself. If there is more you wish to tell me, talk on, my son."

"Did I tell you Dante bashed her head in?" Nicholas silently studied the Priest to see if his words bothered him. "You know Father, seeing her that way made me realize what kind of monster Dante is. So, this morning when I got out of the shower and I looked in the mirror and I looked hard at myself. I thought about what I wanted to do to Dante, but for some strange reason I was overcome with disgust and fear. Because at that moment I realized my heart was empty and I felt disgust because I realized I would become a monster just like Dante, if I did what I wanted to do, to him."

Nicholas rubbed his face. "But then I realize something else. Through my desire for revenge against Dante I now lived like an outcast in society," he laughed and shook his head.

Father Perez watched Nicholas laughing for several seconds before he said. "Please forgive me for interrupting you Nicholas but I must ask why you feel you are an outcast from those who love you?"

"Why Father? Because I have a beautiful girl who I love and I haven't spent any time with her, I stopped seeing her, I stopped telling her that I loved her, all because I have been consumed by my desire for revenge against Dante."

Nicholas softly chuckled. "You know that I tell myself, my girl couldn't possibly love me, because I was dumb enough to let a monster like Dante Channing frame me. But last night when I held her in my arms. I felt bad for the way, I've been treating her. So, before I came to see you, I sat in my car and I ordered her some red roses and I don't know why I did that. Was I feeling guilt, or was it because of my seeing that dead girl's body?"

Father Perez touched Nicholas' shoulder but kept silent.

Nicholas hung his head. "You see Father, my life, my heart is empty. I don't even know why I sent Maëlle the flowers."

"No, I don't see what you see Nicholas. You just told me about your act of kindness and love to your girl Maëlle, you sent her flowers. Can't you see that? That is not the act of a man whose heart is empty?"

"I did that out of guilt!"

Father Perez was calm when he said. "If it makes you happy to believe that your act of kindness and thoughtfulness in buying flowers for your girl was out of guilt, then be happy and believe that, Nicholas."

Father Perez's calmness seemed to provoke Nicholas' rage. "That don't' mean nothing! My buying her flowers!" Nicholas yelled trying to make himself believe what he was saying. "Don't you see, Father? Don't you know what will happen to me when I take my revenge on Dante?" He asked and then paused. "I will become a monster just like Dante, and no one in the world will ever love me. Because I will commit the ultimate sin, murder!"

Nicholas eyes glazed over as he gave an icy stare and in sinister low voice said. "When I find Dante, I'm going to kill him, just like he killed that girl, Holly Chen!"

Father Perez leaned over and placed his hand on Nicholas shoulder. "Don't you see Nicholas, God believes you can change your desire for revenge against Dante, and that's why he had you come to talk to me."

Nicholas shook himself out of his trance. "Yeah, well I didn't hear God say that to me," he said angrily. "And you know what else Father Perez?" He asked but didn't wait for a response. "Maybe I don't want to change! Did God tell you about that?"

Father Perez patted Nicholas's shoulder and breathed deeply and said. "You know Nicholas, The Tibetan Book of the Dead says, *"Death is a mirror in which all of life's mysteries are reflected"* and I believe God let you see that dead girl, Molly Chen, for a reason. But only you can discover that reason. But to do so, you'll need to find your special place of silence and peace, to seek out that reason, and that answer that you seek. I cannot give it to you. You may come and sit here in my favorite spot here, anytime you like. Or you may seek out your own calming favorite spot elsewhere," Father Perez said as he stood up. "Both of those choices are yours to make Nicholas."

Father Perez Senior looked up to the sky. "The sun will be

going down soon. I will leave you now Nicholas, you may stay in my favorite spot, as long as you like. If you fall asleep here tonight. I won't wake you. But I will make sure you are covered with a blanket or two so that you will be warm.God be with you, Nicholas."

Nicholas watched until Father Perez disappear into a building on the other side of the garden. He leaned back and got comfortable. *This was a very nice spot, it looked like God's garden,* Nicholas thought to himself as he stared at several rows of chocolate daisies, Queen of the night, and evening primrose. "Yeah, this spot is nice," he whispered to no one but himself as he reached into his pocket and pulled out the key and looked at it.

Nicholas turned the key over in his hand. He rubbed the key over and over again, wondering if doing so would do some good. Out of nowhere recognition hit him as he remembered Dante Channing had kept a storage locker, but where? He needed to think hard and try and remember.

No sooner did Nicholas make his discovery; he noticed a car pulling into the parking lot. Father Perez Senior had been right, there were benefits to having a view of the parking lot.

Immediately Nicholas quietly rose out of his tranquil spot and stayed low as he made his way unnoticed out of Father Perez Senior's favorite spot in the garden.

47

Chapter 40

Thomas & Kienan ...

That same day, Thomas watched as Kienan made his way to their table at Franciscan Restaurant, on the wharf in San Francisco.

"Kienan, I'm so glad you could make it. You didn't have to come all this way. I could have drove down to San Jose to see you."

Kienan sat down. "No worries, I had a really boring meeting in Burlingame, and lucky for me, your call helped me, to make the best decision of the day and sneak out of there. Besides the sound of your voice made me curious to know about what's been going on."

Their waiter walked over. "Sir, can I get you a drink?"

"Ah, yeah. I'll have coffee, hold on a minute," Kienan said and looked at Thomas.

"Thomas did you order already?"

"Yes, I did."

"Let, me guess," Kienan said. "You got the slow-roasted boneless short rib, right?"

Thomas smiled. "Yes, I did, how did you know?"

"Because the Franciscan is famous for them," Kienan said. "Waiter, I'll have the short ribs also, make it everything like he ordered," he replied pointing at Thomas.

The waiter said. "He ordered his Caesar Salad with his meal, is that alright with you too?"

Kienan nodded. "Yes."

"Very well, coming right up," the waiter said as he made his exit.

Kienan focused on Thomas. "Okay, Thomas tell me about the body in the Sacred river again."

"Well, like I said, when I spoke with you on the telephone. Nicholas called me and said he wanted me to get him inside the morgue in Sacramento to view the body and I got my contact, Fred Longhorn, to get us in. Fred told me he had his assistant Al Johnson do the autopsy on the girl. We learned her full name, was Molly Tameka Chen; she was half-Chinese and African American and from what they discovered she had a very personal tattoo in Chinese alphabet on her back that spelled the name Dante, and Fred told me the girl had a mother, who lived in East Palo Alto and a father named Leroy Jones, who lives in Oakland. In the car ride back to Nicholas's car. Nicholas told me he had suspected the girl had been dating Dante before her death. Then I went to East Palo Alto and saw her mother and she confirmed her daughter had been dating Dante Channing. She had pictures of them together and everything. As to the girls father, Leroy Jones, I haven't been able to make contact with him yet."

At the end of Thomas' story, their waiter brought over their food.

Kienan looked down at his steaming hot plate of slow-roasted boneless short rib, Yukon Gold mashed potatoes, with zucchini and his side Cesar salad. "Mmmm, everything smells delicious."

"Yes, it does," Thomas agreed. "Shall we as they say dig in?"

"Don't mind if I do, my good man," Kienan joked in a playful British accent.

A half hour later.

"That meal was excellent," Kienan said. "But Thomas, I have to tell you. I've been thinking about what you told me, and I get the feeling that there's something you haven't told me?"

Thomas took a sip of his coffee and swallow hard. "I'm sure glad you and I have only ordered coffee because what I'm about to tell you may not make a lot of sense."

"Go on, I'm listening," Kienan said.

"That night, after I took Nicholas to the morgue. I couldn't get to sleep so I got up and poured myself a snifter of brandy. Then I went back to bed and I had the strangest dream. There was this old man and he was dressed in a vintage old-fashioned dogtooth tweed blazer, standing beside my bed, and he said something about my having a key and that I should call you and so I did. And like I said at the beginning it all just doesn't make any sense. Because at some point in my dream I must have woke up and when I did, there was that old man, from my dream wearing the same vintage old-fashioned dogtooth tweed blazer, and then he disappeared right in front of me, like a ghost. "

Kienan leaned back in his chair and said. "I believe you. You see the old man in the vintage old-fashioned dogtooth tweed blazer, is, I mean was, Nicholas' father, Louis La Cour. He was a ghost. I've seen him before too. In fact, he's the reason I hired you to take this case and find Dante."

"Whew!!" Thomas whistled out. "Thank God, because I thought I was going crazy."

Kienan lean his elbows on the table. "Now tell me about this key he mentioned. Where's the key? "

Thomas sighed heavily. "That's just it. We didn't find a key in the dead girls' personal effects. I looked personally," he said. "And the only other key I found was the one I told you about before. The one that went to Ace Kong's other storage unit, over in The Alameda. "

"Yeah, I remember your telling me about that key to that storage unit and you're not finding anything in it," Kienan said. "Think though, did Nicholas look through any of her personal effects before you did?"

"No," Thomas said shaking his head. "The girl's personal effects, where her clothes, boots and jewelry. The jewelry was worth a lot of money and they kept them locked away. I had to be escorted to see them. I left Nicholas back down in the morgue with the body."

"Thomas, didn't you tell me they had dissected her body parts and placed them in bags?"

"Yeah, I did. But, what of it?" Thomas asked before his brain clicked into gear and he looked back at Kienan.

"Bingo!" Kienan declared. "What if there was something, she maybe had swallowed..."

"Or shoved into a cavity of her body, like her vagina or rectum," Thomas said. "Women drug mules do that all the time."

"I'm thinking her stomach. She could have swallowed something," Kienan said with a shake of his head.

"But Nicholas didn't mention seeing... Wait a minute, Now, that I think about it, Nicholas was acting kind of strange in the car ride back to his car. But I thought it was trauma from seeing the dead girl on the morgue slab."

"Is there any way you can check and see if Al Johnson found anything during his autopsy?"

Thomas shook his head. "Yes, the first thing I need to do is to call, Fred and ask if Al Johnson did find anything," he said pulling out his cell phone and dialing a number.

"Hello Fred Longhorn, it's me, Thomas."

"Hi Thomas, how are things?"

"Great Fred... Things are great. Fred can you do me another favor?"

"Sure, what is it?"

"That girl, Molly Chen, I don't remember if you told me if your guy Al Johnson found anything unusual in her stomach or other body cavity. when he did her autopsy, did he?"

"Hold on a minute Thomas, I'll check," Fred said.

A few minutes later, Fred returned to the phone.

"Thomas, you still there?" Fred asked.

"Yes, I am," Thomas said.

"Yes, Al found a key in her stomach and he said he placed it in a small clear bag, that he marked and attached to the front of the bag with her stomach in it. The curious thing is the bag with her stomach is still here, but not the small clear bag with the key in it, it's disappeared."

Thomas looked back at Kienan.

"Thanks, for your help Fred, I'll be in touch if I need you again."

Kienan rubbed his chin. "Looks like my brother-in- law has been busy. We need to find him, fast."

48

Chapter 41

Quinn, I got a bad feeling...

That same afternoon, Quinn pulled his car into the driveway of Kienan and Lacey's home and opened his cell phone and dialed their number.

The phone rang and was picked up on the first ring. "Hey Lacey, how are you this beautiful afternoon? Are you busy?"

"Quinn, is that you? Oh, it's so good to hear your voice. I'm not doing anything. In fact, I was planning on calling Maëlle, and seeing if she wanted to go to dinner."

"That sounds great, in fact, I'd love to treat the two of you to dinner today, that is of course if you two don't mind me tagging along."

"Really! I'm good for it. But we have to check with Maëlle," Lacey said.

"Great, Lacey do you think I can come inside while you call Maëlle?"

"Sure, where are you?"

"I'm sitting in my car in your driveway."

"Quinn, why didn't you tell me earlier, of course. Come in."

Quinn got out of his car and walked to the front door.

Lacey met him at the front door and opened it for him. "Quinn, I'm calling Maëlle right now," Lacey said, holding her cell phone.

"Hello Maëlle? It's me, Lacey, I have you on speaker phone. Say "Hi" to Quinn."

"Hi Quinn, say what are you and Lacey up to?

"That's just it, Maëlle," Lacey said. "Quinn's taking us to dinner. You want to go?"

"Sure do. I'd love to go; I'll meet you at your house, I'll be there in twenty minutes."

"Alright, see you soon, goodbye," Lacey said hanging up the phone.

"So, Quinn, can I get you something to drink. I still got some fresh coffee left."

"A cup of coffee sounds great," Quinn said, as he followed her into the kitchen.

Lacey poured both of them piping hot mugs of coffee. "The cream and sugar are over their on the counter."

"None, for me. I like my coffee black," Quinn replied.

"Suit yourself," Lacey replied. "Come into the family room Quinn and have a seat. We can see Maëlle's car when she arrives from the window. So, tell me, Quinn what's been up with you?"

"Nothing much," Quinn said as he followed Lacey into the family room and watched as she took some kids toys off the sofa and chairs and made room for him to sit.

"Congratulations, I heard you took some French cooking classes and earned a certificate."

"Thank you, Quinn, yes, I now have my Culinary arts certificate. I can open up a catering business if I want too."

"Or a Tea and Fine Bakery Café, like you used to talk about all the time, when you were growing up," Quinn said.

"Wow, you remembered. Yes, that is what I really want to do. But in the meantime, I no longer get strange looks from Kienan about my cooking," she joked.

"Quinn laughed. "So, Kienan's the reason why you took a cooking program?"

"Well, yes and no. Kienan did say at first that my macaroni and cheese didn't taste like Grand *mere* Catherine's but the real reason I went to Culinary arts school was to take my mind off of Nicholas being in prison," she sighed. "And you know Quinn, it helped."

"Speaking of Nicholas," Quinn cleared his throat. "He's the reason I want to take you and Maëlle out to dinner. I've been worried about him, and I mean really worried about him."

"Really?"

There was an eerie silence that was broken by the loud hoking of a car's horn.

Lacey looked up at her window. "Maëlle is here."

She watched as Maëlle headed for the front door and got up and walked over and unlocked the front door.

Lacey and Maëlle exchanged hugs.

"Lacey guess what?" Maëlle asked but didn't wait for a response. "You never will, so I'll tell you, Nicholas sent me the prettiest bouquet of roses!"

"Really?" Lacey replied. "Sounds like my brother is changing."

Maëlle giggled. "Yes, he did. I got three dozen of them."

"You counted them? Why did I ask?" Lacey declared. "Of course, you did."

"Where's Quinn?" Maëlle asked.

"Quinn's in the family room, come on," she said with a wave of her hand.

Quinn rose as Maëlle and Lacey returned to the family room.

"Maëlle it's good to see you," Quinn said.

"You too, okay Lacey get your purse I'm ready to go eat! What restaurant are we choosing?" Maëlle asked but didn't wait for a response. "I know let's go to that new infusion restaurant at the mall called the Banana Boat!"

"Are you kidding me?" Lacey said. "Maëlle the Banana Boat is a place for parents to take their kids. It's a pizza parlor with a giant banana walking around blowing up balloons for kids."

"Oh, I didn't know that. I just drove past it a couple of times. I did notice a bunch of kids were going inside. Anyway, that's it, for my knowing about any new restaurants," Maëlle exclaimed with a wave of her hands. "I'm still starving though. What are we going to eat?"

"Ok, ladies, I'll take over come let's get in my car and we'll go to our old standby. Which by the way you both love?" Quinn said opening his car door.

"Now the only thing you have to decide is who's getting in the backseat."

Lacey rushed over and grab the handle of the front door. "Looks like I'm sitting in the front seat."

"Whatever!" Maëlle exclaimed as she got into the back seat.

"Now sit back and enjoy the ride ladies. "I'm picking the restaurant."

Forty-five minutes later, Lacey and Maëlle were sitting side by side munching on Baby Back Ribs."

"Quinn how's your prime rib?" Lacey asked.

"It's excellent! I'm so glad I picked this place; I haven't been here in years and the food still tastes great," Quinn replied.

"Here! Here!" Maëlle declared. "Let's make a toast to Henry's Hi-Life! The best American food joint in San Jose even after all of these years!"

"I agree!" Lacey declared.

"I second that motion!" Quinn replied.

The three friends toasted their glasses.

"Hey Quinn, guess what?" Maëlle giggled. "Ahhhh! I can't hold it in. Nicholas sent me a three-dozen red rose bouquet, they are the most beautiful flowers ever and a box of See's Candy, nuts and chews. A big box too!"

"Really? Nicholas sent you all that. Where's our share of the See's candy, Maëlle?" Quinn asked.

"Your joking right Quinn?" Maëlle asked.

"Quinn ain't joking," Lacey replied, licking barbecue sauce from her fingers. "Where's the box of See's candy Maëlle? We want some."

Maëlle hung her head. "Come on you guys, you know Nicholas' ain't the most romantic frog in the pond. Can't I just enjoy my box of candy?"

Lacey laughed. "You know what that means, Quinn? Maëlle probably got them sitting in the middle of the living room, sitting on the coffee table like a shrine, the flowers, the box of See's Candy, and let me guess. A picture of my brother."

"A ten by twelve picture of your brother," Quinn teased laughing.

"Tell us Maëlle, did you take a photo of your flowers and candy and post it on Instagram?" Lacey laughed.

"Very funny, Lacey. I didn't post it on Instagram. I posted it on Facebook. You know how proud I am when your brother gives me something, we all know Nicholas ain't the most thoughtful Don Juan Latin lover, that ever lived. In fact, he's his cheap cousin, *Barato!*"

Lacey and Quinn roared with laughter. Soon Maëlle joined in.

Finally, Lacey stopped laughing. "Maëlle do you want to know why Quinn wanted to take us out to dinner today?"

"Alright, why?" Maëlle shrugged.

"He's worried about Nicholas," Lacey said.

"Really? You know Lacey, come to think of it. I am too," Maëlle replied. "Nicholas has been acting really strange for a while and yesterday..."

Instantly Maëlle clammed up.

"Maëlle what were you going to say?"

"First, I want to know why Quinn has been concerned about Nicholas," Maëlle said.

Maëlle and Lacey looked up at Quinn.

"Well, for starters, Nicholas never returns my calls. I've been calling him for weeks. I even went to see Father Perez Senior of the Church of the Good Shepherd, after I saw him and Nicholas talking together at Nicholas' welcome home party, I thought maybe he's been talking to Father Perez," he took a sip of his drink and said. "But Father Perez didn't tell me anything. He said something about Nicholas making a strange confession and that he couldn't share it. And then said something strange like he really wasn't sure if it was a confession or just a bunch of rattling on by Nicholas, because when he was talking to him, he wasn't focus, his mind was all over the place."

"That's exactly how Nicholas has been with me," Maëlle declared. "Like he's not focused but worried about something."

Quinn nodded. "Well, anyway Father Perez would only say that he was deeply worried about Nicholas and that he thought something bad was going to happen."

"Father Perez Senior told you that?" Lacey asked.

"When did you see Father Perez Senior?" Maëlle asked.

"Oh, when he told me that it was about a week ago." Quinn said.

"This is serious!" Lacey exclaimed.

"Why do you say that?" Maëlle asked.

"Because, Grand *mere* Catherine did a reading for me and Kienan a while ago, we went to her concerned about Nicholas too. You see, I was also worried. I had been having these visions, about Nicholas. And well, Grand *mere* Catherine pulled a tarot card, during her reading."

"What card was it, Lacey?" Maëlle asked.

Lacey looked between Maëlle and Quinn. "It was the death card. Grand *mere* Catherine said something was going to happen."

"I've been having a feeling something bad is going to happen too," Quinn replied.

Quinn turned and focus on Maëlle. "Maëlle you said Nicholas had been acting strange and then you stopped in the middle of telling something. What was it?"

Maëlle's eyes looked sad. "Ahhhh, well Nicholas spent the night with me, last night. He called me up earlier in the day, before he came over and he was practically begging me to let him come over and spend the night. Well, when he got there. I could see he was upset, maybe even traumatized. He'd gotten Thomas to take him to the Sacramento County morgue to see the dead body of a girl. A dead girl who used to be Dante Channing's girlfriend."

"What?" Lacey declared. "If Thomas took Nicholas to the Sacramento County morgue then my Kienan knows all about it! The sneaky rat never told me a thing!"

"Lacey and Maëlle, I didn't tell you everything. I saw Father Perez, today before I came over to your home, Lacey. At first, I wasn't going to tell you because I didn't want to worry you. But now after hearing what has been said here today. I am worried, in fact, I'm scared because of what Father Perez said earlier," Quinn declared. "Father Perez said, we needed to find Nicholas, before he does something, bad! Lacey, you need to call Kienan, now!"

49

✦

Chapter 42

Nicholas

Later that same night...

Earlier that day Nicholas had wanted to sit in the garden at the Church of the Good Shepherd and watch the sun go down, but he couldn't. After seeing Quinn park his car in the parking lot and walk into the garden heading for Father Perez's little home, he had hidden himself and sneaked back out to his car and drove away. He had been glad he hadn't parked his car where Quinn could have discovered it.

Nicholas had had to content himself with watching the sun set at Coyote Point Beach just past Burlingame, California. A city right below San Francisco.

The sun had set long ago, as Nicholas sat in his car watching the ocean. Father Perez Senior had been right, sitting for a while in a calm quiet place did wonders for making a man think straight. He remembered the drawings he had made days earlier, in his room. At the time he couldn't think of why the name of the church St. Mary had been clouding his mind.

As he'd sat there and thought about it. It had all made sense to him. He'd been there before with Dante. He had helped Dante move some of his belongings there years ago.

A smile crept across his face when he'd remembered that Dante Channing had kept a storage locker in San Francisco, in a storage facility directly across the street from old St. Mary's Cathedral. He had also recalled what Dante had said the day he'd helped him unload some stuff in his storage unit. *Dante had said that the storage unit was big enough for a man to live real comfortable in it.*

Now his mind was made up. He knew what he had to do. He checked his watch it was ten minutes after ten o'clock pm, at night. Traffic should have long died down on highway 101, heading into San Francisco by now. He could be in San Francisco in less than a half-hour. He started his car and headed for the freeway. He was a man determined to have his revenge.

50

Chapter 43

Quinn he ain't heavy he's my brother...

With Quinn and Maëlle watching her attentively. Lacey quickly dialed Kienan's number. He picked up on the first ring.

"Kienan! Quinn went to see Father Perez Senior, and he believes Nicholas is out looking for Dante, to take his revenge!"

"Lacey, I already know about that. I'm out trying to find him," Kienan blurted. "Where, are you woman of mine? Are you safe?"

"Yeah, I'm safe. I'm with Maëlle, and Quinn. We're here having a late dinner, at Henry's Hi-Life."

"Lacey hand Quinn your phone and tell him to take me off the speaker," Kienan said.

"I hear you, Kienan," Quinn replied, taking Lacey's phone. "In fact, I'm going to walk outside so our conversation is private," he said giving Lacey and Maëlle a wink.

Once outside Quinn said. "Ok, Kienan I'm alone the ladies are inside sitting at our table."

"Good," Kienan said. "Look Quinn, this is serious. I'm with Thomas we're at the Franciscan Restaurant at Fisherman's Wharf, we were just about to leave, but we've been trying to figure out where Nicholas could be. Thomas discovered some old tunnels beneath Chinatown, he believes Dante Channing has been hiding there and we think Nicholas is heading there to look for him."

"What do you need me to do?" Quinn demanded.

"First I need you to take Lacey and Maëlle to Grand *mere* Catherine's. I'm sure that's where my kids are today. Somehow if you can leave them there and then come to San Francisco and help me and Thomas look for Nicholas it would be a great help."

"You can count on me Kienan," Quinn declared.

"I know I can count on you Quinn, once you get here. But you have one big problem that may prevent you," Kienan replied.

"Oh, and what's that?"

"Keeping my wife, Lacey from knowing what you are up to. My fear is that if Lacey discovers you are leaving to come help us look for Nicholas, that hard-headed woman of mine, might try and follow you."

Quinn chuckled. "I hear you loud and clear, Boss man. No worries, I'll have everything under control. But when we hang up, I need you to do me a favor and called Grand *mere* Catherine and tell her you need for her to make sure Lacey and Maëlle stays put at her house when I drop them off."

"Mmmm I like you're thinking Quinn, that sounds like a great idea," Kienan replied.

"Excellent," Quinn said.

"Oh yeah, Quinn, call me when you reach San Francisco, tonight."

"I will, Kienan, I'll say goodbye for now," Quinn said hanging up Lacey's cell phone.

Quinn walked back into the restaurant and up to their table.

Agitated Lacey went to stand up. "Quinn, what did that husband of mine say to you in private that he didn't want me and Maëlle to hear?"

"Calm down Lacey and have a seat. Here's your cell phone. Can, I at least pay the bill. Where's our waitress," he said motioning his hand.

Quickly their waitress walked over. "Could I have the check please?"

"Sure, thing sir. I'll be right back," their waitress said as she hurried away.

"Quinn, I want to know everything Kienan said to you," Lacey demanded.

"Ahh, stop making demands Lacey, now where are your children?"

Lacey snapped her mouth shut and stared angrily back at Quinn.

"Kienan wants to know that his children are safe and sound and then he said I could take you to him, but first I have to get something he needs from Grand mere Catherine," Quinn lied, easily reverting back to his old ways.

"Oh, okay, they are at Grand *mere* Catherine. I can check

on my kids since you need to go there," Lacey said and then turned and looked at Maëlle.

"Maëlle, do you mind riding to Grand *mere* Catherine with me to check on the kids?"

"No, I don't mind. In fact, my plan is to stick close to you tonight. That means if you're going with Quinn to look for Nicholas, I'm going too," Maëlle replied.

Quinn smiled a mischievous smile as their waitress brought over the check. After paying her he put on his best poker face. He knew both women were going to be in for a rude surprise later.

***

A half hour later, Quinn pulled into the driveway of Lacey's childhood home and watched as Grand *mere* Catherine met the three of them at the front door.

"Hello Grand *mere* Catherine, Kienan said you had something for me to take to him," Quinn said with a wink. "Can I please use your bathroom?" Quinn asked. "Those sweet teas I had at dinner are running through me."

"Oh! Oh, yes, I remember," Grand mere Catherine said winking back. "The bathroom is still where it's always been, right down the hallway, that way," she said pointing.

"Shhhhh! Don't make a lot of noise the babies are sleeping," Grand *mere* Catherine declared.

"Come on into the kitchen let me warm you all up, if you're planning on going out and trying to find Nicholas."

Lacey and Maëlle dutifully followed Grand *mere* Catherine into the kitchen.

"Lacey, I found a couple of your heavy sweaters in your old

room, they are there on the chair. I figured you and Maëlle, might get cold while you're out looking for Nicholas."

"Thanks, Grand *mere* Catherine. Say, I smell hot chocolate," Lacey said.

"I do too," Maëlle declared. "It smells like the kind you used to make for us when we were kids."

"It, is. It's right there on the table. I made some earlier. I'm not so sure if it's still hot, now," Grand *mere* Cather replied. "You might need to warm it up in the microwave."

Instantly Lacey walked over to the table and gently touched the pot. "It's still hot," she said grabbing a mug off the tray and pouring her some.

"Save some for me Lacey," Maëlle declared reaching for a mug.

"Mmmm this stuff is delicious"

"Look at the tray of candy!" Maëlle declared. "Grand *mere* Catherine, you never let us eat candy like this."

"Those are sugarless gummy bears," Grand *mere* Catherine declared. "I'm a great grandmother and I have a right to spoil my great grand young ins!"

"Well we young and we will be eating some," Lacey declared grabbing a hand full of gummy bears."

"Hey, don't take all of them," Maëlle declared.

Grand *mere* Catherine watched Lacey and Maëlle's shenanigans and started humming as she opened the dishwasher and started putting away dishes.

Lacey threw another hand full of gummy bears in her mouth and chewed.

"Hey! Lacey save some for me," Maëlle declared. "You're going to eat all the gummy bears!"

"I can't take all of them Maëlle, look how much is on the tray. Dawg! These are heck of good!" Lacey declared chewing with her mouth opened.

Maëlle smiled. "Girl I'm in seventh heaven, I got my mug of the best hot chocolate in the world and I am eating sugarless gummy bears."

Quinn entered the kitchen and walked over to Grand *mere* Catherine, and whispered something in her ear.

Grand *mere* Catherine looked at him and looked at the clock on the wall and whispered back. "It won't be long now."

It took less than fifteen-minutes for the sleeping potion in the hot chocolate and gummy bears to take effect.

Lacey and Maëlle laid sprawled out on the family room sofa.

Grand m*ere* Catherine walked over to where Quinn was standing.

"You know Quinn, I feel I need to say this. I see so much of your father, Louis, in your eyes. And so much of myself in that spirit of yours. I know my son kept from you that he was your father, which wasn't the right thing to do. I never agreed with him on that. But he thought he was doing the right thing," she paused. "I need you to know, Louis made sure you were here at your home with us as much as he could. My son Louis loved you with all his heart and I do too," Grand mere Catherine said.

The moment was intense as Quinn pulled his grandmother into his arms and said. "I know," Grand mere Catherine, I love you too. It's alright, I'm going to find my brother, that's why I'm here."

Grand mere Catherine, squeezed Quinn a little tighter before she pulled out of their embrace and said. "Quinn, I want to show you something I found in Nicholas' room when I was putting away his laundry."

"Your still doing Nicholas' laundry?"

"Don't hate the player Quinn, hate the game," she said with a giggle. "How else can a nosy old grandmother snoop through her grandchild's belonging?"

"Yeah, I'll admit that does sound pretty resourceful, so what have you got?"

"This!" Grand *mere* Catherine said thrusting a piece of paper in his hand with one letter "D" the numbers four, seven, one and the word storage unit."

"Huh! You think Nicholas has a storage unit?"

"Quinn, I thought you were smarter than that. No, I think the letter "d" stands for Dante. And the fact that pretty much everybody has storage units these days, well I believe Dante had one too. Those numbers four, seven one must be connected to it too and I believe that's where Nicholas has gone off to. Off to find both the storage unit and Dante."

Grand *mere* Catherine squeezed Quinn's hand as her eyes pleaded. "Quinn, please check this out for me. It has to be something."

Quinn let out a soft whistle. "Why do you think that?"

"Because I know my Nicholas, he was fixated on those numbers for days. He didn't think I was watching him, but I was. Then I found a drawing on a piece of paper Nicholas threw away." She pulled the drawing from a pocket in her apron. "Here it is. See, he drew church on the corner and a storage unit across from it. He wrote "ST" and Mary. I believe he meant the name of the church is St. Mary's. But then before that, Lacey and Kienan came to me a while ago and ask me to do a Tarot reading because they were worried about Nicholas and I pulled the Owl. Some say the Owl helps people see an alternative way of life. But in the Ten of Swords Tarot Card the Owl Spirit signifies endings, it is the announcer of Death!"

Grand *mere* Catherine clasp Quinn's hands tightly, "When we lived in Louisiana, we believed in a watcher watching the watcher. I need you to be my watcher tonight. I need you to go and find your brother, Nicholas," she let go of his hands and then grabbed him in a tight embrace.

Quinn swallowed hard. He knew the hug she gave him was genuine. He knew he spoke the truth when the words rolled off of his tongue. "I'll find him Grand mere Catherine, I promise."

Slowly Grand *mere* Catherine pulled out of the embrace and patted Quinn on the shoulder. "Be safe Quinn, you'd best get going. Don't worry about Lacey and Maëlle," she said looking back at the two women fast asleep on the sofa. "They'll sleep for hours, with the number of gummy candies sleeping pills they ate."

Quinn nodded his head as he made his exit. One thing was sure, Grand *mere* Catherine was a conning woman.

51

Chapter 44

Funny how life works...

The first thing Quinn did when he reached San Francisco was to call Kienan on his cell phone.

His phone rang once.

"Hello, Quinn, are you in San Francisco yet?"

"Hi Kienan, I'm almost there I just pass the San Francisco Airport."

"Good," Kienan replied. "Thomas and I are about to go inside some tunnels he found under a place called the Hard Rock Candy store, it's on the corner of Washington and Grant street, do you want to join us?"

"Well, I would but I promised Grand *mere* Catherine, I'd check out a storage unit by old St. Mary's church. Do you know anything about one?"

"Old St. Mary's church," Kienan repeated out loud. "I'm not familiar with... Hold a minute Quinn, Thomas, said he has."

Quinn could hear Kienan speaking to Thomas and then

he heard Thomas mention yeah, *I saw a storage unit by old St. Mary's Cathedral on Sacramento Street.*"

"Did you hear that Quinn?" Thomas said the name of the church is old St. Mary's Cathedral and he saw one near it," Kienan replied.

"Yeah, I heard him, St, Mary's Cathedral on Sacramento Street, I'm going to go and check it out. If I don't find anything, I'll call you and find out your location, and join you, alright?"

"Yes," Kienan replied. "That sounds like a plan. Goodbye for now Quinn, and thanks for coming to help."

"No, problem," Quinn said hanging up his phone and pressing his GPS finder in his car and dialing in the word "St. Mary's Cathedral".

Quinn smiled softly as his car's navigation system loudly chimed out. *"Your route has been calculated. Please proceed on Highway 101, to San Francisco."*

52

Chapter 45

Revenge!

Nicholas had taken his time driving from San Jose to San Francisco that night, on purpose because it gave him time to think. Now he sat in his car in the darken alley behind old St. Mary's Cathedral.

St. Mary's Cathedral was said to be California's first Cathedral with a clock-faced tower and a tranquil inner sanctuary.

But Nicholas wasn't interested in seeing a priest. Tonight, he remembered what the numbers four, seven and one had stood for and now he was ready to go check out his hunch. He was sure he would find what he was looking for in the storage unit facility on Sacramento street.

Nicholas smiled as he grabbed his backpack filled, with a pair of brass knuckles, a switchblade, a ten-inch hunting knife, a black light-weight baseball crowbar baton, a sub-compact 9-mm gun, leather holster and a compact flashlight.

Nicholas looked at the sub-compact 9-mm gun, it wasn't

his weapon of choice because it meant a swift end to a situation he didn't want for Dante. He wanted to take his time with Dante. He wanted him to feel the torment and pain he had put him through.

Quickly, he placed the switchblade in his jean pocket, along with the brass knuckles. He placed the ten-inch hunting knife in a protective sheath, that he placed in his leather holster along with his sub-compact 9-mm gun and the compact flashlight. He placed the short black light-weight baseball crowbar baton, under his jean jacket, where it fit neatly on a hidden hook.

A few minutes later, the chill of the night air swept over Nicholas as he quickly walked down Sacramento street to the storage unit on the corner. He watched the building and noticed the last customer had left hours ago. He walked up to the security entrance and punched in the numbers 471, a red light flashed it was the wrong code nothing happened and then he remembered and used the *471, enter and the light on the door flashed green as the door popped opened. Nicholas smiled to himself, as he walked down the empty storage unit looking at the numbers. He was all the way to the end in the back where the hallway would turn, when he saw it, an arrow painted in white paint with black numbers 450-500 this way.

A few steps later and there it was, 471. He pulled out the key, he'd gotten from Molly Chen's stomach bag and placed pushed it in the door and turned it. The latched shot opened and he lifted the metal roll-up door and walked in closing it down behind him. He turned on his flashlight and flooded the room with light.

The storage unit was enormous. It looked to be the size

of a huge loft apartment. There were rows of boxes neatly stacked. He walked over and opened the first box. The box contained Dante's business suits. Nicholas knew they were expensive. But they weren't what he was looking for.

Nicholas opened another box and gasped and said out loud to himself. "Damn Dante, you had a Star Wars collection!"

He opened more boxes and more boxes and started on a third row.

Finally, Nicholas' reached for another box and opened it. It contained a collection of comic books; they were rare and expensive. "These are a collector's item. Now I see where you were spending all of our business' money!"

Frustrated. Nicholas started to scream as he kicked over several boxes. Instantly he froze when he spotted the cover over a car behind several boxes that had fallen over.

Nicholas walked over and lifted the cover on the car. It revealed Dante's favorite car. A fully restored classic 1966 Ford mustang Shelby. He shook his head the car had to be worth one hundred and fifty-thousand dollars, easily.

He walked around the car. There was another cover over a large item. He lifted the cover and revealed a baby grand piano. There were several other large items covered.

Slowly Nicholas began to lift them too. He discovered a very expensive office desk and chair pushed neatly into the back corner of the room. He walked over and sat down in the chair. He thought it was odd that the desk and chair had not been pack away for storage. There were no covers on them and the chair rolled easily. He was sure it had been used regularly.

He got up and went to walk around the desk and immediately noticed when his shoes hit the echoing sound of metal against metal. He stomped a couple times and then focused his flashlight down and saw the trap door.

Cautiously Nicholas lifted the trap door and saw the ladder leading down into a tunnel. Before descending he pulled a pair of brass knuckles out of his pocket and put one on his fighting hand, just in case he needed to land a wallop of a punch. He stuck his head in and felt the cold gush of air. Slowly he descended down the ladder.

It was dark and musty in the tunnel and for one moment Nicholas couldn't decide if he should go left or right and then out of nowhere the smell hit his nose before he knew it.

It was the smell of someone smoking but it wasn't a regular cigarette or marijuana. Instantly Nicholas smiled to himself It was the bold bitter coca flavor of a Kentucky Cheroots. That cigarillos brand was Dante Channing's favorite.

Slowly and quietly Nicholas followed the scent as every muscle in his body tensed ready.

A sudden movement in the dark in front of him shot adrenaline throughout his veins. He knew he'd found Dante; he could feel it deep within his soul.

He grabbed the man in front of him by the neck and flung him around. "Hey Dante! Winner! Winner Chicken Dinner! Looks like you owe me a chicken dinner!"

"What the hell?" Dante gasped in surprise and yelled in shock. Instantaneously recognition hit him.

"Nicholas? How the hell did you find me?"

"Someone sure gave you a bad plastic surgery job! Even I can tell that ugly mug is you, Dante! Aren't you glad to see me?" Nicholas yelled landing his fist covered with brass knuckles.

Dante's yelled in pain as his cheroot cigarillo flew from his mouth and fell to the ground.

Blood ran down Dante's face, as he looked up at Nicholas. "You fucking ruined my life, you bastard!"

Nicholas laughed. "Now that's funny Dante. Real funny, because as I recall I'm the one who went to prison for your backstabbing ass," he laughed.

Dante exhaled hard as if a light went off in his head as he rose up off the ground and charged at Nicholas hurling his body through the air and butting his head into Nicholas stomach screaming. "I hate you!"

The move caught Nicholas off guard and both men landed on the ground.

Nicholas recovered quickly, rolled away from Dante and pulled out his short black light-weight baseball crowbar baton, and jumped up. He roared like a lion capturing his prey and whacked Dante hard in the chest.

"OOO! WOOOO...OOOuch Shit! Damn Motherf—ker! That hurt!" Dante yelled out in pain.

Nicholas landed another blow with his elbow to his head.

"Aagghhhh Shit" Dante screamed, as blood scattered. "You're hitting me with brass knuckles and a pipe. What kind of sick monster are you Nicholas!"

Quickly Nicholas gripped his short black light-weight baseball crowbar baton and rammed it into Dante's gut and watched him ball over.

"I'm not the kind that bashes in the head of a defenseless

woman, like you did, Dante! This is for Holly Chen!" He yelled as he landed another blow.

Dante coughed several times as he rolled on the ground and then started laughing. "Fuck you, Nicholas! Holly Chen deserved to die. You don't know what that double-crossing bitch tried to do to me!"

"Listen to you. Always the victim! You're still a whinny piece of shit, Dante!"

"Fuck you Nicholas! You ain't no better than me!"

Nicholas kicked Dante hard in the ribs. "Fuck you back Dante!"

Dante screamed out in pain. "Have mercy, Nicholas, please! Have mercy!"

"Did you give Holly Chen any mercy, Dante?"

Dante didn't respond and Nicholas kicked him hard again. "Did you hear what I asked you, Dante? I can't hear you!"

"No!... No!" Dante coughed out. "No, I didn't. I didn't show Holly Chen any mercy. That Bitch stole from me! She used me!"

"Shut up! You sick twisted Narcissist why do you always have to play the victim?" Nicholas yelled.

"I am the victim... I'm always the victim!" Dante yelled. "Look what I built! Look what I made! I made a fortune, I built an empire! And this world tore it apart! It tore me down! This world has treated me mean!"

"Damn Dante you sound just like a whining malignant narcissist! "

"I was a powerful man, I had everything and you ruined me!" Dante yelled.

"There you go again, Dante, whining. You think you obtained absolute power!"

"No, Nicholas, I did obtain absolute power! I was the way my life should have been. Women desired me! They wanted me! I was on top!"

"Really, Dante?" Nicholas asked but didn't wait for a response. "You desire power and you thought you were powerful, but you were like all the rest. Just pretending to be powerful because you want to believe there is no limit to your lust, greed and power and thus it becomes the means to your deepest ruin. For to obtain the absolute power, you must become your own absolute ruin, for you want the impossible!"

"Shut the Fuck-up! Nicholas! You don't know my desires!"

"But I do know one thing, Dante!" Nicholas declared. "Do you want to know why I'm doing this to you Dante?"

"Why? ... Why?" Dante asked between coughs.

"I'm doing this to you because I want to know why you did this to me, Dante? Since, I was your friend!"

"I was your friend! I was your friend!" Dante laughed out mimicking Nicholas. "Nicholas you had everything I ever wanted."

Dante's eyes flickered over as he wiped blood from running down his face, as he crawled up off the ground. "Maëlle loved you and yet you treated her like shit. I bet you didn't know I was in love with her, did you? But she didn't even know I was alive," his eye glassed over as if he was in a trance. "While you were away at prison, I arranged to meet Maëlle one afternoon when she got off that stupid job, she had taken to make ends meet. I turned on my charm and I told her all I wanted to do was help. I knew she'd fallen on hard times once you went to jail. I told her I knew that job she taken wasn't paying her any money and that I was willing to give her ten-thousand dollars a month to come and work for me. She didn't even have to work full time just come in and show up and I'd give her the money."

Dante coughed several times and then continued. "Then that calculating Bitch told me she'd come to work for me for twenty-thousand dollars a month, if I'd agree and I did. Then she showed up to work and said she couldn't stay unless I answered her one question truthfully."

Dante rose up off the ground and put his hands on his knees as if he was catching his breath.

"What question did she want you to answer?" Nicholas inquired.

"She assured me that if I answered her, my answer would be between just the two of us, she wouldn't tell anyone what I said. She promised me, she'd stay and work for me as long as I wanted her too. Do you want to know what she asked me?"

"I know you're dying to tell me," Nicholas replied.

Dante took a deep breath. "She asked me if I had set you up and framed you and my dumb ass answered yes, I had. Because I believed her, I thought she was a woman of her word. Then that Bitch told me, she lied she'd had her fingers crossed. She said she would never work for me and that I was lucky she didn't have a gun, or she would have shot and killed my ass right on the spot. She said if I ever came near her again, she'd tell Kienan and Quinn and they'd find someone to take me out! Can you believe that Bitch? I grabbed that bitch and twisted her arm and I told her if she ever told anybody I had told her what I'd said. I'd kill her ass!"

Dante laughed out loud. "That Bitch was so scared of me by the time I let her go, I knew she'd never tell a soul what I had done to her."

Nicholas kept his gaze hard and steady on Dante as if he was in a trance. And then all at once he yelled out a loud roar like a lion on the African plains, he lunged forward on Dante striking him with his fist. "You fucking bastard! How dare you put your hands on my woman!"

Frantically Nicholas kept punching Dante as blood splattered, hitting him over and over again with his brass knuckles, until Dante swooned back at forth like a drunken bum on a street corner.

Finally, Nicholas stopped and stared at him. He watched as Dante slowly crumble over to the ground.

Nicholas stood there breathing hard. He looked at his body and realized he was covered in blood. "Get up Dante!"

"Nicholas please! Man, I'm sorry," Dante stammered out moaning. I'm hurt man. I'm hurt," he said, praying he was buying himself some time, while he got his baring's.

"You're not sorry Dante! I can see that now!"

"No... No, Nicholas. I'm sorry man. I'm so sorry," Dante pretended, and with all his might he then lunged at Nicholas with a left punch.

"You stupid piece of shit, Nicholas!" Dante screamed landing a punch.

Nicholas ducked the second punch Dante tried to land, just in time and grabbed the arm Dante swung at him with and twisted. A loud cracking noise sounded as Dante screamed in pain and fell to the ground flopping around like a chicken with a broken neck.

"Ou! OOO! OOOOOuch! Oh! Shit! You broke my arm! You Motherfucker! You broke my arm. Look at the blood pouring from my body!" Dante screamed in pain. "Fuck it! Fuck it! Go ahead and kill me Nicholas! Get that shit over-with! Kill me now!" Dante begged out moaning.

"You're right!" Nicholas yelled. "You need to die Mother-fucker!"

Instantly Nicholas yelled as he went to swing his short black light-weight baseball crowbar baton, and bash in Dante's head and then it hit him fierce, a familiar scent from long ago filled the air. The moment felt surreal as Nicholas felt like his body was reacting in slow motion. Something was stopping his body from moving forward.

After the overwhelming smell filled the air, the soft tin-kering of a bell seemed to chime out of nowhere as Nicholas felt a strange deathly icy cold wind shoot through his body right before recognition hit him. He knew what the smell was, it was the smell of his dead father's favorite aftershave and then he heard his name called.

"Nicholas! Stop! My son! My son! Stop!"

Startled. Nicholas swing stopped in mid-air at the sound of his name being called. He quickly looked around. No one was standing there.

Silence hung all around.

Light started to form. Shimmering mist of diffuse light began to focus and take form. Then in an instant a man ap-peared before him. He was dressed in a familiar old-fashioned vintage dogtooth tweed blazer,

Recognition hit Nicholas. It was Louis, his dead father, the man who raised him as his own.

"Dad?"

"Nicholas, I love you son. Don't do this!"

The moment was surreal like a dream except Nicholas saw Dante laying on the ground bleeding but breathing hard with is eyes open crying and Louis, his dead father had just told him he loved him.

All anger and revenge melted away deep inside Nicholas' body as he stood their staring as the ghost of Louis, until it disappeared.

"I'm sorry Nicholas! I swear man, I swear to God I'm sorry for what I did to you man! Please get me some help... I'm bleeding to death," Dante moaned and cried over and over in a soft whimper.

Breathing hard Nicholas slowly lowered the short black light-weight baseball crowbar baton, as he looked down at Dante lying bleeding on the ground. He was better than what he was doing. He was loved and he had someone who loved him. He turned and walked back the way he came.

He found the ladder and climbed back up through the trap door and left it opened as he walked over to the chair by the desk and sat down and lowered his face into his hands as he leaned on the desk.

***

A few minutes later, the door of the storage unit went up as light flood the storage unit as footsteps walked in and over to the desk where Nicholas was sitting.

"Nicholas! Thank God, I found you. Are you alright?"

Slowly Nicholas lifted his head at the sound of the familiar voice.

"Quinn? How did you find me?"

"It's a long story," Quinn said placing his hand on his shoulder. "Are you alright? You're covered in blood."

Nicholas looked down at his hands. "I guess, so," he said as he looked back at the trapped door.

Quinn noticed the trapped door and kneeled down in front of Nicholas and said. "Nicholas, my brother, I have to ask you something. If I go down that trap door, will I find Dante dead or alive?"

Nicholas turned his head to the open trap door and curiously looked at it for several seconds before he finally said. "Dante's alive, but he probably wishes he was dead."

Quinn stood up and breathed out loud. "Kienan and Thomas are somewhere in the tunnels looking for you. I need to call them and let them know I found you and see what Thomas can do to keep this out of the news. You okay with my doing that, brother?"

Nicholas tilted his head and looked up at Quinn. "Yes, brother, I'm alright with whatever you have to do."

Quinn went to dial his phone.

"Quinn, can I ask you something," Nicholas said.

"Sure," Quinn said.

"Can you tell Kienan, I'm going to marry Maëlle, and that I need you and him to be my best men, so Maëlle know I'm for real this time? I'm threw being an idiot where Maëlle's concerned. I'm going to marry her and be the kind of man she deserves."

Quinn smiled. "You got it brother, I'm on top of that right now. My phone is ringing."

"Hello Kienan, I found Nicholas! "

"Thank God! Where are you?"

"I'm right where Grand *mere* Catherine said to look. The storage unit right across from old St. Mary's Cathedral, unit 471. Tell Thomas we need an ambulance for Dante, he's still alive. Can you see what Thomas can do to keep this out of the papers?"

"You got it! That's Thomas' specialty. We'll be right there!" Kienan yelled. "We are on our way."

***

An hour later, "Alright, Kienan, my clean-up crew is almost done ceiling off the entrance to this unit. It won't be recognizable in the tunnels and Dante was carried back to the Hard Cock Candy Store, that's where the police found him, lying in his bed hidden in the wall, Thomas said, as he drove Kienan back to his car.

"Good, are you sure they'll be no trace back to this unit?" Kienan asked.

"Yes, I'm sure. My cleaning crew are experts, and you don't have to worry about Dante Channing leaking anything to the police, about Nicholas' involvement in his beating. Apparently, a lot of people had Dante Channing on their hate list. The word on the street is that Dante owed a bunch of money he couldn't pay back to a Chinatown loan shark, who sent a bunch of young thugs to beat him up. Not to mention that girl he killed, who's full name was Holly Tameka Chen-Jones, well even though she dropped her father's name off of her adult identification. Her African American father, still claimed her as his daughter. And I learned Mr. Leroy Jones, was very upset when he learned his daughter had been killed. Also, Mr. Jones is a member of the notorious west coast Shot Callers, a gang of O. G's, based out of Oakland. Apparently, her father was the one to make her give up her life of prostitution. But he never gave Dante Channing permission to kill his daughter, so the street says he may have had some young bloods beat the living shit out of Dante Channing. others say, that he put a hit out on him. Anyway, like I said, the police are not in a hurry to find his perpetrators."

Kienan exhaled. "Thank God, looks like this thing with Dante and Nicholas is finally over."

"Yes, it does. Are you going to stop by where Quinn's taken Nicholas?" Thomas inquired. "I think you should, to make sure he's okay and if he needs medical attention you have the name and address of that doctor in Los Gatos, you can take him too."

"If you think I should then I'm headed to check on Nicholas, now," Kienan replied. "Thanks again for all your help, Thomas, I don't know what I would have done without you."

"You're welcome, here's your car. Now get going. I'm going to go back and check on my cleaning crew and then I'm heading home to get some rest, drive safe Kienan,"

"You too, Thomas," Kienan said walking over and getting inside his car. He watched as Thomas sat and watched him start up his car and drive away, before Thomas made a U-turn in the middle of the street and headed in the opposite direction.

53

Epilogue

Six months later....

Maëlle knew it was the happiest day of her life and that she had picked the best venue to have her wedding. Wente Vineyard in Livermore, California looked picture perfect for her wedding event.

"Look at it, Lacey! This place looks like it was sat up for royalty to be married! It's like my dream come true! I feel like a princess getting ready to marry her prince," Maëlle gushed excitedly.

"Yes, I have to agree, the Wente staff has treated us all like royalty. I'm so happy for you Maëlle, but did you have to invite so many people? "

"My guest list had only four-hundred people for the ceremony. The rest are only for the reception and that was Aunt Joan's doing. I didn't have any say so in it."

"Okay... Okay, Now come on, we have to get going your Uncle George is waiting to walk you down the aisle."

Lacey felt Maëlle's body tense the moment she mentioned walking down the aisle.

"Stop it Maëlle. Don't tense up on me, you have nothing to worry about. My brother is not running out on you this time. We've got him hand-cuff to Quinn and Kienan, he's not going anywhere."

"What? That's so embarrassing! My groom has to be hand-cuffed! I can't go out there!"

"Maëlle, calm yourself. I'm only joking!" Lacey said. "Now come on!"

***

Minutes later Lacey delivered, her best friend Maëlle, onto the waiting arm of her Uncle George. Her Aunt Joan's husband.

"Oh, Maëlle, you are beautiful. Your father would have been so proud to see you today. God rest his soul."

"Thanks Uncle George. I feel so blessed having you here representing Dad."

The music started playing.

"Maëlle, it's time. Are you ready?"

"Yes, Uncle George, I'm ready let's get me married!"

They headed for the aisle leading to the altar and got in step when they were signal to do so.

Maëlle looked down the aisle and saw Nicholas as he stood there between Kienan and Quinn, just as Lacey had said. Maëlle wondered if he really was handcuffed to the both of them. She knew she'd soon find out.

Maëlle saw her Aunt Joan sitting on the front pew on the bride's family side, already crying. She did her best not to look at her, afraid she would start crying too.

With each step Maëlle felt terrified history would repeat itself. For one moment her eyes locked with Nicholas, she could tell he knew what she was thinking.

As soon as she reached the altar, Nicholas stepped forward and clasped her hands tightly in his, as Uncle George took a step back, Nicholas leaned over and whispered in Maëlle's ear. "I will never ever leave you again! Never! You understand," he whispered and then leaned over and kissed her forehead.

Maëlle looked up into his eyes and nodded. "Thank you!"

The minister began their vows. "Dearly beloved we are gathered here today, in the presence of God, to witness..."

***

Hours later, Maëlle knew Nicholas loved her by the way he was looking at her as they walked hand in hand threw their reception party, greeting their guest.

"What are you thinking Mrs. Nicholas La Cour?"

"I'm thinking this magic is real!"

"Magic! What magic are you talking about woman of mine?"

"Did I hear someone say, magic?" Aunt Joan inquired.

"Yes, you did Aunt Joan, my new fickle wife just told me this magic is real. I don't know about you, but do you think my new wife think that I am under the influence of a love potion or something?" Nicholas joked.

Aunt Joan smiled. "Nope my Maëlle ain't thinking that. I can tell. Her skin is glowing, and her eyes are sparkling from the real thing. The magic of love!" She laughed. "Nicholas don't you know you can't buy real love in a bottle of love potion. The real feeling of love is down to the bone deep and intoxicatingly more powerful than any drug known to man."

Aunt Joan threw back her head and laughed. "My baby Maëlle is truly happy with the magic of love! Thank you, Nicholas, for making my baby happy!"

Aunt Joan started to cry.

"There she goes, crying again! Come on Joan, let me take you to the dance floor," Uncle George said, leading her away.

A man walked over. "Nicholas, congratulations to you and your new bride."

Nicholas looked at the man and smiled. "Thank you, Ross, I'm so glad you could make it."

The man was Ross Goldman, Nicholas' attorney.

"I would not miss it. You and your bride look so happy," Ross, said. "Besides, I thought you would want to open this, before you started out on your new life, together," Ross said handing Nicholas a letter.

Nicholas' hand clasp around the envelope Ross handed him as Maëlle looked on.

"Go on open it," Ross said.

Nicholas looked at Maëlle and said. "What do you think? Do you think I should open it Maëlle?"

Maëlle nodded. "Yes, open it now."

Nicholas opened the letter and breathe out in a whistle. "Whoa! Ross, the State of California, made out a check to me... For four and a half million dollars?"

"Yes, Nicholas, I've already had them deposit it into your bank account. It's their way of saying sorry for all they put you through. I know it's not the ten million you lost when Dante Channing framed you. But I figured we' get the rest of it back from the accounts Dante opened in the Cayman Islands and all that stuff he had in the storage unit."

"On behalf of me and Nicholas, I want to personally thank you Mr. Goldman for everything you've done to help my Nicholas," Maëlle said as she reached out and embraced Ross Goldman in a hug.

"Yes, Ross, I agree," Nicholas declared. "I'm just so shocked that you got compensation for my false imprisonment. Thanks again."

"You're welcome Nicholas," Ross said. "I guess I should get out the way and let you get on with greeting your guest."

Nicholas and Maëlle watched as Ross was swallowed up by the throngs of well-wishers.

"Looks like this is turning out to be my lucky day, Maëlle," Nicholas declared.

The crush was great with the throngs of greeters wishing the newly married couple well.

All at once Maëlle and Nicholas were no longer in the close proximity of each other as the room was filled awash with congratulations wishes.

"Oh, God! Maëlle you look so beautiful," a plump middle age woman said with happy hysteria.

"Cousin Leila, it's so good to see you," Maëlle said giving her a hug.

"Cousin Guthrie is going to be so mad he missed seeing you. He just ran to the little boy's room again."

"Sounds like Cousin Guthrie been drinking too much beer," Maëlle said.

Cousin Leila sighed "You should have not had free beer sugar dumpling; you know it's Cousin Guthrie's weakness."

"You're the only one I let call me sugar dumpling, Cousin Leila, "Maëlle laughed. "It's a happy occasion so I guess we should let Cousin Guthrie drink as much beer as he wants. He's not driving home, is he?"

"Of course not, sugar dumpling. I've got the keys safely in my purse."

Cousin Leila became misty eyed. "I just can't get over how beautiful you look."

"Yes, she does," someone said. "Maëlle please let me take a picture with you, before you leave this section."

"Juliet Cornell! Girl, I'm so glad you made it!" Maëlle yelled.

"I knew you'd make a beautiful bride, Maëlle, I won't keep you long, I know everyone wants a chance to hug the bride. Hold on a minute and let me get that man to take our picture with my camera.

"Sir can you take our picture?" Juliet asked a man standing nearby.

"Sure," he said.

"Just push this button right here," Juliet said, and then rushed over to pose with Maëlle.

Maëlle stood there stunned at seeing the man who was taking her picture. She couldn't believe Paul Lombardi, was invited to her wedding.

As soon as the picture taking was done, Juliet hugged Maëlle and said. "Girl, I know you have a busy day today, so I won't take of all of your time. Let's agree to chat after you get back from your honeymoon."

"Sure, it's a date," Maëlle said, watching her friend get absorbed into the crush of people at her wedding.

All around her everyone was too high on congratulation hysteria to notice the man closing the distance between them.

"What the hell are you doing at my wedding Paul?" Maëlle asked through clenched teeth.

Paul grinned sheepishly as he stared down at her. "I'm here by way of an invitation that was sent to Lawrence Mc-Cready, as I'm sure you know he is an excellent friend of your Uncle George. Anyway, as you know Lawrence McCready plus one is always his girl, Dominique Bledsoe, and when Lawrence can't make it Dominique always call me. When I heard, Lawrence had an invitation to your wedding. I made it a point to make sure Lawrence would not be able to make it."

Maëlle could feel her heart beating fast. "You shouldn't have come Paul."

Paul's eyes narrowed as he sucked in his breath. "I love you, Maëlle. You shouldn't have married Nicholas. You should have married me."

"What did you say?" Maëlle asked.

"You heard every word I said," Paul hissed out in a whisper, as his mouth quirked in a humorless smile. "This is no joke, my beautiful bride. I can wait to have what really should be mine. Don't worry, I won't make a scene," he said turning and disappearing into the crush of people.

Maëlle felt her body sway from the shock of what she'd just heard. She couldn't believe the day she was having and for some strange reason she felt like she could no longer hear the sound of all of the noise in the room, the laughter, the music. All seemed to be fading away. She drew in a deep breath and raised her hand to her forehead. "Can someone get me a glass of water?"

"Somebody gets some water!" Somebody yelled. " I think we have a Bride down over here!"

***

Twenty minutes later...

"Maëlle I told you to do two things today, one stay hydrated, and two eat something," Lacey declared.

"Lacey did you see anyone standing around me before I fainted?" Maëlle asked.

"No, no one. In fact, someone said you were talking to yourself before you fainted," Maëlle.

"I don't think I was talking to myself. I'm sure I was talking to someone," Maëlle said. "In fact, I think I was talking to Paul Lombardi."

"Paul Lombardi, that half Italian half African American policeman, you dated years ago," Lacey said. "Girl you must have been hallucinating. I don't recall Paul, being invited to your wedding. You were just malnutrition and dehydrated. I told you to eat something before you put on that dress. I knew that dress was too tight!"

"Ha! Ha! Ha! Anyway, I'm fine now, thanks for the protein bar, I needed it," Maëlle declared.

Just then Nicholas closed the distance between them and walked over and sat down next to her. "Maëlle are you sure you're alright?"

"Yes, Nicholas, I'm fine."

"Good, because we still have a wedding reception going on around us and I promise to stop by this last table and take photos with you by my side."

"Is that the table with the quarterback for the Raiders sitting at it, you've been talking about?" Maëlle asked

"Yup! Baby it is! We gonna it get our wedding photo with a quarterback, Whoa!" Nicholas sung out doing a happy dance.

"You know I got to have that picture with the Raiders quarterback!"

"Alright, Nicholas. Let's go."

Nicholas grabbed Maëlle's hand. "Come on honey, this is the last table we promised to take photos with, "he said leading her over.

As they approached the table a young mother stood up holding the hand of a little boy who looked to be about two or three years old.

"Greetings and thank you for coming to our wedding.I'm so sorry I don't remember your names," Maëlle said.

"Hello Nicholas, and Maëlle, I'm not sure if you remember me, I'm Mimi Mondragon. Lucy Mondragon's sister."

Maëlle elbowed Nicholas. "Oh, my goodness yes I do. I'm sorry but I don't remember inviting you or your family."

"Your Aunt Joan invited me. It's just me here with my nephew, little Quinn," she said as she turned and looked at the little boy standing beside her. "Quinn, say hi to your Aunt Maëlle and Uncle Nicholas."

Nicholas and Maëlle looked at each other and then looked at the tiny little miniature Quinn standing in front of them.

Maëlle gasped. "Oh, my God! He has Quinn's eyes and look he's wearing the cutest miniature black framed glasses, just like Quinn used to wear, when he was a kid!"

"Ahhhh, Maëlle dear! Take a real good look at him," Nicholas replied. "This little fellow looks exactly like Quinn! Even without the cute miniature black framed glasses."

"You know Nicholas, I believe you're right," Maëlle replied staring at the child in disbelief.

Nicholas cleared his throat and said. "So, Mimi! I take it

this little dude has the same eye aliment as Quinn. Hence that's the reason for the glasses?"

"Yes... Yes! He does," Mimi replied. "That's why he's wearing glasses. His eye exams are in the envelope with his other medical records."

Nicholas rubbed his face in disbelief. "Tell me this isn't the child Quinn has been looking for?"

"Yes, he is the son Quinn has been searching for. The one he had with my sister Lucy Mondragon. My sister Lucy Mondragon hid him from Quinn with my mother's sister family in the Philippines. My Aunt Dollie didn't know the truth behind what Lucy had done, nor did anyone else in our family," she said reaching and pulling out a large envelope. "Here is little Quinn's birth certificate and passport. My mother and father sent me here to apologize for Lucy's behavior and to give big Quinn back his son."

"What?" Maëlle asked dumbfounded.

"Are you saying you giving Quinn back his son?" Nicholas inquired.

"Yes, I am leaving little Quinn with you as I have been instructed to do so. In this envelope is all of his health information, birth information, everything you need, please take it."

From the sound of urgency in her voice, Nicholas spoke up. "Why are you doing this? Has someone made you?"

Puzzled and bewildered Mimi said. "Yes, I thought you knew, that is the reason I am here."

"Knew what?" Nicholas and Maëlle said in unison.

"That I was supposed to bring little Quinn here today and leave him with you. Or else the curse that has been brought down on my family will not be lifted."

"Curse? What are you talking about, Mimi?" Maëlle asked.

Nervously Mimi looked around. "A woman named Angel went to see my Aunt Dollie and her family in the Philippines," Mimi hesitated and looked around nervously. "She placed my Aunt Dollies' husband and oldest son in some kind of coma. The hospital can't help them they don't know what's wrong with them. Before I came her another one of my aunt sons went into the same coma along with one of my own brothers. The woman named Angel said the curse will continue in my family to all the males until we return little Quinn. That's why I'm here and I thought you knew, because the woman named Angel was here at your wedding. I saw her in the church."

"Wait a minute you saw Angel, here at our wedding?" Nicholas inquired.

"Yes," Mimi said. "Ask your Aunt Joan, she was talking to her before the ceremony started."

Bewildered Nicholas and Maëlle looked at each other.

Then Mimi said. "I have to leave, so I'll leave little Quinn with you. The suitcases with his clothes are at the front desk. They said they would keep them for me. Please tell Angel, my family and I have done what she asked. Please have her lift the curse."

Mimi stooped down and hugged little Quinn. "Quinn, these nice people will take you to your father, Big Quinn, remember I told you, you will live with your father, Big Quinn? Now, give Aunt Mimi a hug."

The little boy nodded and hugged Mimi.

"Go on, now to the pretty lady, this is your Aunt Maëlle and your Uncle Nicholas. They will take good care of you."

"Okay," little Quinn said as he walked over and place his hand in Maëlle's. "Hi Aunt Maëlle, can I go and see my Dad, now?"

Maëlle had to choke back tears. "Yes, of course you can. That's the first thing we are going to do," she said looking at Nicholas.

Nicholas swallowed hard. "Honey, let me go and find Quinn."

"No, Nicholas, I think we should go someplace private and we get Lacey, or Kienan to find Quinn and bring him where we are at. This is a family matter."

"Your right Maëlle," Nicholas said.

Before Nicholas could move his sister, Lacey's voice carried across the room.

"Nicholas and Maëlle, what are you too up to? You're holding up this production, everyone is missing you guys on the dance floor," Lacey called.

"Lacey, we need you, "Maëlle yelled.

Lacey quickly closed the distance between them.

"Maëlle did you forget this is your wedding or are you babysitting for someone else's kids? What, mine wouldn't do? If you wanted to babysit, mine are always available."

"This isn't a Ha! Ha! Moment, Lacey," Maëlle said leaning over and whispering. "Lacey take a good look at this little boy. Who does he look like to you?"

Lacey looked down, and then stooped down level to the little boy. "Why hello handsome, what's your name?"

"My name is Quinn Darnell Rosolado Rolandis Jr., what's your name?"

My name is Lacey...," Lacey's mouth dropped wide opened. "Oh, my God! Did you hear what he said?"

Quickly Lacey stood up and took charge, Nicholas, you two take Lil Quinn back to your room, the one where you changed in. I'll go and find Kienan and Quinn and meet you back there," she said and then shook her head. "No! No! Wait, maybe you two should go to the dance floor and pretend like nothing happened, and I'll walk around with Lil Quinn, looking for Big Quinn!"

"Stop panicking Lacey, this wedding is almost over anyway. They won't miss us on the dance floor, everybody out there is already stone cold drunk," Nicholas said. "How about we all look for Quinn, and when we find him, we all walk back to my dressing room and handle our family business, in private."

"No!" Lacey yelled. "That's not a good idea."

"What's wrong with going to my dressing room?" Maëlle asked but didn't wait for a response. "Oh, yeah, I forget! I just remembered my dressing room is messy as heck. Don't nobody want to go in there. In fact, I wasn't planning on going back there tonight myself. Nicholas' dressing room it is, we all agree."

Nicholas realized the moment required someone to take charge. He knew it was up to him to handle the matter. "No dressing room, it's agreed family, we will all look for Quinn, together, right now," he declared. "Come on family let's go!"

Nicholas lead the way, and a few minutes later they spotted Kienan first.

"Hey Kienan, have you seen Quinn?"

"Yeah, he just went inside to the bar, the one out here ran

out of Tsingtao. They offered to go get him one inside, but he told him he didn't mind walking."

"Okay, well come on Kienan, fall in line. We're all off to find Quinn," Nicholas declared. "Family business!"

"Big family business!" Maëlle added.

Kienan fell in line with his wife and asked. "So, Lacey what are we doing? Somebody lost their kid?"

"Yup, they sure did, and we found him," Lacey replied.

"I was just kidding," Kienan said. "You serious?"

"Yup, I am, "Lacey declared as she kept up one step behind Nicholas and Maëlle.

Kienan glanced at his wife then at the little boy holding Maëlle's hand. "Wife, you're not going to tell me anything, are you?"

"Shhhhh! Kienan, you'll know in a minute," Lacey said.

A few minutes later, the small party reached the bar inside and found Quinn standing with his back to them leaning over the bar.

Nicholas loudly cleared his throat. "Hey Quinn, "he called. "We have a surprise!"

"Yeah, what is it?" Quinn asked without turning around, as he took another sip of his Tsingtao.

Nicholas looked down at his nephew, as the little boy looked up at him. "Say little man, what did you say your name was again."

"I told you my name is Quinn Darnell Rosolado Rolandis Jr."

"What the Hel —?" Kienan blurted.

"Kienan, we don't curse around children," Lacey scolded.

Quinn was just about to take another sip of his Tsingtao,

when the little boy spoke, he stopped his drink in mid-air and slowly turned around.

His mouth dropped opened wide as he stared back at the miniature version of himself.

Quinn blinked several times as if in disbelief. Slowly he walked over and kneeled down in front of the little boy.

"Hello Quinn Darnell Rosolado Rolandis Jr, I love your glasses, their cool," Quinn said as his voice choked with emotion.

"Thanks, Mister, no one ever told me my glasses were cool, before. I like that," the little boy smiled.

Quinn felt his voice crack with emotion. "So, tell me, what brings you to this wedding today?"

"I'm looking for my Dad," the little boy said.

"Wow! Is that a fact. Do you want to know what my name is?" Quinn softly asked, his voice laced with emotion.

The little boy nodded. "Sure, mister."

In a soft voice, which cracked with emotion Quinn said. "My name is Quinn Darnell Rosolado Rolandis. I bet you can't guess what I'm looking for, can you?"

"No," the little boy said shaking his head.

Quinn's voice was laced with emotion. "I'm looking for my son, and guess what?"

"What?" The little boy curiously asked.

"I think, I've found my son?"

The little boy squealed. "You're my Dad, aren't you, because you have the same name as me."

"Yes, I am son," Quinn choked out. "Is it alright with you, if I give you a hug?"

The little boy smiled and nodded. "I was hoping you were a father who like to give hugs.," he said rushing into his arms.

Quinn looked up at his family, as he hugged his son, with tears running down his eyes and said. "I don't know how yawl did this, but you have made me the happiest man alive! I love you guys!"

THE END

54

About the Author

J.A. Jackson is the pseudonym for an author, who loves to write deliciously sultry adult romantic, suspenseful, entertaining novels with a unique twist. She lives in an enchanted little house she calls home in the Northern California foothills. Her love for cooking and writing come from her Southern roots of Louisiana and Arkansas. She spent over ten years working in the non-profit sector where she wrote grants, press releases and contributed many stories to their newsletter. She was their Newsletter editor for over ten years. She loves growing roses, a good pot of hot tea, chocolate, magical stories, suspense stories, ghost stories, and reading Jane Austen again and again in her past time.

Contact: J. A. Jackson P. O. Box 1494, Clovis CA 93613

Email: jerreecejackson@yahoo.com

https://twitter.com/jerreece

https://www.facebook.com/pages/Jerreece-Ann-Jackson/204377496289139?ref=hl

https://medium.com/@jerreecejackson

https://mailchi.mp/1be4f2939d63/author-j-a-jackson-aka-jerreece

Also by Jerreece Jackson

Diamond at Midnight!

Growing up on the mean streets of Chicago prepared Diamond Dunbar for almost anything. With her sights set on a college education, she's ready to live the dream. Dance, lies and dirty betrayals...

When Sizzling, Steamy, meets sweet sensual then turning scorching HOT!

When A Taker Dreams!

Cierra Cantrell has had little experience with men.

After following the advice of her mother, Cierra agrees to accept family friend Isabella Duvall's offer for help in obtaining a marriage of convenience.

When Isabella's gorgeous brother Ryker —shows up, Cierra can't stop dreaming about him. With nothing left to lose, Cierra walks headfirst into the unknown. But things aren't always as they seem.

Sometimes life is not that simple. Love can be complicated.

Mistress of Desire & The Orchid Lover Book I

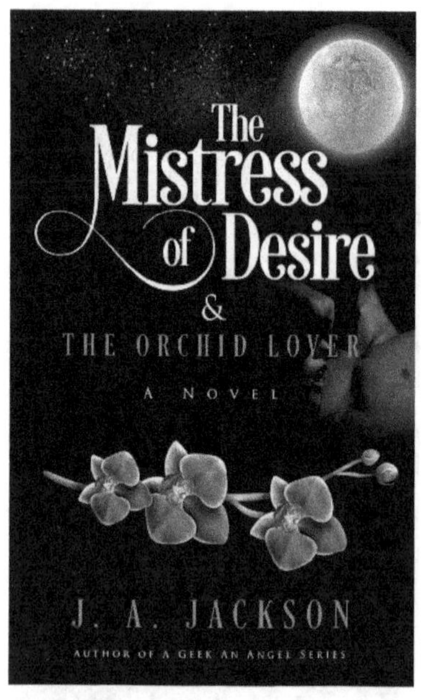

A kind heart is a dangerous thing to possess in the raw, power-hungry, bubbling cauldron known as Silicon Valley. Discover, as beautiful Camille Baptiste finds out the truth. All she ever wanted was to be loved. **Better know your friends or you might get burned.**

Mistress of Desire & The Orchid Lover Book II

Neither Tiara Blake or Delmar Devereaux has a past to be proud of. With a joint history packed with dishonesty, black-mail—and a juicy, torrid love affair—the pair didn't expect their paths would cross again.

After a torrid love affair, shady businessman Delmar Devereaux disappeared from Tiara Blake's life, leaving her to raise their twin sons on her own. So, when he shows up unannounced one day, her first instinct is to kick him to the curb.

www.ingramcontent.com/pod-product-compliance
Lightning Source LLC
Chambersburg PA
CBHW060755210726

48292CB00013B/153